Praise for Philip Kerr's *Prayer*

"Here moral complexity is raised to a new high in a contemporary psychological thriller that is eerily terrifying and disturbing"
—*Library Journal* (starred review)

"A fright-filled meditation on faith . . . The book entertains and makes you think."
—*The Dallas Morning News*

"Provocative . . . Evocative phrasing is another plus in this exceptional thriller."
—*Publishers Weekly* (starred review)

"A rum beast that uses the cozy familiarity of the thriller form to buttress a fantastical supernatural plot. . . . As fans of his Berlin-set Bernie Gunther novels will know, Kerr is a details man. His deep-level research brings Houston and its environs to dusty, sun-bleached life. Martins's narration, too, is deftly handled—*Prayer* demands to be read more than once."
—*The Guardian* (London)

"Tantalizingly creepy."
—*The Observer* (London)

"When Kerr goes off-piste, as he does here, the freedom sends his imagination into some very peculiar places. Who else could make a crackling thriller out of the current debate between religion and atheism? . . . What if the Almighty exists, but is horrible? The story unfolds at a white-knuckle pace, with a sense of the unknown that is genuinely disturbing."
—*The Sunday Times* (London)

"A real page-turner that may just have everyone rethinking the monumental power that faith can provide or . . . take away in the blink of an eye."
—*Suspense Magazine*

Praise for Philip Kerr

"[Kerr] demonstrates his skill in historical research. . . . A compelling read."
—*The Washington Times*

"This is the most intelligent brand of crime fiction, and there is moral complexity here in spades."
—*The Daily Beast*

PENGUIN BOOKS

PRAYER

Philip Kerr is the author of ten Bernie Gunther novels, as well as the forthcoming *Lady of Zagreb*. Most recently, *A Man Without Breath* made the *New York Times* bestseller list and *Field Gray* was a finalist for the 2012 Mystery Writers of America's Edgar Award for Best Novel. Kerr has also been a finalist for the Shamus Award for Best Hardcover Fiction and he won the British Crime Writers' Association Ellis Peters Award for Historical Crime Fiction. Under the name P. B. Kerr, he is the author of the much-loved young adult series Children of the Lamp. He lives in London.

PRAYER

PHILIP KERR

PENGUIN BOOKS

PENGUIN BOOKS
Penguin Group (USA) LLC
375 Hudson Street
New York, New York 10014

USA · Canada · UK · Ireland · Australia
New Zealand · India · South Africa · China
penguin.com
A Penguin Random House Company

First published in the United States of America by G. P. Putnam's Sons,
a member of Penguin Group (USA) LLC, 2013
Published in Penguin Books 2015

THE LIBRARY OF CONGRESS HAS CATALOGED
THE HARDCOVER EDITION AS FOLLOWS:
Kerr, Philip.
Prayer / Philip Kerr.
p.   cm.
ISBN 978-0-399-16765-2 (hc.)
ISBN 978-0-14-312709-3 (pbk.)
1. United States. Federal Bureau of Investigation—Officials and employees—
Fiction.   2. Serial murderer—Fiction.   3. Psychology,
Religious—Fiction.   4. Psychological fiction.   I. Title.
PR6061.E784P78   2014   2013038817
823'.914—dc23

Printed in the United States of America
1   3   5   7   9   10   8   6   4   2

BOOK DESIGN BY AMANDA DEWEY

For Nicholas B. Scott,
a true Scot but a real friend

Prayer is not an old woman's idle amusement. Properly understood and applied, it is the most potent instrument of action.

—MAHATMA GANDHI

When the gods wish to punish us, they answer our prayers.

—OSCAR WILDE

The wrath of God lies sleeping. It was hid a million years before men were and only men have power to wake it.

—CORMAC MCCARTHY, *BLOOD MERIDIAN*

PRAYER

PROLOGUE

It was a bright cold day, but as if it were midsummer, I had given up my usual gray clothes of lambswool and thick flannel, and had been dressed for innocence in white cotton like all of the other children in the cathedral.

I was trembling, but not just because of the freezing temperature in St. Andrew's; I was also trembling because there was a mortal sin in my heart—or so I imagined.

The gray stone interior soared above my neatly combed hair like the hall of some ancient castle, and the air was filled with the smell of candles and incense. As the church organ played and the weak voices of the choir mumbled strange words that might have been Latin, I walked slowly and reverently up the center aisle toward the Friar Tuck–size bishop with my small, sweaty palms pressed together as if I were a little saint—although in my own eyes I was anything but that—just the way my mother had shown me.

"You do it like this, Giles," she had said, showing me exactly how.

"As if you were trying to press something very flat in your hands that you must hold close to your face so that the tips of the fingers are just touching your lips."

"You mean like Joan of Arc, when they burned her at the stake," I asked.

My mother winced.

"Yes. If you like, Giles. But if we think about it, I'm sure you can find a nicer example than that, can't you?"

"How about Mary Queen of Scots?"

"Someone who's not on their way to execution, perhaps. Please try to think of someone else, Giles. A saint, perhaps."

"Surely the saints are only saints because they were martyrs first," I argued. "That means most of them were executed, too."

My mother made an exasperated face. "You've got an answer for everything, Giles," she muttered.

"A soft answer turns away wrath," I said. "But grievous words stir up anger. Proverbs 15:1."

Quoting the Bible was a useful trick I had learned in Bible class. We had to learn a text every week, and it hadn't taken me long to work out that quoting from the Bible also had the effect of silencing critical adults. More usefully, it had the effect of deterring the unwelcome attentions of Father Lees. He tended to leave me alone out of fear of the text that I might utter when confronted with his priestly hands—as if God were speaking to him directly through my innocent mouth. Because of my knowledge of the Bible, my father called me Holy Willie and sometimes "precocious," and told my mother that in his opinion teaching children what was in the Bible was a bad thing. She ignored him, of course, but in retrospect I think Dad was right. There's a lot in the Bible that shouldn't ever have been translated from the Latin or the Greek.

A long line of us boys and girls shuffled up the nave of the cathedral. We must have looked like one of those Korean Moonie weddings where hundreds of couples get married at once.

Of course, this was not my child wedding but my own confirmation—the moment I was to declare my desire to renounce Satan and all his works, and to become a Roman Catholic—and, for everyone else in the cathedral of St. Andrew's, it seemed to be a very happy day. Everyone else except me, perhaps, because there was something about the ceremony I didn't like; not just the pansy white shirt and shorts and school tie—which were bad enough—but something else, too; I think you could say I had a feeling of deep foreboding, as if something terrible were about to happen that was not unconnected with the commission of the possibly mortal sin I was contemplating.

I was twelve years old and being precocious meant I was also possessed of "a bit of an imagination"; that was how my parents described children like me who exaggerated some things and lied about others. Certainly, I had my own ideas about almost everything. These ideas were sometimes influenced by what I had read in a book or seen on television, but more often than not, they were simply the result of deep and often wrong juvenile thinking that was at least the product of an independent mind; any lies I did tell were usually told with good intent.

Thanks to Father Lees, I had been well schooled in the Roman Catholic catechism and in the meaning of confirmation, which you can read all about in the Acts of the Apostles, chapter two. Every Wednesday for the last month I'd been taken to Bible class where Father Lees had told us how, shortly after Pentecost, the apostles had been hiding away in some locked room because they were afraid of the Jews, when suddenly they heard a noise that sounded like the wind but was, in fact, the sound of the Holy Ghost. Next, small tongues of fire appeared like little blue butane-gas cigarette-lighter flames above the heads of the disciples and they were all filled with the Holy Ghost and began to speak in foreign languages that, according to my older brother, Andy, was not unlike what happens in *The Exorcist*.

Now, I didn't like ghosts and ghost stories any more than I would care to have been left alone in a locked room with Father Lees, and I certainly didn't care for the idea of having any spirit—holy or otherwise—come inside my body and light me up "like a little candle for Jesus," which was how the creepy priest described it to us in Bible class. In fact, the idea terrified me. Nor did I much like the possibility that I might never again be able to speak English, but only some baffling language like Chinese or Swahili that nobody else in Glasgow would be able to understand. Not that Glaswegians are easy to understand themselves; even other people from Scotland have a hard job with the accent and the lack of consonants. Speaking the English language as it is spoken in Glasgow is like learning to spit.

So I had made a plan that was going to save me from the strong risk of ghostly possession and speaking in tongues—a secret plan I discussed with no one other than my own conscience (and certainly not my mother) and that I now put into action.

When it was my turn to be confirmed, I knelt in front of the bishop and, as soon as he had anointed my forehead and slapped my face with his nicotine-stained fingers—rather harder than I'd been expecting— to symbolize how the world might treat me because of my faith, and Father Lees had given me the red grape juice and wafer that was the blood and body of Jesus Christ, I stepped around the granite pillar of the church and, while everyone's eyes were on the boy immediately behind me who was now being confirmed, quickly wiped the holy oil off my forehead and spat the dry wafer off the roof of my mouth into my handkerchief.

One of my school friends saw me do this, and for quite a while afterward my nickname was "the heretic," which I rather enjoyed. It gave me a wicked, worldly aspect that I fancied made me seem sophisticated. Apparently unconsumed hosts—which is what you call the wafer when you don't actually swallow it—are very useful for the commission of satanic rites or devil worship. Not that I was interested in worshipping the devil. I think that even then—and possibly thanks to Father Lees—I saw God and the devil as opposite sides of the same grubby coin, although for a long time I think I managed to make a pretty good fist of being a good Christian.

Now, it's said that no sin goes unpunished, and my own evil act was certainly punished because as I pulled the clean, folded white square of handkerchief from my trousers into which I was preparing to gob the body of Christ, something fell out of my pocket, though I wasn't aware of it at the time. This was my new St. Christopher's medal, made of solid Hebridean silver, a commemorative gift from my mother that was engraved with my initials—including the initial of the saint's name I had taken for my confirmation, which was John, who was the brother of James, and which was my own baptismal name—and the date of my confirmation. The medal was distinctive in several other respects, too; my mother had had the medal specially designed by Graham Stewart, who became, eventually, quite a famous Scottish silversmith. I even know what it looks like, because my brother still has the St. Christopher's medal from his own confirmation, which took place a couple of years before mine: the head of St. Peter is a copy of a drawing by the celebrated artist Peter Howson.

Of course, the loss of the silver medal was soon discovered, and although my mother never found out the exact and probably blasphemous circumstances that accompanied its disappearance, for a while I was obliged to pray every night that I might find it again.

HOUSTON, TEXAS

✠

PRESENT DAY

ONE

From the outside, the Cathedral of the Sacred Heart resembled a prison. With its high windows, gray seamless concrete blocks, and a freestanding bell tower, Sacred Heart did not look like a promising place for a talk with the Almighty. I walked through the doors into the mercifully cool marble interior and was greeted by a handsome African-American wearing a priest's collar and a welcoming smile. He informed me that Mass would begin in thirty minutes and confessions in ten near the Sacred Heart transept.

I thanked the priest and passed inside. I hardly wanted to tell him that it was a long time since anyone had heard my confession. I wasn't even a Roman Catholic. Not anymore. I was an evangelical. And I was there to pray, not to attend Mass or seek absolution for my sins.

The prayer was a mistake. I should never have given it wings. As soon as I saw the weirdly modern stained-glass windows and the plastic figure of St. Anthony of Padua, I ought to have turned and left. Compared to the Catholic churches of my youth, this place felt too new for a talk with God about what was troubling me. But where else was I to go? Not to my own church—the Lakewood. That was a former basketball arena. And among the architectural eyesores that constituted the fourth-largest city in the USA, St. Anthony himself would not have found anywhere better than Houston's Catholic cathedral to come nearer to God. I was certain of that much anyway, even if I was less certain that I wasn't just wasting my time. After all, what was the point of praying to a God who—I was almost convinced—wasn't there at all? This was what I had come to pray about. That and the state of my marriage, perhaps.

I picked a quiet pew facing the Sacred Heart transept, knelt down, and muttered a few holy-sounding words; looking up at the simple stained-glass window with its red, comically disembodied sacred heart, I tried my best to address the problem at hand.

"Breathe in me, o Holy Spirit, er . . . that my thoughts may all be holy. Act in me, o Holy Spirit, that my work, too, may be holy . . . Which it isn't. How could my work ever be holy? I see things, o Holy Spirit—terrible things—that make me doubt that you could ever exist in a world as fucked up as this one. And I know what I'm talking about, Lord.

"Take that heart on the transept window up there. Oh, I know what it's supposed to mean, Lord: it's the Holy Eucharist and symbolizes the love that is God who, out of his love for us, became a man on Earth. Yes, I get that.

"But when I see that heart, I remember Zero Santorini, the Texas City serial killer who used to cut out his victims' hearts and leave them beside the bodies on a neat little nest of barbed wire. (It was a nicely sadistic touch, the barbed wire—very Hollywood; it was useful, too, because it's the thing that helped us to nail him. The wire was galvanized eight-inch field fence, and Santorini bought twenty-five yards of it from Uvalco Supply in San Antonio.) Sure, I can delude myself that I'm doing your work, Lord, but it really doesn't figure that you could have been around for any of the seventeen poor girls Santorini murdered.

"It's true that most of those girls were drug addicts and prostitutes, but nobody deserves to be killed like that. Except perhaps Zero Santorini. According to him, he actively encouraged most of those women to pray for their lives before he murdered them; and when you didn't show up with a lightning bolt in one hand and your Holy Spirit in the other, he figured you'd given him the go-ahead to shoot them with a nail gun. The irony of the situation, of course, is that Santorini was looking for some sort of sign that you do actually exist; that in an extreme situation such as the one he had engineered, you might just have put in an appearance and allayed all of his very reasonable doubts.

"I believed his story, too. In a way, his actions struck me as kind of logical. He even took pictures of these poor girls as they knelt on the ground naked, with their hands clasped in prayer, which seemed to bear out his story. You, on the other hand—well, I've got a hundred good reasons to disbelieve you.

"If you are there, then all I'm asking for is some help to believe in you. I'm not asking for a sign, like Zero Santorini did. And I'm not asking for an easier life or an easier job. I'm just praying for the strength to deal with the life and the job I already have. The fact is that in my ten years with the Bureau not once have I seen you fixing something that needed fixing. Not once. And I just get the impression that if all the brick agents on Justice Park Drive stayed in bed one morning then this city would be in a bigger fucking mess than it is right now. I certainly don't see you taking on the loonies I have to deal with in Domestic Terrorism, Lord: the white supremacists, the Christian militias, the sovereign citizens, the abortion extremists, the animal-rights and eco warriors, the black separatists, and the anarchists—to say nothing of the Islamists that the guys across the hall in Counterintelligence are having to keep an eye on these days. I don't see you worrying about any of that, Lord. In fact, I don't see you at all."

I got to my feet. It was time for me to leave. The cathedral was filling up. A priest quietly approached the altar and lit some candles, and upstairs in the organ loft someone started to play a Bach prelude.

Leaving the transept, I walked back up the aisle to the south front, pausing only to collect the parish news bulletin from a pile by the door, and then I went out into the heat of a typical Houston summer evening.

❦

Home was a new-built stone-and-stucco house southeast of Memorial Park on Driscoll Street. From the tower bedroom that served as my study, I had a good view of a suburban Houston street of reassuring ordinariness: a sidewalk lined with several palm trees scorched by the relentless sun and neat lawns that were nearly always smaller than the shiny SUVs parked beside them.

It was a nice house, but I couldn't ever have afforded it on an FBI salary, which was why Ruth's father, Bob Coleman, had bought it for us. In the beginning, Bob and I had got along pretty well; but that was before I was dumb enough—his words, not mine—to have turned down a well-paid position with a prestigious firm of New York attorneys to go to the academy at Quantico and train for the FBI. Bob said he would never have given his blessing to our being married if he had thought I was going to throw away a legal career out of a misguided sense of patriotism. Bob and I don't see eye to eye on any number of issues, but my working for Big Government is just one more reason for him to dislike and distrust me. Then again, I feel the same way about Bob.

I dumped my stuff on the breakfast bar and kissed Ruth for longer than either of us was expecting, after which she let out a breath and blinked as if she had just turned a cartwheel, and then she smiled warmly.

"I wasn't expecting that," she said.

"You have a strange effect on me."

"I'm glad. I'd hate to think I bored you."

"Never."

I went into the bathroom to wash up.

"Did you have a good day?" she called after me.

"It's always a good day when I come home, honey."

"Don't say that, baby. It reminds me of all the things that could go wrong when you're out of the house."

"Nothing's going to go wrong. I've told you before. I'm blessed." I sprayed some antiviral sanitizer on my hands; I must have thought the stuff was an antidote to the kind of lowlife scum I spent most of my time trying to catch. "Where's Danny?"

"Playing in the yard."

When I came back into the kitchen, Ruth had the Sacred Heart parish newsletter in her hand.

"You were down at the cathedral?"

"I was in the area so I decided to drop in and see if Bishop Coogan was there. You remember Eamon Coogan?"

"Sure."

Currently the archbishop emeritus of the Archdiocese of Galveston-Houston, Eamon Coogan was an old friend of my mother's from Boston, which is where my family had moved after we left Scotland.

I went to the refrigerator to fetch a cold beer.

"And was he?" she asked sweetly.

"I don't know."

She laughed. "You don't know?" And then she guessed I was lying, because Ruth always knew when I was lying. After Harvard Law, Ruth had worked as an assistant DA in the New York District Attorney's Office, where she had demonstrated a real talent for prosecution and cross-examination.

"Oh," she said, "I get it. You went there for confession, didn't you?"

"No." I jerked the top of the beer bottle off and sucked the contents down.

"To pray, then." She grinned. "Why can't you go to our own church to do that, Gil?"

"Because it doesn't feel like a church. You know, whenever I'm in there, I feel like looking for the commentary box and a hot dog salesman."

She laughed. "That's not fair. It's just a building. I don't think God needs stained-glass windows to feel at home."

I shrugged.

"Is anything wrong, honey?"

"No, but I think maybe I just answered your first question about what kind of day I've had."

Danny appeared at the back door and, seeing me, launched himself in my direction like a human battering ram; I had time only to cover my balls with my hands before his large and surprisingly hard head connected with my groin.

"Daddy," he yelled, and wrapped his little arms around my legs.

"Danny. How are you doing, big guy?"

"I'm good," he said. "I haven't been bad at all. And I didn't hit Robbie."

I caught a look in Ruth's eye that seemed to contradict this spontaneous denial.

"Robbie?"

"The Murphy boy," she said. "From across the street." She shook her head. "They had a small disagreement."

"I told you. I didn't hit Robbie. He fell over."

"Danny," said Ruth. "We talked about this. Don't lie to your dad."

"I didn't."

I grinned. "You stick to your story, kid," I said. "Don't ever fold under questioning."

I turned the boy around, stroked his fine yellow hair, and gently pushed him further into the kitchen.

Danny went to the sink and washed his hands. Ruth was already serving dinner and this was my cue to remove the Glock on my hip. Ruth had nothing against guns—she was from Texas, after all—but she always preferred me to take it off before I sat down for dinner and said grace.

I said a prayer before every meal in our house, but on this occasion my heart wasn't in it. Instead of our usual grace—"Great God, the giver of all good, accept our praise and bless our food"—I found myself uttering something less worshipful: "For well-filled plate and brimming cup and freedom from the washing up, we thank you, Lord. Amen."

Ruth tried to control a smile. "Well, that's a new one," she said.

After we'd eaten, I put Danny to bed and read him a story and then went into my study in the tower, which is where Ruth came and found me later on.

"Can I fetch you another beer, baby?"

Ruth didn't drink, but she didn't seem to mind that I did. Not yet.

"No, thanks, honey."

She stood behind me and massaged my neck and shoulders for a while.

"You seem kind of distant tonight."

Suddenly I wanted to tell her everything—I had to tell someone—but I could hardly have done that without risking an argument. The church was an important part of Ruth's life.

"You remember I told you about that motorcycle gang of white supremacists who call themselves the Texas Storm Troopers?"

Ruth nodded.

"We've been running a wire on a bar the gang uses in Eastwood. Well, today I heard three of them discussing some murders that were committed back in 2007. Two black women were raped and murdered on the Southside."

"How horrible."

"I wasn't going to tell you. But it was clear from their conversation that it was the Storm Troopers who carried out these murders."

Ruth shrugged. "So, that's good, isn't it? Now you can arrest them."

"We already sent someone up for those murders. A guy named José Samarancho. I worked Violent Crimes for a while when we first moved to Houston, remember? It was our task force that helped to convict him."

"Then this evidence should help to clear him, shouldn't it?"

She still didn't get it, and I could hardly blame her for that.

"It would have cleared him if José Samarancho was still alive. They executed him last month up at Huntsville."

Ruth sat down at my desk and pursed her lips. "That's awful. But you mustn't blame yourself, sweetheart. It's not your fault at all."

"Of course I blame myself. I've thought about nothing else all day." I shook my head. "I was there when he got the juice. I was there, Ruth."

She frowned. "But if he was convicted in 2007, you might have expected that he'd still be alive. I mean the appeal process can take years, even in Texas."

"José Samarancho was a car thief. He was unlucky enough to steal a car that belonged to one of the two dead women, so his forensics were all over it. The car had been left in the parking lot where the Storm Troopers kidnapped the women. Samarancho stole cars to feed a drug habit that caused him to have blackouts; and when we presented him with the evidence that he'd been in the murdered woman's car, he agreed he might have committed the murders and confessed to something he hadn't done because I put it in his mind. His fucked-up brain

even managed to dredge some drug-fantasy memory of his murdering
the women and by some fluke he got the details right. He didn't appeal
the death sentence because he thought he'd done it and therefore
deserved to die." I shook my head bitterly. "Even while he was strapped
to the gurney with the juice plugged into his veins, he was praying to
the Lord to forgive him. The poor dumb idiot died still believing he'd
committed two horrible murders and expecting that he might be going
to hell."

"So, what's your point?"

"I don't know." This was cowardly of me, of course, but I thought it
was best to defuse the situation, for all our sakes.

"Everyone has doubts now and then," she said, squeezing my hand
fondly. "It's what makes faith what it is."

She knelt down beside my chair so that she could put her head on
my lap and let me stroke her hair.

"You're tired and you've had a bad day, that's all. Come to bed and
let me make it right."

"A bad day. Is that how you describe it when someone gets put to
death on my call?"

"It wasn't your call. You talk like nobody else was involved here.
There were attorneys and—"

"I can't excuse the part I played in that man's death. God knows I'd
like to."

"But God can. That's the whole point."

"Maybe there is no God. Maybe *that's* the whole point."

"You don't believe that, honey. You know you don't."

"Don't I?" I sighed. "Actually, that's something I think I do
believe."

TWO

The Houston FBI building was just outside the Loop—which was what locals called I-610—in the northwest part of the city. Close proximity to our only near neighbor, a Wells Fargo bank, might have made the people there feel a little more secure until you remembered that it was the FBI HQ in Oklahoma City that Timothy McVeigh was targeting when, in 1995, he detonated the bomb that killed 168 people and injured more than six hundred in revenge for what happened at Waco. I can't answer for Wells Fargo, but our own security was tight. The seven-story FBI building was made from green-tinted quartzite and was clad in a special heat-reducing glass that was also bulletproof. And that's a comforting thought in a state where people own more than fifty million firearms.

If mentioning this gun-owning statistic seems like my bitching about it, that's because, like almost everyone in this hard-baked but quick-witted city, I'm from somewhere else. Houston is somewhere you go to, not somewhere you come from, and this is particularly true of people at the FBI. After graduating from the FBI Academy, most of us go where the Bureau tells us, and not where we would necessarily choose. Consequently, Houston is not a city that I or many of my colleagues know well. Not that there's very much to know. The city of

Houston is just a lot of overheated freeways, underground parking lots, roadside churches, air-conditioned shopping malls, isolated and bone-dry parks, country clubs for rich folks, and boxy high-rise buildings. Galveston is less than an hour south by car, but after the last hurricane, it's hardly better than a ghost town. The Gulf Coast has little to recommend it but the road north back to Houston.

Approaching the shiny downtown skyline, you would shield your eyes against the reflected sun and, while comparing the cityscape to New York's and Chicago's, you might just consider that the need for control of city planning is even more urgent than the need for gun control. It was these tall buildings and not anything involving drugs and firearms that were the biggest crimes in Texas; and our own field office was no exception.

Inside, the FBI building has the cool, unhurried air of a museum. There's even some indifferent modern art, a few behind-glass exhibits, and a gift shop where you can buy everything from an FBI pen or a set of gold FBI cuff links to a coffee mug. Elsewhere there is more or less all that an agent requires to make life more convenient: a barbershop, a hairdresser, a doctor, a dentist, a bank, and, of course, a well-equipped gymnasium. Thanks to Ruth's father, she and I enjoyed a membership to the Houstonian Club and the use of a gym that was as big as a car factory, but they didn't like you bringing guns in there. I never much like leaving my gun in the car, even when I'm playing tennis, so I preferred to begin my day with a workout in the office gym and then breakfast in the Bureau canteen. I was usually at my desk before eight-thirty a.m.

We're a smart-looking lot in the Bureau. Unless we're in the field, most men wear white shirts and quiet ties, and we polish our shoes and mind our manners, and to that extent we're still Hoover's children. The biggest difference from Hoover's day is the number of women in the Bureau. We call them split-tails on account of the kind of skirts they usually wear. There are more than two thousand women in the FBI, including my own boss, Assistant Special Agent in Charge Gisela Delillo.

Gisela was from North Beach, San Francisco, and another ex-lawyer, like I am. I'm not sure what Hoover would have made of her, but I liked Gisela. Kind of. She was destined for one of the top jobs. As soon as I had collected my files and notes, I went down to her office for an informal weekly case review. She was ten years older than I am, but I'm still young enough to like that in a woman.

Gisela was sitting in the corner of a long leather sofa with her shoes off and her bare legs tucked under her shapely behind. She wasn't particularly tall, but she had a very tall way of walking, like a ballet dancer with an attitude. Her hair was as black as crow feathers and heaped on top of her head. She looked like Audrey Hepburn's dirty sister.

She had a cup of coffee balanced on the palm of her hand—a proper little cup with a saucer and a spoon. She took a noisy sip of it and nodded at a neat red espresso machine on her bookshelf.

"You want one?"

I shook my head. "You heard about the Storm Troopers?"

"I read the field report. You must feel terrible."

"I'll get over it."

"That's why we come to work, isn't it? Because we're optimists."

"Right now my optimism needs glasses. And I'm not just talking about José Samarancho. There's a lot of hate going around this city. And not enough peace and love. Reminds me. Let's talk about Deborah Ann Blundy."

"She's the Black Liberation Army felon on the Most Wanted, right? Shot and killed a cop in D.C. back in 1975."

"Since then, she's been living in Mexico. Only we had a tip-off from someone who used to be in the BLA that she's living right here in Houston. The *Shaft* and *Super Fly* generation of black separatists don't have much in common with today's black activists. But it is possible she'll try to make contact with them. If that happens, I'm confident my source will let me know."

"Okay. What else?"

"Did you read the E.C. I sent you about the HIDDEN group?"

"Yes. But remind me what it means."

"Homeland Internal Defense Delivering Enforcement Now."

"I can't see that catching on in a hurry."

"Okay, it's not NATO or the IRA, but they're just as serious. They're all ex-military. They've got contacts and they've been trained to use the ordnance they're trying to get ahold of. The Switchblade. Basically, it's a tactical drone armed with a three-pound warhead and launched from a two-inch-wide tube you carry around in a backpack. You guide it onto the target via a little camera on the drone's nose. You just fold it out and fire. With a four-foot wingspan, it's not much bigger than a toy plane. Yours for just ten grand."

"Who are they gunning for?"

"Seems they've got a beef with the Jews. They believe that the Gulf wars were fought at the behest of the Israelis and that all their buddies who were killed in Iraq were the victims of a Jewish conspiracy. It's anabolic Christianity. Jarheads for Jesus bulked up with anti-Semitism, Internet conspiracy theories, American exceptionalism, and too much protein."

Gisela sighed and drained her espresso cup. "Sure you won't have one?"

"I think I will now. Our information is that they're planning to fire one of these Switchblades at Congregation Beth Israel on North Braeswood Boulevard."

"That's a nice area." Gisela placed a cup under the dispensing nozzle and pressed a button. The machine made a grinding noise and then vomited a stream of dark brown aromatic liquid.

"It is right now."

"We got this case from RCFL, right?"

Gisela handed me the coffee cup on a saucer with a little napkin and a spoon.

"From Ken Paris?"

The Bureau has more acronyms than Dow Jones. If it didn't, we'd be there all day and the bad guys would escape while we were still saying Regional Computer Forensics Lab. Ken Paris was a Special Agent at the RCFL, a few blocks north of Justice Park Drive. He and his team of geeks spent nearly all of their time copying data from a variety of digital devices seized in the course of criminal investigations and then analyzing it for evidence.

"Galveston police arrested some kids who were running an illegal service provider out of an old oil tanker moored in Trinity Bay."

I sipped my coffee and paused for a moment. "They should put that machine of yours on a crash cart at the DeBakey Heart Center. Gives quite a hit, doesn't it?"

Gisela smiled.

"After Ken had image-scanned all the servers," I said, "he started going through the accounts of their illegal clients. In addition to a huge amount of Internet porn, he found the HIDDEN website and their e-mails to and from an illegal arms company in Costa Rica. Army CID thinks that maybe these are the same people who stole a consignment of Switchblades from a military warehouse in California."

"Tell me they don't yet have this Switchblade."

"I don't think they've raised enough money. But now that their illegal Internet provider's gone, I'd like to get a wire on the HIDDEN leader. A guy named Johnny Sack Brown. The only trouble is we think he's using Skype for all his communications, which is peer-to-peer and offers no central location for us to get a wire on. At least that's what Vijay in DCS Net is telling me."

DCS Net was the Bureau's very own point-and-click surveillance system—simply a matter of choosing a name and telephone number on a computer screen, and clicking a mouse to tap the phone. It worked on landlines and cell phones and provided near high-fidelity digital recordings.

"Now tell me what's happening with those Earth Liberation Front people."

I started polishing my spoon; I'd finished the coffee but it helped to keep my fingers busy.

"Get anything out of them?" she asked.

"I don't think either woman is interested in a plea bargain. I showed them the CCTV footage of them setting fire to the Galveston Island ranger station and the housing development next to the bird sanctuary. They're both clearly identifiable, but they laughed in my face."

She nodded. "Okay. Now I've got something for you."

"If it's another coffee, I don't think my heart can stand it."

She shook her head. "When you first came to the Houston field office, you worked Violent Crimes, didn't you?"

"I haven't forgotten. I still get the interesting dreams."

"Gil, I want you to go see Harlan Caulfield. He seems to think there might be some religious aspect to these serial killings."

"Is Harlan looking to dump this on DT?"

"He's looking for some new ideas, perhaps."

"Are you sure about that? The last new idea they liked here in Texas was lethal injection."

"An irrational attitude directed against any class of citizen could affect your security clearance, Martins. And you might try to remember that Harlan is from Texas."

THREE

Where the fuck is San Saba anyway? Is it near anywhere?"
Harlan Caulfield leaned back in his chair and clasped
his big hands behind his pear-shaped head.

"Is it near anywhere? San Saba is the pecan capital of the world,
son. Otherwise it has no special characteristics."

"I'm glad I asked."

"We'll make a Texan out of you yet, son."

"That's what I'm worried about."

"How's your stomach these days?" he asked, coming around the
desk. He was holding a PowerPoint wireless presenter in his fingers.

"Are you about to show me some of your clients, sir? Because if you
are, I think you need to offer me a caution first. Never did much like
the sight of a dead body."

Harlan grinned. "I knew there was a reason I didn't like you, Gil
Martins." He sneered. "I'll tell you when you're going to see some heavy
shit, okay?"

He pressed a button. A series of faces, male and female, appeared
on the monitor of his PC.

"Kimberley Gaines, Gil Kever, Brent Youman, Vallie Lorine Pyle,
Clarence Burge, Jr."

But I already knew who and what they were. Their smiling year-book faces appeared regularly on the front page of the *Chronicle*; these five were the victims of a killer who was still active in the Houston-Galveston metropolitan area—all of them shot dead over the last six-teen months.

"What all of these people have in common is that they were all good people. And I do mean good people. Normally serial killers tend to prey on the weak, the disadvantaged, or the delinquent. But these five were not only upstanding members of the community, they were also a lot more than that.

"Kimberley Gaines was a member of the Unification Church and a registered nurse. A former Peace Corps volunteer, she recently returned from Haiti, where she'd been involved in a relief fund's cholera treat-ment center. At the time of her murder, she was about to travel to So-malia as part of a United Nations effort to help the victims of a food crisis in the Horn of Africa.

"Gil Kever was the founder of a drug-and-alcohol rehab center for homeless people here in Houston. He was not a member of any church or faith-based initiative. As well as running the center, he also raised all the money. Two years ago Kever received a humanitarian award from the Texas chapter of the Drug Free America Foundation.

"Brent Youman was America's only barefoot doctor. In China, where the idea originated, barefoot doctors are essentially farmers with paramedical training who act as primary health care providers at the grassroots level. Brent Youman was a fully qualified M.D. who walked around Texas treating people who couldn't afford a doctor. Which is probably everyone who isn't a member of the Houstonian Club." Harlan frowned. "You're a member of the Houstonian, aren't you, Martins?"

"My wife, Ruth," I said. "She's the one with all the money. If it wasn't for her, they would kick my ass out of there."

Harlan closed his eyes and smiled. "You'll forgive me if I hold that picture in my mind for a moment."

I smiled. "Drop by sometime and we'll have a game of tennis."

"My days of playing tennis are behind me." His eyes narrowed. "Brent Youman. Just before his murder, he'd been nominated for some prize for people who have made an outstanding contribution to public health. He won the award posthumously and it was presented in absentia at a special ceremony during the World Health Assembly."

I shook my head and moved my BlackBerry at right angles to my pen and my notepad; there wasn't anything really wrong with the way it was lying there before, but I can't abide my stuff looking any other way than neat and tidy; besides, it was something better to do with my hands.

"Sounds as if he was a helluva guy."

"You're beginning to get it. Look, nobody deserves to be murdered. Well, maybe a few. But there are some people whose behavior leads you to suppose that they deserved better than a bullet in the head. Vallie Lorine Pyle and Clarence Burge, Jr., were no different. Vallie Pyle was the founder of Kidneys 'R' Us. That's not a joke, by the way, but an altruistic kidney donation network based here in Houston. Since donating one of her own kidneys to a complete stranger, Vallie Pyle had organized the donation of almost seventy kidneys before she was murdered. Clarence Burge was a Catholic priest from Texas City. After Hurricane Katrina, he gave up the church and set up a construction company to rebuild schools that were destroyed. Working mostly by himself, he succeeded in rebuilding five."

"What do the behavioral science guys have to say?"

"That the victims were picked because they were morally distinguished. That the perp is someone who hates good people. Or is someone jealous of their goodness, who would like to be good himself."

"A crime like this makes a lot more sense if the perp thinks of himself as someone evil fighting against the forces of good. A sort of hellfire club, devil's disciple sort of guy."

"Which means what?"

"I used to be interested in that kind of shit," I said. "You know, books about devil worship?"

"Are there any Satanists or devil worshippers around that you know about?"

"Oh, I'm sure there are. This is America and there's a First Amendment right to practice any kind of religion."

"I'm not talking about religion, Martins," said Harlan. "I'm talking about witchcraft and shit like that."

"Under the First Amendment, anyone has the right to call more or less anything a religion. Today the Salem witches could probably claim protection under the Free Exercise Clause, even if they were guilty. But there aren't any such groups I know of in Texas that demonstrate predication—whose ideology would make them federal meat. But I can look into it for you, if you like."

"I'm all out of good ideas on this one. Lousy ones, too, if I'm honest. So, go ahead."

I collected my stuff off his desk and started to get up from my chair.

"Wait a minute," said Harlan. "You don't get to leave until you've seen the whole show."

He picked up the PowerPoint presenter and started to move through some grisly-looking mortuary shots. All of the vics had been shot at close range several times with a small-caliber weapon—that much was plain from the entry wounds in their heads and faces. Brent Youman had taken one bullet through the eye, which had burst out of its socket like an oyster hanging off the edge of its shell. The exit wounds were rather more spectacular; the back of Vallie Pyle's skull had been blown clean away to reveal a whole damn butcher's counter of brain and tissue.

"They were all shot with a .22-caliber Walther," said Harlan. "Firing a flat-nosed short round from a weapon fitted with a Gemtech sound suppressor. He almost always shoots at night or first thing in the morning and operates just out of range of any CCTV cameras."

"So he doesn't want to get his picture in the newspaper."

"Oh, I'll get him. Even if I have to walk around the city in a nun's habit singing hymns, I'll get this sonofabitch."

I thought about making a joke about that and then flicked the idea away. Harlan was much too unpredictable to meet head-on with a joke about cross-dressing FBI agents.

"I see the first victim was shot on June 29," I said.

"What about it?"

"It's the feast of St. Peter and St. Paul. In the Roman Catholic calendar of saints, it's a holy day."

Harlan handed me a printed sheet of paper. "Any of these other dates mean anything to you?"

I glanced down the list. "No."

"You a Catholic, Martins?"

"You could call me an atheist who goes to church. Or maybe an agnostic. I don't know."

Harlan grinned. "My wife, Molly, is the one who's sweet on Jesus. I just go along because it's easier than having an argument and missing Sunday dinner. By the same token, she comes along to see the Astros although she stopped believing in them a long time ago."

"That's the kind of atheism it's easy to understand."

Harlan let that one go; the case for believing in the Houston Astros was, by any measure, indefensible.

"Which church is it that you go to, son?"

"Lakewood."

"The hell you say. Lakewood's my church." Harlan smiled again. "How come I never saw you there, Martins?"

"That's a little like asking how come you never see me at the ball game. Astros would be glad of a regular crowd like the one they get at Lakewood."

"Is that how you and your wife met? At Lakewood?"

"We met as law students at Harvard. We were neither of us particularly religious then. Until we lived in Houston. We started going to Lakewood Church because we were both believers then. Me included. Although in my case, I've really forgotten why."

"Now I get it. You blame Texas for giving her the sweet talk about the Lord's love, don't you? She's got her pussy all wet for Jesus and you figure it's us who have messed her panties up."

"No."

"Sure you do. It's as obvious as a turd in a punch bowl." He shook his head. "Let me tell you something, son. This has got nothing to do with Texas." Harlan grinned. "Plenty of Texans don't believe in God. Haven't you figured it out? That's why we have so many guns. In case he's not there."

FOUR

I n most churches I could have dozed through the Sunday-morning service and no one would have noticed. But Lakewood was an inter-active sort of church, and the service was more like a Las Vegas show. It was loud and demanded lots of audience participation, singing or just bouncing with the joy of Jesus. When we'd first started going there, I liked that. But not lately. Personally, I couldn't have felt less like bouncing if my feet had been nailed to the floor.

By contrast, Ruth was in a state of ecstasy. Her eyes were closed, a beatific smile illuminated her face, and her hands were raised in the air as if she were hoping to catch a few beams of God's heavenly grace. She was putting her whole being into singing along with the choir and the twenty-piece rock orchestra—aka the Lakewood Church Worship Team—not to mention the huge and rapturous congregation that was also involved in this deafening act of modern worship. The words to all of the Lakewood worship songs—no one called them hymns, because you can't sell hymns on a ten-dollar CD in the church shop—were streaming onto a giant screen above our heads, but Ruth hardly needed them. She knew the words the way I know a meaningful Miranda warning.

Of course, Ruth was hardly alone in her ecstasy. Near the front of the church, and just a couple of rows behind the pastor and the Barbie with a Bible who was his Alabama rose of a wife, it seemed that everyone was more than a little touched with the Holy Spirit. People were clapping their hands and touching their hearts and punching the air and shouting "Hallelujah!" as if they'd just won the Texas state lottery or sent a third man named Bush to the White House.

Everyone except me, that is. I sat down whenever I felt I could get away with it; and when I was standing, I was smiling a shit-eating grin every time one of my proclaiming neighbors met my shifty eyes. But it was Ruth's eyes I most wanted to avoid. I sat down and bowed my head and hoped it might be mistaken for prayer.

Feeling an elbow dug in my side, I opened my eyes with a start and met Ruth's penetrating stare; and satisfied that she now had my attention, she nodded at my crossed leg where the Velcro ankle holster carrying my baby Glock 26 was now fully exposed.

I shrugged sheepishly and placed my feet on the floor so the Glock was no longer in sight, but it was too late; Ruth was shaking her head. I had been judged and found wanting. Especially so on top of the even more inexcusable offense I had given the previous evening. While I was watching the Celtics on TV, Ruth had vacuumed my study and discovered my secret store of carefully arranged but forbidden books. Not a collection of choice pornography, but a small library of "new atheist" authors who argued that religion should not simply be tolerated, but actively exposed as a fraud by rational argument—guys such as Richard Dawkins, Daniel Dennett, Christopher Hitchens, and Houston's very own iconoclast, Philip Osborne. Ruth regarded these writers as the Four Horsemen of the Apocalypse.

"Honey," she said, brandishing a copy of *God Is Not Great*, which I thought the best of all my atheist-porn books, "I can't believe you're reading this. I thought ours was a Christian home."

"Ruth, it is. I see the tithe that leaves my bank account for Lake-wood Church every month."

"Not if you're reading books by Richard Dawkins and Christopher Hitchens."

"Do you really think that reading a book by Christopher Hitchens makes you an atheist? Reading the Bible doesn't make you a Christian. There are plenty of atheists who read the Bible."

Reluctantly, I turned the sound off on the game to give her my full attention, which I didn't want to do as the Boston Celtics were my team, but there was now no way of avoiding this discussion. Not any longer. We both knew it was long overdue.

Ruth sighed. "And what if Danny asks you about atheism? And about Charles Darwin. What are you going to tell him?"

"You want to tell him that creationism provides all the answers, then that's fine by me, that's exactly what we'll tell him. I think a kid needs religion when he's growing up. I mean, I know I did."

"And when you're an adult, what? You put away childish things?"

"Look, what I believe is of no real importance here compared with what I am prepared to pay lip service to, for the sake of family harmony."

"What if I wasn't here? If I had a car accident and I wasn't around anymore. What would happen then?"

"In a situation like that, who can say how anyone will react?"

"Is this what you're telling me?"

"I was watching TV, remember? You're the one who set this crazy debate into motion."

"You think it's crazy to talk about the moral welfare and education of our son?"

"It seems to me we're having a fight that neither of us can win. After all, you can no more prove the existence of God than I can prove he doesn't."

For a moment Ruth looked as if she were trying to swallow something indigestible, and I felt sorry for her because I could see the dilemma she had—that we both had. Whereas before we had loved each other because of what we had in common, it was beginning to look as if we were going to have to love each other in spite of our differences. My own parents had managed this very well. Maybe that's why I felt that this present difficulty was not at all insurmountable.

Ruth tossed Hitchens's book onto the La-Z-Boy and went out of the TV room without another word. This suited me fine as the Boston Celtics were now back in front.

But then, right after Sunday-morning service, she started it all up again.

"Well, that was embarrassing," she said.

"Sorry."

"Actually, it wasn't the gun I was referring to," she said. "No, you looked like you were a million miles away. That's what I'm talking about. We used to worship like a family, and I just had to look at you, Gil, to know that your heart was in it, too. But not anymore."

She was right, of course. And I didn't need to insult her intelligence by denying it. I sensed another argument was coming my way so it was fortunate Danny was already asleep. After 140 minutes of Lakewood, I could hardly blame him. I was looking forward to a Sunday-afternoon nap on a lounger at the Houstonian Club myself.

"Perhaps if we didn't sit so close to the front, that might not be so obvious. I'd feel more comfortable if we sat at the back."

"I like being close to the front," she said. "It feels like I'm nearer to God."

"I think God notices the cheap seats, too, don't you?"

"Maybe we should speak to someone."

"I don't think holding hands with a Lakewood prayer partner is going to help, Ruth."

"All right, then. Perhaps if we prayed together about this, Gil, just you and I. The way we used to pray."

The last time Ruth and I prayed together had been when we were trying to have a child. Ruth's idea, not mine. She'd suffered a miscarriage and took happy pills for a long time after that. She also experienced difficulty in becoming pregnant again, and she eventually thought the Lord might be of some assistance. This was what got us both going to Lakewood. We went to church and we prayed for another baby, although when I say we prayed for another baby we didn't just do it in church, we prayed in bed, too. Whenever we made love, we would ask the Lord for his blessing, and there's nothing quite as unerotic as that: the whole sex-prayer thing more or less killed our sex life. Having Jesus in bed with the two of us gave me a real problem and obliged me to take Viagra in secret, which is probably the only reason she got pregnant at all—but for Ruth, Danny was the miracle that proved God's existence. Since then, we've been pretty regular at Lakewood. Which is more than I can say about our sex life.

"I'm certainly willing to give prayer a shot," I said reluctantly.

Ruth sighed loudly. "What prompted you to read those books anyway?"

I shrugged and shook my head, although I knew perfectly well. I had started flirting with atheism more than a year ago, around the same time I had started an affair with a certain lovely Profiling Coordinator in Washington, D.C., where I had been given a temporary duty assignment. Ruth had chosen to remain behind with Danny. The Profiling Coordinator's name was Nancy Graham, and she and I had met after a debate at Georgetown University—the subject of the debate was "There's No Point in Praying," and the two antagonists were the British journalist and antitheist Peter Ekman (for the motion) and the former archbishop of Canterbury, Lord Mocatta (against the motion). Ruth knew about the Profiling Coordinator because I had stupidly told her and, for that very same reason, I hardly wanted to bring up the subject of Washington and the TDA again.

Ruth never ever mentioned Nancy Graham. But I knew the affair had hurt her deeply, and instead of seeking out a divorce lawyer as another woman might have done, Ruth had taken refuge in her religious faith. The affair was over, and I was deeply sorry for what had happened, and Ruth said that she had forgiven me for it, but I knew that the pain of my having had an affair was never far from my wife's thoughts.

❧

You might think that Texans are violent. Not a bit of it. The high incidence of gun ownership gives people some useful pause for thought. Most Texans are friendly, well-adjusted folk, endlessly hospitable and always polite. By contrast, the Scots are preternaturally aggressive. Many would pick a fight with a brick wall, which happens more than you might think. Scotland is the most violent place I've ever been. There's something in the air, perhaps, that makes Scotland one massive fight club. If gun ownership was as easy in Scotland as it is in Texas, the population would soon be decimated.

When my family left Scotland in 1990, the country was in one respect not much different from the Scotland of 1590 because it was divided by religion into two bellicose and bigoted camps—Protestant and Roman Catholic. In this ancient feud it always mattered more what you were than who you were and, at the sharp end of the divide, things were every bit as bitter as anything in Northern Ireland. But while religious hatred was as deep as in that other conflict, the violence in Scotland was usually limited to the fierce tribal rivalries that continue to exist between Scotland's largest football teams—both of them based in Glasgow—Rangers and Celtic. At "Old Firm" matches between these two teams the strictly segregated fans now hurl insults at one another where once they hurled rocks and bottles. But God forbid that you should be a Rangers fan who finds himself astray in Celtic territory or vice versa; and in such circumstances murder is not uncommon. For many decades sectarian football violence has been Scotland's dirty secret and few of the tourists visiting there ever have any idea of the horrors that lurk underneath my home country's threadbare and bloody kilt. I exaggerate, of course, but only a little. Then again, I am completely and utterly biased. And now let me explain why.

My father, Robert, is an orthopedic surgeon and, until his retirement last year, was a professor of orthopedic surgery at Tufts Medical Center. Prior to this, he was a surgeon at Glasgow Royal Infirmary and perhaps the leading Scottish specialist in the field of sports injuries. In 1988, when I was twelve years old, my father—a fairly prominent Roman Catholic—treated a famous footballer named Peter Paisley for a chronic knee injury that threatened to end his career. Paisley, a Protestant, played for Rangers Football Club. Following several operations, Paisley returned to the team and helped Rangers win the Scottish Football League title for four years in a row; but not before my father had received death threats from aggrieved Celtic supporters, not to mention an explosive device that almost blew off his hand.

I didn't find out about the bomb until we had left Scotland forever, but I remember coming out of our house one morning to find my father's Jaguar covered in graffiti. Soon after that, my parents and I, and my three brothers and two sisters, went to live in Boston where my dad had wisely accepted the position at Tufts. He has never returned to Scotland and probably never will.

The move was something of a wrench for us all. And it was only later that I was able to see how being a Catholic had defined me in the eyes of my Scottish friends. Of course, none of this mattered in Boston, and my religion soon seemed less important as I learned to think of myself not as a Scot, or a Scottish-American, or even a Catholic, but as just an American; in the USA what seemed to matter more than where I was from or what religion I practiced was where in life I was going.

After we came to Boston, my father stopped being a Catholic altogether.

After graduating from Boston College and Harvard Law, I went to work as an intern with a firm of New York lawyers, DLB&B, but I was already coming to the conclusion that I was more interested in working in law enforcement than in becoming an attorney. Nine-eleven only underlined that. DLB&B's offices were in the old WTC 7, which was badly damaged when the North Tower of the WTC collapsed; it caught fire and fell some six or seven hours later, by which time I was quite certain that I wanted to serve my country in some way. The following Monday I put in an application to join the FBI.

After Quantico, I had four years working in Counterterrorism in NYC. All we did was work to make America safe. I even learned to speak Arabic. I can speak the language reasonably well—although my Italian is better—but I found it hard to read and write, which is what the Bureau wanted most: agents who could read intelligence documents in the language, so that was that. The Bureau always figures it knows best where a man's talents really lie. And in 2008 the Bureau sent me to Texas to work in Domestic Terrorism.

After more than ten years with the Bureau, however, I'm still just a Supervisory Special Agent and nothing more. Fact is, I might be an ASAC right now if only I'd been willing to work in the Chief Division Counsel's office, but being a lawyer with a badge wasn't why I joined the Bureau. My boss, Gisela, is an ASAC—an Assistant Special Agent in Charge—and so is Harlan Caulfield; but the field office boss, the Special Agent in Charge, is Chuck Worrall, who doesn't like me at all. And maybe, if I am being honest here, it's not just because I didn't want to work in the CDC's office.

You see, Chuck is from Washington, and he was previously Nancy Graham's boss. After our affair was over, Nancy Graham resigned from the FBI and it's my opinion that Chuck held me responsible for the loss of a very promising agent.

⚕

From Lakewood we went to the Houstonian Club, where Danny went down the water slide and Ruth swam fifty laps. Ruth is a beautiful swimmer, very elegant, with a flip turn a dolphin would be proud of. I sat under an umbrella and read a newspaper and watched the other guys around the pool watching Ruth. She's worth a look. In her swimsuit she has a physical grace and a presence that always reminds me of an Olympic athlete.

When Ruth was through swimming, she came and lay next to me under the umbrella. She played with the hair on my chest while I stroked her head. Ruth is a very loving woman. It's not her who has the sexual problem, it's me. It's said that most men prefer their wives to be a lady in public and a whore in the bedroom. Well, I've got a saint in the bedroom, the kitchen—pretty much everywhere you can think of. You try fucking a saint. What else do you call it when the minute after you've fucked someone they start reading the Bible or saying their goddamn prayers?

When we arrived back at Driscoll Street, Ruth made meat loaf. After dinner, I played an Xbox game with Danny and put him to bed; then I watched TV and fell asleep in my chair. I didn't hear the telephone ring, but Ruth answered it in case it was the Bureau. It wasn't uncommon for the office to ring on the weekend given the DT caseload, but it wasn't the office, although I might have wished it was.

"It's Bishop Coogan," she said, handing me the telephone.

It had been months since Eamon Coogan and I had spoken, and

while I was surprised to have him call me, I tried to look more surprised than I was. This little pantomime was for Ruth's benefit as I hoped to avoid a scene with her the moment the call was over; I guessed she would assume his call was connected with my earlier declaration of disbelief and that I had already tried to bring my doubts about God to the bishop. I pressed the speakerphone button on the handset so she could hear all of our conversation in the hope it might save me the trouble of a denial.

"I'm sorry to interrupt you on a Sunday evening, Gil. I was hoping I could ask you to come and see me. In private. There's something important I'd like to discuss with you. I know it's short notice, and you're probably very busy, but would now be possible?"

I glanced instinctively at my watch. It was already seven-thirty.

"Nothing's happened back in Boston, has it?"

"No, no. Nothing like that, Gil. It's something I need to ask you about in your capacity as a federal agent."

The bishop was South Boston Irish and, despite his having lived in Houston for several years, some of his vowels sounded as wide as the Charles River. When he said "ask," he sounded like JFK.

"Yes, sir. But would you mind telling me what it's about?"

"It's hardly a subject for the phone, I think. Come over to the bishop's residence in an hour. Just sound your horn and I'll come out. I was thinking, perhaps, we could go over to O'Neill's."

It was just like Eamon Coogan to suggest that we go to an Irish bar.

"All right. I'll be there in an hour."

I rang off and looked at Ruth.

"What do you suppose that's all about?"

"If you ask me," said Ruth—much to my irritation, she could always mimic a Southie accent perfectly—"it's perfectly obvious what it's about."

I shrugged.

"It can only be about pedophile priests."

"What?"

"You don't think it goes on here, just like in Boston and Chicago?"

I put my arms around her waist and kissed her back. For a while, she let it happen and then pushed me gently away.

"God, I hope that's not what it's about," I said, wrinkling my nose with disgust. "It's really not something I feel comfortable talking about. He's my mother's oldest friend."

FIVE

B rian O'Neill's bar was the only Irish pub I'd ever seen with two palm trees out front, but inside things were more authentically Celtic, with the best draught Guinness in the city and perhaps the worst service anywhere west of Dublin. The place was popular enough, although, even by Texas standards, most of the bar's customers looked as if they could have survived a couple of Irish potato famines.

No less in size was Bishop Coogan, who made any room he was in look small. He was sitting in a very fat-old-womanish way, all chubby-fingered and splay-legged, with the sleeves of his huge black jacket rolled up over his forearms and the waistband of his equally enormous black trousers riding just under his armpits. The priest's collar around his neck was almost invisible under his chins. He looked like a sumo wrestler at a wake.

I set a second tray of drinks down on the table in front of him and one of the whiskies instantly disappeared. Now that our small talk about Scotland and Northern Ireland was exhausted, I was impatient for him to get to the point. I was especially intrigued by the old duffel bag he had brought with him.

"So, Bishop, what's in the bag? Is it guns you're bringing me or the loot from the Woodforest National Bank robbery? The Buick that's parked on the drive in front of your house looks like the getaway car on that one."

"Sorry to disappoint you, Gil, but it's just a lot of newspaper clippings, a couple of books, and some printouts off the Internet. One way or the other, I seem to be spending a lot of time on the Internet these days."

"You and me both, sir."

"The papers and the books are for you."

Coogan unzipped the bag and handed me a paperback book titled *All the Possible Gods*. The author was Philip Osborne. As soon as I saw it, I laughed.

"Only an hour or two ago Ruth was giving me hell for reading this book. And several others like it."

"Oh? Such as?"

"Dawkins, Hitchens, Peter Ekman." I shrugged. "Sam Harris, Dan Barker, Daniel Dennett . . ."

Coogan chuckled. "That's virtually the whole pantheon of disbelief you have there."

"Why the hell do you want to give me this book?"

"Philip Osborne is a friend of mine," said Bishop Coogan. "Or at least he was."

"You say that like he's dead."

"He might as well be. He's confined to the Harris County Psychiatric Center here in Houston. I visited him a few days ago and spoke with his doctors who described to me a case of psychogenic malignant catatonia resulting in permanent cognitive impairment. They've concluded there must be actual damage to the frontal lobe of his brain, although there's absolutely no identifiable trauma that might normally have caused such a state of mental breakdown."

Coogan's familiarity with all these medical terms impressed me, at least until I remembered that before becoming a priest, Coogan had been a medical student at Tufts in Boston, where he had been taught by my father.

"So he didn't fall and nobody hit him," I said. "But you're going to tell me what did happen."

"I'm not sure I am. But I'd like to tell you what I know, Gil. And why I wanted to talk to you about it."

"Go ahead, but"—I shrugged—"I don't see how I can help. At the FBI we have jurisdiction over violations of federal law. And so far I can't see there's anything federal here. If you want, I can put you in touch with the right people in the Houston Police Department."

"Fidelity, bravery, and integrity," said Coogan. He was quoting the Bureau's motto. "Perhaps I should go ahead and add patience to that little trio of the better human qualities." He laid his hand on the book. "It's not a bad book at all. As a matter of fact, it was me who gave him that title. Or at least recommended it as a title."

"*All the Possible Gods?*"

"It's from a quote by Stephen Roberts. He's another of your so-called new atheists. As if they make any more sense than the old atheists."

"I think that perhaps I'm not as patient as you think I am, Eamon." I looked at my watch pointedly.

"About a month ago Philip turned up at my house in an agitated state. When I asked him what was wrong, he said he hadn't been sleeping. That was obvious. And when I suggested he see a doctor and get some sleeping pills, he told me he couldn't because he was already taking Xanax and that whenever he did sleep he had terrible nightmares. I asked him if he could account for this change in himself and he shook his head and said something strange. Well, for him it was strange—I might have said it was impossible. He asked me if I would pray for him."

Coogan sat back for a moment. "Gil, you could have knocked me over with a feather. It was awful, that's what it was. You see, I'm a man first of all, and a priest second. So there was no bloody rejoicing about a lost sinner. I felt sorry for the poor bastard."

"So what happened after he came to your house?"

"My praying for him seemed to give him a bit of peace of mind. But only for a while." Coogan searched his pockets. "I need a cigarette. Let's go outside."

It was hot on the terrace. We moved away from the tables where a few of the bar's more heat-resistant customers were eating and drinking under the shade of some black-and-white umbrellas; we stood at the edge of the tree-lined road. Quickly and expertly Coogan made a roll-up and tucked it into the corner of his lopsided mouth, where it remained until it was the size of a lost tooth. Meanwhile, he continued to tell his story.

"A couple of months ago, Random House—his publisher—launched his latest book at a party at the Hotel ZaZa. The book is called *More Faith in a Shadow*. It's kind of like the other one. A drive-by shooting outside the gates of heaven."

"At least that sounds like a crime, Eamon."

"The party had started at around seven. But at eight-thirty there was no longer any sign of Philip. Soon afterward, everyone on the terrace heard a commotion that seemed to come from the direction of the plaza. The plaza is a small island of trees and bronze figures just a few yards away. It was a dreadful commotion—like the sound of an animal in distress. I think it was the doormen who crossed the road to investigate. Anyway, they came back to inform us that it was Philip Osborne and that he appeared to be in a state of hysteria. Some of the guests went to see what we could do and an astonishing sight awaited us: Philip was cowering underneath the cupola of a little monument, whimpering like a dog. His hands and face were covered in blood and he was pleading with some invisible figure to leave him alone.

"When I tried to touch him, Philip let out such a scream that it quite put the fear of God into everyone. Philip then attempted to strangle one of the doormen and it was at this point that an HPD patrol car arrived. One of the officers was about to Taser him when suddenly he gave up the attack and took off across the road into some nearby fountains. And that's where we found him a few minutes later—lying on the surface of the water, staring up at the sky, and quite unresponsive to all external stimuli, almost as if he were dead. He's been like that ever since."

By now I had remembered the story in the *Chronicle*—only the report had suggested the author had been drunk, and since it wasn't unusual for drunks to take a swim in the fountains on Montrose Boulevard, I had paid little attention to it. It all sounded unfortunate, but I was still at a loss as to why Bishop Coogan was interrupting my Sunday evening with this.

"There was blood—Philip Osborne's blood—all over that little plaza, as if he'd run around banging into one thing and then another like a crazy man. He gashed his arm and—"

"Well, there you are," I said. "He must have hit his head on something as well."

"But there were no contusions on his skull. Just a few scratches on his face from the branches on the trees."

"And the blood on his hands?"

"He'd tried to climb the monument."

"Did the police find any assailant?"

"No. The police think it was a simple case of stress, overwork, too much Xanax mixed with too much alcohol. A Britney-style breakdown that ended up being rather more damaging than a photo spread in *Us Weekly*."

"Look," I said, "I'm sorry about your friend, but however you want to cook it, Eamon, Bishop, sir, this meat's HPD."

"And if I told you that this is hardly an isolated case? That there have been similar cases—fatal cases—in other states?"

"I'd probably say what I said earlier. People go MIA when their heads are upriver. That's just the way it is."

Coogan was shaking his own outsize head. "No, no, this is different, Gil. I'm sure of it. I can feel it."

"That might be a deeper source of religion, but it won't do for my boss. We need evidence."

"And I've got it. In my duffel bag there's a file full of evidence. Just promise me that you'll take a look at it."

"All right. But I can't promise to act on your material. That way I won't disappoint you. On top of everything else."

"You're thinking you're maybe an atheist and that I'll mind and be disappointed, is that it? God's got an electronic tether on you, Gil. And for the rest of your life it'll be there around your ankle so that he can come and get you when he's ready. Once it's on, it stays on and there's nothing you can do about it. You could wander to the end of the world, Gil, and it'll still be sending God a signal once or twice a day forever."

SIX

A lot of people at the Houstonian Club know I'm an FBI agent and I am often given information about some alleged crime that turns out to be a whole bunch of crap. It's an occupational hazard, I guess, but whenever I'm in the club, it's not very long before one of the members or even one of the staff approaches me with a story that usually obliges me to step off the running machine and make a few notes: to do anything else would not be good for the image of the Bureau. As would my telling any of these people to fuck off. In order to escape the possibility of any unpleasantness at the Houstonian, I try to stay off the club radar; by using a professional set of picklocks to get in and out of a service door near the parking lot, I can more or less come and go and still keep out of the computer system, thus avoiding any "hot tips" and general bullshit. If no one knows you're there, they can't come and find you.

I had too much respect for Bishop Coogan to brush him off as just another crackpot in a long line of crackpots; however, for Ruth's benefit, that's exactly what I did when I got home. Dismissing Coogan's "tip" was a quick way of dismissing what she always imagined was the case: the power that the Church of Rome still had over me. But as soon as I was alone again—Ruth always went to bed early on a Sunday night—I opened the bag and started to read.

There were clippings from *The New York Times*, *The Boston Globe*, and *The Washington Post*; but mostly I was looking at copies of web-pages reproduced on Coogan's printer. All of these papers had been neatly hole-punched and filed in strict chronological order so that I was quickly able to gain an impression of just what had convinced him that there was something fishy going on.

When I had finished reading through the file, I fetched a pad of paper, read the contents again, and made some notes. Just before midnight I poured myself a scotch. I don't normally stay up late and drink scotch, but you don't expect a bishop to point out what a lot of law enforcement officers had overlooked.

It was a sultry night with the air temperature still in the high seventies. I opened the window in my little tower and leaned outside with my glass. I lit a cigarette and smoked it quickly in the hope the smell might not reach Ruth's nostrils.

I called Coogan at the bishop's house on my cell. "I just wanted to say I'm sorry I sounded skeptical."

"You were just doing your job. What happens now?"

"There's a process, a way of doing these things. You might say I have to convert some people to our way of thinking."

"But you do agree with me?"

"There's something, yes. But don't get your hopes up. I can't promise to come back to you on this for a while."

"I understand. You've got your own archbishops and cardinals, just like I do. Anything else I can do?"

"Well, I would say that you could pray for me if I thought for one minute it would do any good."

That was when I heard something in the doorway and looked

around to see Ruth standing there. It seemed like she'd been there for a while—long enough to get hold of the wrong end of the stick because she was looking pretty pissed at me.

"Eamon, I've got to go."

"Good night, son, and God bless."

ЯΒ

"So what were you talking about with Bishop Coogan?"

"Those papers he gave me. I think there's more to it than I thought."

"It sounded to me as if you and he were discussing your own crisis of faith, honey."

I shook my head. "No, it wasn't anything like that. I'm sorry, did I wake you up?"

"I smelled the cigarette."

"That's why I was smoking it out of the window."

"It still comes in the house when you breathe out."

"All right, in future I'll try not to do too much of that." I shrugged. "What's the matter?"

"I guess I'm a little puzzled that you can talk about things with Bishop Coogan that you don't seem able to discuss with me."

"I already told you," I said, stifling a yawn, "that's not what he and I were talking about."

She unfolded her arms and took my hand in her own.

"I was thinking, Gil, maybe we could . . ."

She hesitated long enough for me to get the wrong idea. I put my arms around her and tried to kiss her.

"I didn't mean that," she said. "I thought maybe we could pray. Now. Together."

I sighed and put a better face on my disappointment. "I really don't think that's going to help right now, sweetheart."

"It's okay for Bishop Coogan to pray for you, but not me. Is that it?"

"Look, you can pray for me all you want, honey. And so can he. His was a professional courtesy, I imagine. But I don't want to pray with anyone. Not anymore. Not ever. I just can't, Ruth. I don't have the words. God isn't there for me. Perhaps he never was."

⚭

They say God moves in a mysterious way, but I have to admit I was more than a little surprised by what happened over breakfast.

Danny was watching television before Ruth drove him to school. I had a slice of toast in one hand and a cup of coffee in the other, and Ruth was fixing my tie for me, and perhaps it didn't help that the tie was one she knew I had acquired during my temporary duty assignment in Washington, D.C. If she suspected that Nancy Graham had bought it for me, from Michael Andrews Bespoke—which she had—then she certainly didn't say so. But this time she did a lot more than merely straighten my tie. The green eyes I knew better than mine flicked up and down between the knot of the tie and my face, and each time I met them they seemed a little sadder than before; then she swallowed a lump in her throat the size of an egg and a tear appeared on one eyelash. In the same moment a terrible fear went through me and, recognizing all at once that something was very wrong, I started to cover her forehead with kisses and to apologize for the previous evening.

"I'm so sorry about last night, babe," I said. "I shouldn't have said what I said. It was unforgivable."

"Yes, it was," she said, and tightened the silk knot of my tie just a little too much. "I could strangle you because of what you said last night, Gil Martins. And I hate having that feeling about my husband. I don't recognize myself in your eyes. We used to be such good friends, you and I. But now all I feel is your overriding hostility."

"Come on, Ruth, it's not you I feel hostile toward," I said. "You know I love you. I've always loved you. Even when I made that mistake in Washington, I still loved you."

"Do you see what you've done, Martins? You and this precious job of yours? Do you see where you've brought me? Where you've brought us?"

"Let's not talk about my job again, Ruth."

"And I am not going to talk about it. I give you my word on that. I'll never talk about your job again. Not now, not ever."

As she let go of my tie, I put down the toast and the coffee, cupped her hands in mine, and lifted them to kiss the tips of her fingers.

"Forget what I said last night. Look, if you want to pray, let's pray. All right? I'm ready. We'll kneel down and pray and ask for God's help, just like you wanted."

I knelt down and tried to make her kneel with me, but Ruth stayed up on her feet and turned away. "You have to leave," she said.

Still kneeling in front of her, I glanced at my watch. "No, it's okay, honey. I'm still early. Besides, this is much more important than opening a new case."

"No, Gil. You don't understand."

"Come on, honey, I'm trying to say sorry."

"I mean you have to leave this house. For good."

"What?"

"You heard me."

Suddenly, I felt like I had stepped off the top of the J.P.Morgan building without an elevator. Like one of those jumpers from the WTC on 9/11. There was nothing underneath me except hundreds of feet of empty air.

I stood up. "What the hell are you talking about, Ruth?"

"I didn't want this," she said. "I tried. I really did. But you have to leave this house, Gil."

"You're shitting me."

I don't know why I said that because Ruth wasn't the type to say anything like that lightly. I grabbed her by the arm and pulled her toward me, but already it felt like she wasn't my wife anymore and that love and understanding were behind us and that even now we were each returning to our separate pasts and who we had been before we ever met and that what we were to each other for more than eight years was gone.

She shook her head, firmly. "No," she said. "I am not."

"What, are you crazy?"

"I'm not crazy, no. But I will be if I continue living with you, Gil. The fact is, I can't believe in something I hold to be important and still be around someone who doesn't believe it at all."

"Nobody dumps their husband because he's no longer a fucking Christian. It's positively medieval."

"Well, there you go again. Nobody, huh? 'Do not be unequally yoked with unbelievers. For what partnership has righteousness with lawlessness?'"

"Ruth? You sound like a fanatic. The sort of people who come out with this kind of thing? We call them Christianists at the Bureau. They're just as crazy as Islamists only they sing cheesier songs. I can't believe that's you, Ruth. Listen to yourself."

Ruth closed her eyes. "Listen to myself, he says. Nobody else talks to me. Not you. Not anymore. You tiptoe around me like I'm some kind of minefield."

"This isn't about God or my loss of faith, is it?" I said.

"Well, that certainly doesn't help."

"It's about her, isn't it?"

"Why don't you say her name? I'm sure you can't have forgotten it, Gil."

"I thought we were over all that."

"And with God's help, I really think we might have been. But that's not to be, I can see that now."

"God's got nothing to do with what happened in Washington."

"With what happened? No, you're right about that much, Gil. But I really thought he might help us to shape a future for ourselves. I need God and Lakewood Church because I really can't do this by myself. I'm not strong enough. And you don't help, Gil. You're so detached from me—from me *and* Danny. Well, you have your work to think about, of course. And I don't deny that yours is important work. You are helping to keep our country safe. It's work anyone can be proud of. But with you, it's more than just work—it's a refuge, a sanctuary, a compulsion. You come back and you're all closed up and neat and tight and secure, like a gun safe. But what have I got? Where else can I take refuge but in God and Lakewood? I'd like to know. And don't say the club. I'm not like those other Houston women who spend all day in the spa having their nails done and reading *H Texas.*"

"You were a fine lawyer. You could go back to work, Ruth."

She shook her head.

"You were good at it."

"Only you thought so. But I didn't have the teeth for it. I was too forgiving to be a decent prosecutor. That's what the DA said."

"You could get a job in private practice."

"It wasn't all right for you, but it might be all right for me, is that what you're saying? You're joking, of course. People in law firms these days put in twelve-hour days and more. I made a choice, Gil. A choice to be a wife and a mother. Besides, I really don't want to leave Danny with a nanny."

"Lots of women do."

"I didn't try so hard to have our child just to farm his care out to a stranger."

"All right. I understand that, honey. But please, let's try to work this out."

"Work it out." Ruth smiled a weary little smile. "What do you think I've been doing these last few months? What do you think I've been doing? I've been desperately hoping that I could see some sign that you were happy with just me and Danny. That you'd forgotten about her. Nancy Graham. There, I said her name. I lie awake at night and see it written in the atoms of air above our bed. But I know you haven't forgotten her. I can see it in your eyes. It's not just God and the church that you don't believe in, Gil. It's me and Danny. It's our life in Houston. It's us."

"Oh, that's nonsense, Ruth."

"Is it? I don't think so. Your atheism is a symptom—an important symptom—of something much more profound. Of a deeper fracture between us as a couple. Maybe you can't see it. But I can and I just don't want to deal with it. Not anymore. You think you can humor me with—what was it you said? With what you are prepared to pay lip service to for the sake of family harmony? Well, I'm through with lip service. And I'm through with you. I want more than just lip service from my marriage. I want a connection. I want a union. I want a conversation. I want—I want you gone."

"Do you honestly think I'm just going to walk out of here without a fight? No way."

"As you like," she said. "But don't you think we've done enough fighting? That's why I'm telling you that you have to leave."

"This isn't over, Ruth," I said, grimly picking up my car keys.

"Yes, it is," she said.

"We'll talk about this when I come home tonight."

"No, we won't," she said.

"Yes, we will," I said. "Not to talk about it. You think that's what God wants? Not to give me a chance to put things right."

"You should go," she said.

SEVEN

Working late kept my mind off what was happening at home. Ruth and Danny were no longer there. She was already back with her parents; their home—a twelve-hundred-acre hilltop ranch in Corsicana—was the first place I telephoned when I discovered Ruth was gone, and it was all Bob could do not to sound pleased when he said that she didn't want to speak with me. He always felt that Ruth could have done better than pick me. I suppose all fathers feel that way about their only daughters; but it's not often they tell you as much.

Corsicana is less than two hundred miles north of Houston and I thought of driving there to straighten things out, but I stayed in Houston and told myself she'd come home when she was good and ready. After that, I only called her cell and I must have sent her about a hundred texts but she never answered. Every marriage has its ups and downs. I figured that Ruth just needed time and space to get her head around what was important in her life. There was plenty of space in Corsicana.

A couple of times I sent Danny some books and a new Xbox game from Amazon so he'd know I was thinking of him; I knew they were delivered all right, but he didn't reply, either—or at least Ruth didn't allow him to send me a text or an e-mail, which struck me as mean. It was odd how quickly I felt removed from them both—almost as if they had ceased to exist, so much so that I started to question just how much I had loved them. Would I have risked the affair with Nancy Graham if I'd been the loving husband and father I ought to have been? Was that how it was for most men when their marriages end? I asked a few of the guys around the office and the consensus was that it wasn't them who had ceased to exist, it was me. After a while, they said, you're just some guy who used to live with them but who still pays for stuff and you might as well get used to this. But I certainly didn't want to.

It helped a lot that I could throw myself into my existing caseload as well as a closer investigation of what was in Bishop Coogan's file; and in this I was lucky enough to have the assistance of Anne Goldberg, who was by general consensus the best investigative analyst in the Houston field office. As a member of our Field Intelligence Group, Anne handled the collection of raw information such as telephone records, webpages, bank details, and, of course, criminal backgrounds; as someone who'd worked as a journalist, Anne was very good at getting information out of other journalists—they're always cagey about sharing information with the FBI. So she had several conversations with reporters from *The New York Times*, *The Washington Post*, and *The Boston Globe*. Her greatest skill, however, was her ability to see patterns and shapes in assembled data, and this was the main reason why brick agents like me wanted to work with her. No one could make a link chart like Anne Goldberg.

It's not just bits of information that we like to connect in the Bureau, it's each other, too. There are no lone wolves at the FBI. The brick agent I worked with in DT was Helen Monaco and, like me, she was ex-Counterterrorism. Helen's first case had been working undercover on an FBI yacht in the Mediterranean; her role had been to act as the eye candy while a sting on some al-Qaeda Arabs went down. It was plain to see how someone thought she could play that role to perfection. Helen Monaco was everyone's fantasy desert-island partner. In an effort to play down her looks and be taken seriously, she now wore weak-prescription and possibly unnecessary glasses, little or no makeup, and severe business suits, but no one was fooled by the Betty Bureau shtick. Helen Monaco could have worn a used trash-can liner and she'd still have looked like a hot babe. Not that I entertained any intentions toward her. Besides, I had the strong impression that she'd already been warned about me by Chuck Worrall. He had my card marked as a hustler, and until now, I'd thought that was good. It helped to keep my feet on the straight and narrow for Helen to think of me as someone with whom it wasn't safe to share an elevator car.

Helen had one other qualification that marked her out as an excellent partner. During the undercover operation on the yacht, she'd shot two al-Qaeda when they drew on one of her colleagues. One of the men she shot died; the other's driving a wheelchair around the supermax prison yard in Florence, Colorado. Result.

The three of us—Anne, Helen, and I—started to work the Philip Osborne case on Monday; and by Thursday, we had enough information to take it to the ASAC. I asked those two along because I figured that all three of us made a more convincing argument in favor of a proper investigation than just one line supervisor. Besides, I had a theory I wanted to test; actually it was Helen's theory. Helen said that Gisela Delillo always gave me a harder time when there were other female agents present—almost as if she were trying to prove that there was nothing between us.

While I lined some sharpened pencils up in neat little ranks beside my Bureau leather folder, Gisela made all of us coffee and then invited me to make the case against our unsub—the as yet unknown subject of an FBI investigation.

❀

"This is the strangest case for investigation I have ever presented," I began. "Almost three weeks ago, here in Houston, the writer Philip Osborne suffered an acute shock that has left him mentally impaired, perhaps permanently. No explanation for how that shock came about has yet been discovered. At first it was assumed that he'd been attacked. But if so, it's not clear how. Or by whom. There were some superficial wounds on him, only these would appear to have been self-inflicted. But there's a lot that's not clear here so I'm going to have to ask you to be patient, boss."

"I'm always patient with you, Martins," said Gisela, and she grinned at Helen and Anne. "I guess it's the only way, huh?"

I let that one go. When you're just a line supervisor, you let it go more often than you pick it up. Besides, my theory about her was already starting to amount to something: in front of other women Gisela liked slapping me down.

"As you may know," I said, "Philip Osborne was gay and his two most recent books were both about atheism. In the last few years he's managed to upset a lot of people. But everything I've read about him makes me think he gets a kick out of that. At first I wanted to dismiss what happened as a celebrity crack-up. But I was wrong. My friend Dr. Eamon Coogan, who is the emeritus Catholic archbishop of the Cathedral of the Sacred Heart, drew my attention to a number of recent homicides that display some interesting similarities. The other victims were also what you might call enemies of the conservative right: a senior consulting obstetrician, an evolutionary biologist, and a philosopher and cognitive scientist. But at present no connection has been established between any of these cases."

"If the other three were relatively well known," said Gisela, "and you're arguing a connection, how come the newspapers haven't done that? They're usually not slow to spot a trend."

"Because they all look like natural causes. But Coogan thinks there are circumstances that bear further examination and share common features with what happened to Osborne. And so do I."

"Is there any other field office interested in investigating a connection?"

"No," I said. "This will leave Houston as the office of origin."

"If we take it on," said Gisela. "Don't jump the gun, Gil."

She smiled at me, but that was the second time in five minutes that I'd been whipped. I wondered if Helen and Anne noticed it, too.

"All right. I'm still listening. But start here in Houston. With this Osborne guy. If any of this is connected, he's what lets us buy the blinds."

I knew to my cost that Gisela was a skilled poker player, although it was rare that she ever talked like one. But it seemed like another way of reminding me that she was holding all the aces in this meeting.

After setting out the facts as reported by the HPD officers who had attended the scene at the Hotel ZaZa, I described the visit I had made with Helen Monaco to the Harris County Psychiatric Hospital.

"Dr. Andrew Newman, the medical director, gave me a diagnosis of Osborne's condition. The guy is in a catatonic state. He doesn't move at all and appears to be in a frozen state of being that Newman thinks is psychological rather than neurological. Specifically, he thinks something induced an extreme fight-or-flight response—a stress response— that caused his adrenal hormones to kick in on a massive scale and induce a sympathetic nervous system dynamic. There's a third strike after the fight-or-flight pitch: you freeze. You know, the rabbit caught in the headlights kind of shit. But humans do the same thing. And if that isn't resolved, it builds up, sometimes really quickly, and you enter a shock state that is designed to protect you from something worse, per- haps. Usually you come out of it. Sometimes quickly, sometimes not so quickly. And in Osborne's case it's clear Dr. Newman doesn't have the least idea if he'll be like that for eighteen days or eighteen months."

"So, what, is he just lying on a bed staring at the ceiling?"

"They keep him strapped on a bed for his own safety in case he does snap out of it all of a sudden. But like a piece of Play-Doh, Osborne's body can be contorted into any posture, which he'll maintain for several minutes, or until you move his limbs or his head in some other direction."

I felt Helen shiver beside me.

"And all the time he just stares straight ahead as if he were dead," I said. "Only he's not. All his vital signs—heart rate, pulse, blood pressure—seem to indicate that he's perfectly normal. It's like he's imprisoned inside his own body. But there was one thing that was odd, and it ties in with the fight-or-flight response described by Dr. Newman. Quite soon after he was admitted to the hospital, the doctors took a blood sample. Adrenaline is often measured in blood as a diagnostic aid. In any of us right now, the level is probably ten nanograms per liter. That can increase by as much as ten times during exercise and by as much as fifty times during extreme stress, to five hundred nanograms per liter. Osborne's body contained about ten thousand nanograms per liter, which is apparently the amount they might administer to acute-care cardiac patients with a hypodermic. To inject that amount of adrenaline in a short period you'd need a large Epipen or a cardiac needle; and yet there is no sign anywhere on Osborne's body of a hypodermic mark. Nor any evidence that an inhaler was used. No Epipen or inhaler was found at the hotel, or the plaza, or on Osborne's person. Newman hasn't ever seen that quantity of adrenaline occur naturally, but he says that doesn't mean it couldn't happen. He hasn't ever seen a case of acute catatonia like Osborne's, either."

"That is strange," said Gisela, scribbling something down on her pad.

"He also recently applied for a concealed-handgun license."

"Nothing strange about that," said Gisela.

"Except that he was a vocal opponent of the NRA and gun owner-ship in general," I said.

"So something had him scared." Gisela looked at Anne Goldberg. "Anything on his telephone records, Anne?"

"Not a thing that shouldn't be there. All of the numbers were in his address book."

"E-mails?"

"The guys at the lab are looking over his computer to see if there are any clues there," I said. "But that's going to take a little time. Until then, here's what we know about the other three.

"Dr. Clifford Richardson ran the Silphium Clinic in Washington, D.C. Until his death six months ago, he was one of the country's lead-ing obstetricians. He was also a former president of the American Gy-necological and Obstetrical Society, and an internationally recognized authority on clinical obstetrics. Following threats to his life in Utah during the late 1990s, Richardson came to live and work in the capital, opening a clinic just a few hundred yards north of the White House, on Sixteenth Street where, he assumed, there might be less opposition to abortion."

"If it wasn't for people like him," said Gisela, "I don't know what women would do in this country."

"He was wrong," I said. "About there being no opposition in D.C. The Silphium Clinic has been regularly picketed as a so-called abor-tion mill by self-styled sidewalk counselors from pro-life groups and D.C.'s Catholic University of America. They try to talk women out of having abortions, and pray for women who are coming out of the clinic having had one."

"It sounds like harassment," observed Anne.

"Which is why there are cops on the scene," I said. "And pro-choice escorts. Or 'deathscorts,' as the pro-life people call them."

"Oh, brother," muttered Anne. "There are times when I wish we could bring in Jesus for questioning and ask him if he wouldn't mind disowning some of these stupid pricks." She looked at me. "Sorry, Gil. I know you go to church."

"That's all right. Matter of fact, you didn't say anything about him that I haven't been thinking myself. And just for the record, people, I'm no longer a churchgoer."

Gisela sat back in her chair. "What does Ruth think about that?"

I was about to make a remark about how thought didn't seem to be part of my wife's decision when the failure that was my marriage choked the words in my throat. I thought of Danny, and I swallowed hard and felt my eyes begin to blink as if I didn't quite trust them to stay open without displaying more emotion than was appropriate for a case meeting with my ASAC. There followed a longish silence that grew more revealing and eloquent by the second as I tried to get a grip.

Gisela's quick, poker-player instincts read the tell that was in my eyes and guessed the whole story, or at least half of it.

"Oh, my God," she gasped. "Gil. Has Ruth left you?"

I shook my head but my face and fluctuating Adam's apple said different. "I'd really rather not talk about it right now. One way or another, it's been a difficult week."

"Look, do you need a minute?"

I took a deep breath.

"No, I'm fine," I said, and suddenly, for the moment, I was.

"Cliff Richardson lived in the Watergate complex," I said. "His apartment had a balcony with a view of the Potomac. On Friday, February 21, of this year, Richardson was late finishing work at the clinic. His receptionist described him as unusually preoccupied. After filling the tank of his car at a gas station, he arrived home at about nine o'clock, parked in the underground parking lot, and took the elevator upstairs.

Despite what you may have read, security is good at the Watergate. His neighbors reported seeing or hearing nothing unusual. It was a cold night and there was snow on the ground, but not enough to break a man's fall from the eleventh floor. The following morning one of the gardeners found Richardson's body in some bushes beneath his balcony. He had a ticket for a concert the following evening and a full refrigerator. The same day he apparently jumped off his balcony he also ordered some books from Amazon that arrived on the same morning his body was discovered."

"What you're saying," said Gisela, "is that none of this behavior was consistent with a man who was going to kill himself."

"Correct," I said. "The Metro Police Department attended the scene and—with some difficulty, I might add, for there were several locks on the door—they entered Richardson's apartment, where they found no suicide note and no signs of a struggle. The TV was still on, and there was a meal cooked in the microwave oven. Because of these contraindications to suicide and Richardson's previous history, MPD decided to treat the death as suspicious. Inquiries were made in Utah. And people who had been picketing the clinic were interviewed. There's also a CCTV in the apartment block and everyone who went in and out of the building that day was accounted for and cleared. None of them had any connection with the pro-lifers outside the clinic. Having failed to turn up any leads, the MPD concluded that Richardson had committed suicide and closed the case. But there was one unusual thing the police noticed in Richardson's apartment. A Torah scroll open on the sideboard in a kind of pride of place. You know? The sort they use in a synagogue, written on parchment paper in ancient Hebrew, with wooden rollers 'n' all."

"So?" said Gisela.

"Richardson wasn't Jewish," I said. "According to his daughter, he wasn't even religious. She couldn't explain why he owned such a thing."

"It was a Sefer Torah scroll," said Anne. "They're expensive. Richardson bought it on eBay about two weeks before he died. And he paid seven thousand dollars for it."

"Which is strange," I added, "when you consider that he read not one word of Hebrew."

"Strange, yes," admitted Gisela. "But not evidence of murder."

"Next we have Peter Ekman, a prominent British journalist who became an American citizen after 9/11. He was a former editor of *The New Republic*, the author of many books and an irreverent daily news blog called *Ekman: Hack* that appeared on *The Daily Beast*. Until his death in April this year, his blog was receiving five hundred thousand hits a day."

"I didn't even know he was dead," said Anne.

"Apart from politicians, Ekman regularly went after religion. The week before he died, he wrote a piece about the Baptists that drew sixty-five thousand complaints, which is a record for *The Daily Beast*. Ekman was the kind of guy who would say things no one else dared to say. And he got away with it because he was funny. Famously, he was on *The Volker Walker Show* on HBO with Pastor Ken Coffey, the evangelist, and Coffey got so angry with Ekman that he suffered a seizure and had to be taken to the hospital. That got Ekman in a lot of trouble with the religious right. I once saw him debating with the former archbishop of Canterbury, Lord Mocatta, at Georgetown University, and he was extremely funny and trenchant. But the biggest stink he attracted was with the Muslims when he blogged about Angela Merkel, the German chancellor, when she gave a press freedom award to Kurt Westergaard— the Danish guy who drew the caricatures of the prophet Mohammed."

"Always a mistake," said Anne.

"Actually, Ekman used his blog to compare the Danish cartoons with ones that used to appear in the newspapers in Nazi Germany, but even though he was defending them, he still managed to piss off the Muslims by reproducing the cartoons."

"Some people you can't help," said Anne.

"All right," said Gisela. "Ekman was funny. But he had a smoking-related illness. Emphysema, wasn't it? And I remember that he had a heart attack. So why are we talking about him?"

"After the Muslims threatened his life, he decided to take some precautions regarding his personal security; and he had a panic room built at his home. The room had its own generator and an alarm button connected to the local police. That should have saved his life. Instead, his wife came back from the city one day to find him dead in there. The police concluded that the room wasn't properly ventilated and that this caused carbon monoxide poisoning. He was sixty-two."

"Why was he in the panic room in the first place? Do we know?" asked Gisela.

"No. And he didn't sound the alarm. Or if he did, it didn't work and no one came. The front door was locked. So were all of the windows. No footprints in the garden. No broken tiles on the roof."

"Recent threats?"

"Ekman's wife told the police he received threats all the time, mostly on the website or in the mail, but that she wasn't aware of anything out of the ordinary. Then again, she thought Ekman probably wouldn't have told her if there had been. He tended to treat that kind of thing as an occupational hazard. Anyway, the Tarrytown PD handled the investigation with the assistance of the Bureau of Criminal Police from the New York staties."

"So, an accidental death," said Gisela.

"Ekman had a pet cat," I said. "The cat was found dead, too."

"It figures," said Gisela. "Carbon monoxide poisoning. That stuff is invisible and odorless."

"Except that the cat wasn't found in the panic room but outside, in the gallery where the panic room was concealed."

"Maybe," said Helen, "when the door of the panic room was opened, a pocket of gas came out. Not enough to trouble Mrs. Ekman, but just enough to affect the cat."

"There you are, Gil," said Gisela. "I think Helen just solved your felinicide."

"Hey, I thought you were supposed to be on my side," I told Helen.

"I am," she said. "But it just occurred to me. Maybe, unbeknownst to Mrs. Ekman, the cat followed her into the panic room, took a deep breath of the gas, came outside again, and died."

"All right," said Gisela. "Let's try to keep the speculation to a minimum, folks. Gil. You said there was a third case that caught Bishop Coogan's eye. Why don't you tell us about that?"

"Willard Davidoff was a professor of human evolutionary biology at Yale University, the vice president of the American Humanist Association, a celebrated author, and a well-known atheist. In 2009 he was listed by *Time* magazine as one of the hundred most influential people in the world. Just before Christmas last year, Davidoff gave a lecture at the Boston Public Library. His subject was 'The Evolution of Superstition and Religion,' and he argued that today's religions are not a matter of divine revelation but of natural selection, in that only the strongest religions have survived by virtue of their fitness, which he defines as their willingness to exterminate other religions."

"That must have gone down well in Boston," said Gisela.

I grinned. "Actually, the lecture was a sellout. Afterward there was a party to which all of Boston's Brahmins were invited. Before it ended, his publisher reported seeing Davidoff on one of the upper floors, talking to himself. She spoke to him and he ignored her. He was known to be an irascible character, so she was used to this and left him alone. No one saw him after that, and it was assumed he had gone back to his room at the Four Seasons. It's a ten-minute walk. You could do it with your eyes closed. But the following morning a dog walker found Davidoff's body in Olmsted Park, which is an hour's walk in the opposite direction. He was still wearing his Rolex and carrying a wallet with three hundred dollars in it, so it was clear he hadn't been mugged. His neck was broken and he appeared to have fallen out of a tree. His clothes were heavily stained with tree moss and there was bark underneath his fingernails."

"Was he drunk?" asked Gisela.

"They found about a bottle of red wine in his system," I said.

"That would sure make me drunk," admitted Helen.

"The question is," I continued, "was it the bottle of red that Davidoff drank in the Boston Public Library that persuaded him to walk three miles in the wrong direction on a cold night and then to climb a tree? Or was it something else? Someone on Huntington Avenue said they thought they saw a man answering Davidoff's description running in the direction of the park at about ten-fifteen that night; and a nurse at a nearby hospital claimed she saw what could have been Davidoff almost getting knocked down by a city cab."

"So what did the BPD have to say about it?"

"He came out of the library and walked in the wrong direction. When Davidoff realized he was lost, he chased after a cab, got lost some more, and found himself in Olmsted Park, where he met an accidental death. They picked the obvious explanation because the most obvious explanation is usually the correct one. Which is that Willard Davidoff climbed a tree when he was drunk and became one of the fifteen thousand Americans who died from falls last year."

Gisela tapped her pen impatiently on her notepad. "And I can't honestly say that I disagree with that."

"Come on, boss," I said. "This is a Yale professor, not some kid from the Skull and Bones. On a cold winter night in Boston, is climbing trees the normal behavior for an internationally famous sixty-five-year-old evolutionary biologist?"

"You know, it might be," said Gisela. "He was climbing a tree looking for some rare beetle or a piece of fucking tree bark, but it's what biologists do, Gil. On the other hand, perhaps the tree afforded him an excellent view through an attractive young woman's bathroom window. That's biology, too."

"Don't you think all of this is a coincidence? Each one of these guys seems like he was afraid of something. Three of them end up prematurely dead within six months of one another. It's who and what they are that gives me an itch here. And I'm not the only one who wants to scratch it, boss. It was Bishop Eamon Coogan who put me onto this, remember?"

"Need I remind you of something you should have learned at Quantico, Agent Martins?"

That was me being bitch-slapped. Any mention of what I should have learned at the Academy always left me feeling like I was never going to make ASAC.

"Gil, I flip a coin ten times and it comes up heads all ten of them, do I whisper conspiracy? Or do I shrug it off as a coincidence? We're the Federal Bureau of Investigation not the Foolish Bureau of Ingenuousness. Your request for a case file is an investigator's Oscar Wilde line. One's unfortunate, two is careless, and three is Title 18."

Title 18, of the U.S. Code, Section 351, was what empowered the special agents and officials of the FBI to investigate violations of federal statutes.

"Helen? What do you think?"

Helen shifted uncomfortably on her chair and crossed her long legs, as if that might afford her some time to come down on one side of the argument or the other. I already knew Helen was in favor of further investigation. The question was, would she fold in the face of Gisela's ace: Gisela was the boss.

"What you said about coincidence makes sense," said Helen. "But sometimes it seems to me that life shows us what we need to know. Before I came into this room, Gil had me convinced there might be a real fire at the end of this smoke trail. Now I'm not so sure. On the other hand, if it were me, I'd probably trust his instincts, for a while at least. Maybe a week or two. Just to see what his nose turns up. Couldn't do any harm. Might even do him some good."

Gisela looked at Anne. "What do you think?"

"I get a nose for things, too," said Anne. "I like patterns. I believe in them. I see connections where there are no connections. I hear what you say, boss, but I've an idea that there will come a time—not too long from now—when computers will make the idea of coincidence and randomness seem obsolete, and we'll see things for what they really are. Coincidence will seem logical."

Helen and Anne were right, of course. But so was Gisela. I made it three-to-one in favor of further investigation, although Gisela's one was more than three, of course. I could tell she was a little disappointed that the sorority had sided with me, but that's how it is, and maybe Anne and Helen had just had more time to think about the case than Gisela had.

"I have to justify this to Chuck and I don't want him making me look like some breast-Fed dancing around her handbag," said Gisela. "Gil Martins is not the guy wearing a new set of balls here. I am, and I want to keep them for a while. If I do decide to green-light a domestic terrorism inquiry, what's your next step, Gil?"

"Swoop down for a closer look. Helen and I would go to Washington, Boston, and New York. See if we can't dig up more on those three deaths than the local police did. Hope that the lab guys find something on Osborne's computer. And pray that we get a lead, I guess. Or maybe another victim. If someone is behind this, I doubt they'll be satisfied with three deaths and one case of acute catatonia. Either way, I figure we can chase down all the facts in a couple of weeks. As it happens, I think you can spare me. Army CID's got an informer alongside Johnny Sack Brown and they're keeping us up to speed with the HIDDEN group's plans to acquire a Switchblade system. Chicago FBI's chasing up a lead on those two ELF fugitives."

Gisela nodded.

"Okay," she said. "That's all for now, folks. I'll think about what you've all said and let you know my decision when I've made one."

EIGHT

A week later, with nothing to show but a handful of expense receipts and inconclusive field reports, my swoop felt more like a belly flop. We'd struck out in Washington and New York, and now that we were in Boston, it looked as if we were going to strike out there, too. The only consolation was that we were staying with my mom and dad at their large South End house—a ten-minute car ride away from the Boston FBI office in downtown where we endured the silent mockery of our colleagues. Cops and feds have the hardest eyes in the world. Every time I looked at one of these guys, I knew they were thinking the same thing: *You flew up from Houston to investigate the death of a guy who fell out of a fucking tree?* We didn't find anything of interest in the police report at headquarters on Cambridge Street; and we didn't find much at the scene of Willard Davidoff's death in Olmsted Park. Except, perhaps, the tree itself.

"That's a fifty-foot sycamore," said Helen. "I wouldn't try to climb that tree on a summer's day. And I'm someone who likes climbing."

"You do?"

"Sure. I go bouldering sometimes at the Texas Rock Gym on Campbell Road."

"Bouldering?"

"It's climbing without a rope."

"That sounds like a description of my career in the Bureau."

"It can be pretty exhilarating, if that's what you mean."

"Sure. Until you fall."

"And you think that's what happened here. To you? With this investigation?"

"I'm still in the air, perhaps, but the outcome of that already looks clear enough."

"We learn from our mistakes. Isn't that what they teach us at the Academy?"

I shrugged. "I always liked this park."

"Ever bring any girls here?"

"Just you."

"My lucky day, I guess."

"Not so far." I looked back at the tree. "This is the right tree, yeah?"

Helen turned and looked at the Boston Police Department cruiser parked on Jamaica Way. "That's what they said. They found tiny pieces of tree bark and moss on his clothes. And bits of his skin on that branch."

I shook my head. "Yes. But how the fuck did he climb a tree like this?"

Helen took off her jacket and handed it to me. "Only one way to find out. You test a theory with an experiment. That's scientific method. Galileo."

"Yeah, well, be careful, Helen. Galileo discovered gravity. Just make sure you don't discover it, too."

"Actually, you're wrong." Helen took hold of the tree trunk and looked up for a handhold. "Galileo proposed that different bodies would fall with a uniform acceleration."

"Same kind of shit."

"The point is that between Galileo and Aristotle there were just a lot of guys with theories they never bothered to test."

"I knew there was a reason I never brought any girls to this park."

Helen jumped up, caught a branch, and pulled herself up with one arm and then two.

Instinctively, I went to help her.

"Don't touch me," she said sharply.

"Sorry." I snatched away my hands and clasped them penitently behind my back.

"I meant—I have to do this on my own, like he did; otherwise there's no point." She swung her legs up and hooked the branch she was holding with her calves.

"Yes, of course. Stupid of me."

She let go of the branch with one hand and pulled her skirt up around her waist, affording me a spectacular view of her underwear.

"This park is sure looking up," I said.

"I can see that *you* are." Helen took hold of the branch again and wrestled her way around until she was sitting on top of it.

"I'm just assisting in a scientific experiment," I said.

"And what's the conclusion, Galileo?"

"You're a good-looking woman."

"From where you're standing."

"True. How old are you, Helen?"

"Twenty-seven. Why?"

"Willard Davidoff was twice that age and more. If he climbed this tree, I'm George Washington."

"That was a cherry tree."

Helen swung down, dropped onto the grass, and then pulled her skirt over her tan thighs. "'Sa matter? Never seen a pair of panties before?"

"Sure. You'll find my DNA on most of the lingerie shop windows in Houston."

"Right. Who needs sniffer dogs with you around, huh?"

"It wasn't my nose I was pressing up against the glass," I said.

"Well, that's all right then."

"I sure wouldn't like you to get the wrong impression about me, Helen."

"No, everything's quite clear to me now, Agent Martins. I'm beginning to understand your wife."

"I wish I had your capacity for understanding. I don't mind telling you, Helen, I'm having a tough time figuring how the BPD could ever have confused a sixty-five-year-old science professor with Indiana Jones."

Helen inspected her hands for a moment before spitting on them and then rubbing them on a handkerchief I handed to her.

"I never did like science very much," I said.

"Too intellectually demanding for you, I suppose."

I grinned. "You're not supposed to talk to me like that. I'm your supervisor."

"That's what makes it such fun."

"Let's get out of here before you say something you'll regret."

We walked back to the rental car we'd left parked behind the BPD cruiser. The two gumps praying into their styrofoam coffee cups regarded us with obvious amusement. They were both from the Irish Riviera—some shit suburb—overfed shiesties with breath like sour mash.

"Fucking guy fell out of a tree, I guess," I said.

"O! Light dawns on Marblehead."

Both of the cops laughed but that was okay. Cops have to have their laughs. Maybe cops most of all.

❀

I had good reasons for not wanting to eat at home. For one thing, my monosyllabic answers about Ruth and Danny had been noted by my mom and dad, and I hardly wanted to expand on our trial separation—which was how Ruth's lawyer had described it. To do that, I might have had to mention my own infidelity and Ruth's religious fanaticism. This was still a touchy subject with my father. I didn't want to upset my parents—they seemed so much older and more decrepit than I remembered. But Helen wouldn't hear of it. Besides, she was more interested in my parents' home than in food.

From the outside, at least, it was like any other town house in that part of Boston: tall, with bay windows, a stoop, and climbing ivy that was no good for the red brickwork, not that my father cared much about that; on the inside, however, they had made the place look like a real home from home, which is to say it was an exact facsimile of the house we had lived in back in Glasgow. There were stained-glass skylights, soft tartan furnishings, a lot of solid Victorian mahogany furniture, and, on the walls, several dull Scottish landscapes and several portraits of unforgiving, stone-faced ancestors and relations, including my father's brother, Bill.

Not long after leaving Scotland to live in Boston—I was fourteen—my father gave me some advice that I've always tried to stick to.

"Be slow to take offense, Giles. Learn how to be tolerant and how to live and let live. Remember this: intolerance, bigotry, bearing a grudge—these are all the things we're leaving behind." This was rare advice from my dad; he wasn't ever one for telling people what to do. In consequence, I'm difficult to provoke, which, from the Christian point of view of turning the other cheek, is good, I suppose. But it also made a few people believe that I didn't care about anything very much. So everyone was surprised when I joined the Bureau. Nobody was more surprised than my dad; no one was prouder of me, either. And he never seems to tire of telling me so. "America has been good to our family, Giles," he would say in an accent that—even after more than twenty years—still sounds as if he lives in one of the nicer parts of Glasgow. "I'm very glad that you've chosen to pay her back."

Looking back at things now, I understand there was a lot more to the advice he gave me as an adolescent than just the desire to stop me from turning out like a lot of my countrymen. More important, he didn't want me becoming like my uncle Bill.

By now Uncle Bill must be seventy-six years old and I haven't seen him since we left Scotland in 1990; I'm almost certain my father hasn't, either. You see, my uncle Bill went mad and is still confined to an asylum somewhere in Scotland. One time, not long before my family left Scotland, my father came back in tears from a visit with Bill, swearing he would never go again. My own memories of Bill are as vivid as if I had seen him yesterday. For almost ten years he was a doting uncle, but he gradually became a frightening person for anyone to meet, even his nephews and nieces. I remember the furious but entirely silent arguments Bill had with people who simply weren't there. There's a proper psychiatric term for what was wrong with Uncle Bill, but my dad says that it was just a case of someone having an abnormally heightened sensitivity to the disappointments of everyday life. That's an easy situation to find yourself in if you happen to live in Scotland. Once I asked Dad who it was that Bill believed he was arguing with, and Dad told me he thought it was probably one of his other personalities. Another time Dad said he thought it might be God or the devil, and when I asked which he thought was more likely, Dad just shrugged and said, "It's all the same thing." That was before my dad announced his own atheism, but all the same, you could see the writing on the wall even then.

In retrospect it seems to me that Bill's madness dates more or less exactly from the moment of my confirmation, or my nonconfirmation, depending on the way you look at it. After all, spitting out the host and wiping the holy oil off my forehead is not exactly the behavior of a devout Roman Catholic. Even Bishop Coogan didn't know about that. For a long time afterward, I told my young self that God had punished me for my precocious act of blasphemy—he knew very well how fond I was of Bill—by punishing poor Bill with madness. Even today it's no more or less persuasive a piece of reasoning for someone's madness than a lot of others you'll hear in any church.

Sometimes these things run in families.

⊞

My cell shifted on the dinner table as if an earthquake was in progress, startling my parents.

"Hello, this is Special Agent Gil Martins."

"This is Cynthia Ekman." The voice was a little breathy but sexy and English with a hint of American, like whiskey with a splash of ginger ale, the way my mom and dad always drank it.

"Peter Ekman's wife," she explained. "Widow."

"Mrs. Ekman. I'm sorry we missed you when we were in New York."

I stood up and moved away from the dinner table, beckoning Helen to follow and, at the same time, touching the speakerphone icon on the screen of my Bureau BlackBerry so that she might listen in on the conversation.

"My son was graduating from Oxford University and I went over to England for the ceremony. But I'm back in New York now."

"My colleague, Agent Helen Monaco, is here with me and listening in on this conversation. It'll save me describing it to her afterward. We're in Boston right now."

"I'm very sorry for your loss, Mrs. Ekman. Both Agent Martins and

I have read a lot of your late husband's writing. Which we greatly admired."

Helen and I were at a window overlooking Worcester Square. In the little tree-lined park below, the moon was reflected in the surface of the water underneath a fountain dominated by an ugly group of crudely realized figures that is supposed to be two Boston ladies out for a walk with their pain-in-the-ass children.

"I saw your husband debate the former archbishop of Canterbury in Washington, once," I said. "You might say he helped to turn me off the church."

Mrs. Ekman sighed. "Then I'm sorry for *your* loss, Agent Martins. In the face of my late husband's militant atheism, I managed to retain my own religious faith. To have been married for ten years to a man like Peter and still call myself a Muslim, well, that took some doing. Look, the reason I'm calling is that there was something not quite right about what happened to Peter. He didn't die accidentally, the way they said he did. I'm sure of it; and I assume that you yourselves might have some doubts, too."

"What makes you think that the police might have been wrong?"

"I've found a journal he was keeping up until he died. A secret journal I didn't know about. Having read it, I'm sure there was more to his death than met the eye."

"Have you told the police about this journal?"

"No."

"May I ask why not?"

Cynthia Ekman sighed. "My husband was having an affair. And I don't trust the police not to show the diary to someone in the press. When Peter died, there were several stories in the *New York Post* that could only have come from the police. The News Corporation and Peter had a feud that went back years. And now that he's gone, they'd love to smear his memory with some shit like this. The diary is principally about his affair; but from time to time he mentions something that makes me think he was scared. Really scared."

"Okay," I said. "Do you want to send us the diary?"

"I have to trust someone with this, but I can't yet bring myself to trust people I've never met. Perhaps if you came down to New York, we could meet and I could read you extracts from the diary here."

NINE

Tarrytown is an affluent village in the New York county of Westchester and occupies one of those spacious coves that indent the eastern shore of the Hudson. Not far from this village and halfway toward the village of Sleepy Hollow was the quiet acre of land on which stood Cynthia Ekman's house. Surrounding the house was a small forest of flowering dogwood, cherry, pear, and, in larger number, tall white pines. The tapping of a woodpecker was the only sound to break in upon the uniform tranquillity. It seemed like a promisingly sequestered spot for a writer to take up residence, especially one with some hard-core urban enemies. In the early-evening twilight, we approached the house in the Taurus we'd hired at LaGuardia.

"Do you feel it? That sort of drowsy, unreal feeling in the air?"

I grinned. "You've been listening to that fucking guy behind the front desk at the Doubletree hotel. According to him, this place is like one big Tim Burton movie and abounds with haunted spots, local tales, and morbid superstitions. You ask me, Helen, they trade off shit like that. Headless horsemen, witch doctors, things that go bump in the night. It's good for business, that's all. Brings in the tourists."

"You don't believe in the supernatural?"

"Me. No. Not anymore. I don't believe in anything I can't shoot."

"Maybe that's because you've never shot anyone. After you've shot and killed someone, it becomes a whole lot easier to believe in all kinds of shit. That guy I shot on the boat? For a long time afterward, I had the weird idea that he was still around. I would start to hear music and voices in the air—the same music and voices I heard on the boat at the time the whole thing went down. And a couple of times I even thought I saw him. Like he was holding some witchy power over my mind."

We caught sight of the house and I steered the car down a long winding gravel drive. It was an old two-story wooden colonial with an exterior stair and a wooden deck that looked as if it afforded a fine view of the grounds and glimpses of the Hudson River.

We got out of the car and walked up to the front of the house.

"And now? Do you think about him still? The Arab?"

"No. That's the first time I've thought about him in ages. And certainly the first time I ever talked about him to anyone other than the Head Fed."

The Head Fed—Dr. Sussman—was the psychiatrist to whom the Bureau assigned you after you'd shot someone, to make sure you weren't crying into your Starbucks about it.

"Well, I'm very glad you shared. I think it's important I know what you've been through and vice versa."

"What exactly have you been through, Martins, that wasn't wearing a split-tail skirt?"

We walked up the steps and knocked on the door.

"That was cruel. True, but cruel."

The door opened and a good-looking woman in her forties was standing there. Very tall, with a thin frame, a face like an almond, a neck as long and sinuous as the Horn of Africa, and skin the color of unpolished copper, she looked like a model. She was wearing a red blazer, gray slacks, leopard-print kitten heels, a white shirt, and a silk scarf. She greeted us warmly and, ushering us inside, led us into a double-height sitting room that had more books on the shelves than a room in *Architectural Digest*. Helen and I sat at opposite ends of a long couch while Mrs. Ekman moved a book off the chair where she had been sitting. Choosing the edge to perch on, she faced us demurely with hands clasped in front of one knee. The lamplight, bright on the glass of some framed movie posters and even brighter in the diamond studs in Mrs. Ekman's earlobes, glinted on Helen's glasses as she looked one way and then the other before glancing up at the gallery, as if to remind herself that this was where the panic room in which Ekman had died was located.

"You've been here before, of course," said the widow, watching Helen carefully.

"Yes," said Helen. "The last time we were here, your housekeeper let us in to take a look around."

"So you'll already know that's where he died. Up there."

Both of us nodded. The CSI pictures of Ekman's dead body were still in the file in my briefcase, but more unpleasant, they were also lodged inside my head. I've seen quite a few dead bodies in my brief career with the FBI; a lot of the time the bodies are fucked up and in poor condition. Ekman's body hadn't had a mark on it, but there was something about the body that profoundly disturbed me—something grotesque about the dead man's face. When people are dead, they're dead, and usually that's all you can say about them. But this particular cadaver's face seemed to look at you in a very concentrated sort of way. It sounds absurd, but it was as if the face contained something more than just the story of one death—it was almost as if it had something to say about the nature of all death, a truth, perhaps, about the nature of eternity and our place in it. That all sounds pretty weird, I guess; and it is. But I sincerely hoped that Mrs. Ekman had never seen the pictures of her husband's dead body.

"Would you like something to drink?" she asked. "I have some wine open."

"No thanks," I said.

Mrs. Ekman was already on her feet again, and helping herself from a bottle of white wine that was open on the sideboard.

"I never used to drink wine," she said. "Probably I wouldn't ever have started if Peter hadn't drunk so much of it. I used to finish a bottle just to stop him from finishing it, you know?" Bearing a glass of golden liquid, she came back to her chair and sat down, this time more comfortably than before. "My husband wasn't exactly a fan of the FBI. Under the Freedom of Information Act he managed to get a copy of the file you had on him. He wrote to your FOIA Request Record/Information Dissemination Section somewhere in Virginia, obtained the file, and then wrote an article about it on his blog."

I nodded.

"You've seen Peter's FBI file?"

"I've looked at it, yes. But just recently and only because he's dead. The Bureau tends to keep files on foreign nationals, people who've signed a political petition, previously been a member of the Communist Party, or who've hung out with a foreign dictator. Peter qualified on all four counts."

Mrs. Ekman took a large sip of white wine, frowned, and then answered her own question. "Of course. He wrote a book about Hugo Chávez, didn't he? Another mistaken judgment on Peter's part. He always thought the best of politicians until, inevitably, they let him down just like the rest of us did. Only, Peter always took that kind of thing very personally." She smiled. "But don't get me wrong. He was very proud of that FBI file. He loved talking about it at smart dinner parties. He thought it made him seem edgy and subversive. Even though he wasn't like that at all. In a lot of ways, Peter was very conservative. As I'm sure you know if you've read some of his stuff."

"Yes, I do know. But it's not us he was afraid of. It was someone else, you think?"

"He was definitely afraid of something."

She shivered a little and, collecting a cashmere shawl off the arm of her chair, wrapped it around her shoulders.

"Sometimes this place gets a bit lonely and one starts to imagine things. We used to joke about it, Peter and I. The Sleepy Hollow syndrome, we called it. It's a lot easier to joke about that sort of thing when you don't live on your own."

"Are you afraid of something now, ma'am?"

She shrugged. "Your husband dies, sometimes you forget he's not here. You imagine he's in the kitchen. Or in his study. Like he always was. Or, sometimes, you imagine—other stuff."

Cynthia Ekman shook her head. "It's an old house. Sometimes it creaks a bit, that's all. I'm sure that there's no one who has it in for me, the way they might have had it in for him. Not anymore, anyway. It's been a long time since anyone threatened me. At least five years."

"We didn't know about that," said Helen. "I'm sorry. I'm afraid that all of our attention has been on your husband's death."

"I'm originally from Somalia," said Mrs. Ekman. "I was born there and then sought political asylum in England to avoid an arranged marriage, before coming to work here in the States as a translator at the United Nations. Then I wrote a book about the treatment of women in Islamic society called *Among the Odalisques: Breaking Out of the Seraglio.*"

"I read that," said Helen. "You're Cynthia Shermarke?"

"Yes."

"I enjoyed that book," said Helen. "It was a bestseller, wasn't it?"

"Yes, it was. Only the book earned me a lot of criticism in Saudi Arabia and Egypt. Some of it quite violent, really. I had more than a few death threats. These days that's par for the course when you write something people disagree with. After I'd written the book, I met Peter. We married and came to live out here. The panic room was originally supposed to be for my benefit. Little did we think that it would be him who'd feel he needed it."

"Perhaps you'd care to elaborate," said Helen.

Mrs. Ekman smiled and it seemed that Helen at least had won her confidence.

"Yes," she said. "Perhaps I should."

Mrs. Ekman put down her glass and got up to fetch a laptop off a desk. She brought it back to her chair and opened it up on her knees.

While we waited for it to start up, I glanced around the room. A number of handsome cigar boxes occupied pride of place in alcoves like the tombs of unknown French generals. I knew they were cigar boxes because there was a cigar cutter on the top of each one. A crystal ashtray the size of a hubcap was on the coffee table next to a granite table lighter that looked as if it had probably been cracked off a meteorite. And there was an oxygen cylinder with a line and a breathing mask to remind me that Peter Ekman had suffered from smoking-related emphysema.

"He kept the journal on this laptop," explained Mrs. Ekman, as she typed some more. "It was protected by a secret password. Except that the password wasn't so very secret. It was written down in a little notebook where he kept a record of all his passwords. Peter was very careless about that kind of thing."

Mrs. Ekman smiled a patient sort of smile and, for a moment, I had an insight into the kind of relationship they'd enjoyed: him, frequently drunk and disorganized, but fun with it, probably; and her, resourceful and tough, even a little steely, and often exasperated by her brilliant husband, but obviously charmed by him, too. At least she had been until she found out about the affair, I imagined.

"I've highlighted the key passages for you, but for present purposes it might be better if I just read them out loud. I still haven't decided if I'm going to hand this laptop over to you."

I shrugged. "You could just give us a copy on a thumb drive. I have one right here."

"Look, you'll probably understand what I mean when I start reading, all right? And perhaps it would be best if you saved any questions until I've finished."

I nodded. "Sure. Whatever makes you feel more comfortable, ma'am."

She shook her head bitterly. "Oh, believe me, Agent Martins, there's really nothing I find at all comfortable about any of this. And would you say Cynthia or Mrs. Ekman instead of ma'am? It feels condescending. Like you're trying awfully hard to be patient with me. I'd appreciate that, thank you."

As Mrs. Ekman glanced down at the screen, I caught Helen's eye and tried to contain the desire I had to pull a face in her direction. My leash had been snapped hard, and I was still gagging a little and flexing my neck like a corrected mutt.

"There is so much e-mail I get now," read Mrs. Ekman, "that, at times, it feels like a modern variant of the proverbial Chinese curse—may all your messages find you. It's like the opposite of a diaspora. If a thousand roads lead forever to Rome, then I'm equally sure that a thousand e-mails a week seem to lead to me. These days I am resigned to receiving UBE (unsolicited bulk e-mail), UCE (unsolicited commercial e-mail), or *just plain spam from so-called zombie networks that are located all over the world. Routinely, I am promised millions of dollars if only I will send my bank details to some illiterate Nigerian 'phisherman' (for so these spammers are sometimes called); or I am offered some equally improbable means of making my male parts much larger than they are at present. I have grown used to this kind of junk mail much as I have grown used to having gray pubic hair or supplements in the sections of the Sunday* New York Times.

"*Sadly, I am even used to threatening e-mails. In my line of work, they are an occupational hazard and nearly always these are the usual nocent missives about how I have mightily offended the GOP or Islam or God and how he will soon punish me with death. But lately I have been receiving e-mail threats that are very different from the ones I normally receive. Not in their content—no, the content stays the same: God just hates my guts—but rather in the way they seem to behave when they arrive in the in-box of my computer.*

"*Now, I am not a technical person. One of the smaller paradoxes of my life is that I spend so much time using a computer and yet understand nothing at all of how one works. Of course, I have become used to this level of quotidian ignorance. And, like most people who own a laptop computer, I can live with it. Or at least I thought I could.*"

Cynthia Ekman read aloud from the on-screen journal with an obvious pride in her late husband's slightly pompous prose. I hadn't the least fucking clue what "nocent" meant and I was someone who'd been to law school.

"*No, what I find perplexing,*" she said, continuing to read, "*is that I am quite unable to find any one of these e-mails on my computer. Let's call them the Mr. Phelps e-mails, for they seem programmed to self-destruct just as soon as they have been read, almost in the manner of the taped message that used to precede the titles in the sixties television show* Mission: Impossible. *Jim Phelps, the stone-faced leader of the MI force of con men and safecrackers, would play a cassette tape that would then dissolve in a cloud of smoke, as if a hidden vial of acid had erased the secret message forever. It was always the best moment in the entire show, if only because it was always the easiest part to understand.*

"*These e-mails are not viruses, for they seem to have the very opposite effect to the idea of computer malware, which is to run in secret without being shut down or deleted by the user or administrator of the computer system. Trojans, for example. No, my Mr. Phelps e-mails arrive in my in-box, and stay there only until the moment I have read them or until they have remained unread in my in-box for a set number of hours. Indeed, as an experiment, I left a couple of these e-mails unread and both of them had disappeared like snow within twenty-four hours.*

"*So far there have been at least a dozen of these Mr. Phelps e-mails. Naturally, they are anonymous. The words vary but the content is essentially the same: the e-mails are short jeremiads of sustained invective that denounce me and prophecy my imminent death. At first I ignored them. And yet their curious behavior led me to decide that I should share their existence with someone. Obviously, this couldn't be Cynthia. (It's an isolated spot where we live, on the edge of Tarrytown, and when I travel to New York to see Adele, Cynthia is alone out here; it would not be good for her state of mind to believe that once again her life or mine was under threat.) And since Adele knows everything about computers—she is a recent graduate of MIT's EECS and one of the resident chic geeks at work (quite what she sees in me, I have no idea)—I decided to tell her about them.*"

Mrs. Ekman's voice seemed to falter a little at this, the first mention of her husband's lover, Adele; and thinking to pay her back for jerking my collar so violently earlier on, I cleared my throat and said: "Adele. I assume this is the woman with whom your husband was romantically involved."

"He was fucking her."

"Had he been—seeing her for very long?"

"I really don't know. I've only just found out about it myself. From reading this journal, that is. I suspect she was just another little unpaid whore hackette looking to get on in the dwindling world of print journalism. But like I said before, Agent Martins, perhaps it would also be best if you saved any questions you might have until I've finished reading."

"Oh, sure, I remember you saying that. But in the FBI we're trained to think for ourselves and ask questions when we see fit, not when we have someone's permission to do so. We're not as patient as people imagine we are. Do you know Adele's surname?"

"No, I don't know it. But I imagine it wouldn't be too difficult to find out who she is."

"No. I guess not."

"Can I continue with this particular entry?" She shot me a bitter little smile. "Please? I'm nearly finished. There are two more after this one."

"*Adele lives in a nice condo on Eleventh Avenue, just around the corner from the office. She was intrigued when—we were in bed at the time—I told her about the Mr. Phelps e-mails and, her professional interest piqued, she insisted on my turning on my laptop so that she could take a look for herself. But naturally, there was nothing to see in my in-box and I do believe she half thought I was imagining the whole thing. Sweetly, Adele offered to monitor my e-mails for me, in the hope of identifying one of the Mr. Phelps e-mails herself, but that would mean giving her my password and, as much as I'm fond of her, I don't quite trust her enough to let her through the front door of my life like this.*"

Mrs. Ekman paused.

"That's the end of the first entry," she said. "The first relevant entry, that is."

Mrs. Ekman finished the glass of wine she'd been drinking and poured herself another.

"Interesting," said Helen. "I haven't ever heard of self-destructing e-mails."

"Me neither," I confessed.

Mrs. Ekman shrugged dismissively. "If that's what they were," she said.

"Do you think they might have been something else?" I asked.

"Well, I'm not a computer expert," she said. "But it strikes me that Adele was. This little whore he was seeing; she knew about computers, right? If you're looking for who might be behind this whole thing, you could do worse than look at her. She could easily have had access to his laptop. Like I already told you, Peter wasn't exactly clever about keeping his password a secret. She could have installed something on Peter's computer without his knowing anything about it. Something that could have erased e-mails selectively."

"Yes, I suppose that's possible," I said. "But what's her motive for doing such a thing?"

"Peter was famous. Influential. There's no end of help he could have been to someone just starting out in the world of journalism, like her. So maybe she cooked the scheme up to scare him and put him in her power."

It sounded like lunacy, but I nodded anyway, and so did Helen.

Cynthia Ekman shrugged. "Then again, if he had decided not to promote her career, then maybe she might have been bitter. And, maybe, she thought to teach him a lesson. I don't know."

"You've got more maybe there than Buddy Holly and the Crickets, Mrs. Ekman," I said.

"Was he scared?" asked Helen. "By these Mr. Phelps e-mails?"

"Perhaps the simplest answer to that question is just to read the next entries in the journal," said Mrs. Ekman. "This first one was written on a Monday, exactly a week before he died. May I?"

I stifled a yawn. The Mr. Phelps e-mails were interesting and I was looking forward to describing them to the lab guys at the office; but hearing Ekman's journal read aloud reminded me of what I'd always thought about the man: that he was a bit of a flosser—like a woman with a great badonkadonk who walks along the street and gives her shapely behind an extra wiggle just to drive some street-corner homeys crazy.

"Go right ahead, ma'am."

"*More on my strange Mr. Phelps e-mails. In the beginning these were just generally threatening: 'Almighty God has judged you and found you wanting and you will soon die a horrible death at the hands of God's number one angel and be condemned to hell eternal.' That kind of thing. But now it seems that I have a rendezvous with death at the end of the month. Like a visit from the rent collector. My time allowed is just seven days from now. Which is good, I think, because at least after a week has elapsed and I'm still standing then perhaps these e-mails will disappear for good.*

"*Adele thinks I should go to the police, but cops don't like it when you can't give them evidence. Adele has looked for some trace of these e-mails on my computer and come up with nothing. And I can't see the police being able to find what she cannot. Of course, this latest twist—the prediction of my death—is just best practice for the people trying to scare me. Good close-up magicians make predictions based on choices they have already forced on their spectators, just as in tribal societies the witch doctor always lets his victim know well beforehand that he's going to be a victim. It's simple voodoo logic. Thankfully, I'm not all that gullible. And I've been threatened before. Nothing came of it the last time; and more than likely nothing will come of it this time. Perhaps the best defense against threats to one's own person is, quite simply, an assertive life. So, with apologies to Sam Beckett, I must go on . . . I'll go on.*

"Tuesday. Beset with uncertainty. And the curious sensation that I am not alone. Especially when I am alone. Cyn has gone back to London for a while, to work on her new book. Leaving me here, haunted by the most grotesque conceits. A couple of times these fancies found me touring the garden with a pistol in one hand and a flashlight in the other. Of course, I found nothing. Not even a footprint. All the same I think I would have been quite relieved to have found an assassin hiding in the shrubbery instead of nothing at all. Because it doesn't quite feel like nothing at all. And that's the problem. I have an imagination like any other man and it's easy to see a murderer or a demon in every shadowy corner. Especially here, in the faux-creepy village of Sleepy Hollow. Even as I write this, the clock ticks on the mantelpiece with an uncanny loudness, marking every second between here and next Monday night, as if my life were nearing the end of its measured time. Ridiculous, I know. Things are not so bad in the daytime, but of course, the darkness brings one's imagination truly alive, sharpening the rest of the senses the way blindness is said to improve the hearing so that every noise, every movement, every smell takes on a new and sinister meaning. Everything conspires to leave me feeling unsettled and out of joint in a place where I am normally so comfortable and at peace.

"Quite unnerved by my own company—this has never happened before—I called Adele and took the train into the city and had lunch with her at Michael's. There were lots of people I knew and the atmosphere was so metropolitan and sensibly Gothamish that all thoughts of death threats were quite dispelled. Probably I've been drinking too much. And possibly the drink interferes with the steroids I've been taking for my emphysema. Not to mention the Xanax I've been taking. And the Viagra, of

course. After a delicious lunch, it was back to Adele's apartment for sex. Stayed the night. Oddly, the sex was brilliant, which makes me think that my problems aren't physiological but mental; and with my mind distracted, my body just reacted to her the way it's supposed to.

"Friday. Returned to Tarrytown for the weekend, without a thought for Mr. Phelps and the threatening e-mails. My relaxed state of mind lasted only until about halfway through the train journey, when my car emptied at Irvington and I was left to finish the journey alone. What is it that Hughes Mearns wrote? 'Last night I saw upon the stair, / A little man who wasn't there. / He wasn't there again today. / Oh, how I wish he'd go away.' Well, it was like that walking home from the train station. I could have sworn I was followed, but every time I looked around to see who it was, the road was empty. A couple of times I stopped and found myself addressing thin air, challenging whoever was there to come forward and identify himself. But worst of all was that night. I switched out the light in my bedroom and distinctly heard the sound of someone else breathing. It might have been me, yes. But I don't think so. Anyway that was the last time the light went off. And since then, the entire house has stayed lit up like a Christmas tree. I guess this makes me an easy target for anyone with a sniper's rifle, but I can't help myself. The fear of the less probable seems to override my fear of the more likely. 'Twas ever thus, perhaps. But to quote Horatio, what I have seen or perhaps not seen, 'is wondrous strange.'

"Sunday. Today I know I heard something that wasn't there. Possibly saw it, too. In the garden. And then in the house. Half a dozen times I started to call the police and then stopped myself. They would only think I'm crazy. Of course, it's quite possible I am going mad. Cyn's always suggesting as much and I can't say I blame her. That's half the reason she went to Europe—to get away from me. Of course, in Hamlet everyone thinks the prince is mad, and it's a better play if we think that, too. I

always think that it's Shakespeare's play that informs The Turn of the
Screw. *There's not much difference between Hamlet and the governess.
How does James himself put it? 'The strange and sinister embroidered on
the very type of the normal and easy.' Lately that could be a description
of my own everyday life. The strange and the sinister and the normal and
the easy. It's the juxtaposition of the two that makes for something really
creepy.*

"*Saturday. I am thinking I will spend the night in the panic room. I
am almost embarrassed to admit this; after all, it was for Cyn's benefit
that we had the panic room installed, not mine. I must be a wuss. I am a
wuss. (It's not Beckett, but it'll do.)*"

Mrs. Ekman paused for a long moment before she added haltingly,
"And that was his last entry before he was found dead here in the panic
room."

"Did you think your husband was crazy, Mrs. Ekman?" asked
Helen.

"All husbands are crazy," she said. "But a man would have to be
fucking mad to remain single, don't you think? Considering what a
wife is prepared to do for him." She shrugged. "I really don't know,
Agent Monaco. Helen."

"Did your husband take drugs?" I asked. "Recreational drugs."

"He used to take them. When I first knew him, he was addicted to
cocaine."

"I'm just trying to establish if some of his paranoia was caused by
drink. Or by medication, perhaps. He suffered from emphysema, didn't
he? What was he taking for that?"

"Steroids, mostly. Xanax. That was for the anxiety caused by not
being able to get his breath. Pure oxygen. You saw the nebulizer."

"Well, it can't have helped him mixing alcohol with those, can it?
And whatever else he might have been taking. Viagra? Of course,

emphysema means you don't get enough oxygen, which can cause hallucinations. But if one night you're alone and you finish the bottle on
your own, then maybe you get hold of your cylinder and you take too
much pure oxygen; and because your lungs aren't working properly,
then you can't breathe off the excess carbon dioxide that this quickly
produces. Now, that also causes hallucinations, doesn't it?"

I knew I was on safe ground here. One of my grandparents had died
from smoking-related emphysema.

"Yes, what you say is certainly possible," admitted Mrs. Ekman.
"On the other hand, if you pay attention to the tone of that first journal
entry, I think you'll agree that he seems quite rational. I do believe that
the Mr. Phelps e-mails were quite real."

She shook her head and closed the laptop.

"But if you think all that, Agent Martins, then it puzzles me what
the heck you're doing here."

"It's our job to be skeptical," I said. "Until we see some evidence
that proves otherwise. But that is what we're looking for here despite
what I said just now. I was just playing devil's advocate. I can see now
that having a copy of the journal on a flash drive wouldn't be ideal. So,
if we may, we'd like to borrow your husband's laptop and have the FBI's
own computer forensics laboratory in Houston take a look at it and see
if they can find anything on it that your husband's friend, Adele, could
not. It'll be returned to you just as soon as possible. Undamaged. And
everything that's on it will be treated with complete respect and in
confidence. What they'll do is make a complete mirror-image copy of
everything on the laptop's memory and hard drive, and then use that to
work on. We can get it couriered back to you in a day or two."

Mrs. Ekman hugged the laptop to her breast for a moment as if it
were Ekman himself.

"You'll never know it's even happened," said Helen. "Our people
are really careful. You can trust them. I give you my word on that."

Mrs. Ekman seemed to think about it for another moment and nodded. "I guess that'll be all right."

She handed Helen the laptop. "The password is Balliol. That's
B-A-L-L-I-O-L."

Helen put Peter Ekman's laptop in her briefcase. It was a Briggs &
Riley, with more sleeves than a hippie's record collection.

"I have a question," said Mrs. Ekman. "You guys are from the
Houston FBI, right? Peter was never in Houston in his life. Which can
only mean you think there's some connection between what happened
to him and something that happened in Texas, right? You still haven't
explained how you people are involved in the first place."

"There's a possibility of a connection with another incident," I said
vaguely. "Only I'm not at liberty to comment on that right now."

Mrs. Ekman shrugged. "I guess we're used to that in this country:
the FBI holding out on us."

"We're not holding out on you, Mrs. Ekman," insisted Helen, who
disliked any implication that the FBI was anything like the CIA. "It's
just that we don't yet have anything concrete to tell you. I give you my
word that just as soon as we do, I'll tell you about it."

"And you'll be sure to speak to this little bitch he was screwing,
won't you?"

"Just as soon as we're back in Manhattan," I said.

We thanked Mrs. Ekman for her cooperation and then went out to
the car. Dusk had turned the sky a fiery, almost hellish, color, as if a
volcano had erupted half a world away. The bats Ekman had written
about in his diary were very much in evidence now, flitting silently
through the squeaky twilight like the stuff that nightmares are made of.
My skin crawled a little at the sight, and as we drove away from the
house, I told Helen that it was easy to see why Peter Ekman had had an
affair.

"Oh, really?" she said. "Why is that?"

"From what I've heard about Ekman, he was much too metropolitan for a place like this." I shrugged. "Thoreau or Emerson he wasn't."

Helen nodded. "It is kind of elemental, isn't it? Out here it's easier to believe in the devil than in God."

"Sometimes I think God is just the devil pretending to be nice."

TEN

The RCFL building at 13333 Northwest Freeway is a five-story glass box that most resembles a wide-screen TV positioned on a patch of grass that looks like a small concession to nature in an area dominated by anonymous buildings and noisy high-speed trucks and automobiles. It's just a seven-minute drive northwest from the Houston field office, but it might as well be seven hours. If the atmosphere in the FBI building at North Justice Park Drive is loud, busy, and frequently combative, the atmosphere in the forensics lab is altogether more low-pitched and quiet, like a public library in a town full of illiterates. Most of the geeks employed by the RCFL pay little attention to looking as smart as us feds do. What would be the point? The only people they ever speak to are field agents like me, demanding—the analysts would say—the impossible, and you don't need to be wearing a tie and a pair of shiny shoes to go messing around inside someone's Dell.

Through a door beyond a desk that could have fronted any regional field station, things quickly turn very different from the usual FBI office. There's a room full of wide shelves on which rest a couple of dozen large removal crates, each of them containing a computer or hard drive that was bagged in pink plastic by the investigating LEO, just in case something falls off or out. And beyond this reception area is a long, brightly lit floor given over to very private-looking workstations that are more like monastery cells in a RadioShack, each of them the almost hermetic province of some CART or RCFL geek whose job it is to mirror-image a suspect computer and identify a file document or digital image that can be used as evidence in a court of law. The workstations are wraparound workbenches with high shelves on which stand a variety of operating PCs and Macs, while under these benches are boxes of wires, leads, and flash drives that are the spatulas, scalpels, and tweezers of this less gruesome but no less vital forensic work. In truth, magna brushing f-powder onto a nonabsorbent surface in search of latent prints already looks like last year's episode of *CSI*. These days our most commonly left fingerprints are digital ones, whether it's a cell phone signal in a Speedy Mart during a robbery or a Facebook page with a picture of the perp holding a MAC-10, a newspaper with a story about the robbery, and some stolen bills. I shit you not.

Ken Paris was the prince of the geeks at RCFL. A Bureau man for thirty years, he was KMA: Kiss My Ass, which basically meant that since he was coming up on retirement we needed him a lot more than he needed us. But Ken loved his work. Just the week before, he'd been in court giving evidence against a twenty-three-year-old man from Galveston, Rhys Conroe, Jr., who had been distributing thousands of images of young boys being sodomized by a variety of adults. On Ken's evidence, Conroe had been convicted and sentenced to 220 months in federal prison without parole. That was what made the job worthwhile for Ken, the idea that creeps like Conroe were out of circulation, and this was also why he was an advisor to Project Safe Childhood, a Department of Justice initiative launched back in 2006. Ken hated jackos and tot bangers the way most of us hate roaches, and he was already on the Internet trail of some of the sick bastards Conroe had been supplying with images.

Ken was from Little Rock, which is why he sounded so very like Bill Clinton. If you closed your eyes, it was almost as if the ex-president was alongside you in the room. Ken even looked a little like him, too. In his late fifties, he was tall, with a huge head, small blue eyes, an easy smile, a tsunami of silver-gray hair, and a nose like a shapely woman's ass on a barstool. He'd always been interested in computers and, until the mid-1980s, he had worked for Apple; then, disappointed by sales of the Macintosh, he turned down the opportunity to buy shares in the company and joined the FBI. "I've always been lucky that way," he would joke.

I found him at his desk, attaching pictures of startling obscenity to an FD-302—a field document that would eventually be produced in court as evidence.

"Hey, Ken, what's cooking?"

He closed the lid on the laptop he had been working on and shook his head. "The Conroe case, part two. It seems we have some local elementary school teachers who were involved in this degenerate shit. As soon as a jury sees just one of these JPEGs, they'll convict. They always do. Just so they won't have to look at them anymore. Can you believe that? Fucking schoolteachers."

"In my day you gave them an apple, not your cherry."

"You're here about Peter Ekman's computer, aren't you?" he said. "Good writer. Nicely argumentative. If a little wordy, for my money."

"Self-destructing e-mail. How about it, Ken?"

"I hadn't heard about it before."

"So they do exist."

"Oh, sure. There are several companies offering this kind of business e-mail service. Which is really what it is: a service. Primarily, it's a way for a company to track e-mails it sends out invisibly, and to know if and when documents are opened and forwarded. A tracking report can contain a whole lot more than that, too. Date and time opened, approximate geographic location of the recipient, his IP address, URL clicks, how long the mail was read for, how many times the e-mail was opened, how many computers it was read on. Almost anything except how big the recipient's dick is. And maybe, a few years down the line, when we get more video e-mail, we'll know that, too. An SDE doesn't use spyware, malware, or a virus. It's not illegal and it doesn't breach any privacy regulations."

"Wait, wait. You forgot to put the cherry on my ice cream. This tape will self-destruct in five seconds. Good luck, Mr. Phelps."

"I was coming to that. The e-mails are configured to delete themselves at a certain point. You can set the maximum number of times the message can be viewed, the amount of time that the message actually exists, or both. You can compose a message that will delete itself after the first time it's viewed, after ten seconds, one minute, or ten minutes, or after one view or ten views. It's really up to the person composing the message to set the destruction criteria. And there's no sulfuric acid required. Mr. Phelps doesn't even have to look around to check that no one is looking."

"But if you're a legitimate business, Ken, what the fuck?"

"Actually, there are many perfectly good and entirely legal reasons why anyone might use SDEs. How do you know that your personal information is safe on the mail recipient's PC? You send someone your CV, but you don't want them making free with your personal details if you don't get the job, shit like that. SDEs give you an extra level of security. With the ability to create and send self-destructing messages, your most personal correspondences can't ever end up in the wrong hands. And they can't remain in someone's in-box for nine years like some of the e-mails on Ekman's computer. Nine years from now, two businesses that work well together now might be bitter rivals. And once a message is self-destructed, it's gone. Not even the person who wrote the message can retrieve the original."

I shook my head. "But this wouldn't apply to you."

"Your faith in me is very touching, but please notice I don't wear a white coat and a stethoscope. There's only so much medicine I can do with a flash drive and a USB cable."

"When a file is deleted, the file system puts a marker in the file management system to let the system know; but that wouldn't apply to the backup drive. And Ekman had a backup drive. Surely all you have to do is find the digital cavity where the binary data is hiding?"

"What I gather from one of the SDE companies I spoke to is that someone subscribes to the SDE service, and when they want to send a self-destructing e-mail, they send a link that looks like an e-mail. The recipient would access the e-mail via that link, at which point the tracking and destruction criteria set by the sender apply. The e-mail never actually resides on the recipient's computer, therefore conventional forensics can't find it."

I winced. "You're sure about this?"

"I looked through Ekman's Dropbox, his Microsoft Windows Registry, and the Microsoft Outlook files: In-box, Deleted, Unread, Spam, Junk E-mail, AVG Virus Vault, you name it, I looked at it. And while it's true there are some threats in the mail, these are old threats that go way back to 2005. Islamic stuff. And before that, to 2002, when he had some threats in the UK from animal-rights extremists concerning favorable comments he'd made about people who wear fur. But nothing at all as recent as you suggested. I checked through the hiberfil. I checked Ekman's temporary application cached files. I checked all of the SDE companies I found on Google, looking for a search string. I checked through the machine's unallocated space. I even looked in all his digital cavities. Nice phrase, by the way. I must remember that one."

"How many of these SDE companies did you find on Google?"

"'Bout a dozen. And Gil, those are just the legitimate ones. You can bet there are at least as many illegitimate outfits offering an SDE service, for whatever reason. That's the thing about the Internet; there's always more shit than shinola. But you'd need a court order to inspect the database of the legitimate service providers. And even then there's no guarantee you'd actually find a damn thing. Best you can do is hope that you find yourself a likely suspect, impound his computer, and we get lucky and find that he accessed the self-destructing e-mail website either by viewing the index.dat file—which stores the Internet history— or by webpage remnants left behind in cache."

I let out a sigh and sprang up off Ken Paris's chair and went to the grimy window and looked out at the less than inspiring view. If John Ford's movies were to be believed, Texas was once a place of wide-open plains, red rivers, and relentless big sky. Maybe the sky was still the same, but the rest was now silent speeding cars, half-empty parking lots, and go-fuck-yourself office buildings carrying on all manner of local Houston business: auto sales, pipeline machinery, home construction, real estate. Real estate. Shit. I was going to have to look for somewhere to live, and soon. Somewhere that wasn't home, where I could practice my heroic solitude; that seemed stereotypically Texan, at least. Like any other brick agent at the Bureau, I'd managed somehow to screw things up at home. Irrevocably, it seemed, if the last agonizing conversation with Ruth was anything to go by. I had been informed that I had thirty days to get out of the house on Driscoll Street before she changed the locks and dumped my stuff on the sidewalk.

"My wife, Ruth. She filed."

"Well, that's the Bureau for you. We always get our man. It's just our women who get away." Ken waved a finger at me as I left. "Just don't let your kid get away, all right?"

᠙

Dear Danny,

I'm writing this letter to you now to explain myself to you since lately I haven't been able to speak to you very much. You're too young to read this right now so I'm going to keep this letter until you are older. By the way, you'll notice that there's a postmark on the sealed envelope; that's just so you know that I really was thinking of you a lot when I wrote this and that I'm not trying to pretend you were more important to me than perhaps you've grown up thinking you were. I don't know how old you are at this present moment, which makes this letter even more difficult to write, so forgive me if I just go ahead and try to speak to the man I think you will become.

I am so proud of you, Danny, and I love you very much and I've always wanted the best for you, son. So does your mom. We both want that. Until you have a son of your own, it's hard to know how wonderful it feels to be someone's parent and what a sense of human mystery that provokes—by which I mean the question of how any of us are here at all. Frankly, I have no more idea now that I'm a man than I did when I was a boy.

But inevitably, when I look at you, I see myself, and I often imagine my own dad looking at me in turn. It's only now that I'm your dad that I can really understand him the way I tried to do when I was his son. He was a good father, and while I've tried to be a better one, I'm not altogether sure that I've succeeded. I think that's true for a lot of guys. The fact is that it's both an honor and a great responsibility to be a father and there are times when perhaps the responsibility weighs a lot more heavily than you might imagine. You want to pass on some hard-won wisdom and a wealth of good experience to your son, but sometimes you feel that all you're doing is giving orders and advice and not much in the way of love. You have to learn a lot of stuff when you're a kid, but what no one ever tells you is how much more you have to learn when you're a parent. I guess you could say I've had to learn more being your dad than I ever had to learn being someone's son. Who'd have thought it? Frankly, being my dad's son was easy in comparison with how much more difficult it must have been to be my dad. I thought he had all the right answers—not all of which I agreed with. It's only now I realize that he didn't have all the answers and how—in a good way—he was making it all up as we went along. I think all fathers do that. Life presents so many temptations and problems that there's just not enough time to always get things right. And the fact is I don't have the answers, Danny—none of us has as many answers as perhaps we need—but I do recognize the questions. They're the same questions that I asked when I was a boy. They're probably the same questions that all sons ask their fathers. I guess what I'm saying here is that you're a lot more like me than perhaps you realize.

Don't mistake what I'm telling you, Danny. I don't want to make you like me. You're not me just as I wasn't my dad. Look how different we are. We're different, but he's always the one guy I know who's most like me. The one guy who loves me just as much as I love you.

As I write this, your mom and I haven't been getting on too well lately and we're living apart. None of that is your fault. It's my fault and, to a lesser extent, your mom's. I sincerely hope that we can patch things up between us and live together as a family again, but with each passing day I fear the worst—that

something has broken between us that can never be repaired. I
won't go into the details right now except to say that no matter
how much they might love each other sometimes people find
their beliefs and principles forcing them apart. I think I believe
one thing and your mother believes something else, but the one
thing we can agree on is you: we both want what's best for you.

I promise to write again when I have time. But for now,
that's all. I love you.

Your loving father

ELEVEN

The following morning, checking through my voice mail, I found an urgent message from Andrew Newman, the medical director at UTHCPC, asking me to call him at his office.

"Uh, thanks for calling us back, Agent Martins. I appreciate it. I'm sorry to tell you that Philip Osborne died at 4:31 this morning. I have to say it came as a real surprise to us here at Harris County Psychiatric. We were pretty sure we had him stabilized. At least physically. It's too bad. I was a major fan of his writing."

"What was the cause of death?"

"Cardiac infarction. Followed by a massive pulmonary edema. It looks like his heart just stopped."

"I see. So, did you try to revive him?"

"No. There are certain occasions when it's clear there would be little point in trying. I don't want to go into too many details, but I'm afraid this was one of those occasions."

"All right, sir. Can I ask you this: Would you say that his death was caused by the same mental trauma that put him in an acute state of catatonia?"

"From the amount of adrenaline we found in his system, sure, that would be my guess. But it is just a guess, you understand, Agent Martins. There will, of course, have to be an autopsy."

"When will that be?"

"First thing tomorrow a.m., I would imagine."

I was about to hang up the telephone when I realized that Newman was still on the line.

"It's probably nothing important," he continued, "and in a way it's nothing unusual, but for a brief moment, just before he died, Mr. Osborne regained consciousness. According to the computer monitoring him, and the nurse who was summoned by his patient alarm, he was conscious for almost four whole minutes."

"Did Osborne activate that alarm himself?"

"No, it's automatic. His conscious state would have activated an alert on the duty night nurse's computer, which summoned her to his room. Not that she really needed it under the circumstances."

"What circumstances were they?"

"Er, he screamed. And kept on screaming, like he was taking a dive off a tall building. That's what I've been told. The nurse was pretty spooked by it. Then again, it's not that unusual for people to scream in a psychiatric hospital. But perhaps it's a little unusual to scream for so damn long. According to the nurse, perhaps as long as four minutes."

"You mean he screamed for the entire time he was conscious again?"

"Yes."

"I'd like to speak to the nurse if I may, Dr. Newman. What's her name?"

"Nurse Kendall. But she'll have to call you. Her shift was supposed to end at midday, but she was sent home early."

"Oh? Why is that, sir?"

"The screaming was followed by a massive pulmonary edema. I guess it shook her up a bit."

"What exactly is a pulmonary edema?"

"Usually, it's caused by heart failure. As the heart fails, pressure in the veins going through the lungs starts to rise. And as the pressure in these blood vessels increases, fluid is pushed into the air spaces in the lungs, which interrupts the normal intake of oxygen in the lungs. He coughed up some blood. Onto Nurse Kendall, who happened to be bent over his bed at the time."

"So she got some blood on her uniform. Isn't that what you might call an occupational hazard?"

"Yes. But it's like this, Agent Martins: The guy coughed his guts all over the woman. She was covered in blood. Like someone threw a beer glass full of it over her. It's possible there was some preexisting cardiomyopathic condition. Or lung ailment."

"I wouldn't be so sure about that, Dr. Newman. He wasn't a smoker. And he had kept himself reasonably fit. He was still only in his forties, I believe."

I thanked Newman and reminded him to have Nurse Kendall call me and send me the result of the autopsy.

I put the telephone down and stared at my computer for a moment before Googling "pulmonary edema" and "Philip Osborne."

The stuff about pulmonary edema was disquieting and convinced me that sometimes the human body goes wrong in a spectacular way.

The Web images of Philip Osborne showed a man with a large bushy beard, and also without a beard, and he looked progressively stronger and more buffed than he had been in his twenties. The man had biceps like a stevedore, but these were not as big as the biceps of the other gay man he was sometimes pictured with—a very muscular-looking guy, also with a beard, holding Osborne's hand, both of them wearing the same white linen shirt and blue pin-striped pants. It looked like one of those beachside civil ceremonies that you read about in the celebrity magazines, and I wondered why there was no mention in the case file of this man, whose name was John Cabot; and so I Googled him, too, and discovered that they had indeed been civil partners and that Cabot had died of AIDS more than five years ago.

There were also a couple of more recent pictures of Osborne shaking hands or sharing a joke with Bishop Coogan, and remembering that they had been friends, I thought to give him a call.

"Sorry, Eamon. But Philip Osborne died this morning."

"Thank you for telling me. I'll go over there and say a prayer for him. Since Osborne was admitted, they're quite used to seeing me at that hospital. Did they say how he died?"

"The doctors say he had a cardiac arrest that occasioned a pulmonary edema. But whatever happened left an experienced night nurse feeling like she needed to go home."

"Look, I have to go now. There's a little local difficulty we're having here right now. Which is why His Eminence is here with me now. Perhaps I might discuss that with you when I call you back."

"By all means, Bishop."

I put down the telephone and then headed for the men's room to wash and sanitize my hands while asking myself what the "little local difficulty" might be that required a federal agent to advise a bishop. Returning to my office a few minutes later, I met Jesus Guttiérrez coming the other way.

There were five bomb techs working in the Houston field office and Guttiérrez—the Gut—was the most experienced, despite also being the youngest and least senior. He was wearing a blue field jacket, and since DT agents and bomb technicians often worked the same cases, I stopped and asked him if there was something going down I should know about.

"It's probably nothing," he said, quietly shifting his bulk from one foot to the other like an impatient boxer. "But we got a call from the Pasadena police. It seems like someone found a suspicious object in the Armand Bayou Nature Center, and Mel and I have to go down there and check it out."

Mel Karski was the Gut's line supervisor.

"It's a strange place for a suspicious object," I remarked.

Guttiérrez shook his head. "This job has JAWOFT written on it in neon letters," he said.

JAWOFT was "just a waste of fucking time," like most of the investigations that came the way of the FBI's bomb technicians. Every time the Counterterrorism guys flushed out some raghead with a bomb in his sneakers or his underpants, the FBI's bomb technicians were obliged to field more false alarms than a maternity hospital.

"But surely the alternative is worse," I said.

"You sound just like Mel. He's checking out the van before we go all the way down there. I don't know why they think this is BT shit. There's no package and there're no wires or panties on show. What do the Pasadena cops think I'm going to do with this thing? Kick it, maybe. Or try to make it fly again."

"Fly?"

"They said the object looks like some kind of fucking model airplane. Hell, it probably is a model airplane. Like I'm an expert on fucking UFOs."

"Is that how it arrived in the nature reserve? It flew there?"

"Looks like, yeah. Lucky it landed in the wetlands, otherwise it might have started a fire."

I went back to my desk. There was something about what the Gut had said that troubled me. A moment passed before I realized that Vijay Persaud was hovering over my desk and that he'd asked me a question. Vijay worked in DCS Net, the FBI's dedicated wiretap system.

"What's that you said?" I asked.

"I asked if I could have a word with you?" he said. "In private."

"Now?"

"If that's okay."

I stood up. And grabbed my jacket, and my cell phone.

"That's cool." Still hardly listening, I started running down the hall. "But it'll have to wait."

"Where are you going?" Vijay shouted after me.

"The Armand Bayou Nature Center," I said. "In Pasadena."

※

Mel Karski steered east off the Sam Houston Parkway onto Genoa Red Bluff Road. The van was none too clean, with empty fast-food bags and cigarette packs on the floor and a piece of chewing gum stuck to the dashboard like a shiny gray limpet that had lost its shell. For a while, I rested my head on the passenger-side window; at least I did until I realized that the bird shit on the outside of the window was actually on the inside. After that, I kept my hands in my pockets.

"You should wash this van," I said. "It's like a petri dish in here."

"Blends in nicely the way it is," said the Gut.

The land on either side of the highway was uniformly flat and arid, and apart from the odd McDonald's restaurant, gas station, trailer park, and rig hauling a tank full of milk or pesticide, or maybe both, it was mostly empty. There was the occasional church, too, of course; you never have to drive more than five miles in Texas before you find a place of worship.

A few minutes later we were heading off the main road into the ABNC, which is one of the largest urban wildlife refuges in the United States and named after the river or bayou that runs into Galveston Bay. A white Pasadena Police Ford Crown Vic was waiting for us at the visitor center and two cops wearing black uniforms led the way on foot along one of the meandering trails to where the suspicious object had been found. The local police had missed their breakfast in order to wait for us and they weren't feeling very gabby about anything very much, which suited me fine. It gave us a chance to enjoy the quiet and the sea breeze off the bay a mile or two to the east. It made a pleasant change from the heat and dust and in-your-face cacophony of the city. The ranger didn't say much either, although it's possible we might not have heard him on account of the sizable mustache that covered his whole mouth. Possibly it was this that scared a big white egret out of the tall grass that grew on either side of the trail; as it took off and headed south across Clear Lake, it blotted out the sun for a moment.

At the end of the trail we climbed aboard a pontoon boat, which wasn't much more than a rectangular deck with handrails and a steering wheel on top of a couple of long floats. As the ranger started the engine, something living sank silently under the emerald carpet of weeds that covered the surface of the water and moved slowly away with an almost indiscernible wake. On the other side of the bayou the ranger nudged the bank with the square bow of the boat and let us step off onto dry land. He stayed on the pontoon and the cops showed us to the clearing where the object had been found. One of the cops drew his pistol and looked around carefully.

"They use this clearing to leave meat for the gators," said the other. "Which is how they found it in the first place."

"That's a comforting thought," said the Gut. "I wondered why the ranger stayed on the pontoon."

It was about the size of a large dead egret and similarly colored. Two feet long with a four-and-half-foot wingspan. The tailspan was maybe two-thirds that width. The fuselage was long and cylindrical and unmarked and resembled nothing so much as a small cruise missile. Most of the ground underfoot was waterlogged, which probably explained why the object hadn't scorched the grass when it landed.

"The hell is that?" said Mel, kneeling down beside the object. He carefully laid a hand on the metal fuselage and then quickly took it away again. "Hot. Most likely from the sun, though." He squinted at the rear end of the thing and made a noise. "Interesting. No sign of combustion back here. Looks like it might be electrically powered." He leaned over the front. "Jesus. There's a little camera in the nose."

"It's called a Switchblade," I said, "and it's the latest in high-tech battlefield wizardry: a miniature drone that you can take out of your backpack and deploy quicker than a grunt's fucking mess tin. You just fold out the wings like a picnic table and then use a miniature guidance system to fly it through someone's bathroom window. Assuming the hajis have bathroom windows. The Pentagon calls this little toy plane their magic bullet."

"Looks like one hell of a bullet," said the Gut. "Sure give some Big T a wake-up call."

Big T was what people like the Gut who'd served in Afghanistan called the Taliban.

I shrugged. "This one must have been unarmed, otherwise it wouldn't have been found."

"All the same," said Mel, "we'd best let the army deal with it. This looks like one for the Too Hard Box. Okay, Gut?"

The Gut nodded. "I only fuck with that which I know of and about this I know fuck all. I'll call Explosive Ordnance Disposal at the army base when we get back to the van."

"Yeah. Do that."

"Even so, I'd like to hang around and see how they do it, if you don't mind, boss. Just in case there's a Windows upgrade I don't know about."

Mel nodded. "Sure, be my guest." He glanced up at the blue sky. "Question is, what the fuck is this thing doing all the way out here? With no targets. No hajis. No bathroom windows. Just floating handbags."

"We had a report from Army CID of a group of terrorists, ex-military, called the HIDDEN, who were trying to get ahold of these weapons."

"You mean they're Americans?" said Mel.

I nodded. "That's right. Americans. The most dangerous fucking terrorists of them all. They're planning to use these weapons against the local Jewish community."

"The Jews," said Mel Karski. "It's always us. As if we didn't have enough to deal with from Big T and the Reverend Al Qaeda."

"My guess is that this was a test flight," I said. "They could have sat in a Starbucks on Sylvan Beach while flying this bird around the whole of the bay area. Or maybe the vendor arranged a quiet little demonstration for one of the bad guys."

I had my cell phone out and was about to dial a number.

"Either way, it means I now have to telephone my ASAC to arrange a quiet little demonstration of how the FBI handles a five-star crisis."

"Uh, no, you don't. Not here, Agent Martins. Not next to this fucking thing. Better switch it off right now." Mel turned toward the two cops. "You, too, boys. Just in case. Wouldn't want a detonation signal hitching a ride on our cell phones, now would we?"

"Can that happen?" asked one of the cops, edging away from the Switchblade.

"Oh, yeah," said the Gut. "Matter of fact, it happens all the time in Afghanistan and Iraq. More angels get made that way in coalition country than in Bedford fucking Falls."

TWELVE

I spoke to Gisela about the abandoned Switchblade and she agreed that we couldn't afford to wait on the Army CID informer they had working in the HIDDEN group to bring us up to speed with the terrorists' plans. We had to assume that HIDDEN was now in possession of the weapon and that at any moment it might carry out an attack on Congregation Beth Israel on North Braeswood Boulevard. It was a Thursday and in less than twenty-four hours the synagogue would be full of people. It was imperative that we arrest the group as quickly as possible. At the same time, we knew the HIDDEN group was already heavily armed and, given its military background, it seemed reasonable to assume that the members were likely to put up a violent resistance. All of which suggested that we were going to need full tactical support.

HIDDEN's leader, Johnny Sack Brown, lived in an apartment complex on South Gessner Road, on the southwest side of Houston. It's an area frequented by local gangs—the Cholos and the Broadway Sureños—especially at night when the Southside starts to kick off. From the number of five-point stars, black rosaries, and descending pitchforks I saw graffitied on some of the local buildings, I figured the Cholos were in the ascendant. Either that or there were some militant Rosicrucians figuring to move in.

Together with some HPD from the seventeenth district who knew the area well, we checked over the site on Google Earth and Google Maps, and decided to park our vehicles in front of the Episcopal Church of the Epiphany about two or three hundred feet from the target building, and deploy from there. This church looked less like somewhere you'd have met Jesus or St. John the Divine and more like an all-night place where you might get a prescription filled or a hamburger served up. From the church, one team was going to approach the apartment complex from the north, another team would go in from the south, and a third team from the west. On Google Earth, the apartment complex constituted a couple of dozen concrete boxes, each with one small apartment on the ground floor and another identical one on the floor above. Some of the little houses even had chimneys, although it was hard to see how these might ever have been of use in a city as warm as Houston.

When the operation went down at six the following morning, these houses seemed no less unprepossessing. South Gessner Road is a four-lane highway with all the charm of yesterday's doggy bag. Across the road is a You Lock It self-storage building, and from the general look of the neighborhood, it was a useful facility to have in an area where none of the doors and locks gave the impression that they could have resisted an assault by a determined two-year-old.

Almost as soon as the doors of the bus opened, the team moved quickly into positions with everyone trying to keep their minds on the job at hand. But this wasn't easy. On average, the Tac Team is called up maybe once or twice a month; and it was an unfortunate coincidence that I had called for a deployment on the morning that another probable victim of Houston's serial killer had been found in Memorial Park. This meant that several field agents were hauled off duty with Violent Crimes to come and serve on my Tac Team operation with the result that the latest murder investigation, headed by Harlan Caulfield, was immediately stretched to the limit. It made for a very difficult morning and there were rumors of a stand-up row between Gisela and Harlan about which investigation took priority. Harlan was just trying it on for size, of course; once a Tac Team op has been called, it always assumes precedence. No one wants to risk an agent's life by deploying a half-strength squad. Not for a dead woman in a park.

In any event, not even a single shot was fired. Johnny Sack Brown and his two friends offered no resistance and they submitted to being arrested and driven to a holding cell at the Bureau field office as meekly as if they'd received gold-embossed invitations to go there from the governor of Texas himself. There was, however, no sign in the apartment of a Switchblade, or any other weapons for that matter, not even a sidearm; and the Tac Team went back to the office feeling less than elated. It was only when I searched Johnny Sack Brown's desk drawers and discovered a receipt from the You Lock It self-storage facility that I guessed where the group was keeping their new toys. Ten minutes later I was on the other side of South Gessner Road with a couple of our newest brick agents, opening an outdoor storage unit with climate control and a roll-up door, and unpacking an arms cache that included not one but six Switchblades.

It was still early. I hadn't eaten breakfast yet, but I was too psyched to be hungry. I jumped in the car and was driving back to Justice Park Drive with the good news about the Switchblades when my cell rang. It was Bishop Coogan.

"I was at the hospital," he said. "To pray for Philip Osborne. I called you last night, like you said I should, but you weren't answering your cell."

"Sorry about that, sir," I said. "I meant to call you back only we had something real important going down last night."

"I've seen a good many passings, you understand, Gil. It's not everyone who dies with the smile of the saints on his face."

"Meaning what?"

"To be frank with you, Gil, he didn't look at peace with the world. Sure, there's a great comfort to be had in a fellow's last prayer, you know. To die in the arms of the Church, so to speak. And Osborne didn't have that. I hate to see a soul that's not at peace when it passes over. And he certainly wasn't that. You remember that when you pick up your next book by Richard bloody Dawkins."

"Fair enough, Bishop. Look, you said there was something you wanted to speak to me about. A little local difficulty, you called it."

"That I did. I need some advice, Gil. Perhaps you could drop round to the house again sometime. Tomorrow, maybe. I'll be here most of the day."

"Sure. Come to think of it, I should take some time off. I need to see a real estate agent and look for somewhere to live, among a lot of other things."

"Are you two kids moving house, Gil?"

"Ruth wants me out of her house, sir. And she wants a divorce, too."

"Why did she do that?"

"I kept my virtues in one pocket and my vices in the other. I guess that was fine until she started going through my pockets and discovered I wasn't quite as virtuous as she imagined."

"I don't suppose there's any use in my offering to speak to her on your behalf."

"Hell, no." I laughed. "I think she dislikes Catholics as much as she hates heathens like me."

"You're no heathen, Gil. You might think you are now. But when you turn away from God, it's only a circle you're making and before long that same circle will put you back in front of him. You see if I'm wrong."

It was hard arguing these things with a bishop, even one as worldly as Eamon Coogan.

My route back to the office took me onto the Southwest Freeway and then north up the 610. About halfway there I saw blue and red lights, and then two FBI Evidence Response Team trucks as they turned off the opposite lanes onto North Post Oak Road and Woodway Drive. They were obviously headed for the serial killer's latest crime scene, and thinking I might loop around and follow them, I decided to make a right onto Memorial Drive. I placed the cherry on top of the car roof and put my foot down. It wasn't that I thought I could add anything important to the investigation, but I hadn't yet seen the killer's work firsthand and, after all, Harlan Caulfield had asked for my opinion once before, so I wanted to show him that I was still willing to help. Besides, I was still feeling a little guilty about stealing some of his men.

The trucks were easy to spot as they came barreling east along the road and I was quickly on their tail. They veered south onto Memorial Loop Drive and pulled up in front of three practice baseball diamonds, right next to a mobile command center—one of the big blue-gray motor homes with a satellite dish on top that look as if Tom Cruise might be resting inside between takes. Some cops were doing an excellent job of keeping a line of looky-loos at a distance. Already there were several TV cameras set up to scavenge the scraps from the police and FBI tables to make the whole ghastly scene complete. You could almost smell the scent of a fresh kill in the air above the crowd's eager, bobbing heads.

Trusting in my cherry, the cops waved me on through like I was someone who mattered and I pulled up next to the MCC just as Harlan came out with an e-cigarette in his mouth. With no flame or combustion involved, e-cigarettes were about the only thing you could smoke in Memorial Park, or almost anywhere else for that matter. Harlan took a drag of his tobacco-free, smoke-free, smell-free cigarette. It was just harmless water vapor with a little nicotine mixed in, so you could get the taste without insult to the throat or other people. I didn't mind offering an insult to anyone.

"I was right about Saint Peter, wasn't I?"

"What makes you say so, Martins?"

"Come on, Harlan. Everyone in the office knows that's what the boys in Violent Crime have nicknamed your serial killer." I nodded at the news crews. "Everyone except them, that is."

"That's one newspaper headline I never want to see," growled Harlan. "So keep your mouth shut about that. I'd better have a word with my team. And stamp on someone's kiwifruit, very hard."

"Another victim who was on her way to collecting a halo?"

"That she was." Harlan sighed. "Caroline Romero founded the Robbie Center when her boy Robbie disappeared. He ran away from home when he was twelve and she's never seen him again. So she and her husband, Manolo, used some of their not inconsiderable fortune to found the center in order to try to prevent abductions and runaways, and to recover missing children. Since they started fifteen years ago, they've helped find more than three hundred missing kids and reunite them with their parents. And if that isn't worth a damned halo, I don't know what is." He took a drag on the cigarette. "She lived on Crestwood Drive, about a mile west of here. Nice house. Nice people. She had other kids, but losing one isn't something you get over, I guess. She never did anything bad to anybody. That's what all her neighbors say."

"How'd it happen?"

"She was shot with a small-caliber weapon, same as the others. Last night she went out jogging and she didn't come back. No one saw a fucking thing, of course. Leastways, not so far."

"Is it possible that your killer feels that he's on the side of the angels? Could the reason he's killing these people be that he actually thinks he's doing God's work?"

Harlan looked at his e-cigarette and shook his head. "You're taking this atheism a little too far, aren't you?"

"No, no, Harlan, listen. It makes complete logical sense when you think about it. That is, if you believe in heaven and in God's rewards for the righteous—the whole nine yards. I mean, if heaven really is heaven, then maybe the killer believes he's just helping his victims to their reward sooner rather than later. Maybe he thinks he's doing them a favor."

Harlan frowned. "That's the stupidest idea I ever heard."

"You're not a serial killer, Harlan. You don't think like a crazy person. But we both know lots of people who do think that heaven is a real place and can't wait to get there. Didn't those Muslim terrorists who flew those planes into the Twin Towers believe that they were going to find seventy-two virgins waiting for them in heaven?"

"I never did see the attraction of virgins all that much."

"Harlan, maybe the killer thinks he's gathering these victims to the Lord. Admitting them to heaven. Bringing them to their reward. Exactly like St. Peter."

"You are one sick bastard, Martins. Do you know that?" He grinned and punched me gently on the shoulder. "But frankly, that's the best theory I've heard in a long while. And as good as any other one I've heard since I started to work this fucking case."

"Just maybes is all it is, Harlan. Just maybes."

"Ain't you heard? Maybe is how we get this show on the road."

"Maybe."

"Uh-huh. You had breakfast?"

"Nope."

"Good. Then let's go take a look at the scene."

❦

Caroline Romero's murder brought Saint Peter's death toll to six and had the effect of triggering the use of the Houston field office's Crisis

Management Operations Center, from where the resources of all local law enforcement agencies investigating the killings would in future be coordinated. The CMOC is a large windowless room on the second floor. It's like the Situation Room at the White House, only bigger and actually better equipped with dozens of PC terminals and flat-screen TVs along the walls so that information is more easily obtained and, more important, shared among the fifty federal agents and cops that the CMOC can accommodate. No one likes to set up the CMOC when another operation is going down. The crisis manager running the CMOC wants to feel that he's got first call on all of the local Bureau resources, which is why, when we met outside the elevator in the front hall, Doug Corbin thought to tap a nail in my ear.

Doug Corbin had a personality that belonged in a tissue. He'd nailed my ear before and took more delight in doing so than he ought to have done.

"I could use a heads-up, Agent Martins," he said, standing much too close for comfort, "the next time you try to swat a fly with half the fucking CMOC Team."

"Well, sir, it certainly didn't seem like it was just a fly at six o'clock this morning."

"Says who? You? You're just a line supervisor, Martins, not Bob Mueller."

"And I cleared it with my ASAC, sir. Gisela Delillo. Why don't you take it up with her if you're unhappy about what happened?"

"Is that supposed to reassure me that you know what you're fucking talking about?"

"We had good intel that the suspects weren't the kind to give themselves up without a couple of dozen guns in their faces."

"Really? The gun cupboard was bare, is what I've just been told."

"You heard wrong. I've come straight from the lockup, where my subject was keeping six mini–cruise missiles and enough guns and ammo to resupply the Alamo. And neither I nor Gisela knew that the CMOC was open for business when we called the op."

"You just make sure you speak to me before you even think of calling an op again. I don't like opening up a CMOC with just a couple of kids who are straight out of the Academy and a secretary who stinks of fucking mothballs. I don't like waiting around for people to show up like it was the first day of school. And I sure as hell don't like you."

Toward the end of this conversation, Vijay Persaud—the guy from DCS Net—appeared next to my shoulder.

I let Corbin take the elevator by himself. The thought of inhaling his lousy breath was too much for me. I'd kind of hoped that Vijay would get into the car alongside him but he didn't.

"You should take that up with the AA," he said. "You know I'm the chapter representative."

The AA was the FBI Agents Association.

"Thanks, Vijay. But I do believe I will forget all about this. I never did like kids who went crying to their mothers because someone called them fat."

"Awright." He paused. "Uh, Gil? We need to talk. Urgently. Remember?"

"Well, go ahead and talk, Vijay. This is the FBI, not the locker room at the Houstonian Club."

"Actually, no. We have to do this in private, I think. Would you mind if we found a meeting room and talked there?"

I hesitated.

"Like I say, it's urgent."

"Okay, Vijay. I hear you. But right now I got something urgent of my own waiting for me in the interview room downstairs. Probable terrorist by the name of Johnny Sack Brown. He was planning to fire a guided missile through the window of a synagogue right here in Houston. So why don't I come and find you when I'm through with him?"

"Awright. Please do, Gil. Like I already said, it's kind of urgent."

I let that one go. But I wanted to tell him that in the FBI it's always fucking urgent.

⁂

Johnny Sack Brown was a "No comment" kind of guy with muscular folded arms and a rolled-up newspaper of a manner. With almost every question Gisela and I asked him over the course of the next two or three hours, he clenched the fist that was manacled to the table and then politely uttered his mantra of antipathy and estrangement. On his chest was a tattoo of startling obscenity featuring an old and presumably divine figure with a long beard and the sentiment "God has a hard-on for Marines," while on one forearm was an American eagle clutching a banner on which was written "jesUS our sAvior." These tats intrigued me, and for a moment I sought to turn the one-sided conversation away from the Switchblades I'd found in the lockup on South Gessner Road, in the hope that I might get Brown to talk about anything—anything at all.

"I've often thought about getting a tat myself. Only I can't seem to think of a sentiment that I like enough to endure the pain."

Brown stared us both down like we were the ugliest dogs he'd ever seen.

"I assume you wouldn't have those tats if you didn't believe in God. Is that right?"

For once he did not reply "No comment" to a direct question, and thinking to press ahead with this line, I added, "No, I guess you can hardly say 'No comment' about a question like that. Not without denying your religious faith. Although, of course, because of *Miranda*, a court can construe silence as a tacit denial. Perhaps you didn't know that. So, I'm going to ask you again, sir. Are you a Christian, Major Brown?"

After another long moment, he said: "I'm a Christian, Agent Martins. What of it?"

"I sure didn't mean any disrespect to your faith. I used to be a Christian myself."

"What are you now?"

"Oh, I'm an atheist, sir. But you know, I can't help wondering what God would have made of what you were planning to do. I can't figure how your God can have a hard-on for Marines who are prepared to murder his chosen people."

"God punishes his people when they do wrong."

"It's one thing to chase the money changers out of the temple; it's another thing altogether to fire a guided missile through the temple's fucking window."

There was a cold steadiness about Brown I found daunting. He was hardly the fanatic I had imagined. He gave the impression of a man who had thought a great deal about what he had planned to do. And he didn't look in the least bit troubled by his situation. He was going to be a hard man to break.

"I tell you what I don't understand," said Gisela. "What I don't understand is how someone as intelligent as you could plan to commit the mass murder of men, women, and children just because they were Jews. It just doesn't follow."

"Isn't that for you to find out?" said Brown. "You and your shrinks from Behavioral Science." Then he smiled, leaned back, and folded his arms as best he was able and said not another word.

We tried asking more questions but without result; and after a while, we concluded the interview, switched off the tape, and Johnny Sack Brown was taken into the sally port and handed over to the custody of the United States Marshals Service for transport to a federal detention center.

"We'll let them all boil over the weekend in FDC," she said, reclaiming her gun from its locker. "The shrinks can assess our friend Johnny on Monday. There's nothing like a couple of nights behind bars in the detention center to make a man more talkative."

I stifled a yawn.

"You need to go home," she said. "You were up half the night working on the Tac Team op. Go home and I'll see you on Monday."

I sighed and shook my head. "I can't. I've got Vijay Persaud from DCS Net who wants to talk to me about something."

"It's late," said Gisela. "Chances are he's gone home himself. Forget about it until Monday. If he's still around, I'll speak to him."

"And Corbin's been chewing my ear about taking agents from the CMOC for the Tac Team."

"Fuck him," said Gisela. "Tac Team ops come first. No dead feds. That's standard protocol. I'm going to take this up with Chuck. I'm tired of that fucker Corbin trying to ramrod my agents. Just because he's the crisis manager doesn't mean he runs this field office." She smiled. "So, go home."

I went to the men's room and washed my hands and face carefully. Questioning suspects has that effect on me.

THIRTEEN

I t was early on Saturday morning. Somewhere along Driscoll Street a dog was barking, but mostly I had only the noise of my own shallow breathing and the death-watch ticking of the travel alarm on the bedside table for company. It sounded like a frenetic metal beetle chewing into the rotten wood of my life. My sense of being on my own now was always worse at that time of day. I was lying in bed and staring across the wasteland of a king-size mattress separating me from Ruth's pillow where her blond head ought to have been. I hadn't slept well since she had left. For the last hour I'd lain awake, making plans for one and trying my best not to feel sorry for myself. The weekend was shaping up nicely to be a piece of shit. But for the fact that I urgently needed somewhere to live, I'd have gone to the office.

Probably it wasn't a good idea, but in the absence of any better ones I decided I was going to go to Lakewood the following morning. Not to make my peace with God, but in the hope I might meet and make peace with Ruth. I'm not sure where she was, but she wasn't in Corsicana. Someone had told me he'd seen her and Danny in church the previous Sunday and I thought that while she was there maybe she might be more inclined to do unto others—i.e., me—as she would have others do unto her. But it seemed like a slim hope and most of all I just wanted to catch a glimpse of Danny. I figured Ruth would be more disposed to give me the time of day if I was able to tell her that, as requested by her lawyers, I'd moved out of the house. So, before driving to see Bishop Coogan, I put some clothes in a bag with the intention of moving into a motel while I looked for a place of my own to rent. I had plenty of ideas about that. I just didn't have plenty of money.

I took a last look at the house, remembering our life there. Mostly I just stood in the doorway of Danny's room and stared at his little bed and the less favored toys he'd left behind when he and his mother took off. Coming back downstairs, I reflected that I'd never liked the place that much—mainly because I'd had so little to do with choosing it— but for a while, until I fucked things up with Nancy and my new atheism, we'd been happy there. Hadn't we? And now? Did Danny ever miss home? Or me? I wondered about that: at his grandpa's house in Corsicana there were horses and ponies for him to ride, a tree house and a swimming pool the size of a wheat field. A small boy can forget about a lot, including his absent father, when he has his own pony.

I drove slowly away and steeled myself not to look back, as if I were Lot himself. I just fixed my eyes on the road ahead and then put my foot down. I headed northwest to the bishop's residence on Timber Terrace Road, which was off Memorial Drive. It was a sprawling modern house in a quiet leafy part of Houston close to St. Mary's Seminary where, when he wasn't working at the chancery of the archdiocese, Coogan performed some occasional academic function for which the house was the reward, I suppose. And a handsome reward it was, too, with a wide curving drive, a satellite dish on the roof, and a kidney-shaped pool, not to mention access to the Cardinal Beran Library, where Coogan was researching a book he was writing.

A housekeeper—possibly a nun—holding a duster and canister of furniture polish in her hand, opened the bishop's heavy wood-and-glass door and admitted me to a comfortable book-lined study that smelled strongly of cigars and beeswax; outside the library's elegant bay window a sprinkler hissed like a snake, hard at work keeping a carpet of emerald lawn well watered.

Coogan appeared in the doorway, mopping his brow with a handkerchief as big as a pillowcase; as usual, he looked like a fat Elvis trying out a strange new all-my-trials-Lord costume for a one-off show at the Vatican. We shook hands. In Coogan's big mitt mine felt no bigger than a cat's paw.

"Had breakfast?"

"Seems you read my mind, Eamon."

"You've lost weight. That's easier to read than your mind, Gil. It's not home cooking you've been having, I'll bet." He put his big hand on my shoulder. "Come through to the kitchen and we'll get Mrs. Harris to cook something for you."

I followed Coogan through the hall and into a well-appointed kitchen where the woman who had answered the door was polishing a stainless-steel cooktop in the center of a granite counter as big as the nave of a small and very clean church.

"Mrs. Harris?" said Coogan. "Would you cook Mr. Martins a huge breakfast, please?"

"Certainly, Your Excellency."

"I've asked her not to call me that," Coogan told me. "It makes me sound like I should be wearing a pith helmet and carrying letters of introduction to the queen, but she just ignores me."

Mrs. Harris ignored him; she was already preparing my breakfast; and within twenty minutes it was served, and very good it was, too. Coogan watched me eat it with vicarious pleasure, almost as if he could taste every bit of it that went into my mouth.

"So what did you want to talk to me about, Eamon?" I asked. "Do you mind if I smoke?"

"No, go ahead. I like the smell of cigarettes."

I lit one and waited. "And?"

He shrugged. "It doesn't matter. The archbishop and I have resolved the matter ourselves. Father Breguet, one of the priests at St. Benedict's seminary, was suspected of having embezzled some church funds. Anyway, we thought it over and decided not to press charges."

"You're going to let him get away with it?" I frowned. "Mind if I ask why?"

For a moment, I had the impression Coogan was picking his words with care.

"His Eminence and I concluded that it wasn't nearly as much money that went missing as we had earlier supposed."

"Hardly a federal matter, I'd have thought."

"No. But you're the only law enforcement officer I know well enough to talk about these things without having a lawyer present."

I grinned. "Well, I can't complain about the food."

"As it happens, there was another reason I had for going ahead and letting you come here."

I sighed. "I'm not looking for eternal reassurance. Just some place to live."

"Then you really have moved out."

I nodded. "This morning, before I came here. Ruth was about to throw my ass onto the street. A woman can do that when she's got custody of your kid. And when she's got her daddy's Benjamin Franklins bankrolling her. She always seems to know the very best moment to twist the knife in a man's guts."

"Well, I'm no expert when it comes to women," he said.

I let out a long sigh and slapped my full stomach. "So, after I've left this wonderfully spic-and-span house of yours, Eamon, I'm going to find a motel and then look for an apartment somewhere."

"Now, I might just be able to help you there, Gil. Mind you, it's not exactly convenient. But it might tide you over for a while."

"Well, my online search criteria are straightforward enough. They come down to this: the cheaper the better. I'm going to need what money I've got for a divorce lawyer. Look, it's very kind of you to offer to help me, Eamon, but I don't think life in a seminary would suit me right now. These days the only thing I pray for is to win the Texas lottery."

"I was thinking, there's a house you can have. All to yourself. And for as long as you want. It's hardly ideal for a man who works in Houston. But if you're needing to save money, I'm thinking for a while it might suit you."

"I dunno, Eamon. I'm kind of particular about things being clean, you know?"

"An empty furnished house. With five bedrooms and a small garden, and it's as clean as a whistle. Rent-free, too. Until you find something more permanent here in Houston. Which won't take you long. You can move in today if you're interested."

"Of course I'm interested. But there's just one catch, right? This is where you tell me the house is haunted."

"It's in Galveston." Coogan put his hands in his pockets, pushed his belly out, and smiled, awaiting my response.

I thought for a moment. Galveston wasn't exactly around the corner, and it was even farther away from Ruth and Danny in Corsicana. Fifty miles south of Houston, the largest seaport in Texas was only just starting to recover from Hurricane Ike. The place was virtually a ghost town. I've seen tumbleweed that looks more cheerful than Galveston, and so living there was hardly ideal. There was all that and the fact that I'd spend two hours on the I-45 every day. But what else did I have to do with my spare time? And there are major advantages to living almost anywhere when it's rent-free, even in a disaster zone. Rent-free is as cheap as you can get. And useful when you don't have the least fucking idea where you're going to be spending the night. Besides, the true fact of the matter was that I had little stomach for the business of actually looking for a place to live. From what I'd heard, rentals were nearly always filthy. That part of finding a new place really appalled me. And I certainly wasn't exactly looking forward to spending days cleaning a new apartment.

"It's a dump, right? Like the rest of Galveston. Ike took the roof off and left the basement full of water. Either that or there's still no electricity."

Coogan shook his head. "Actually, it's not a bad house. A bit quiet. Most of the neighbors moved out after the hurricane and they haven't come back. But all of the damage was repaired and the house was redecorated only last year. There's a wide-screen TV. A power shower. A fully renovated kitchen with all the modern conveniences. Until recently, the place was occupied by a priest who liked his wine and his creature comforts. Father Dyer. He's in a Texas City nursing home. For retired members of the clergy. And I had the place professionally cleaned after he left, so right now it's immaculate."

"Immaculate?"

"Immaculate." He paused. "Look, Gil, none of the lazy so-and-sos in the seminary even wants to set foot in Galveston. They're looking for somewhere with a little more action, here in Houston or in Dallas. Somewhere with some people. With some Catholics. And I can't say that I blame them. The only regular congregations to be found in Galveston are the goddamn cranes and turtles. The house is close to the old cathedral. So you'd be doing me a favor if you could keep an eye on the place. Kind of like a caretaker. We've had a few problems with looters down that way. Bastards stealing lead off church roofs, shit like that. A tenant with a Glock might be just what the doctor ordered. If you like, we can drive down there now and take a look at the house."

"Well, yeah, that'd be great, Eamon. If you're sure you can spare the time."

Coogan made a face. "I'm celibate, right? And there's no damn game this weekend. So what else am I going to do with my frigging Saturday?"

I grinned. "It's true what they say. If you want to lose your faith, make friends with a priest."

FOURTEEN

God and BP have a lot to answer for in the Gulf of Mexico. But calling Galveston a ghost town was misleading. Even the ghosts looked like they'd jumped on a train across the Galveston Causeway, retreating inland and north back up the Gulf Freeway for a more congenial city to haunt, such as Houston or Dallas. Most of the ghosts anyway; about the only place that seemed as if it might still be home to a spook or two was the Catholic diocesan house where Bishop Coogan had taken me the previous day—the place where it seemed I was going to live for a while, in the absence of something rent-free that was any better.

From the outside, things did not look promising. It was a turn-of-the-century three-story wooden house with a corner turret roof, wrap-around balconies and verandas, and a white picket fence. The house was much larger than I had imagined, and like a lot of old places in Galveston, it belonged properly in a less congenial part of Amityville. I've seen creepier-looking houses, but only on the cover of a novel by Stephen King.

Inside, however, things were very much more agreeable. The place was spectacularly clean—Coogan hadn't exaggerated about that. And the house was as well-appointed as he had promised it would be, with a wide-screen television, a well-stocked wine cellar, and a handsome library; it was nicely furnished, too, with a large and very comfortable bed, some fine Spanish rugs, and lots of leather furniture. I even liked the framed prints that were on the walls, although many of these pictures were of religious subjects. Coogan said they were by an English painter called Stanley Spencer, whom I'd only vaguely heard of: his *The Resurrection, Cookham* was pleasantly ordinary, while his *Angels of the Apocalypse* looked like a group of wives heading home from a Weight Watchers meeting.

In spite of these creature comforts, I did not sleep well on my first night. The tree out front was perfectly shaped for a hanging—an effect enhanced by a piece of ancient rope that was tied around the sturdiest bough; it was badly in need of pruning and, stirred by the Gulf breezes that had once made Galveston a better place to live than Houston, the branches tapped against the upper windows all night long. Being made entirely of wood, the house creaked like a wrecked schooner as it cooled after the high temperatures of the day, so that there were several times during the night when I felt obliged to get up and check what I already knew—that I was the only person in the house.

I wasn't just the only person in the house. The general ghostly effect of my new home was enhanced—if that's the right word—by the fact that most of the other houses in the neighborhood were boarded up and empty. I could have fired a whole clip out of the window and no one would have turned a hair. Galveston was getting back on its feet was the rumor at the local gas station but not so that anyone would have noticed. I've been in noisier boxes of cotton than Galveston.

Every time I looked out of a window I had the idea I might see a bunch of zombies coming along the street. At the local bodega on Strand Rear Street, by the greenish harbor, the guy behind the cash register was from some shit-hole town in Russia's Arctic Circle; he joked that Galveston reminded him of home, and I believed him. I couldn't have felt more cut off if I'd been manning a camp at the North Pole. And that particular Sunday morning, when I drove out of Galveston, I never thought I'd actually be glad to be heading for Lakewood Church.

I wasn't long off the island across the causeway when my cell rang. It was Helen Monaco.

"Where have you been, Martins? I was ringing you at home all day yesterday," she complained. "And you weren't answering your cell or your e-mails."

"Gee, Helen, it sounds like you were worried about me."

"Where the hell are you, anyway?"

"Galveston," I said. "It's where I'm living, as of yesterday. That's why you couldn't reach me at home. I've moved out. I should have called the office and let them know but this is my first day off since Ruth left me."

"Galveston? What the hell are you living there for? Are you tired of life or something?"

"It's actually quite a nice house, in the day. And rent-free, too."

"If I'd known you were that desperate, you could have had my couch."

"Ah, that's what you say now. But late at night, when we'd had a few drinks and you started coming on to me. Well, who knows how that might turn out?"

"And here I was, feeling sorry for you, sir."

"Don't. I'm doing just fine feeling sorry for myself all on my own."

"You're in the car. I hope I'm not going to spoil your Sunday."

"Every day feels like Sunday in Galveston. That's why I'm driving back to Houston."

"Yesterday morning I got a call from a guy I know in HPD. On Friday night they busted a forty-one-year-old Caucasian woman named Gaynor Carol Allitt for causing an automobile accident after she ran a red light on North Post Oak and Woodway. It was nothing serious. Just a couple of fenders bent is all. It seemed as if she might have been spooked by a patrol car that was heading for Memorial Park to check out this latest murder. At least that's what the two patrolmen thought. But when they questioned her, she became almost hysterical and told the two officers she wanted to confess to a murder."

"To the serial killings?"

"To the murder of Philip Osborne."

"But she's a loon, right? She has to be."

"That's what the police thought. So they fluttered her. And the polygraph said she was telling the truth. That's when they called me. And when I spoke to her last night, she sounded pretty reasonable; like she was in earnest. She didn't give any details, but she's sticking to what she told HPD. She told me she heard about Osborne's death from the TV news and felt guilty about it. Which is why she confessed in the first place."

Suddenly the idea of going to Lakewood did not seem so very important. Besides, I already knew in my gut that I was probably wasting my time. Texting Ruth that I was out of her house on Driscoll Street looked like the easier option—one that wouldn't have required me to wear a tin hat.

"Where is she now?"

"They transferred her to Travis Street. That's where they did the polygraph. Apart from that, the only reason HPD is still holding her is because I asked them to. In their opinion, she just doesn't look right for murder and belongs in a hospital. After all, it's not like Osborne was actually murdered. At least as far as we know he wasn't."

"You want to meet me at the Coney Island on the corner of Dallas?" I asked.

"Sure."

"I'm on my way."

❧

Surrounded by other tall modern buildings, 1200 Travis Street was thirty stories of honey-colored stone already hot to the touch. The ground-floor lobby was enclosed by tall plate-glass windows with big logos and outsize community slogans. Except for the cops going in and out of the front door in their sky-blue shirts and navy blue pants, the general impression was of an international advertising agency rather than the headquarters of the Houston Police Department. I parked the car, and peeling the shirt away from my back, I flung my jacket over my shoulder and headed for the Coney Island on the opposite corner. I wasn't much of a cook, and with nothing in my refrigerator after just one night in my new home, I was ravenously hungry.

Inside, Helen was at a corner table. Her blond hair hung loose about her powerful-looking shoulders, which were left bare by the light sleeveless dress she was wearing. I sat down opposite her and nodded affably at a half-eaten fat pill and an empty coffee cup.

"Looks like you've been here awhile, Agent Monaco."

"Not really. But I could use another cup of coffee."

The waitress came over, poured some more coffee and some water, and I ordered greedily. I handed the sticky plastic menu back and, as soon as the waitress was gone, I took out a little bottle of antibacterial hand gel and rubbed some into my hands.

Helen smiled.

"Same old Gil Martins."

"What?" I said.

"I wouldn't worry about the germs. The cholesterol in your order'll kill you. That or those cigarettes you've started smoking again. I can smell them on your clothes."

"You know, with a nose like yours, you should work for the FBI."

My breakfast arrived and Helen did a good job of restraining her horror while I ate it.

Helen said, "Don't mind me. I love to watch people make pigs of themselves."

"Sorry, but I haven't eaten since yesterday afternoon," I explained. "There's no real food to be had anywhere in Galveston."

"What's the house like?"

"Creaks a lot. Especially at night. But otherwise quite comfortable. Cops expecting us?"

"At eleven o'clock. The detective's name is Kevin Blunt."

When my breakfast was over, I fisted my chest and paid the check.

We went outside where the heat hit us like a prairie fire, crossed the street into the cool of the HPD building, and announced ourselves to the Bratz doll who was the receptionist.

A few minutes later, Inspector Blunt came down and took us to a windowless interview room. He was the heartless authority-figure type with a neat line in crusty dialogue that lived up to his name. He was wearing ostrich-skin cowboy boots and a blue linen blazer with gold buttons that had little rattlesnakes on them, probably good likenesses of his children.

"You ask me, you're wasting your time," he said, inviting us to be seated. "A murderer?" He shook his head. "I've worked homicide for twenty years and in my opinion this woman's got JDLR stamped on her forehead. JDLR for murder, in case there's any doubt."

JDLR is one of those acronyms in law enforcement's glossary that are—most of them—designed to stop the great American public from knowing as much about us as they'd like to know; it means "just doesn't look right."

"If you feebees think it's worth it, then go ahead and be our guest," he grumbled. "Hell, we love to cooperate with the Bureau. It actually makes us feel like we're important. But in the absence of any evidence other than Miss Allitt's improbable confession, I can't hold her after today. Hell, we're not even treating Philip Osborne's death as suspicious. And I've got better things to do on a Sunday than chaperone an interview with a woman who is frankly delusional."

"We're certainly grateful for your cooperation, Inspector," I said.

Wearily, he picked up a telephone and asked someone on the other end of the line to bring Gaynor Allitt along to our interview room.

"You want to know what I think?" Blunt said after a while.

"You're the homicide expert, not me."

"Only a few months ago we had a guy in who confessed to a murder and he seemed to know a hell of a lot of details about the case; we fluttered him the way we fluttered Gaynor Allitt, expecting the polygraph to show that he was lying, right? Only he wasn't lying. Not according to the machine. He really thought he'd done it. And so, for a while, did we. They say you don't look a gift horse in the mouth. But then we did because the DA told us to. And it turned out the guy had a gold-plated alibi for the murder. So that was that. And a little later on we discovered he'd taken some medication and fallen asleep in front of the TV. Slept all the way through a rolling news station and twenty or thirty news bulletins about the murder. So many that when he woke up he was convinced he really had killed someone."

I nodded.

"I'm just saying that fooling yourself is what being human is all about, right? It's the price we pay for having the kind of brain that invents explanations for stuff. I believe in human gullibility and not much else. The only wonder is that we don't get more of this kind of Looney-Tunes shit. Crackpots who confess to murders they didn't commit."

I smiled patiently but I was getting a little bored with Blunt's Dr.

Phil show. I looked at my watch and drummed my fingers on the table until I remembered the number of lowlifes who had probably touched it.

Blunt shrugged. "This is a big building," he said. "It can take a while to bring a sub all the way up here." He looked at his watch and was speaking again when the door opened.

⸭

After a few routine questions and answers that were supposed to try to make her feel comfortable, I asked Gaynor Allitt if she wanted an attorney present. She declined, as she had done the previous day; and because at this stage neither Blunt nor the FBI was inclined to believe that she had committed anything other than a traffic violation, it hardly seemed necessary that we find her legal representation.

She was a tall woman with shortish red hair and plucked eyebrows. Well-endowed, she wore a plain purplish dress, too much green eye shadow, and a large gold crucifix around her freckled neck. There was an indignant aspect to her not unattractive face, and from time to time, when she refused to answer a question, her unevenly shaped chin would adopt a pugnacious cast. She would blush deeply and within a few seconds her long pale neck would turn blotchy, as if she'd swallowed something hazardous, such as a truth that she wished to conceal. To that extent, she was easy to read. She couldn't ever have played poker; everything on her broad shoulders was one big tell.

"On Friday evening you informed two HPD police officers that you murdered Philip Osborne," I said. "What made you tell them that you'd murdered him?"

"I made a mistake, okay? When I heard the siren, I don't know why but I really thought they were after me. Which is why I ran the red light. After I hit the other car, I was pretty shook up, I guess."

"So it was on your conscience. Osborne's death."

"Yes," she said. "But it was the police I told and not the FBI. I can't see why you should think this is a federal matter."

"That's our affair," I said.

"I think I have a right to know why you and not the HPD are questioning me. Since I've waived my right to legal representation—for the moment—there's no reason not to tell me, is there?"

"You seem very well informed, Gaynor. These finer points of jurisdiction are sometimes confusing even to us."

"I'm a court reporter at the Harris County District Court on Franklin Street."

"The Bureau is involved in this case because Philip Osborne had received several threats against his life from extreme right-wing organizations. That's the kind of thing we're obliged to investigate." I was lying about that. But I couldn't see that anyone listening to the tape would have a problem with this. "Now, perhaps you might like to tell us why you murdered Philip Osborne. And then perhaps you might explain to us exactly how you did it."

Gaynor Allitt shook her head.

"For the benefit of the recorded tape," said Blunt, "the subject is shaking her head."

"I'm sorry, but isn't that what you told those cops?" I said. "And Police Inspector Blunt, here? That you murdered him? Or have I made a mistake?"

"I never said anything about anyone being murdered; Philip Osborne wasn't murdered," she insisted. "He was killed because he was an ungodly man."

"Why do you describe him as ungodly? Is it because he was a prominent Democrat? Or because he was prominently gay?"

"It wasn't the main reason."

"Oh? What was the main reason he was ungodly?"

"Because of the things he wrote and the things he said. And by the way, Agent Martins, you're wrong about his politics; he was no Democrat. Lately, he was something of a hawk. Certainly as far as Iran is concerned. His ungodliness stems from something else. Because the fool has said in his heart, 'There is no room for God.' Psalm 10:4."

"Is that all? He was ungodly because he was a fool?"

"Because Philip Osborne was an atheist who actively tried to turn others away from God. We're talking about someone who had made it his life's work to defame God, to ridicule the followers of Jesus Christ, to undermine Christian teachings and Christian morals. Philip Osborne was killed because he was a wicked man, Agent Martins."

"The jails in Texas are full of wicked men. Most of them much more wicked than Philip Osborne."

"But not as dangerous. And after all, they're behind bars. That man believed in everything that was opposite to God's law. In Revelation 21 it says that the cowardly, the unbelieving, the abominable, the murderers, the sexually immoral, the sorcerers, the idolators, and all the liars shall have their part in the lake that burns with fire and brimstone, which is the second death. That's what is meant by ungodly."

"And yet if you killed him, that makes you a murderer, too, doesn't it?" I said.

Gaynor Allitt colored. It was clear I'd touched a nerve.

"God's laws take precedence over anything enacted by us. We must obey God rather than men. Acts 5:29."

"You sound like you must read the Bible a lot, Gaynor," I said.

"Yes."

"But the power that rules this country is ordained by God, isn't it? And if you really did kill Philip Osborne, that makes you a criminal not just in the eyes of the law but in God's eyes, too."

"God's law is unchanging," said Gaynor. "Man's laws can change from one day to the next. And if there is a conflict between God's law and man's law, a Christian is best advised to keep God's law."

We went on in this vein for at least another ten minutes before I tried to get down to some real facts.

"Let's suppose for a moment," I said, "that you did kill Philip Osborne. Are you confessing to us now because you feel guilty about it?"

"In a way, yes," she said quietly. "I'm not strong enough to do God's bidding without feeling the human weakness of remorse. I don't want to have any more deaths—I mean I don't want to have his death on my conscience."

"It's a little too late for that, isn't it?" said Helen. "He's already dead."

"Let's talk about how you killed him," I said. "At the moment, the police aren't actually treating his death as suspicious. Sudden, perhaps. But not suspicious. Would you care to tell us what the police might have missed that would make Osborne's death the subject of a criminal investigation?"

"No, I would not."

"Come on," said Blunt. "Give us a break here, Gaynor. We're only human, you know. Perhaps there was something we missed with Philip Osborne's death."

"I'm not confessing so that I can help you," she said simply. "Frankly, I figure that you ought to be able to do your own job without my help."

"Ah," I said. "Now I get it. You want our help." I smiled and sat back on my chair. "Yes, I begin to see everything."

"How's that?" Gaynor Allitt was looking annoyed with me now.

"Something is weighing on your conscience and so you figure that you need to talk about it with someone. So that you can feel better, perhaps."

She didn't answer.

"But we can't help you unless you help us first, Gaynor. With some basic information."

Again she remained silent.

"Maybe you think you can confess and that'll be it," I said. "You'll have got what you wanted, and because we have absolutely no evidence against you, we'll have no choice but to release you."

Gaynor Allitt looked away and sighed. "That's not it at all," she said.

Blunt leaned forward on his chair and examined his fingernails.

"I think this whole bullshit story is just a piece of attention seeking," he said. "I'm surprised that Agents Martins and Monaco are being so patient with you, Miss Allitt." He laughed. "If you weren't a court reporter, I'd be inclined to have a doctor come and give you a mental examination. Or charge you with obstructing justice. Maybe I will charge you anyway. That's a serious offense in this state, lady. Under the Texas Penal Code, it carries a maximum penalty of twenty years. I shit you not."

"I know what I know," she said. "And please refrain from the use of bad language. It's not necessary and I find it offensive."

For a long moment, silence reigned; Blunt was reaching for the tape to conclude the interview when Helen spoke.

"Wait a minute," she told him. And then she quietly said to Gaynor Allitt, "Gaynor, I think I really do believe that you want our help. And you know we can help you, but if that's to happen, then you really have to trust us."

Allitt sighed and wiped a tear away from the corner of one eye and then the other. Then she produced a handkerchief and wiped her reddening nose.

"I'm afraid," she said.

"Of whom?" asked Helen.

"I can't tell you." Allitt smiled bitterly and shook her head. "I'm sorry, Agent Monaco. I really can't. But I don't want to go home. Especially today."

"What's important about today?" Helen asked.

"It's Sunday. I don't want to be at home on a Sunday. I feel God's presence with me more on a Sunday. And when I'm alone."

There was something in her demeanor that reminded me of the way I'd been feeling the previous evening at the diocesan house in Galveston. A sense of nervousness.

"If you don't mind my saying so, Gaynor," I said, "you sound like you're telling us you're afraid of God."

"Let's just say that there's more reason to fear God than perhaps you can possibly imagine."

"So when you say you fear God, you don't mean it in a respectful way," said Helen. "In other words, it's not a manner of speaking, the way a pastor in a church might utter that phrase. You mean it in a real way. Is that correct?"

"Yes. That's right. And I do fear him, very much. I fear Almighty God as I would fear his hurricane or his flood or his plagues or the power of radioactivity. I fear God's angel. I fear the Lord's power and his wrath. I do fear him, yes, very much so."

It was almost as if her fear was infectious, because for a moment all of us fell silent; then I realized where logically all of this was heading— at least by the logic of what she believed.

"Was it God who killed Philip Osborne?" I asked her.

"Yes," she said.

"Did you ask God to kill Philip Osborne?"

"Yes."

"How?" I asked. "How did you ask him?"

"If ye shall ask anything in my name, I will do it," she answered. "John 14:14."

"Let me be clear about this, Gaynor," I said. "Are you saying that you prayed to God for Philip Osborne's death?"

"Yes."

"And God killed him, in what way?"

"I'm not sure. But I think God probably sent his angel of death to do his bidding. Just like in the Book of Exodus, chapter twelve."

"Jesus Christ." Blunt uttered a profound sigh and looked up at the ceiling.

"No, not Jesus Christ," she insisted. "God. There's a difference."

"Right," muttered Blunt.

"The effective, fervent prayer of a righteous man avails much," said Allitt. "James 5:16."

"You're saying that you killed him with prayer?" I said.

"Yes. He was killed by my prayers."

"That's quite a claim, Gaynor," said Helen. "And you'll forgive us if we find it a little hard to believe."

"Blessed are those who have not seen and yet have believed."

"Maybe that sort of thing was easier in biblical times than it is now," objected Helen.

"Nevertheless, it's quite true. I mean, it would explain a great deal, wouldn't it?"

"How do you mean?"

"The circumstances of Philip Osborne's death weren't normal either, were they?" said Gaynor Allitt. "The only thing the newspapers said after that incident at the Hotel ZaZa was that he had suffered a breakdown. But we know he ran away from something he was very afraid of."

This was true. Out of respect and admiration for one of their own, the newspapers had only reported Osborne's "breakdown"; nothing of his acute fear in the moments that led up to his collapsing in the fountains or in the minutes before his subsequent death had ever appeared in print.

"And until he died," she went on, "he was in a state of catatonia that his doctors couldn't explain. Isn't that correct? Something terrified him. And something killed him, too, eventually. But it wasn't a revolver, was it? And it wasn't poison. No, it was something much more powerful than any human weapon."

Blunt was rolling his eyes; and I could hardly blame him for that. What Gaynor Allitt was saying sounded mad. And yet there was something about the way she said it that made it seem almost believable.

အ

After Gaynor Allitt had been taken back to the holding cell downstairs, Police Inspector Blunt collected his coat off the back of his chair and put it on wearily.

"That woman is whacko."

He was grinning broadly and shaking his head with the air of someone who had thought he'd seen and heard it all—at least until he'd seen and heard Gaynor Allitt.

He had my sympathy. But I wasn't smiling—not yet; and neither was Helen.

"What do you make of her, Gil?" she asked.

"I really don't know what to make of her, Helen. In some ways she seemed rational. Even perceptive. Did you notice that when I deliberately described Osborne as a Democrat she pointed out, correctly, that on many issues of foreign policy he was actually ultraconservative? It was *what* she said that sounded fucking crazy. Not the way she said it."

"But not everything she said sounded crazy," objected Helen. "She certainly seemed to know things about Osborne's death that weren't in the papers."

"She could have found out that shit on the Internet," objected Blunt. "You can find anything on the Internet. The other day I even saw my own wedding video on YouTube. Haven't seen that fucking horror movie for twenty years."

"Maybe she did," said Helen. "Maybe not."

"Come on," said Blunt. "You can't kill someone by praying that they will die. Not even in Haiti. If prayer worked, my second wife would weigh a hundred pounds less than she does now."

I checked my notes and leaned across the desk to the tape machine. "About twenty-two minutes in, Gaynor Allitt said something else that was interesting and then corrected herself." I started to wind the tape back. "I made a note of the position. Here we are." I hit the play button.

"Are you confessing to us now because you feel guilty about it?"

"In a way, yes. I'm not strong enough to do God's bidding without feeling the human weakness of remorse. I don't want to have any more deaths—I mean I don't want to have his death on my conscience."

I stopped the tape. "She said 'any more deaths.' Plural."

"She did, didn't she?" said Helen. "Are you thinking what I'm thinking?"

"That perhaps she prayed for more than one death? Yes. Peter Ekman, perhaps? Clifford Richardson."

I told Blunt about the other cases we thought might somehow be connected.

Blunt listened patiently and then said, "You don't actually believe any of her bullshit, do you?"

"That she killed Philip Osborne with prayer?" I said. "No. But surely you'll concede that prayer is prima facie evidence of intent to kill. Just because she says that it was prayer that killed Osborne doesn't mean that's how he died. There may actually be a guilty act that we simply haven't yet discovered."

"You're chasing shadows," said Blunt. "One thing I've learned in Homicide is that it's the obvious suspect who's nearly always guilty. You catch a guy with a smoking gun in his hand, it's dumb to go and check and see if Colonel Mustard has a fucking alibi."

"Perhaps," I conceded. "But if there's one thing I've learned in

Domestic Terrorism it's that it's in the nature of conspiracies to seem improbable."

"It's a pity we have to let her go," said Helen. "I don't think she wants to be released."

"Do we have to let her go? I don't know."

"What?" Blunt was horrified.

"According to your own polygraph, she's not lying."

"Sure, she believes she's telling the truth. A lot of crazy people do. I could convince myself that I'm fucking Napoleon, but who would believe me?"

"The polygraph is only inadmissible when a defendant objects to it or when it violates a defendant's Sixth Amendment right to obtain favorable witnesses." I shrugged. "I can't see how Gaynor Allitt could object to it since it proves she's telling the truth."

Blunt read my mind.

"Oh, no," he said. "Not me. If you think I'm going before a judge to explain why I want to keep this crazy bitch in custody, you're even more deluded than she is."

"She said she doesn't want to go home," argued Helen. "She's clearly frightened of something. Or someone."

"So am I," Blunt said. "I'm frightened of my wife falling on top of me from a height of more than two feet. I'm also frightened of going into court and being made to look like an asshole by some smart-aleck lawyer. Look guys, Gaynor Allitt has already been charged with the traffic violation. So there's no reason to hold her for anything else. And now that I've heard what she's got to say, I want that woman out of my store within the hour."

"What about a court order for emergency protection, Gil?" Helen said, ignoring him.

"Against what?" I shrugged. "There's no domestic violence here."

"A mental health warrant?"

"She doesn't strike me as constituting a risk to herself. All the same, we might persuade a judge to issue an order into custody for a mental illness examination. The polygraph result could only help to make the case."

Blunt was still shaking his head.

"Why not?" I asked. "You said yourself she's crazy."

"People look and sound crazy right up until the moment they get into court, then they always manage to keep their shit together while you end up looking like a fucking Nazi."

"Yes," I said. "But all you have to do to obtain the court order is show reasonable cause. After that, she can be held for up to twenty-one days."

"The only way you'll get an MO for that woman is if she cooperates. And she didn't strike me as the cooperative type."

"He's right, Helen. If she opposes the order, there's no way a judge is going to consider that she's crazy enough to be detained in a mental hospital."

"She might cooperate," said Helen. "That is, if she really is frightened."

"Yes, she might. And then what happens?"

"She's a goddamned liar," said Blunt. "And that comes back to bite you in the ass."

"Sometimes you have to lie in order to tell the truth," said Helen.

"Oh, that sounds good," said Blunt. "Did they teach you that at Quantico, honey?"

"We could interview her again," said Helen.

"You're wasting your time," said Blunt. "Jesus, I wish I had the case-load you people seem to have. Maybe you've got nothing better to do. Me, I'm going downstairs to sign a release form. And then I'm going home to enjoy what's left of Sunday."

Then he went out of the interview room, leaving Helen and me alone.

"So what do we do now?" asked Helen.

"Let her go."

"What happened to getting a court order?"

"Oh that." I grinned. "I was using Detective Blunt to help me with a small experiment. I wanted to see if there might be a way that any of this doesn't sound completely crazy."

"And there isn't, is there?"

"If I was to telephone the FBI counsel and try to explain all this, he'd probably have my badge."

"It's Sunday. Maybe he's at church. Maybe he even believes in God. In which case he might just believe that there is something in Gaynor Allitt's story."

"I never met a lawyer yet who didn't put evidence ten yards ahead of belief. Me included, by the way. Not for a minute do I think that Philip Osborne was killed by that woman's prayers."

"So, we let her go."

"Yes. But it's a Sunday. Which is fortunate for us."

"Why?"

"If you were a Christian fanatic, where would you go on a Sunday?"

"Church."

"Precisely." I absently applied a little more hand gel to the palms of my sweaty hands, filling the air with a sharp clinical smell. "I think I'd like to find out a little more about what kind of church she goes to and the company she keeps there. Wouldn't you? You know, there might be other Christian fanatics like Gaynor Allitt who think the same way as she does."

FIFTEEN

We waited for Gaynor Allitt and then drove her home; it seemed the best way of keeping an eye on her. The house was just outside downtown in Houston's greater east end and was part of a small gated community of two-story town houses only a couple of minutes east of Minute Maid Park. I pulled up in front of the double garage that constituted the ground floor and switched off the engine.

"Well, thanks for the lift. And for trying to help."

"Wait a minute," I said, and took out my wallet. "Here's my card."

"You don't believe me, do you?" she said. "About Philip Osborne?"

"It's not that we don't believe you," I said. "It's just that our superiors won't believe us. My career's in enough trouble as it is without retailing your story, Gaynor."

"I guess it does seem a little far-fetched."

"Just a bit," I said. "Perhaps if you gave us something a little more concrete to go on."

She smiled bitterly. "Perhaps I will give you something concrete. I mean really concrete, that you can't ignore. Only not right now. Later, perhaps. After spending the night in that police station, I feel like I need to take a bath."

"Of course," said Helen.

"Look," said Gaynor. "You've both been very kind. I appreciate the fact that you took me seriously. Unlike that jerk back at the police station. Blunt." She opened the car door. "I'll pray for you. I'll pray for you both."

We watched her climb a little flight of steps at the side up to the front door and go inside the house.

"I'm not sure how to take that, in the circumstances," I said.

"I think she meant it kindly."

"Let's fucking hope so, in view of what she maintains happened to Philip Osborne. God might be pretty pissed at me."

I started the engine and moved the car just around the corner onto Cline Street, from where we could still watch Gaynor Allitt's front door.

"Why should God be any different?" said Helen. "These days everyone sounds like they're pissed at you."

"Define everyone."

"Your wife, your father-in-law, Chuck, Doug Corbin, Gary Greene."

"Greene? What's his fucking problem?"

"I don't know. He told me you've been ducking him."

"That's bullshit."

"I saw him yesterday morning and he was asking for you. Said you'd promised to speak to him and Vijay Persaud, but that you'd ducked them then."

Greene was the ASAC in charge of the Cyber Crime Task Force.

"He said he'd tried calling you at home, with no result."

"Like I told you, I don't live there anymore. Besides, if it really was urgent, he'd have called me on my cell phone or on my office Black-Berry." I frowned. "Wait a minute."

I took out the BlackBerry.

"I was out of range until you called me, Helen. Since then I've had it switched off because we were interviewing Gaynor. Shit. It looks as though he called me three times." I sighed. "The one day I take a day off and everyone wants to get hold of me."

I pressed a button to return his call.

"He's on voice mail. Gary? It's Gil Martins, returning your call. I moved out of my house, which is why I didn't pick up your message until now. Get back to me." I dropped the BlackBerry back in my pocket.

For a while we sat in silence—or as near to silence as could be achieved in that area. From time to time, a Harris County Sheriff's patrol car would put on its siren and move noisily up Clinton Drive.

"I can keep an eye on this one if you want to lie down. We could be here awhile. I've got ten bucks that says she's in there until this evening, at the earliest."

"Look, you heard her. She said she was going to take a bath."

"When a woman says that, she means she's going to bed. She didn't want you thinking she was a lazy slob, that's all. If you knew the first fucking thing about women, you'd know that."

"Are you saying I don't know anything about women?"

"You know shit about women—sir."

"Come on, Helen. This woman is not just a Christian soldier, she's one of God's Navy SEALs. At least that's how she thinks of herself. And God's special warriors do not go to bed on a Sunday morning."

"We'll see, won't we?"

"Okay. Ten bucks. Look, Helen, I've got nothing better to do. But you. I don't figure it. Shouldn't you be climbing walls at the rock gym or modeling bikinis for the CIA?"

"Maybe I wanted to tell you when you got to Coney Island this morning that a man without a nose could have smelled the liquor on your breath."

"I spent last night in Galveston. You should try it sometime. There's nothing else to do in Galveston except drink and watch TV. And by the way, yesterday was a Saturday. Last time I checked I wasn't on duty."

Helen nodded. "My dad liked to drink. A lot. So there are two things I can smell a hundred feet away, Martins. Bullshit and booze. You may have lost your religious faith and your wife, but just make sure you don't lose your self-respect and then your career."

"You know, I like the way you run me down, Helen. I almost think you give a shit what happens to me."

"Yes. That's probably true. And it's always like this with me, Martins. When I do give a shit about someone, I usually hand out an accompanying lecture. Just promise me you won't do any more solo drinking."

I nodded. I was on the edge of making another joke when I saw Gaynor Allitt coming down the little flight of stairs at the side of her house.

"Looks like the first drinks are on you," I said. "That's ten bucks you owe me."

Gaynor opened her garage door to reveal a maroon Ford Explorer; but it wasn't the car she'd been driving when she'd had the accident that had brought her to the attention of the HPD; that was still in the repair shop. It wasn't unusual for Texans to own more than one car; except, perhaps, when they were living alone.

"Didn't see that coming," admitted Helen.

Gaynor closed the garage door and drove quickly to 59. On the Explorer's bumper was a sticker that read DON'T FOLLOW ME, FOLLOW JESUS. She stayed on 59 for about ten miles west until she reached 610, where she turned north. At the Galleria shopping center, she drove down the ramp into the underground parking lot. We followed.

"This may be the largest mall in Texas," said Helen, "but last time I looked there wasn't a church in here."

We parked the car and followed Gaynor Allitt into the mall. With nearly four hundred stores and restaurants and a couple of hotels, the Galleria was the air-conditioned mecca for people from as far afield as Louisiana. Tiffany, Ralph Lauren, Gucci, Chanel, Louis Vuitton, Valentino, Versace, YSL—they all had stores in the Galleria, and although it was Sunday, all of them were open and looked like they were doing good business. For many Houstonians, a Sunday-afternoon trip to the Galleria was something of an institution, but for someone like Gaynor Allitt, going to the shops on the Lord's day would have been a sin. I'd described Gaynor Allitt as God's Navy SEAL; and it was like discovering that a Navy SEAL couldn't swim.

The two of us stood on an escalator and followed her up to level one. It was like being inside a cathedral—a real Texas cathedral, with a proper glass atrium and thousands of worshippers. In my father's house there are many mansions and mostly these belonged to big fashion houses selling overpriced accessories.

"Who buys this stuff?" I asked, as we came past Burberry and then Valentino, both of them empty of customers.

"Women, of course. Women who want to look good."

"Those are the six most expensive words in the world."

"Maybe she's going to the Microsoft store."

But Gaynor Allitt kept on walking, past Giorgio Armani, Salvatore Ferragamo, and Bulgari; and both of us were surprised when she went into Yves Saint Laurent.

"It costs nothing to look," said Helen.

"That's what I say." I took an ostentatious glance at Helen's bare legs and nodded.

"You're pathetic." But she was laughing while she was peering through the YSL window. "Maybe the St. Joanna routine was an act."

"If it was, then I'm kind of interested to see the next one, aren't you?"

"Yeah. I'm ten bucks down. There's got to be something in this that'll help me pull it back."

Standing in the Ralph Lauren store opposite YSL, we fought off a determined sales assistant with polite negatives and, when these didn't work, with Bureau ID. Helen explained to the perma-tan blond who persisted in trying to engage us in sales conversation that we were keeping a suspect under surveillance; finally we were left alone and spent the next half hour looking out of the store window, which must have been strange for those who paused to look in.

"I still don't figure it. You saw what she was wearing at the police station. I'd have bet you she couldn't even spell Yves Saint Laurent."

"And she's a court reporter, too. That's ten bucks I could have won."

"Why don't you take a look through the window and see what she's doing?"

Even as I spoke, Gaynor Allitt came out of the shop, but she wasn't wearing the dress she had been wearing half an hour before. Now she was wearing a belted dress with a bold jaguar print.

"That's quite a transformation."

"It certainly is," said Helen. "And by the way, that's a three-thousand-dollar dress she's wearing, if my memory serves, and it usually does in these matters."

Gaynor Allitt paused and then turned to her left. She went only a few yards however and then walked into Jimmy Choo.

"Good call," said Helen. "Now she needs some better shoes."

"How much better?"

"Eight or nine hundred dollars."

"This is turning into quite a Sunday."

Another thirty minutes passed before a noticeably taller Gaynor Allitt came out of the shop. This time she was wearing a pair of black rhinestone-encrusted sandals with what Helen assured me were four-inch heels.

"Oh, I do like those," she said. "Those shoes are a thousand dollars."

"For shoes?"

"The less shoe there is the more they cost. Not only that, they'll make her easier to follow."

"How do you make that out?"

"Obviously you've never tried walking in four-inch heels."

We followed Gaynor through the Galleria again. "She's all dressed up," I said. "What she needs now is somewhere to go."

We went back to the parking lot and then tailed her out of the Galleria. She drove onto 59 and went east for about seven miles before turning north on Polk Street and then into the Hyatt parking lot.

It wasn't difficult to remain unseen in the Hyatt: the hotel's twenty-nine-story atrium, one of the highest in Texas, was the size of a small airport.

"She seems to be checking in," said Helen. "And without luggage."

"Isn't that the man's job? Checking in?"

Helen looked pained. "Sometimes I wonder about you, Martins. You're assuming her lover is a man when it might just as easily turn out to be another woman."

"Come on," I said. "It stands to reason that someone like her could hardly be gay. She probably thinks all gay people should be stoned."

"The Bible doesn't say anything about gay women," said Helen. "Just gay men."

"Look, I know what the evangelical people of Texas think about gays, male and female. Until recently I was one of them."

"Well, I know, too."

"You're not evangelical."

"No, but I am gay."

I felt my breath stop in my chest for a moment. "What?"

"I'm a lesbian."

"What?"

"I'm a lesbian, Martins."

"Well, Jesus, Helen. What the fuck?"

"I had to tell someone sometime. You're my boss and my friend, so I thought it ought to be you. I thought that maybe you could tell some of the other guys at the Bureau."

"Me?"

"Yeah, you. Is that a problem?"

"No. I'll tell people if you want. Sure. No problem." I paused. "Hey, the desk clerk just handed Gaynor a key."

"You know what I think? That maybe she wasn't exaggerating. She is afraid to be home on her own."

Gaynor Allitt walked across the floor of the lobby into an elevator. Her new heels on the marble floor sounded like a pianist's metronome. Then we watched the car ascend to the twenty-sixth floor.

"So what do we do now, sir?"

"I'd suggest we go up to the Spindletop revolving restaurant and get a cup of coffee, but I'm already feeling a little turned around by your recent revelation."

"You sound a little disappointed, Martins."

"No," I insisted. "Maybe a little. But I'm not disappointed in you, Helen. In fact, I kind of admire you for just spitting it out like that. That's a hell of a thing to keep to yourself all this time. It can't have been easy."

"Comes with the territory," she said.

I glanced at my watch. "I guess that's that. I'll take you back to your car."

We returned to the Hyatt parking lot. It took a little while to get out because the ticket machine wasn't working and the attendant had to come and take my money in person, which meant that it was another fifteen minutes before I was turning right onto Polk Street. We had to wait again, to allow emergency services to pass before turning onto Smith: a fire truck, a couple of ambulances, and three patrol cars.

"Wonder what that's about?" said Helen. "Maybe we should follow." Helen turned around in her seat. "They're stopping in front of the Hyatt."

"False alarm. We've just come out of there and everything was okay."

"We are on the scene."

I cursed, but I was already turning the car around and putting the cherry on top.

I pulled up next to a cop who was already stringing out a line of crime-scene tape. I dropped my window and flashed my badge.

"Hey, buddy," I said. "What's happening?"

The cop glanced at me and then at the Spindletop. "Woman jumped from the top of the Hyatt," he said.

"Jesus." I glanced at Helen who returned a rueful look. "You thinking what I'm thinking?"

"Of course."

I stopped the engine and we walked the length of the Hyatt's façade until, at the foot of the atrium's "window," we came upon a scrimmage of cops and paramedics. Behind them on the ground was a length of plastic sheeting screening something unspeakable. One of the cops turned to face me.

"Yeah, what?"

"We had a woman under surveillance," I said. "Inside the Hyatt. Caucasian, red hair, fortyish, wearing a jaguar-skin print dress. Could that be your jumper?"

"Got a couple of feebees here who think they can identify the jumper," he said loudly.

My BlackBerry was ringing. I looked at the screen.

"Shit."

It was Gary Greene calling me back.

"Gary. Look, I'm sorry, I can't talk to you right now. A sub I've been following has jumped from the top of the Hyatt Regency Hotel. I'll have to call you back."

"Make sure you do," said Greene.

It wasn't much of a conversation, but it was long enough for Helen to move out of my sight. When my eyes caught up with her again, she was staring at what was lying on the ground underneath the plastic, and then so was I, and all of a sudden I was able to understand why they'd needed such a long sheet of plastic.

Nothing ever prepares you for the sight of a dead body. Violent death is rarely ever neat and tidy, but there is something doubly unpleasant about viewing a body that has fallen from a great height; I've never seen anything as fatal as what happens to someone who jumps out of a tall building; and immediately I was thinking about those two hundred souls who were forced to jump from the Twin Towers—the most harrowing and enduring image of the horror that had been unleashed inside. At first I didn't understand the actual details of what exactly had happened to Gaynor Allitt; it takes the eyes and the mind a while to disentangle the awful red and raw human wreckage of what you're looking at; all I knew for sure was that it was Gaynor Allitt. The dress and the shoes she was wearing told me as much. But it took several seconds of horrified contemplation to perceive that when you hit the concrete from a great height everything that's inside your body ends up being on the outside. In Gaynor's case, some of her insides were fifteen or twenty feet away from her shattered body. Most distressing of all, perhaps, was the realization that most of her internal organs and intestines had exited her cadaver from between her legs, almost as if she had suffered some ghastly and giant miscarriage in the street.

Something caught my eye. It wasn't the Jimmy Choo shoe that protruded from a pink mass of leg bone and flesh like a small sea urchin; and it wasn't the jaguar print of the dress that made me think of some big cat incarnadined by the blood of some recently devoured prey; and it wasn't Gaynor Allitt's eyes, which were hanging out of their sockets. It was the card she was holding in her still identifiably human hand. I drew the attention of one of the cops to the card and asked him if I might take a look at it.

"Be my guest," he said. "Just don't remove it from the scene."

I found an evidence glove in my jacket pocket and peeled it on my hand carefully. Gaynor's grip was strangely firm, and I had to bend back one of her fingers to extract the card from her dead grasp.

It was my own business card.

I turned it over, read what was written on the back, and then handed it to Helen, mainly to avert her gaze from the butcher's yard that lay on the ground. Then I took her by the arm and led her away.

She glanced up at the Hyatt tower. "We should go in and check it out. Someone must have pushed her, Martins."

"No," I said.

"What the fuck? Look, she just spent four thousand bucks dolling herself up. Chances are it was for someone who might still be in there."

"No," I said. "Look at the card. It was suicide. Had to be."

"This is your card. Why the fuck have you given me your card?"

"She was holding it," I explained. "Gaynor Allitt. It was in her dead hand. She must have been holding on to it when she jumped. There's something written on the back."

"'Dear Agent Martins. Is this sufficiently concrete for you to base an investigation on?'" Helen pulled a face. "Jesus, you're right. It must have been suicide. I guess that was her idea of a joke."

"I'm not laughing."

Helen returned my card and I gave it to one of the cops along with another business card on which I wrote Gaynor Allitt's home address.

"She'd still be alive," I told Helen, "if I had insisted on trying to get a mental health warrant."

"You don't know for sure that you'd have been granted one."

"No, that's true. But why the dress and the shoes? I don't understand that at all. If you were going to kill yourself, why spend four thousand dollars on your wardrobe? It doesn't make any sense, Helen."

"Yes, it does," said Helen. For a moment she looked like she was going to puke. Then she swallowed and said, "I think I can explain it."

"Go ahead."

"When I was on that yacht in France, one of the other agents told me that his dad had committed suicide. But beforehand he put on his best suit and shoes. He figured his dad had probably wanted to look his best when he died. This strikes me the same way. Maybe Gaynor wanted to feel and look a little bit special—the way only a new dress and a fabulous pair of shoes can make a woman feel special."

We walked back to the car in silence. We drove down Fannin Street and, just short of the Gulf Freeway, we came in sight of the Cathedral of the Sacred Heart.

"You can drop me here, if you like."

Assuming she thought I was getting straight onto the freeway for Galveston, I shook my head. "That's all right. HPD's only half a mile down Fannin."

"I know. That's why I want to walk."

"Sure. Whatever you say. I understand. After what we just saw . . ."

I pulled up at the side of the cathedral. Helen stepped out of the car, and when I didn't drive away, she came around to my window. Behind her was the cathedral's perfectly kept flowerbed, from which a variety of scents filled the air, and above this was an arched window near the organ loft where someone was practicing a Bach toccata and fugue. It seemed like a whole lifetime since I'd been in there to pray that my dwindling faith might be restored, but in truth it was only a few weeks.

"Why didn't you tell me before?" I said.

"About what? Being a lesbian or a Roman Catholic?"

I smiled. "Any more surprises?"

"I think you've had enough for one day."

"Are you going in there?"

"Yes. I thought I'd pray for Gaynor Allitt."

"It can't do her any harm."

"You could come with me if you want. We could pray for her together."

"And miss a quiet Sunday afternoon in Galveston? I don't think so. Besides, your prayer has a better chance of being heard if I'm not kneeling beside you, Helen. If you're going to speak to God, you'd better be seen in better company."

"Oh, I don't worry about that. I'm a lesbian, remember? I really don't think that God understands lesbians at all."

"Then why go in?"

"Because I think Gaynor would appreciate it. You see, Martins, she was a lesbian, too."

I frowned. "Are you serious?"

"Of course. I don't joke about that kind of thing."

"But how can you be sure?"

"You're such a man, aren't you? It was right under your nose and you couldn't see it."

"And you did?"

"Of course."

"You make me sound like an idiot, Helen."

"You're not an idiot, Martins. You're just a man, that's all."

"When you say that, somehow you make them sound like the same thing."

SIXTEEN

I didn't drive to Galveston—not right away. I had questions about Gaynor Allitt I needed to answer. It seemed the least I could do after the note she had left for me on the back of my own business card. I drove to 1127 North Shepherd Drive and the Eleventh Division police station—a low-rise building surrounded by car showrooms and auto-repair shops; after her Friday-night accident on North Post Oak and Woodway, it was to one of these that Gaynor Allitt's car had been taken, and where I was now directed by the desk sergeant.

I rolled on some latex evidence gloves. A mechanic showed me out back to a parking lot where he pointed out a Taurus with a heavily dented passenger door, and then tossed me a set of keys. Unbeknownst to him, it was the keys I wanted. In addition to the car key, there was a Yale and a Ford leather fob with four numbers written on it. I didn't have to be a detective to see that the Yale was the key to Gaynor's front door on Gregg Street, and the numbers were probably the combination for the house alarm.

There was nothing much in the glove compartment or the trunk, but the navigation system's address book contained her favorite destinations. These included her home, the Harris County District Court on Franklin Street where she had worked, and a church near the Johnson

Space Center in Clear Lake. I made a note of the church address and zip code and the four numbers on the key fob and then drove back to Gaynor Allitt's house.

I parked the car on Cline Street, like before, just in case any nosey-parker neighbor paid attention to that kind of thing, but it didn't look like it. Gregg Street was still quiet, which made it even harder to believe what had happened since driving away from that spot.

I went up the side stair, opened and closed the front door, and would have keyed the four numbers I'd noted into the alarm except that Gaynor hadn't armed the system. What was the point when you knew you weren't ever coming home again. I slipped on a fresh pair of evidence gloves, wiped the door handle, and looked around. My search of her house was legal under section 213 of the Patriot Act—the so-called sneak-and-peek provisions; then again, without even an EC or a field report in the name of Gaynor Allitt, it wasn't completely warranted, either. But I had the feeling Gaynor wouldn't have objected to my being there. I wasn't likely to forget my business card in her hand or the sight of her shattered body. I was still in a state of shock about that. At least this was the excuse I was giving myself for the time being until I could think of a better one.

The house was open-plan with polished wooden floors, ceiling fans, and imitation Art Nouveau lamps. There was a big leather L-shaped sofa on one side of the sitting room and a kitchen area on the other. The house had two bedrooms, each with an en suite bathroom, and a handsomely furnished little study with plenty of books, most of them religious. Facing the desk was a video camera on a tripod, but the SD card was missing. Open on the leather-topped desk was a laptop, and a big family Bible. Something about the closet in the spare bedroom caught my eye—an antique double-size wardrobe made of rich flamed mahogany. But one of the doors was covered with a sort of thick heavy curtain resembling an intricately embroidered quilt cover, and although the design was unknown to me, there was something about it that suggested to me it might have religious significance. Drawing the curtain aside, I opened the wardrobe door and was intrigued to discover not a rail of clothes but a small cushioned seat, another Bible, and several rosaries, as if the wardrobe had served some devotional purpose. Curious, I stepped inside and sat down on the little seat, which was quite comfortable; there was a small electric lamp so I switched it on.

The Bible was a rather ancient one, and as big as a desktop PC, with an ornate leather binding that belonged in a horror movie; the rosaries were mostly silver and ebony; on the wooden walls was a cheesy picture of God and a text from the epistle of Paul the Apostle to the Romans: WHO SHALL LAY ANY THING TO THE CHARGE OF GOD'S ELECT? IT IS GOD THAT JUSTIFIETH.

I opened the Bible. Inside its heavy pages was a neatly printed list of names. The list had a one-word heading. The word was "Prayers."

I glanced down the list of names. Most were names I didn't recognize; but I had no problem with four of them and three of these— Clifford Richardson, Peter Ekman, and Willard Davidoff—had been crossed out; the fourth name was that of Philip Osborne. Presumably Gaynor Allitt hadn't had the time—or, given her feelings of guilt in the matter, the inclination—to cross his name off the list like she had the other three dead men's names.

This list was the clearest evidence yet that these four deaths were somehow related; and yet the heading wasn't likely to convince anyone—least of all the Houston Bureau's Chief Counsel—that there was some kind of case to answer. Police Inspector Blunt's attitude to Gaynor Allitt's confession had been salutary in its skepticism. It was one thing to pursue an investigation into four sudden deaths; it was something else again to look into the deaths of four men on the basis that these had been brought about by the prayers of an emotionally disturbed woman who had committed suicide. Real evidence of the kind you could put in a plastic bag and hand to a jury was needed here. I photographed the list with my phone and then put it into my pocket; having checked that the picture was legible, I photographed the interior and exterior of the prayer cabinet—if that's what it was; then I collected Gaynor's laptop and carried it out to the car.

From there, I drove to the Northwest Freeway and the RCFL, where I filled out some paperwork and left the laptop for Ken Paris to take a look at. Then I went to the office, where I logged the prayer list as evidence before calling Gary Greene; and this time I got him, although I regretted doing so immediately.

"Where the fuck have you been?"

I told him I'd been obliged to move out of my house and then spend the morning interviewing a sub who'd subsequently killed herself. These sounded like reasonable explanations to me, but Greene wasn't having any of it.

"Your ass stays right where it is," he growled. "I'm coming in."

"Can't this wait until tomorrow, sir? It's not exactly been a great day. I've still got blood on my shoes."

"Nope. This can't wait. But you can. And your day's about to get a lot fucking worse than just a bit of blood on your damn shoes." And then he hung up.

⚅

Gary Greene was tall—taller than I was—and black, with a head like a bowling ball and the manners of a mechanical pinsetter. Around his mouth there was a light gray beard and a mustache and, on the end of his nose, he wore a pair of heavy framed glasses that added a strong touch of disbelief to the way he regarded me. I had been summoned to his office minutes after his arrival in the building. Vijay Persaud was also there from DCS Net.

The Digital Collection System is the FBI's dedicated surveillance system and allows instant access to all cell phone, landline, and SMS communication anywhere in the United States—and, for all I know, abroad. How it works is classified, but it runs on the Windows operating system and makes wiretapping as easy as buying something on Amazon.

"We've been trying to put your slippery ass in that chair since Friday evening," he said.

I started to explain, but Greene didn't look as if he was interested in hearing my side of things. He waved a hand in front of his face as if he were trying to get rid of some gas—his own, probably.

"You're busy. I get that. Everyone in this building thinks his shit is more important than the next guy's. But we're busy, too, Martins, and given that I should be taking my daughter to Sunday school, you'll appreciate that maybe I wouldn't be here now if you'd made time for us on Friday night."

"Gisela said she'd speak to you."

"Oh, and she did. But it wasn't Gisela we wanted to talk to, Martins. You see, we didn't want to talk to you on Bureau business but in your capacity as a witness."

"A witness? Me? To what?"

"At last you begin to see."

"Maybe you'd better just cut to the chase, sir. I certainly wouldn't like to waste any more of your valuable time."

"You know Bishop Eamon Coogan, is that right?"

"Yes, I do."

"Mind telling me how?"

"I don't mind. Before he became a bishop here in Houston—strictly speaking he's an archbishop, but it's an emeritus position, so it's not like he's a real archbishop, which is one stripe below cardinal—before that he was a friend of my parents in Boston. He trained to be a doctor. My father taught him at med school."

"So you're a Catholic?"

"Used to be."

"But you're still the bishop's friend."

"Yes, I am."

"Close friends?"

"That all depends on what you're about to accuse him of."

"Honest answer."

"A few weeks ago he took me into his confidence," I said. "He put me onto a DT case we've been investigating. He had some suspicions that there was a connection between the death of Philip Osborne and—"

"Yeah, Gisela told me all about that shit." He paused. "And that's all he talked to you about?"

"That's where I was this morning. I was interviewing a woman who claimed to have something to do with it."

"The woman who committed suicide?"

I nodded. "Maybe now would be a good time for you to tell me what this is all about."

"I find it interesting he should take you into his confidence about that and not something else that might have more immediate relevance to him."

"Such as?"

"No, I want to get this quite straight, Martins. Other than Philip Osborne's death and the related inquiry, there's nothing else by way of a possible criminal offense that you and he have discussed?"

"Not really."

"Meaning?"

"Well, when I saw him yesterday, he mentioned something in passing about a priest from the Benedictine seminary in Jersey Village who had been caught with his hand in the cash register. But nothing other than that."

"Was it Father Breguet?"

"Yes. It was."

"He mentioned that in passing. How?"

"Over breakfast. We were having breakfast at the bishop's house on Timber Terrace Road."

"Do you often have breakfast with the archbishop emeritus?"

"As a matter of fact, that was the first time."

"And he said what else? About Father Breguet?"

"Only that he'd considered asking my advice about it. But that he and the cardinal had decided not to press any charges."

"Why not?"

"Because it didn't seem like a very Christian thing to do; and because it wasn't a lot of money."

"That at least is true."

I glanced at Vijay Persaud. He was stick-thin and very handsome in a kind of sad way. So far he'd said almost nothing. But it wasn't difficult to work out how he was connected to this.

"I'm guessing you've been spying on the bishop's phone, Vijay. Which is why you're here."

Vijay looked for his cue to Gary Greene, but he didn't get one; his was just a bit part; this was going to be Greene's show and Vijay was there to give a yes-or-no answer only when Greene required it.

"Father Lawrence Breguet is wanted in connection with allegations of child abuse dating back twenty years to when he was a teacher at St. Benedict's—the boy's school attached to the seminary. We've interviewed a number of victims following the arrest of several teachers who were part of a tot-banger scene here in Houston."

"The Conroe case," I said. "Ken Paris told me something about that. But he didn't mention the Catholic diocese."

"One of those jackos cracked," explained Greene. "He told us about

Father Breguet. And we found pictures on the Father's desktop PC that put him in the same toilet bowl as the others. Only he was on vacation in Italy at the time. At the Vatican, to be more accurate. And it now looks as if he has no immediate plans to return home to Texas on account of the fact that your buddy the bishop more or less told him to stay away. Since then, he's disappeared, but not before removing a sum of cash from local church funds via an online checking account."

"All that's on the wiretap?"

"That and more."

"And you're looking for what—a grand jury investigation against Bishop Coogan?"

"Aiding and abetting the flight from justice of someone who is accused of child abuse. That's a felony."

"And does the bishop know about this investigation?"

"He will tomorrow morning," said Greene. "Only we wanted to speak to you first, Martins. Make sure that everything in the Houston field office is watertight. We wouldn't want any more leaks, now would we?"

"What? You think I'd tip him off? The way you say he tipped off Father Breguet?"

Greene just stared at me, saying nothing.

"With all due respect, sir, fuck you. I'm no snitch. And certainly not for the Catholic Church. But then, if you really thought that, you'd have E. Howard Hunt here tapping my phone, too. Wait a minute." I smiled. "That's what pissed you off, isn't it? About my not being at my old home on Driscoll Street. You tapped that phone, but I wasn't there. And since I've been in Galveston, my cell phone coverage has been nonexistent. That's it, isn't it? You bastard."

I stood up and headed toward Greene's door.

"No one's tapped your phone, Martins," said Greene. "I just wanted to see how you'd react to the news about your friend Coogan. So sit the fuck down again." He paused. "You're not under suspicion of anything."

I sat down, but I felt only partly reassured.

"I wanted to ask you some more about Bishop Coogan. What kind of man is he?"

"You mean is he a jacko, like Father Lawrence Breguet?"

"All right. Is he?"

"To be honest? I haven't a fucking clue. It's not the kind of thing that you talk about. But let me say one thing more: If Coogan is a jacko, then I'll buy a fucking shovel and help you to bury him. Okay?"

"I'm reassured to hear that, Agent Martins."

"Frankly, I don't give a damn about your being reassured. I saw a woman I knew jump from the top of the Hyatt Regency today. Somehow after that, everything seems of lesser importance. And that includes your opinion of me." I shook my head. "One more thing about the wiretap. When you said the wiretap had Bishop Coogan telling Father Breguet to stay away from Houston, you said that's more or less what he said. So my question is this: Which is it?"

"I'm not with you, Agent Martins."

"More or less. Which is it? Or maybe I should listen to the recording and decide for myself."

Greene shrugged. "It might conceivably be argued by the bishop that he was carrying out the cardinal's orders."

I grinned. "Less than more, I'd say. In which case you're going to have a hard job persuading a grand jury to hand down an indictment. A cardinal tells a bishop to do something, he does it. Not to do it would be like a soldier disobeying an order from one of the Joint Chiefs of Staff. It's only my opinion, but I used to be a lawyer and I can tell you that you might be better off prosecuting the Houston diocese instead of the bishop."

"It won't be the first time that a Catholic bishop has been indicted by a grand jury," argued Greene.

"It will be in Texas," I said. "Houston has the third-largest Hispanic population in the United States. Forty-four percent Latin American. That makes Houston a very Catholic town. Unlike Kansas City."

"I'm a Baptist myself," said Greene.

"But it was Kansas you were talking about, wasn't it? Where they indicted that other Catholic bishop? Kansas is a lot more Protestant than Houston."

"And you. You say you're not a Catholic anymore. So what's your denomination now?"

"I don't go to church. Since I don't believe in God, there doesn't seem to be much point in calling myself this or that."

"Hell, Martins," said Greene, "don't you miss going to church?"

"I used to go because of what I believed. Now I don't go because of what I know."

❧

I didn't know much, that was obvious. And certainly not about Bishop Coogan. Ruth was going to be jubilant when she read about the grand jury investigation in the newspapers. Her detestation of the Roman Catholic Church now looked to be utterly vindicated. It just proved what she had always alleged: that the Houston diocese concealed a nest of pedophile priests, just like in Dallas. Of course, I was guilty of no small concealment myself. I ought to have mentioned to Gary Greene that I was now living in the Catholic diocesan house in Galveston. Probably I ought to have vacated the place and moved into a motel; and I was going to do that, just not right away. There was something important I needed to do first. Something that took me three-quarters of the way back to Galveston early that same evening and which made it convenient to stay on for one more night.

⚅

The USA may have ended the space shuttle program, but the international space station mission is still controlled from the Johnson Space Center in Clear Lake City. It's a complex of about a hundred buildings that dates back to a time when Americans looked to the heavens and thought not of Jesus but of the moon and the stars, and wondered how we were going to get there; it seems incredible, but forty years after the last manned flight to the moon, we look up at the sky and think of God and how to lead a life that will please him enough to let us into heaven. If that's progress, then I'm Neil Armstrong.

A mile or two northwest of the Johnson Space Center, the Izrael Church of Good Men and Good Women was a big art deco building on Space Center Boulevard. I don't think there were many guys from the space center who worshipped there. Back in 2007 there was a hostage situation in Building 44 and most of the guys I met then struck me as more inclined to put their faith in the telemetry that brought Apollo 13 back to Earth in April 1970. From everything I've read about that mission, it took a lot more than prayer to bring those guys home. More than anyone, they know there isn't a heaven, I think; there's just the great big glitter ball that we call the universe.

The church had the look of an old airport terminal and, given its proximity to Ellington Airfield, I had no doubt that's what it was; but the control tower had been replaced with a tall glass steeple and there was an enormous bas-relief of an angel above the main entrance. He looked as if he were keeping an eye on the expensive cars that were already parked on the sun-baked lot. Either that or they used him to take the roll for evening service and then go find those careless folks who were still at home watching the ball game. They'd have come along with him, too. He didn't seem to be the kind of angel who was likely to take no for an answer.

Near the entrance there were church greeters—men, mostly, wearing summer suits and carrying well-thumbed Bibles. The greetings were enthusiastic, too. *So far so Lakewood,* I told myself as I passed into the church's mercifully cool interior where the similarity ended and I felt my jaw drop as I marveled quietly at my surroundings for a long time. I've been in plenty of cathedrals and churches but very few that were as impressive as this one. Somewhere an architect was still looking at his fee check, and when he wasn't wondering if he dared to cash it, he was probably congratulating himself on his own breathtaking audacity.

Lakewood was big, but the Izrael Church was so achingly modern it was almost impossible to describe except to say that it was a circular structure with more than a dozen entrances that was dominated by a central chimney cone that rose up into the steeple. The altar was underneath the cone, which probably resembled the large hadron collider in Switzerland. A huge picture of Christ was hanging in the air above the seating area where several thousand people were waiting patiently for the service to begin. It was so like being on the set of a James Bond movie that when the pastor finally entered to thunderous applause I almost expected him to be carrying a white cat.

I sat down near the back and fixed a rictus smile to my face—the kind I'd frequently been obliged to deploy at Lakewood; almost immediately I was on my feet again as the worshippers surrounding me jumped up and began to pump their fists in the air, shouting "Hallelujah." A huge organ started to play and it was quickly clear to me that the pastor of this futuristic church wasn't the type to share the spotlight with a "worship team" of singers and second-string preachers. The music sounded like it was classical and perhaps baroque in origin, although I didn't recognize the composer; but it had to be someone with a taste for the dramatic.

The pastor was in his early forties and wore a white shirt and black frock coat so that he resembled an old-fashioned preacher in a John Ford movie or perhaps an Orthodox Jew, depending on how you look at these things. From the big screen on which his beaming face was projected, I could see that he was handsome with sky-blue eyes, machine-cut features, and a smile like the raiment of angels. His hair was blond and thick, and his voice was deep, with an accent that couldn't have come from anywhere but west Texas, and while his delivery was a tad wooden for my taste, there was no doubting its effectiveness; those around me just lapped it up as if he'd poured his voice onto a heap of warm pancakes.

We sang some hymns. All of the words appeared up on the screen. It was only when our pastor started to preach that I began to understand his angle. Every preacher has one. It's just good business. Billy Graham used to preach about being born again in Jesus; Pastor Joel Osteen at Lakewood preaches that God wants you to be successful; at the Izrael Church of Good Men and Good Women Pastor Nelson Van Der Velden—his name was captioned on the screen above his head— preached passionately about the coming Last Days accompanied by "testimonies" of his direct communications with God, Jesus Christ, and his angels. I have heard many church sermons and could probably work out a reasonably fair scoring system for them if Zagat ever decides to start reviewing church sermons; but even in Texas this was the first time I'd heard a preacher declare that he'd actually met the Messiah in a vision. Pastor Van Der Velden spoke with the complete certainty of one who has taken the trouble of first convincing himself that everything he tells his enraptured audience is the absolute truth. I don't know how else he could have pulled it off and, to this extent, it was like listening to a smoother version of a street-corner hustler working a highly sophisticated permutation of three-card monte. To work a good con like that requires you to partly believe it yourself.

"I hate to repeat myself," he said, grinning handsomely. By now the volume on his charisma was on eleven. "I really do, folks. But some things do bear repetition. When Jesus talked about the good news he didn't mean for us to shut up about it. On the contrary, he told his disciples, 'Go ye into all the world and preach the gospel.' And if the gospel isn't worth repeating every day of the week, every minute of every hour, I don't know what is. No, sir, I'm never going to shut up about God's message.

"You know how when you're at work and you hear someone talking about something they saw on TV? Like *America's Got Talent*? Well, that's how I feel about God's message. Me, I'm the kind of fellow who's liable to say, 'Sure, America's got talent, but where do you think it got that talent from? Why from God, of course.' Man, I love that show, but whenever I watch it, I can't help but think about the parable of the talents. What a great story that is. What a great teller Jesus was, too. Now, there was a guy with an extraordinary talent."

Lots of Amens and Hallelujahs and Praise the Lords.

"Repeating yourself," said Van Der Velden. "Some folks get embarrassed about that. They think it's a sign that they're getting old. Well, by that standard, I must be as old as Methuselah because, if I've repeated God's message once, I must have repeated it a million times." He chuckled. "But who's counting? Another thing you've heard me talk about before is my experience in the Holy Land. How back in 2005 I spent a whole year studying in Israel. I guess you could say that I just had a hunger to see the land of miracles. I was like one of those folks by the Sea of Galilee when Jesus performed the miracle of the loaves and the fishes. I was hungry all right, but like them, I got a lot more than I was expecting. Praise the Lord but I was filled with his message as if I'd eaten a great feast. Because if you seek, ye shall find; and if you knock, then the door will be answered to you, my friends. Amen. Amen.

"Some of you have also heard me speak of two wise man I met in Israel. Not three wise men this time, just two. Certainly these were the wisest men I ever met. One of these wise men was Rabbi Yitzhak Kaduri. Senior Jewish rabbis from all over the world used to come and listen to Rabbi Kaduri, who for years was about the nearest thing there's been to one of those Old Testament prophets; he certainly looked like one. Earlier on I mentioned Methuselah who was famously old, of course. And while Rabbi Kaduri wasn't as old as he was, he was pretty old by modern standards. When he died on January 28, 2006, he was one hundred and eight years old. I'm proud to say I got to know him a little in the last few months of his great life. To be honest, I have no idea what a man like him saw in a young guy like me, except perhaps a hunger for spiritual truth and enlightenment.

"And maybe this, perhaps: that I was a gentile. Of course, there were a great many Jews who listened to Rabbi Kaduri and rightly so, but I think he worried that they would keep his final truth to themselves, or even try to suppress it. So, to that extent, I was just the right guy in the right place at the right time. Nothing more to it than that.

"I expect you know that the word 'rabbi' is generally applied to those who become masters or teachers of the Torah—the name given by Jews to the five books of Moses that begin the Hebrew Bible. When people realized what a wise man Jesus was, they started calling him rabbi, too. Now, like I said, Rabbi Kaduri was the wisest man I ever met. He taught me all kinds of things. Some of those things—hidden things that people like him have known about for thousands of years—I promised him not to talk about. And I have to respect that promise. But one thing he did give me permission to talk about was a vision he'd had. And you can imagine how excited his followers were when he announced that the person he'd met in this vision was none other than the Messiah, because, of course, the Jews have been waiting for the Messiah since before when. And they got even more excited when the rabbi announced that the Messiah was coming soon. He also told them that he knew this person was the Messiah because, in the vision, Rabbi Kaduri was given a message. In Hebrew that message went like this: *Yarim ha'am veyokhiakh shedvaro vetorato omdim.* Now, in English that means that he will lift his people and prove that his word and law are valid.

"Now I've thought about this a great deal and it strikes me that this is exactly what the Messiah would say. And here's another fascinating thing: Rabbi Kaduri wrote down the name of the Messiah and promised that after his death the identity of the Messiah would be revealed. This is exactly what happened. He wrote the name down on a piece of paper and put it in a sealed envelope and gave this to one of his followers who opened it after the rabbi's death. And d'you know something? It turned out that the name that the wisest, oldest, and best-respected rabbi in Israel had revealed to all his followers was the very same name that Christians have known about for more almost two thousand years. Jesus. That's right. Hallelujah and amen.

"Now, as you can imagine, that gave a lot of the rabbi's followers a real big problem. No one likes to admit that they made a mistake. And not just any mistake. Imagine it: The rabbi's revelation meant that they'd rejected their own Messiah, that they'd handed him over to the Romans to be crucified, like it says in the gospels. So what were the followers of Rabbi Kaduri to do in the light of this revelation? Well, I'm sad to say that a lot of them chose to suppress the old rabbi's posthumous message. But of course, the truth will out. Like I say, I think that's one of the reasons that Rabbi Kaduri told me about the details of his vision: because he guessed that maybe some of his own followers would try to keep things quiet and because he knew that I'd tell you people about it. And he was right. The name of the Messiah is Jesus, friends, and he's coming very soon. And when he does, there's going to be a great reckoning. In the Gospel according to St. Matthew it says, 'Even now the ax is lying at the root of the trees; every tree therefore that does not bear good fruit is cut down and thrown into the fire. I baptize you with water for repentance but one who is more powerful than I am is coming after me; I am not worthy to carry his sandals, he will baptize you with the Holy Spirit and fire. His winnowing fork is in his hand, and he will clear his threshing floor and will gather his wheat into the granary but the chaff he will burn with unquenchable fire.'

"I tell you, brothers and sisters, that it's already started, too—this great reckoning that the Bible speaks of. Things are happening in Israel right now—things that were foretold in the Bible—that prove this to be the case. Political events and historical forces that herald the last days before he comes again. His enemies are already in disarray. The day of judgment is at hand when the unrighteous will be condemned as it says in the Book of Revelation. Hallelujah."

I glanced at my immediate neighbors as they muttered "Amen" or "God be praised"; I didn't find them laughable or contemptible because they were ecstatic about something in which I no longer believed myself, but I did pity them. You can bet when people start talking about enlightenment and messiahs that the rock on which their truth is founded can be carried on the back of a mayfly.

I stifled a yawn, wondering how much more of Pastor Van Der Velden's bullshit I could take without heading for the men's room; possibly there was someone outside—one of the greeters, perhaps—who might tell me something more about poor Gaynor Allitt. I was about to risk making an early exit when I caught a glimpse of someone who looked a lot like Ruth and, for a moment, I reflected that I would certainly have preferred a vision of my wife to one of God or Jesus; frankly, I wouldn't have known what to say to anyone or anything more divine than my own wife. But it *was* Ruth; and now that I was certain of it, I realized I had no idea what I was going to say to her when—as seemed likely—we spoke; naturally, she would assume I had followed her here and be none too pleased about that. And I hardly wanted to tell her I was there on Bureau business; not that she would have believed that for a minute. Equally, there was a strong possibility that she would ignore me altogether and that by speaking to her I would cause an ugly or embarrassing scene. None of this was especially troubling to me, however, compared with the fact that Danny was nowhere to be seen and the apparent significance of the man Ruth was standing next to. He was tall and handsome, and wearing a blue suit that was a bit too large for him in the way that the largest size in the shop is too large for anything other than a four-hundred-pound gorilla or Goliath's younger brother. He looked like a football player, or a bodybuilder, or perhaps a small building. From time to time, Ruth would glance up at him—he was six and a half feet if he was an inch—as though in search of his approbation, and he would glance back at her and give it with a broad smile. In that respect, at least, they were like any of at least a thousand other couples in that church; just seeing them made me feel like a fish out of water.

Finally Van Der Velden finished speaking. We had yet more prayers and then a hymn before the show was over and people turned toward the aisles and started to head for the exits. That was when Ruth saw me and her face could not have looked less pleased if the outsize boyfriend had trodden on her toe. Pain quickly gave way to irritation as I pushed through the crowd to reach her.

"What are you doing here?"

"It's not what you think. I didn't follow you. I had no idea you'd be here. Really, I give you my word on that."

"Listen, buddy," said the giant. "Don't make trouble, okay?" He put his King Kong hand on Ruth's shoulder—a proprietary gesture I didn't much care for.

"Really, I'm not here to make any trouble, I'm just trying to speak to my wife, that's all. I don't know what she's told you about me, but all you need to do is give me a minute here. All right?"

The big man glanced at Ruth, who nodded back at him. "It's okay, Hogan," she said.

"Hogan?" I repeated, in spite of myself.

"I'll see you back at the car, okay? I can handle this."

Reluctantly, Hogan walked away, leaving me alone with Ruth and her killing look.

"Where's Danny? Please tell me how he is."

"You're not here on official business," she said.

"As a matter of fact, I am."

"I don't believe you, Gil. I'm not listening to your nonsense. It's obvious that you must have followed me here."

"Ruth, honestly, my finding you here is just a coincidence. But now that we're both here, can't we just talk for a moment? Please. Did he get any of the presents I sent him?"

"He got them, Gil."

"Did he like the Xbox game?"

"It was a little old for him, Gil."

"All kids like the games that are too old for them, honey. That's just how it is. You just have to go with that."

"So tell me: What's the official business that brings you all the way down to Clear Lake?"

"One of the church members here—Gaynor Allitt—is dead. She committed suicide this morning. I came here to speak to someone and see if anyone can explain why she might have done it. You see she was the sub in an—"

But another man—fiftyish, with a broken nose and a pimp mustache—had heard what I said and butted in.

"Excuse me, sir," he said. "I couldn't help overhearing some of what you were saying just now. Did you say Gaynor Allitt is dead?"

"Yes, sir. I did. And she is. Did you know her?"

"Yes, I knew her. My name is Frank Fitzgerald."

"Mr. Fitzgerald, my name is Gil Martins and I'm a Special Agent with the FBI. If you might give me a moment here—"

"Yes. Yes, I will. In fact, you wait right there, Agent Martins, and I'll be right back."

Fitzgerald went away urgently. My eyes followed him long enough to notice that under his coat he was wearing a radio on his hip; it looked more likely than a gun.

"You see," I told Ruth. "He believes me even if you don't."

Ruth shot me a disbelieving look, as if she hoped that the earth would swallow me up forever.

"Where's Danny now?" I asked again, looking around. "Did you bring him with you today? I'd like to see him."

"He's not here. He's back home. When all this is sorted, Gil, I expect you can, but until then, I don't want him disturbed. This has been quite upsetting enough for him already."

"Well, we can agree on that much at least." I glanced around as people continued to file out of the church. "I certainly didn't expect to see you here."

"That's two things we can agree on."

"You know, this church, it's a long way from Corsicana, Ruth."

"I'm not living there."

"Oh? Where are you living?"

Ruth looked surprised at that. "At my house on Driscoll Street, of course. Where else?"

Now it was my turn to look surprised. "Is that where Danny is now?"

She nodded. "Gil, you left a message to say you'd moved out, so I took you at your word."

"Even by your standards, that's fast work."

She looked away; it was easier on her eyes than looking at me and my grief.

"Well, who's taking care of him?"

"He's spending the day at Robbie Murphy's house. He's the boy across the road."

"I remember. He's the one Danny hit, right?"

"That was just boys being boys. Really, they're the best of friends. I'm surprised you even remember that."

"Of course I remember. I still love you both, Ruth. And I want you back. More than anything in the world I'd like things to be just the way they were before. That means no more atheism, no more Richard Dawkins and Christopher Hitchens, no more stupid irreligious remarks. You have my word on that. I'll even come back to Lakewood with you." I shook my head. "Things just got on top of me for a while. You know? Pressure. It got to my head, I think. But I'm all right now."

Ruth looked pained; she was good at that; Ingrid Bergman in *Joan of Arc*; but all the pain in her voice was directed my way. It couldn't have hurt more if she'd used a razor on my ears.

"I believe you, Gil. But we both know you don't believe in God. Don't you see? You'd be living a lie and so would I. How long could we keep the lid on all that? Three months? Six? No, it couldn't ever work. Besides, I don't go to Lakewood anymore. This is my church now."

"Ruth, you can't be serious. These people—they're even bigger cranks than the ones at Lakewood. You're an intelligent woman, Ruth. A lawyer. You're supposed to be hard-headed about these things. Do you really want our son growing up in an environment like this? For Christ's sake, Ruth—"

"It's for Christ's sake that I'm here, Gil. It's a pity you can't see that."

"Don't do this to me, Ruth. Don't do this to our boy, please. A boy needs to have his father around. Just like a father needs to see his son growing up. You're taking all of that away from me. And for what? Because I'm a sinner? Because I'm the chaff that needs to be thrown into the unquenchable fire? Please, Ruth. You may not realize it now, but I promise you'll regret this. One day you'll wake up and realize what was lost."

Frank Fitzgerald appeared at my side again. "Pastor Van Der Velden would like to speak with you, Agent Martins," he said.

"Yeah, sure. Why not?"

I turned to look at the man beside me. Now that I saw him close up again—close enough to smell his breath and see into his eyes—I saw the steadiness and experience in the man, and how deliberate he was, and I knew instinctively that the radio on his hip was a gun after all. Did he wear it for his own protection or the pastor's?

"Right now he's busy meeting some of the many people who've come along here this evening." Fitzgerald glanced over one of my shoulders and then the other, as if trying to see if he could pick out a partner I might have brought with me. "But he's invited you to wait in his private office for a while. Until the last of his parishioners has gone. Would you do that, please?"

Parishioners. I liked that. It made the setup at the Izrael Church sound almost benign, like garden parties and picnics and pink paper packages tied up with fucking string.

"Sure, I can do that," I said. "No problem."

I glanced back to where Ruth had been standing, but she'd already taken advantage of this momentary distraction and had disappeared into the crowd.

Fitzgerald must have noticed the disappointment on my face because he touched my arm in a gesture of contrition; at least I think that's what it was; his grip was as firm as the cinch on a rodeo rider's saddle. He didn't let go of my arm until I started to follow him.

"What happened to her?" he asked.

"Excuse me?"

"To Gaynor. You did say she committed suicide, didn't you?"

"No disrespect, sir, but perhaps it would be better if my explanation could wait until we're in the pastor's office. What happened today was traumatic, to say the least, and I'd rather not go through it all more than once. I'm sure you understand."

"Yes, of course. Then you were with her."

"More or less."

"I shall certainly miss her," he said. "She was a long-standing and much-loved member of this church. And a steadfast Christian."

"I wouldn't know about anything like that," I said.

SEVENTEEN

F rank Fitzgerald walked me through an important-looking door at the top of a flight of stairs; it looked important because it was large and curved like an enormous wooden shield. He left me alone in a high, circular library that was floored in marble and probably designed by an extraterrestrial being with a fetish for brushed aluminum. In the center of the floor, underneath a glass ceiling, was a semicircular desk, and ranged around the room were a series of glass cases containing old illuminated Bibles of the kind that a whole monastery of scribes must have worked on for a lifetime of rainy Sundays. I looked at one of these and told myself that the word of God was a lot more believable when it was written in Latin. Probably the old Roman Catholic Church had been right about that: the minute you allowed people to read the Bible in their native language you were opening the door to interpretation, debate, challenges to doctrine, heresy, and, finally, atheism. There's nothing like reading the Bible to put you off the whole idea of God and religion.

"That's an interesting one you're looking at."

It was Nelson Van Der Velden and he was alone. He came and stood next to me in an invisible cloud of aftershave and sanctimony. He was taller than I had supposed, with good, clear skin and hard blue eyes. Immediately, I had the strong impression I'd seen him some place before, but where?

"That particular Bible was commissioned by the first king of Jerusalem, Baldwin I, in 1100 A.D., to celebrate the establishment of his new kingdom. What makes it especially interesting from a theological point of view is that it's only the Old Testament, which has led some to speculate that the monks who illustrated it were also members of the Knights Templar and Manicheans—which is to say that they believed in the dual nature of God and not at all in the divinity of Jesus Christ. Personally, I just think they ran out of time and money—possibly both. But praise the Lord, it is wonderful, don't you think?"

"Yes, it is." I owned some pretty rare DC comic books myself, but I saw no reason for us to get off to a bad start by telling him that.

"Nelson Van Der Velden," he said, holding out his hand.

"Special Agent Gil Martins." I shook his hand and handed him my business card.

He glanced at it and frowned. "Didn't the little roundel used to be embossed in gold?"

"We've had to make some budgetary cuts," I said.

"Pity. Gold looks so much better."

"I guess those medieval monks thought so, too." I nodded at the Bible I'd been looking at.

"The use of gold was intended to represent the multiple grace of heavenly wisdom. But gold served a higher spiritual purpose, too. It was meant as an act of praise, to exalt the text. Along the way, of course, it did also demonstrate how powerful the owner was."

"I expect J. Edgar Hoover had something similar in mind," I said, and showed him my gold shield. "It's not made of real gold, of course. I wish it was. I'd have hawked it and bought a fake."

Van Der Velden smiled patiently. "Frank tells me that a member of our church has committed suicide."

"Gaynor Allitt," I said. "She jumped from the top of the Hyatt Regency in Houston just a few hours ago."

"Oh my goodness, that's awful."

"Yes, it was."

"Were you there?"

I nodded.

"How ghastly for you. How ghastly for you both." He shook his head. "Gaynor Allitt."

"Did you know her?"

"I'm trying to fit a face to the name. That's not always easy with a membership as large as ours."

"How many is that?"

"Eleven thousand."

"I go to Lakewood, so I know what you mean. There's almost eighteen thousand there."

"Oh, man, that's a good church," said Van Der Velden. "And Osteen's one great preacher. The best. He has a real gift."

I nodded. "Do you remember her now? Gaynor Allitt? Tall, red hair, late thirties."

He winced. "No. I'm sorry, Agent Martins. Under the circumstances, I wish I could. I feel kind of bad that I can't."

"I gained the impression from Mr. Fitzgerald that she'd been coming here for a while. In fact, he described her as a much-loved member of this church."

"Well, if Frank said that, then I'm sure she was. As our membership secretary, he has a lot more to do with the grassroots membership of the Izrael Church than I do." Van Der Velden shrugged. "Me, I'm just the front man. Tell me, Agent Martins, have you any idea why she did it?"

"It's early days, sir. I'm working on a number of possibilities."

"Look, would you mind if I said a short prayer for her?"

The pastor bowed his head and closed his eyes, which gave me an opportunity to study him more closely.

"Almighty Father, eternal God, hear our prayers for your daughter Gaynor Allitt, whom you have called from this life to yourself. Grant her happiness and peace. Let her pass in safety through the gates of death and live forever with all your saints in the light you promised to Abraham and all his descendants in faith. And on that great day of resurrection and reward we know is coming soon, God, raise Gaynor up with all your saints. Pardon her sins and give her eternal life in your heavenly kingdom. We ask this through Christ our Lord, amen."

"Amen," I said. That was for appearance's sake only. I hardly wanted the pastor thinking of me as badly as my own wife did, not while I hoped to get some information about Gaynor Allitt.

The pastor opened his eyes and then nodded in a way that made you think he really had been speaking to God. He was one of those rare ministers of the church who possess that gift and who made it so much easier for you to believe because he believed with such irresistible force; and when he smiled, it was like he was smiling because he'd felt the power of God's love and forgiveness. I almost envied him the apparent strength of his faith and, by extension, I felt a little twinge of shame and regret as I recalled my earlier cynical assessment of his character and calling. The man was more sincere than I had imagined.

"What can I do to help you, Agent Martins?"

"I'd like to speak to Mr. Fitzgerald again, if I may, since—by his own account—he knew her better than you. Having said that, it's incumbent on me to explain just how the Bureau comes to be involved in this case."

"Yes, I must admit, I was wondering that myself." He pointed at a long curving sofa that completed the circle begun by his desk. "Why don't you make yourself comfortable and tell me all about it and then I'll have Frank answer your questions?"

I told Van Der Velden how I'd been investigating the sudden deaths of Clifford Richardson, Peter Ekman, Willard Davidoff, and Philip Osborne; and how Gaynor Allitt had confessed to killing Osborne with prayer.

"Excuse me," he said. "Did you just tell me that she said she'd killed someone with prayer?"

"That's right."

"Prayer to whom, exactly?"

"To God." I shrugged. "At first we were inclined to treat her as a harmless crank. We get a lot of that kind of thing in law enforcement. But clearly she believed what she told us. And in all other respects she was rational. Which is why, when we released her from custody this morning, we decided to keep her under surveillance. You see, it was also clear that she was very afraid of someone. God, perhaps. I don't know. Anyway, that might be why she killed herself."

"Let me get this straight," said Van Der Velden. He was picking his words with care now. "She actually said that she had prayed for the death of this man, Philip Osborne. I assume you mean the journalist and writer."

I nodded.

"Did she explain why she had it in for him?"

"Because he was ungodly. I guess you could say because he was one of the unrighteous you mentioned in your sermon. Those who are condemned like it says in the Book of Revelation."

"But you don't actually believe that Mr. Osborne was killed by prayer?"

"No. This is just a trail of smoke and we're looking to see if there's a real fire underneath it. We thought it might be possible that there was

some connection between Osborne's death and those three others I
mentioned. That someone might have been involved in a more practical way. I know it sounds as if we're grasping at straws. But Gaynor Allitt
did seem to know a lot more about Philip Osborne's death than had
been in the newspapers."

"Did she leave a note?"

"Nope."

"Did she mention this church?"

"No. Actually she was keen to leave your church out of things. I
only found out about you because this address is listed as a favorite
destination on her car's satellite navigation system."

"You were at the service," said Van Der Velden, "so I hope you'll
forgive me if I remind you that we pray *for* people at the Izrael Church
of Good Men and Good Women, not against them. We're an evangelical church, Agent Martins. We believe in the same kind of things they
do over at Lakewood."

"That was certainly my impression, sir."

"I'm relieved to hear it. You know, prayer is absolutely fundamental
to the Christian. There's a poem by an Anglican clergyman named
R.S. Thomas that I kind of admire. It's called 'Folk Tale,' and one of its
lines reads: 'Prayers like gravel flung at the sky's window, hoping to
attract the loved one's attention.' Which puts it very well, I think. God
knows everything already. He probably knows what I'm going to
pray about before the words are out of my heart. You hope he'll listen—
that maybe you can change his mind about something. Once in a
while, I figure, he hears my prayer and maybe answers it, too. That's my
faith. But most of the time I figure he knows what's right for me
and doesn't pay any attention to my prayers. Most of the time, I think,
I'm just flinging gravel at God's window. I guess what I'm saying is this,
Agent Martins: It's hard to imagine anyone using prayer as a lethal
weapon. It would be more than a little impertinent for us to believe

that we could call on God like those Old Testament prophets and bring destruction on our enemies. You see what I'm talking about? I don't doubt the power of God is more lethal than any man-made weapon, but I do doubt that it's a power that anyone but someone like Moses or Joshua is equipped for or, more accurately, is granted the right to handle. I also have to wonder what kind of God would answer such a prayer as the one Gaynor Allitt claimed to have made. If I might quote another English poet, C. S. Lewis? 'May it be the real I who speaks. May it be the real Thou that I speak to.' Frankly, I'm not at all sure who might answer the kind of prayer Gaynor Allitt claimed she made. But I'm absolutely sure it couldn't have been our father in heaven."

⊞⊟

The pastor went to fetch Frank Fitzgerald. He was gone awhile.

For a moment or two, I glanced over the magazines on his coffee table; these were more inclined to the intellectual than the spiritual: *Forbes, The New Yorker, Scientific American.* Then I amused myself by looking at all the books on his shelves. Some of them appeared to be in Hebrew, which convinced me that, unless they were merely for show, Nelson Van Der Velden really had studied scripture in Israel, and not just Christian scripture but Jewish scripture, too. As well as books, there were several framed photographs on the shelves. In one or two of them Van Der Velden was pictured alongside a very old Jewish rabbi, and when the pastor finally returned with Frank Fitzgerald, I asked if the old man was the same Rabbi Kaduri he had mentioned in his sermon.

"Yes. That was taken in Jerusalem not long before Kaduri died. A very remarkable man."

"Would I be right in thinking that you know a lot about Judaism?"

"My doctorate from the University of California at Berkeley is in comparative religion," said Van Der Velden, with no small pride. "I wrote my thesis on Judaism and the Kabbalah. Why?"

I took out my phone and found the photographs I'd taken of Gaynor Allitt's prayer closet.

"You wouldn't happen to know what this is, would you? In particular, the design on the curtain?"

Van Der Velden looked at my pictures and frowned. "It looks kind of like a *parochet*," he said. "That's a curtain that covers the door to the *aron kodesh* in a synagogue—which is a cabinet where they keep the Torah scrolls. Only this particular curtain appears to be upside down. The design you see is a menorah—the seven-branched candlestick that's been a symbol of Judaism since ancient times. Either the person who hung this curtain is ignorant of the design or . . ."

I waited. "Or what?"

"Or it might indicate someone who wished to be blasphemous—in the same way you might hang a crucifix upside down if you were, let's say, satanically inclined."

"The curtain was on the door of a closet where Gaynor Allitt seems to have hidden herself away when she was praying."

Fitzgerald came over and looked at the pictures on my phone. "Never seen anything like that before, Pastor."

"You say she prayed in there, Agent Martins?"

"That's right."

"It does seem kind of obsessive," he said. "And I speak as someone who prays a great deal. What do you think, Frank? Is this the Gaynor Allitt you knew?"

"Not at all," he said. "Look, she was strong in her faith. They say faith can move mountains. Well, maybe it can, but I think you'd have to be a little crazy to try." He shrugged. "Gaynor was committed, even devout, but she never struck me as mad enough to go around praying for folks to be dead."

"It sounds to me like she was suffering a nervous breakdown," said Van Der Velden. "From overwork, perhaps."

"As a matter of fact, she seemed very sane to me. Although—well, I've been going to church for a long time and I haven't ever come across a prayer closet before. If that's what it is. Can you think of any reason why someone would want to pray in something like that?"

"You mean apart from the obvious? Quiet, concentration, it being a special place? My grandma used to pray in bed—it was her way of falling asleep. My daddy used to pray out loud every time he sat in a plane, which didn't exactly make him popular with the other passengers. On top of high mountains, in burning buildings, or on sinking ships—I think the Lord is used to hearing prayers from all kinds of strange places."

"One more thing, Pastor," I said. "In your sermon you mentioned your father. That wouldn't be Robert Van Der Velden, would it? From the Prayer Pyramid of Power in Dallas?"

"We're not the family business people sometimes imagine us to be. My father does things his way and I do things mine. And, by the way, the Prayer Pyramid is closed now, in case you didn't know. The church went bankrupt. The Roman Catholic Diocese of Dallas bought it from the federal court that was administering the windup. They paid fifty million dollars."

"I'm surprised the Catholics had that kind of money to spare," I said.

"Just so you know," said Van Der Velden. "None of that money came my daddy's way. I like to keep things out in the open so people don't think I'm connected with the Prayer Pyramid in any way. Especially as he ended up owing so many people so much money." He grinned and clapped me on the arm. "I wouldn't want the FBI getting any ideas I'm some kind of crook. I love my daddy, but the name we honor here at the Izrael Church is God's holy name, not the name of Van Der Velden."

"I certainly appreciate your candor."

"Well, all right. Got any other questions?"

"Only for Mr. Fitzgerald. Since you say you knew Gaynor better than Pastor Van Der Velden."

"That's right," said Fitzgerald. "I did."

"Did she have any family in the church? Next of kin? Friends?"

"How can I put this without making it sound like I'm speaking ill of the dead? She wasn't a warm person, Mr. Martins. She kept herself to herself. But she was respected. I guess you could say she was the kind of person you admired rather than one you befriended. The kids will be upset, though."

"Kids?"

"She was a teacher in our Sunday school. We wondered where she was this afternoon. It wasn't like her not to show up without letting anyone know. You won't want to speak to them, I hope. It's going to be bad enough telling them she's dead without also explaining that she killed herself."

"No, I don't think there's any need for that."

"Good."

"Gentlemen. Thank you for your time and patience. I wish I could have come here as the bearer of better news. But I have enjoyed seeing your magnificent church. If I'm not mistaken, it was once an airport building?"

Van Der Velden nodded. "One of our wealthier members bought the building for us from Ellington when commercial air services ended there. This used to be the Continental Airlines building."

"Whatever happened to them?" I murmured.

"And please, anytime you're in the area, stop by. Especially on a Sunday. You're always welcome to worship with us."

❧

On leaving the Izrael Church of Good Men and Good Women to drive back to Galveston, I stopped at several gas stations until I found one with a well-stocked grocery store and a large rack of magazines and periodicals—in particular, the current issue of *Scientific American*. I was keen to find a copy because, as I had glanced over the various magazines on the smoked-glass coffee table in Pastor Van Der Velden's handsomely appointed office and registered the name of Dr. Sara Espinosa on the cover, I had realized this was the second time I had seen her name. The first time had been on the list I had found on the floor of Gaynor Allitt's prayer closet, inside her Bible. In anyone else's office, a copy of *Scientific American* would have seemed innocent enough, and I would have written it off as a coincidence my stumbling across Dr. Espinosa's name a second time. But given who and what Van Der Velden was, you'd imagine that this was a magazine a Texas preacher would disapprove of.

I was less inclined to think it was a coincidence when I opened the magazine. The article that Dr. Espinosa had coauthored was described as a frank and sometimes controversial exchange of views between two prominent biologists on how scientists ought to approach religion and its adherents.

I selected a bagful of groceries and the magazine, and I read all the way through the article in the car while I smoked a cigarette.

Dr. Espinosa was a professor of integrative biology at the University of Texas in Austin, and despite her comparative youth and good looks, she was also the recipient of numerous honorary doctorates and international prizes. A few months before, at the Salk Institute for Biological

Studies in San Diego, she and Professor Ambrose Salomon from the University of Cambridge, in England, had debated the most effective way to oppose religiously motivated threats to scientific practice. Espinosa was less inclined than her colleague to achieve a peaceful coexistence between science and religion; and the main thrust of her argument was that the best way of discrediting and eventually destroying all religion was to continue teaching the facts of human evolution and to keep pseudoscientific variants of creationism out of school science curricula. In view of what Gaynor Allitt alleged had happened to Philip Osborne, it seemed reasonable to suppose that any Christianist taking a hostile view of him would have taken a similarly hostile view of Dr. Espinosa.

I was still no nearer discovering the details of how Osborne and the three others had met their deaths; but suspecting a hidden cause as I did, it seemed like a good idea to look more closely at Pastor Van Der Velden and his church—not to mention Dr. Espinosa—because I was already half convinced that she might be in danger.

The following morning, as soon as I was done making my report on the arrest of Johnny Sack Brown and his HIDDEN group, and briefing the shrink who was scheduled to go to the FDC and evaluate his mental state, I would tell Gisela that, in my opinion, there was compelling circumstantial evidence of a conspiracy to commit domestic terrorism. At first, she would probably resist the idea. But she could hardly ignore the list of names in Gaynor Allitt's house, her strange confession, her horrible bloody suicide, the mocking sarcastic message she'd left for me, and the way Dr. Espinosa's name had cropped up on Gaynor Allitt's list and on the cover of a science magazine in Nelson Van Der Velden's office. Surely all I had to do to move the investigation forward was to ask Dr. Espinosa if she had received any threats in the form of self-destructing e-mails, like the ones received by Peter Ekman.

Arriving back at the diocesan house in Galveston, I washed up with some relief and made myself an omelet; after I'd eaten it, I Googled Van Der Velden and then the professor, with a large whiskey in my hand, while at the same time I tried to arrange things in an orderly fashion on the table I was using as my desk. Sometimes it seems I can't work at all unless I get a nice shape to my things: my laptop square in the center, my mouse wet-wiped and placed on its antibacterial pad, my cell phone always on the left-hand side, a clean page open in my notebook, a neat row of carefully sharpened pencils, a new eraser still in its cellophane. I guess we all have our peculiar little rituals when we're at our desks.

It was after midnight when I was through. I drank a second largish whiskey in the hope that it would put me in touch with much-needed oblivion. It didn't and it wasn't long before I was wishing I'd taken Helen Monaco up on the offer of her couch. Which was all it had ever been, of course, an offer to sleep on her couch and not with Helen herself. That much was certain now. But in truth, I probably stayed awake because I had so much else to think about; there were so many programs still running in my head that my body couldn't decide which of them to close down first before sending me off to sleep. And so I just lay there, staring at the shadows that were thrown on the ceiling by a full moon as big as a bowling ball, my poor mind racing with the day's residue of everything that had happened to me since leaving the house that morning: Gaynor Allitt's improbable confession at HPD headquarters; her suicide from the top of the Hyatt; the revelation that Helen was a lesbian; that damning list of names in Gaynor's weird prayer closet; the discovery that the Roman Catholic Diocese of Houston and Galveston was the subject of an ongoing FBI investigation; the announcement that Bishop Coogan was about to become the subject of a grand jury investigation for aiding and abetting the escape of yet another tot-banging priest—even though I was aware of what was about to happen to Eamon, I was, of course, strictly forbidden from contacting him, and besides, DCS Net was tapping his telephones so that to call would have been career suicide—seeing Ruth again; seeing Ruth with that outsize fuckwit, Hogan; the suspicion that she and Hogan were already in some kind of a relationship; the suspicion that the Izrael Church of Good Men and Good Women and its apparently easygoing pastor were involved in some kind of horrible conspiracy to murder the opponents of all organized religion.

If all of that wasn't enough, the diocesan house seemed restless; now and then even the bedroom walls and the floor seemed to shift a little as if the house were trying and failing to get comfortable with me in it. As with the previous night, the place felt about as homey as an almost empty Transylvanian hotel. There was trapped air in the pipes, too, which meant that from time to time the place let out a curious sigh that was kind of unnerving and meant that my dreams, when they came, were not pleasant ones but rather a vivid, if not to say fantastic, outlet for my overactive imagination.

I don't know why, but I dreamed of the Dykebar Hospital for the incurably insane back in Scotland, and my poor mad uncle Bill, who was still confined within its stern gray walls. And I seemed to understand what perhaps I had always really known, which was that the violent but entirely silent argument he was always having with the invisible man apparently standing next to him was actually his trying to tell someone—anyone—something important. *Something important about me.* And now that he had told me, he seemed finally to become calm. Very much at peace now, he put his hand on my face and nodded kindly.

"I couldn't have loved you more if you'd been my own son," he said. "That's why I was so fucking angry. It was because no one would fucking listen to what I was trying to tell them. About you, Gil. About you."

I wish I could remember what it was Bill told me in my dream. But when the alarm clock by my bed went off, I sat up suddenly, covered in sweat, and left almost every memory of what had been said between us on the pillow behind me.

EIGHTEEN

There was a flower on Gisela's desk: one big seductive calla lily in a slender gray glass vase that looked like a golf bag with just one club. But she wasn't looking at her single lily; she was looking unflinchingly at me, as if I, too, were some curious botanical object to be studied with care.

As I told her about Gaynor Allitt and the Izrael Church, she glanced down the list of names I'd found and heard me out with a perceptible reluctance so that even before I had finished talking I knew my arguments hadn't persuaded her.

"Gil, you did a hell of a good job last Friday," she said. "The way you cottoned on to that attack drone they found in the nature reserve so quickly. The Switchblade. That was a very good call. With all of the evidence we have against Major Johnny Sack Brown, I'd be surprised if the DA doesn't go after the death penalty."

"Oh, that makes me feel very good."

"Well, it should. If it hadn't been for you, there might have been a lot of dead Jews in this city and the press would be trying to hang the Bureau's ass out to dry. It was a good job. The mayor and the governor called Chuck to congratulate us. And Chuck called me and said to pass on his own appreciation."

"I guess it was too much trouble to tell me himself."

"He might have done that but for a couple of recent complaints he's had about you."

Gisela was nothing if not frank; I'll give her that.

I nodded. "I might have guessed. Gary Greene and that dumb fuck, Doug Corbin."

"I know, I know. I told Chuck what I thought about Corbin, too. Greene, well, that's something else again. Why shouldn't you be friends with a bishop? It's not like he's the head of a Mafia family, for Christ's sake."

"The way Greene was talking, I dunno. Time will tell."

"Look, Gil. Shit happens in this job. But on the plus side Harlan's really impressed with that crazy theory you came up with on his serial killer." She sighed and then raised a sad smile on her face. "Maybe that's what makes me think this latest idea of yours about Gaynor Allitt and Nelson Van Der Velden might just be a crazy theory too far."

"I don't really see the connection," I said.

"No, and that might be the problem." She paused. "You told Harlan that you thought the serial killer might be on the side of the angels, didn't you? That he actually thinks he might be doing God's work? Gathering good people to the Lord, that kind of thing."

"It was just an idea."

"And now you've got another idea about how people from this church down in Clear Lake City might be killing those they perceive to be God's enemies, yes?"

"So you were listening."

"Isn't it possible that you've become a little bit preoccupied with God and the church?"

"Half the terrorism in this country is done in the name of God, or Jesus, or the prophet Muhammad. Don't tell me, Gisela, tell them. I work in Domestic Terrorism, so if I seem just a tad obsessed with God, maybe it's because so many of our customers are, too."

"There are some crazy people out there, Gil, I'm not denying that for a moment. Which makes it all the more essential that in the Bureau we stay sane."

"Amen to that," I said; but by now I was beginning to smell a rat and the rat was wearing my aftershave.

"Are you still having nightmares?"

"So what if I am? It helps keep your eye on the ball if you know that the guy who threw it has a fucking grenade in his pocket. Where's this going, Gisela? Yesterday Greene almost accused me of being a jacko and an informer for the Roman Catholic Church and now you're saying what?"

"Look, Gil. I'm not a shrink, but it seems to me that a lot of what you said just now—about Nelson Van Der Velden—follows on from your wife's leaving home because you stopped believing in God and going to church. Aren't you becoming a little bit obsessed with trying to prove that God's the bastard, here?"

"I don't see how, since I no longer believe he exists."

"Either way, there's no way we can go to the Chief Division Counsel and make a case for investigating Van Der Velden's church."

"Why the hell not? You saw the list—"

"This is why not."

She handed me that morning's *Houston Chronicle*. On the front of the City & State section, underneath a picture of the governor leading another "day of prayer" in Reliant Stadium, was a picture of a beaming Nelson Van Der Velden at the Texas Children's Hospital on Fannin Street meeting some kids who were suffering from cancer; the headline made plain Gisela's reluctance to go after the pastor as I'd urged us to do: "Clear Lake City Pastor Raises $1 Million for Sick Kids."

"Oh," I said quietly.

"Can you imagine what would happen if the newspapers found out we were investigating him? Chuck would feed me my own ears but only after he'd torn them off the side of my head." She paused for a moment and then winced before adding, "And then it would all come out. Everything. By which I mean your other obsessive behavior. After that, we'd both be in the shit. Me for not picking up on it before and you for—well—your obsessive behavior."

I frowned. "What the hell are you talking about, Gisela? What obsessive behavior?"

"Oh, come on, Gil. You must have noticed it yourself."

"Noticed what?"

Gisela looked momentarily at a loss. "You really haven't noticed? No one else has mentioned this to you before?"

I shook my head. "I don't know about obsessive. I've always been a bit particular about my stuff. Is that what you mean?"

"Well, yes. You are. And it is. Only it seems to be getting worse. When it was just a case of your sharpening a few fucking pencils every morning and lining them up on your desk like your own private army, that was all right, I guess. But lately it's a lot more than that. The compulsive handwashing and sanitizing, the way you always clean the steering wheel in your car with a box of wet wipes you keep in the glove compartment, your addiction to rearranging hotel rooms, the way you tidy stuff up, the way you count out loud while you're taking a leak—at least that's what some of the guys say—the way you won't choose something on a menu if it's an odd number, that one I've seen myself. You're like the little triangular point on the toilet paper in a hotel bathroom, Agent Martins. I could go on, with more examples, I mean. But it seems to me that your little fetish has worsened since your private life imploded. It's as if you're trying to compensate for all your current emotional disorder by making everything else obsessively neat and tidy. That's what I think."

"It's not a crime to keep my desk tidy, is it?"

"No, it's not."

"And maybe it helps to be a little obsessive in this job. Did you think about that, Gisela? Maybe it pays to look for a little bit of order in the chaos."

"Sure, I thought about it. You're my best field agent, Gil. People like you. They respect you. But one or two people have mentioned it, that's all."

"Like who?"

"It doesn't matter. All I'm saying is that I'm your boss, and as a result, I'm responsible for your welfare and maybe, just maybe, you could think about getting some professional help, that's all. Before a small problem becomes something more serious."

"Professional help? You mean see the Head Fed?"

"Well, yes, I think you should go and see him and tell him straight out that you have OCD."

"OCD? What are you talking about? I don't have OCD."

"Gil Martins, listen to me. You have OCD. I know other people who've had OCD. You're just like them. And it's getting worse because you've been working too hard, which, of course, is a corollary of not wanting to go home. You need to see Dr. Sussman and calmly discuss all this with him. And until then, you should take some leave. I talked it over with Chuck just a few minutes ago and he's agreed that you need to take time off. We both think that four weeks would be best. Did you know that it's been six months since you took any time off?"

"Jesus, Gisela, what the hell am I supposed to do for four weeks?"

"You could try taking a rest. Look, it'll be okay. Helen will look after your caseload while you're gone."

"Gisela, if I'd been on vacation last Thursday night, there might be a hundred dead people in a synagogue on North Braeswood Boulevard. You said so yourself."

"Yes, I did. But this is important, too. This is your mental health we're talking about, Gil. You're one of the best agents in this field office, and because we can't afford to lose you, we need you to take a rest."

I tried to swallow what I was feeling.

"Are you okay?" Gisela asked.

"Yeah, I'm okay."

"Good." She paused. "So. You should go home."

But I wasn't okay, not by a long shot. I thought of home for a moment; and then I thought of the dump in Galveston where I was now living; and when I glanced back at Nelson Van Der Velden's handsome face in the *Chronicle*, it seemed like he was laughing at me. You can't argue with a man who helps kids with cancer. Not in Texas. Not anywhere. And how much did you have to make before you could afford to give away a million dollars?

⬥⬥

In truth, I'd always known I had a little bit of a problem with arranging stuff and shit like that, and when it was just keeping things tidy and in their correct place, it had seemed just about manageable, although to be fair to her, it used to drive Ruth mad; but Gisela was right. Maybe it had gotten a little out of hand of late. Of course, that didn't make me feel any better about what had happened in Gisela's office; in fact, I felt as low as I'd felt since Ruth had walked out on me. Maybe lower. I suppose you might say I needed the Bureau the way Ruth needed the church.

I called the College of Natural Sciences at the University of Texas in Austin and asked to speak to Dr. Espinosa. It was one of the last things I intended doing before going home as ordered. I just wanted to check that she was okay. The college secretary told me that Dr. Espinosa didn't take telephone calls on campus and refused to give me her e-mail—not even when I told her I was from the FBI.

"Perhaps I could have her call you back later through the FBI switchboard, Agent Martins? As a way of making sure of your bona fides?"

"No, that won't do. I'm going to be out of the office for a while."

"Then I'm afraid you'll have to put your questions for the doctor in writing."

"Ma'am, I'm calling from the FBI, not *Reader's Digest*. And it is kind of urgent."

"I understand that, sir. Nevertheless, that is the only way you're going to be in communication with Dr. Espinosa. I'm afraid she has very strict rules about who can be in contact with her. Might I ask what it's regarding?"

"It's regarding some threats to her person that she may or may not have received."

"I see," said the secretary. "There is one other way you could speak to her."

"And that is?"

"If it is urgent, like you say, you could always come and meet with her in person. If it's a matter affecting her personal safety, I'm sure she could make time for someone from the FBI."

"When did you have in mind?"

"This afternoon. Say around four o'clock? I happen to know she'll have some free time around then."

"I don't know." I paused. "That's quite a drive." I glanced at my

watch. It was eleven o'clock. Austin was a three-hour drive west of
Houston along the 10 and the 290. I could easily make it there and still
have time for lunch en route. And what else did I have to do?

"All right, yes. I'll be there."

I left a note for Helen explaining that I was driving to Austin and
why, but that after this I was going on forced leave and that she should
call me on my cell if she had any operational questions because I
couldn't remember my number in Galveston; then I put some stuff I
might need into a bag, went down to the parking lot, and collected my
car. I put the bag inside and retrieved a bottle of scotch; after what had
happened in the office, I felt justified in having a little sharpener for
the journey. But just the one. Despite what Helen Monaco thought, I
wasn't yet an alcoholic. I just needed a better reason not to drink than
any I'd had so far. Besides, drinking is an excellent way of controlling
OCD. It's difficult to care very much about your funny little habits
when you're half cut by lunchtime but I'd hardly wanted to tell Gisela
that. Being an agent with OCD is one thing; being a drunk with a
badge is probably something worse.

Licking around the inside of my mouth for a last taste of the scotch,
I lit a cigarette and set off for Austin.

It's an easy drive to the state capital. You're still in Houston and its
apparently endless low-rising suburbs until you cross the Brazos, the
longest river in Texas. After the Brazos, the country is flat farmland all
the way and it's easy to get a little sleepy with the road always lying
straight in front of you right up to the horizon, like a loose gray thread
in a big counterpane of white cloud and blue sky. Austin itself is spread
out in order to preserve the Capitol View Corridor, which is meant to
ensure that you can see the state capitol building from anywhere in the
city. These days, with all the high-rise condominiums, Austin's downtown area is looking more and more like Houston's or Dallas's; but
while the Austonian tower was easily taller, it was the university's

Spanish-looking tower that was without question the most notable—
not to say notorious—tower in all Texas.

As I parked my car near the main university building, I regarded
the temple top of the university tower with forensic interest, trying to
calculate with a marksman's eye an approximate height and distance;
and for a moment, I came to a halt with my gaze fixed on the tower
clock, imagining what it must have been like to have been standing
exactly where I was on August 1, 1966. I think everyone visiting the
university probably does the same thing. We do it for the same reason
that makes us all instinctively glance above when we drive up Dealey
Plaza past the Texas School Book Depository in Dallas. It is human to
be fascinated by such things. To have been in the cross-hairs of some
madman's high-powered rifle sight—what does that feel like? It's an act
of prurient imagination that feeds our appetite for contemplating the
arbitrary impermanence of human life, not to mention the unspeakable human brutality that sometimes occasions it. No doubt the people
up on the tower's observation deck were imagining much the same
thing as I was. We were all traveling back in time to when Charles
Whitman had barricaded the tower's observation deck; and then, with
two rifles and a shotgun, had shot and killed fifteen people.

Compared to the criminal investigation that had prompted me to
drive one hundred and sixty miles from Houston, Whitman's crime
seemed all too real and I briefly reproached myself for the frivolity of
my present inquiry. Surely Gisela was right; I had to be obsessed with
proving religious believers were criminals if I'd driven all the way to
Austin to chase a goose as wild as this one. Maybe I did need help.
But then I remembered the sight of a broken Gaynor Allitt fallen from a
similarly tall building and carried on with my fool's errand. But it can
be a mistake to underestimate the tenacity of a really determined fool.

Or for that matter, the tenacity of a really bad architect. In the main
university building they directed me a short way north of the sniper

tower to the Norman Hackerman Building on East Twenty-fourth Street. This was a very modern building, but in a way that reminded me so strongly of an architect's maquette that I half expected to see it surrounded by scale-model trees made of foam rubber and some Lego people.

They were expecting me at the reception desk; a security tag was already completed in my name, and as soon as I had flashed my ID— this caused much excitement—I was permitted through the turnstile and then into an elevator.

Before I Googled her on my laptop in the car, I'd had an idea that Dr. Sara Espinosa would be Latin American, but from her extensive Wikipedia page, it was obvious that she was anything but that. Originally from Hartford, Connecticut, she'd attended Yale and then won a prestigious UNESCO L'Oréal International Fellowship grant for her work in microbiology and virology; but it was as a debater on scientific and political issues that she was best known. She was a regular on Fox News because she was a frequent and popular target of the American right for her views on the three A's: atheism, abortion, and Afghanistan.

In person, she was taller than I expected, with strawberry-blond hair, a wide mouth, a wry, mocking smile, and a deep, sexy voice; her hands were mannish and her manner brisk, as if she was used to dealing with people less intelligent than she was, which was probably everyone. She was very attractive and not much like the lab-rat women I'd known back at Boston College. She wore black linen trousers, a black linen shirt, and a white cotton jacket that may or may not have been a lab coat.

"Agent Martins, I presume," she said loudly, greeting me at the elevator door. "Only someone from the FBI would wear a woolen jacket in this place and in this weather. I presume that's because you're carrying a firearm. Do you always carry a weapon, Agent Martins?"

A lot of her conversation was like that—as if she knew the answer already or couldn't be bothered to await an answer.

"Yes. It saves getting shot."

She laughed and led me into an expensively furnished office with a wraparound sofa, several desktop PCs, and a wide-screen TV. We sat down. On the wall above her head was a large picture of Charles Darwin—just in case anyone should be in any doubt as to where her sympathies lay.

"Could I see it?"

"Hmm?"

"Your gun. Could I see it, please? I've never seen a real gun up close and yet so many people seem to carry them in Texas. So, I'm curious to know what all the fuss is about. Especially at this university. Lots of people carry guns at UT. Even some of the students. For obvious historical reasons."

"Sure," I said. "If you want."

I reached around to the small of my back, fetched the Glock from my holster, and ejected the double magazine before handing it to her. She watched with fascination.

"There you go, Dr. Espinosa." I started my spiel. "Thanks for seeing me, I'm sure you must be very busy—"

"And do you do that—I mean, take the bullets out of the handle like that—because you actually fear I might shoot you?"

"If you did, I very much doubt it would be on purpose."

"Since we've only just met."

"That certainly didn't stop Charles Whitman," I said.

"The poor boy was suffering from a massive brain tumor when he shot all those people. Did you know that?"

"But accidents do happen. Especially with firearms."

"If what one reads is correct, fifteen hundred Americans a year are killed by accidental firearm discharges. Although that's actually quite small when you take into account that every year thirty thousand Americans die from gunshot wounds. You would think it would be more, wouldn't you? I mean, you can't imagine that there were thirty thousand people shot and killed because another thirty thousand people actually wanted that to happen."

"I can imagine it," I said. "Only too well, I'm afraid."

"Perhaps you can, at that." She weighed the gun in her hand, like she was judging a melon. "How does it make you feel, Agent Martins? When you're carrying it? What I mean is, do you think it has a psychological effect on the way you conduct yourself?"

"You ask some very personal questions, Dr. Espinosa."

"Yes, I do."

"Well, to be honest, I'm glad I haven't had to use it. I have a colleague who shot two people and I think it bothers her a lot."

"I'm glad to hear it." She smiled. "By the way, call me Sara. Or Doctor, if you must. My real name is Sara Hooker, but for obvious reasons I prefer to use Espinosa. You've no idea how puerile student minds can be. As it happens, Hooker is actually a very scientific name. There was a Joseph Hooker who's a distant ancestor of mine who was actually Charles Darwin's closest friend. But that's another story. Luis Espinosa was the name of my third husband. He's from Argentina and I married him because he looked so becoming on a polo pony. I kept his name because when I first appeared in print and on television that's what I was calling myself; back then I still had the romantic notion that we might be together forever. He left me when I stopped paying his debts. In retrospect, I would rather like to have shot him dead, the bastard. I've never met a lazier, more good-for-nothing man in my life than my ex-husband, Luis. And believe me I know what I'm talking about. I have two other ex-husbands to compare him with. Does that shock you, Agent Martins?"

"Not really. Nothing shocks me all that much. Not anymore."

"You have my sympathy. To be shocked by things is one way of gauging how civilized we are. Don't you think so?" She sighed extravagantly. "Well, there it is. Now you know all about me. It'll save you from having to slap me around later." She smiled, handed me back my gun, and watched carefully as I reloaded it, as if seeking instruction. "How many does that thing hold?"

"The magazine? Nineteen nine-millimeter rounds. It's quite a conversation stopper."

"Nineteen rounds. That seems a lot. At least until someone starts shooting at you, I suppose. Then you would want as many rounds as humanly possible, I imagine."

"I could show you how to use it if you like."

Her face brightened. "Would you?"

"Is there a reason you'd like to learn how to use a gun?"

"Not really. Only I think I might be rather good at it. My father was an excellent shot and I take after him in nearly everything else. He was a professor of medicine."

"My father used to be a professor of orthopedic surgery at Tufts Medical Center."

"Oh, my word. I wonder if they ever knew each other. My dad was at Yale medical school. Isn't it a small world?"

"Why didn't your father teach you how to shoot?"

She sighed. "He shot himself. After that, my mother never allowed us anywhere near guns. She wouldn't allow one in the house."

"I'm sorry."

She smiled nervously, as if she had been just on the edge of shedding a tear. "I don't know why I'm telling you these things."

"I'm from the FBI. And it'll save me from having to slap it out of you later."

The smile widened. "Oh, I'm so glad that you have a sense of humor, Agent Martins. One always imagines that federal agents are rather straight, ugly men with bad suits and even worse haircuts. You're none of those things. Tell me, are there many women who work for the FBI?"

"Plenty. My own boss is a woman."

"And how do you like that?"

I shrugged. "I like it fine. Most of the time I don't pay it much regard."

"As a rule, men hate working for a woman. It makes them feel inadequate. It's the same dynamic that ruins a lot of marriages. Women should always pretend to be dumber than their husbands, especially when they're not."

"Actually, I think I've learned a lot from my boss. And from that colleague I was telling you about. The one who shot two subs."

"What would you say you've learned from your female colleagues?"

"For one thing, I've learned something about women." I grinned. "Speaking as a man, you can never know too much on that particular subject."

"True. Most men are fearfully ignorant about women. Especially the women they're married to."

"I know I was."

"Divorced?"

"Not quite. But I will be soon. First time."

"Oh dear. What were you ignorant of? If you don't mind my asking."

"We were regular churchgoers and I fell by the wayside. I stopped believing in God and she didn't. So she threw me out. Simple as that."

Of course, it wasn't, not really, but it made for a neat shorthand.

Sara's jaw dropped. "With apologies to Ford Madox Ford, that's the saddest story I ever heard. Hasn't she heard of love thy neighbor?"

"Since I no longer choose to stand in church beside her, Ruth finds it very hard to think of me as her neighbor at all. I'm more of a kind of tourist from a pagan country who's outstayed his welcome." I shook my head. "I don't know why I'm telling *you* this."

"Because we're having a conversation. Because I asked. Because you already showed me your gun. Because you volunteered to teach me how to shoot. Because you feel you can confide in me. Which must mean there's chemistry of the kind neither of us understands. Well, at least you don't. That's why."

"What kind of chemistry?"

"The biochemical kind. Olfactory receptors. Human beings have four hundred functional genes coded for olfactory receptors and six hundred that we believe are pseudogenes, which means they've lost their protein-coding ability. However, I tend to believe that they're not disabled for everyone; indeed, that some of those pseudogenes are, in fact, fully functioning for many people. Smell is a lot more important in the way we get on with some people and not with others than we might think."

"So now I know why girls fall helplessly in love with me. They're just following their noses."

She smiled triumphantly. "Exactly so. While you're teaching me to shoot, I can teach you some human biology."

"I asked you before if there was a reason why you'd like to learn how to shoot and you told me a lie."

Momentarily, she looked delighted. "How did you know that?"

"You might say my nose told me. You see, Sara, people lie to me all the time."

"Yes, I suppose they must. Or they'd be arrested. Or shot."

"So the reason is . . . ?"

"Well, yes. You're right, Agent Martins."

"Call me Gil. Most people do."

"That's a relief. There is a reason, Gil. Because of who and what I am, or more likely because of what I say—because of all that, there are plenty of people who hate my guts. And who would certainly like to see me dead. There's no real free speech in this country. Not anymore. Certainly not for anyone who speaks her mind on television as I do. Consequently, I'm in constant receipt of death threats. Which is why I employ a mail screening service to examine all my snail mail, and why I run ChoiceMail on my personal computer. That's a permission-based e-mail program that assumes everything is spam unless you tell it otherwise—only approved e-mail gets into your in-box. And it's also why my home is monitored by Smith Protective Services. They're the largest in Texas, and I pay for a full service that gives me access control, video surveillance, burglar alarms, and an armed guard response. At least that's what it says on my quarterly invoice. But lately I've been thinking of downgrading to something more manageable. My own personal firearm might be just the answer."

"Smith is the best," I said. "You couldn't do better. So can I ask why you're thinking of downgrading your personal security at this present moment in time?"

"Smith is the best, yes. But it's also expensive. Also, I don't feel I'm getting as many death threats as perhaps I used to. I must be slipping."

"Or maybe ChoiceMail and the USPS are doing a better job than you think."

"Good point. I never thought of that."

"So there's nothing new on that front that you've become aware of lately? New threats. Hate mail. That kind of stuff."

"There's nothing new," she said carefully, "but I can't imagine that you drove all the way down from Houston for the hell of it."

"No," I said. "It's because your name has appeared on a list of names of people identified as enemies of the church and God. Some of those names have received threats. I'm just checking the others on that list to see if they've been threatened, too. That's all. Nothing more serious than that, Sara. So, given what you've just told me, I think you can relax."

"Now it's you who's lying, Martins."

"No, ma'am, that's the truth."

"I've had three husbands, Martins. It may not rank alongside your own investigative experience of liars in the FBI, but I have an unerring eye for when a man is not telling me the truth."

"Which of them was the worst?"

"Kevin. Number two. He was a Wall Street trader and the only time he ever told the truth was when he talked in his sleep. I heard him praying in church once and I swear even that was a lie. Can you imagine lying to God?"

"I've been doing it for quite a while."

"Not like he did, you haven't. This was someone who believed in God. He was a Roman Catholic and I happened to overhear him in confession—"

"Happened to overhear?"

"All right, I bugged the confessional at St. Patrick's in New York."

I laughed out loud.

"And listened in at the back of the cathedral on a little short-wave wireless transmitter. I bought the whole kit from Amazon for just eighty-five dollars and recorded everything on a memory card. It worked out to be the most cost-effective of all my divorces. Anyway, I heard him confessing his adultery and he only confessed to one of the other women he'd slept with when I happened to know there were at least three. Can you imagine it?"

"I'm still trying to picture you at the back of St. Patrick's with your transmitter."

"But let's not change the subject. We've only just met and already you're trying to deceive me." She paused. "Well, aren't you?"

I said nothing.

"Look, I don't doubt that what you told me was a lie told with good intent, but it was still a lie. So, please level with me, or I shall think you're every bit as secretive as J. Edgar Hoover and that will be the end of the beginning of our friendship."

"All right. And I stand corrected. That list of people I was telling you about? They all have one thing in common—that they are not beloved by the religious right in this country. Up to now, what four of them also have in common is that they're dead. And I think at least one of them you probably knew: Willard Davidoff."

"Well, of course, I knew about Willard. We were friends. He taught me biology, at Yale. But the papers said that was an accident."

"That's what it looked like. He had a drink, climbed a tree, fell, and broke his neck."

"Willard always did like his wine."

"He was sixty-five. Not some kid from the Skull and Bones. I went to Boston and took a good look at that tree. Believe me, I couldn't have climbed it and I'm thirty years younger than he was."

"Actually, he *was* Skull and Bones. But I see what you mean. Although, as it happens, he was quite a vigorous sixty-five. Believe me, I know."

"You mean you and he were . . . ?"

"Yes. For a while. He had a great mind. I like that in a man. And the others?"

"Philip Osborne. Peter Ekman. Clifford Richardson."

"Peter I knew, too. That was very sad. Although I never went to bed with him, we were quite close for a while. And it's fair to say there was one occasion when we almost did go to bed." She shook her head. "Only I thought he managed to asphyxiate himself in his panic room."

"That's what the coroner said."

"But you don't believe that."

"No. He went into his panic room even though there were no signs of an intruder. Not only that, he failed to sound an alarm that would have summoned the police. Look, I'll be honest with you, if any of them were murdered, I have no idea how. I don't know that and I don't know—well, let's just say there's a lot more I don't know than I care to confess right now."

"So, tell me what you do know and maybe I can help." She shrugged. "After all, I seem to have a vested interest in this case since my name is also on that list."

"When I said I was checking the other names on that list to see if anyone else has been threatened, you're the first of those other names I've spoken to. I wanted to take a look at you in person and judge for myself what kind you are. See if you're the kind of person who is easily spooked."

"I understand."

So I told Sara Espinosa everything—from the night in O'Neill's bar when Bishop Coogan had given me his file of clippings and web-page printouts, to the day before in Nelson Van Der Velden's office in the Izrael Church of Good Men and Good Women when I'd spotted the copy of *Scientific American* containing her article.

"Yes, that does seem to have put the cat among the pigeons. They've had a ton of complaints about my piece." She shrugged. "I suppose that's why I write them."

Then I underlined the fact that Richardson, Davidoff, Ekman, and Osborne had all died in fear of something; that Ekman had been in receipt of self-destructing e-mails that threatened his life; that it seemed Osborne had believed he was being chased by something that wasn't there; that Clifford Richardson had thrown himself off his Washington balcony; and that Gaynor Allitt had been equally fearful of something before jumping off the top of the Hyatt Regency. I made it all sound sufficiently mysterious to warrant FBI involvement and the interest of the Domestic Terrorism Task Force. But at the same time, I spared myself nothing by way of criticism—specifically, how Gaynor Allitt's "prayer list" was the only shred of evidence I'd found so far that the deaths of these four were anything other than an unfortunate coincidence.

Sara frowned. It looked like the kind of deep frown you deploy to stop yourself from laughing.

"You know, it might all just be an unfortunate coincidence," she said. "I mean, now and then it's the nature of coincidence to look like something more than that. People want to believe in something more than just a random series of disasters. They want to see the hand of God in nearly everything abnormal."

"Well, that's one way of seeing it," I admitted.

Finally, she could restrain her grin no longer. "Oh, now wait a minute, this is not some personal crusade you're on, is it? It wouldn't be that you're looking to find a better reason to believe in God again, would it? You don't seriously think there is actually something occult going on here. Please say you don't."

"Not in the sense of how most people use that word—of this being a case involving something supernatural, no. But in the true sense of the word? Of there being something hidden and secret? Yes, I do think there is something occult going on here. All criminal conspiracies are occult until we uncover them."

"Yes, you're right, of course. And you're quite right to remind me of the word's true meaning. It's Latin, isn't it? *Occultus*. I seem to remember my own father using the phrase 'occult blood.' Whatever that is."

"In medicine I think it means that when you find an unexplained anemia there may be hidden bleeding."

Sara looked pleased that I'd remembered what she'd perhaps forgotten. "Yes, that's right."

"Just so you know, I didn't stop believing in God to start believing in voodoo. Naturally, I've considered the possibility that there is no connection. That I'm chasing a ghost up a tree. But the list appears to contradict that."

"Yes, it does seem to. Well then, here's what we'll do. We'll approach the problem empirically. It's what you do when you want to test a theory. You carry out an experiment."

"How? How are we going to carry out an experiment?"

She smiled. "Simple. I'll be your experiment."

"How do you propose that's going to work?" I laughed. "Strap you down on a gurney with a heart monitor on your chest and keep you under permanent observation?"

"It's a nice thought," she said flirtatiously.

I felt myself blush a little.

"But no, I was thinking of something altogether more prosaic. I will take extra care in observing the things around me. At home, when I'm driving here. All of the time I'll be looking out for something unusual. And once a week we'll keep in touch by telephone. Do you have a business card?"

I took out my wallet and handed one over. "Call me day or night. Whenever you like."

"Thanks. And if I have anything unusual to report, I'll tell you and we can take it from there, can't we? I also propose that we should meet up in, say, a month's time, and if nothing has happened, then you can sign me off with a clean bill of health, so to speak. Maybe you can give me that shooting lesson, too. Yes, that'd be fun. Meanwhile, I suggest you telephone some of the other names on Gaynor Allitt's prayer list and see if, unlike me, any of them have anything unusual to tell you. What do you say?"

I nodded. But only half of me agreed with her; the other half believed she was humoring me—cleverly finding a way of removing me from her office without embarrassing either one of us.

"Yeah," I said. "Good idea." I stood up to leave. "I seem to have bothered you for nothing. Me and my crazy theories."

"Really, it was no bother at all." She stood up. "Here, I'll walk you out."

NINETEEN

Galveston was once described as the only city on the Gulf Coast you'd want to visit on a rainy day. Now that felt like an awful, tasteless joke because it had been the rainy day to end all rainy days that had ended forever the island city's role as a welcome escape for inland Texas refugees. Nearly everything that had once made Galveston an important tourist attraction was gone; and whereas before it had offered the visitor a unique historical perspective on the slave trade and the Civil War—not to mention a few nice beaches and some sophisticated hotels—now it offered only a salutary example of how our modern climate can ruin a place forever. Galveston looked like a plague town, or one of those habitations in Japan or Ukraine that have been contaminated by radiation, nowhere more so than in the city's restaurants and bars.

The Strand Bar and Grill might just have been the worst bar in Galveston, but I liked it because it suited my mood to be somewhere that felt as fucked up as I did. It was a big empty dance hall of a place with dozens of ugly-looking tables where they served uglier Mexican food. Only the waitresses were less appetizing, which is saying something. Even when the place was half full—which wasn't often—the place felt abandoned. The Strand Bar and Grill was holding on to the idea of a business recovery in Galveston the way a lost dog in a fast river clings to a piece of driftwood; and no one was fooled: the place was a dimly lit anteroom in purgatory.

Another reason I went to the Strand was that I could walk there and back again, although, to be honest, walking there was always a lot easier than walking back. The bar was just a few blocks away from my rent-free diocesan house, which, now that I was on forced leave, I saw little or no reason to abandon. Besides, the house was more forgiving when I'd had a drink or two and it was less inclined to make me feel uncomfortable. There's not half as much to disturb a man when he sleeps during the day. Especially in Galveston. No one ever sent any mail here. Or rang my doorbell. So that when one day it finally happened that someone did ring it, the noise was so loud and surprising to me that I almost jumped out of my skin.

I went to the door expecting to find Bishop Coogan on my porch and braced myself for an awkward conversation with him. The newspapers were full of Father Breguet's escape and the role the Roman Catholic Diocese of Houston and Galveston had allegedly played in that. Instead, I found a FedEx guy standing there with a box in his hands.

I signed for the box and watched the driver go away. It gave me something to do. The brightly liveried FedEx van was probably the most color and noise they'd had in that street all year and I was surprised that one or two of the neighbors didn't come out to investigate the commotion. Actually, I wasn't entirely sure if it was one neighbor or two who were still living nearby; there was an old man who occupied a dilapidated blue house about ten doors down from me and another old man a little farther on from him, but they might easily have been one and the same. Besides, the old man probably thought I was another Roman Catholic priest and I could hardly imagine that priests were all that popular in a place so obviously deserted by God. Then again, the old man might just have been one of Galveston's many ghosts. In a place like this it was hard to tell just who was alive and who was not. I had the same problem whenever I looked in my bathroom mirror. I wouldn't say that I'd completely let myself go, but when you're only grooming for the benefit of the patrons of the Strand Bar and Grill, there are times when it hardly seems worth the effort of opening a package of razors—or, for that matter, a FedEx box from the Portland, Oregon, police. Especially when most of the time you're drunk. So I tossed the box onto the sofa, and after it disappeared under a pile of unwashed laundry, beer cans, and old newspapers, I forgot all about it.

꙰

I've only ever been to Portland, Oregon, once. I went there to interview a suspect and I was in the city for less than eighteen hours. It seemed an attractive enough sort of place and they make some good beer there, but more than that I can't say. I don't know anyone who actually lives in Portland. But clearly someone knew me. I opened the box and emptied out a large envelope that contained a police file and a long cover letter. I fetched a cold one from the refrigerator, lit up a cigarette, and started to read.

> *Dear Agent Martins,*
>
> *I hope you'll forgive this intrusion on your vacation and for circumventing the usual investigative channels. I am a police officer with the Portland police, a detective with twenty years on the force. Helen Monaco at your field office gave me your current home address so that I might send you this police file concerning an investigation we've been conducting here in Portland into the recent death of the Reverend David Durham.*

*Maybe you already heard about this case because there's been
a lot about it in the media—most of it wild speculation.*

*On the face of it, his death seems to have been a freak
accident—certainly that's the official conclusion of this
investigation—but there were several features about it that
struck me as more than a little strange. I'd heard about the
death of Peter Ekman in NYC, and when I contacted the local
PD to discuss one or two similarities between his death and that
of David Durham, they told me about your own investigation.*

*I've been ordered to close the case and, in the absence of any
real evidence that will satisfy my superiors that Durham's death
was not accidental, that is what I will have to do; but I don't feel
comfortable about that. Consequently, I have decided to bring
the very peculiar circumstances of his death—these are mostly
unreported by the media—to your attention, albeit in this
underhanded and off-the-record way. For all the reasons I just
mentioned, I have to remain anonymous; I am nearing
retirement and would very much like to reach the end of my
service with an unblemished record; this would not be the case if
it became known that I had deliberately disobeyed the order of
my superiors.*

The facts are these:

*Four weeks ago the workers at the Columbia Boulevard
Wastewater Treatment Plant here in Portland discovered the
body of a forty-one-year-old Caucasian male floating in its new
dry-weather clarifier. It's a sedimentation tank designed to
remove solids from dry-weather sewage flow. This followed a
report to the local police that a homeless man had been seen
hiding in a storm drainpipe in the Columbia Masonic
Cemetery in the Maywood Park district of the city, about nine
miles west of the treatment plant. When police reached the*

cemetery, they arrived in time to witness the man taken by a
flood that followed a very sudden squall of heavy rain. Until
then, we'd been having the driest summer in Portland since
1968, with record low flows in the streams and rivers. That
sudden squall meant that about an inch of rain fell in just five
minutes, which was enough to wash him away.

Eight hours later, after police had combed the nearby
Columbia River and its canals, the body was found at the local
sewage plant as described. The man was initially identified as
George Gresham but later as David Durham, who'd been living
under an assumed name at the Golden Spikes Motel a mile or
two east of the cemetery. It's not clear why he was staying under
an assumed name any more than it was clear why he had
chosen to get inside a drain. At the time, however, the drain was
dry; and it seems fair to conclude that he was hiding from
something.

Durham was not from Portland and it seems he had no
connection with the city. Prior to his arrival in Portland the
previous day, he had been living and working as an evangelical
pastor in Toronto. But he was very possibly the most
controversial preacher in North America. His religious beliefs
had already put him at odds with a lot of evangelical Christians
when, in 2000, he was appointed as a professor of religious
studies at the University of California at Berkeley. Later, he
published a bestselling biography of Jesus entitled The Jesus Lie
in which he argued that the gospels were inaccurate, that Jesus
was not the son of God, that he was not resurrected, and that
heaven does not exist. His unorthodox reputation was cemented
when he appeared in David Horowitz's 2006 book The
Professors: The 101 Most Dangerous Academics in America.
Following an incident in which Durham burned Horowitz's

book on the university campus—an act for which he himself
later apologized and described as a Nazi act—he was dismissed
by the university.

At this point in his career, he accepted an unlikely offer of a
job as pastor at the Tre Fontane Evangelical Church of Canada
in Toronto in 2007—a church that had already become
internationally known for its progressive-liberal views. This was
largely based on its racial diversity and the important role it
played in providing services for the poor and the homeless and
also for its support for Toronto's gay and lesbian community.
This had often put the Tre Fontane Church at odds with
evangelical religious orthodoxy and so it was probably a good fit
for Durham to go there. Especially since he was an experienced
public speaker. Preaching had always been at the heart of the
ministry at Tre Fontane and Durham quickly established a
name for himself there as the most radical preacher in North
America. He once went on Canadian television and told the
audience that he doubted that God would ever have arranged a
virgin birth or allowed Jesus to walk on water; in the same
interview he described the physical resurrection as a conjuring
trick and the Book of Revelation as the "pathological ravings of
a madman." But while he always remained a very popular
figure in Toronto, he was soon a hated figure among religious
figures in the United States; his life was threatened on more
than one occasion.

This summer he went on a lecture tour of the United States
to promote his new book The Unnatural Nature of Theology.
And because of the death threats he had received from both
Christians and Muslims, his publisher took the precaution of
hiring an armed guard to accompany him. But the tour had to
be cut short when, at a reading in Philadelphia, Durham

appeared to suffer a nervous collapse that his publisher
attributed to his busy schedule. He returned to Toronto, where,
almost immediately, he resigned from the church and
disappeared.

A week after his resignation, he arrived here in Portland.

Durham was divorced and lived alone. His girlfriend in
Toronto, Cassandra Hendrikson, told Portland police that prior
to his disappearance he'd been worried by something; but when
she tried to speak to him about it in a restaurant, he bawled her
out and so she left. She had no idea why he went to Portland;
he'd never mentioned Portland before. It wasn't even on his book
tour. He bought his plane ticket at the airport on the same day
he traveled. This was not a ticket for Portland, however; it was a
ticket for Anchorage. That flight was subject to a lengthy delay,
and instead of waiting for it like everyone else, Durham
canceled his ticket and bought a second one, this time a
first-class ticket for Portland. It almost seems not to have been
very important to him where he went and how much he paid as
long as he went to the opposite side of the country as soon as
possible. He was only carrying hand luggage, which was also a
little unusual for a journey of that length.

On his arrival here in Portland, he told the immigration
officer that the purpose of his visit was tourism. Apparently, he
seemed very tired and could hardly keep his eyes open long
enough for a retinal scan. At the airport, Durham rented a car.
The rental clerk almost didn't let him have the vehicle because
he seemed distracted; he was also sweating a lot and seemed out
of breath. The only reason the clerk finally parted with the car
was because Durham was able to prove he was a church pastor.

After leaving the airport, Durham checked into three
different hotels in the space of twenty-two hours: the Nordic

Motel on Northeast Sandy Boulevard only four miles from the airport; the Palms Motel on North Interstate Avenue; and finally the Golden Spikes. He paid cash up front at each one. At the Nordic, he took a two-room unit because that was all that was available, but he was told to leave by the management. It was drawn to their attention by the guy in the next room that Durham had piled all the furniture in front of the door. At the Palms Motel, he panicked when there was a power outage that lasted only a few minutes, and he checked out immediately. As he drove away in the rental vehicle, he took the side mirror off a parked car. From the Palms, he seems to have driven around for an hour before he stopped at the Multnomah County Sheriff's Office on Southeast Hawthorne Boulevard and demanded to be taken into custody. When the desk sergeant asked Durham what for, he answered that he'd killed someone; and when the sergeant asked him who he'd killed, Durham replied that he'd killed Jesus and that he bitterly regretted it now, at which point, rather comically, the sergeant told Durham to leave before he got himself into trouble. And then he left.

The desk clerk at the Golden Spikes Motel noticed nothing unusual about Durham other than he asked for a bungalow as far away from the road as possible. After checking in, he left his car in the parking lot and then walked west along Northeast Sandy Boulevard to the Columbia Masonic Cemetery, which is about three miles as the crow flies. There's a Best Western Pony Soldier Inn nearby, and before he went into the cemetery, he asked if he might look at a room. They showed him a room and he said he would come back. Then he went across the road into the cemetery where he spent the next few minutes lifting a storm drain cover. At the Sacred Grounds Espresso Bar across the road, John Philips and his wife, Carol, were having a coffee. It

was his birthday and she'd just given him a pair of new
binoculars, which is how he happened to see Durham in the
cemetery across the road. He alerted the manager to what was
happening and the manager called the Multnomah Sheriff's
Office, which sent a patrol car and the two officers who
witnessed the accident.

On that morning's weather forecast there was no mention of
rain—freak or otherwise. Mr. and Mrs. Philips reported that
when they went into the espresso bar the sky was blue and
cloudless; but within ten minutes of seeing Durham in the
cemetery, a thick dark cloud appeared over the whole area that
they described as "ominous and alarming."

Durham's body was taken to the medical examiner's office in
Clackamas where the chief deputy ME performed an autopsy
and identified the body. This was made more difficult by what
had happened to the body after drowning. Both the victim's arms
and legs were broken in several places and, worst of all, his face
was scraped off the front of his skull. All of this was consistent
with the reported force of the storm water in the drainpipe.

Identification was made possible due to a room key for the
Golden Spikes that was found in the dead man's jacket pocket.

Further examination of the victim's remains revealed that he
was suffering from a malignant sarcoma of the heart—an
extremely rare form of cancer. His erratic behavior is now
ascribed to this condition. However, at no point was Durham's
cancer ever diagnosed by a medical practitioner, not in Toronto
nor in Portland; and it seems entirely possible that at the time of
his death Durham remained unaware of his medical condition.
Moreover, Durham had seen his own doctor for a routine
checkup only three months before his death and no signs of
cancer were detected.

There is one last strange and highly unpleasant fact that
marks the death of David Durham. When police entered his
bungalow at the Golden Spikes Motel, they discovered on the
floor a single extruded excrement that was twenty-four inches
long. It seems not unreasonable to speculate that, in the same
way that burglars defecate on the floor of the houses they've
broken into, David Durham did the same because he was afraid
of something.

I stopped reading and went to look for my cell phone; not because
I wanted to make a call—that was impossible due to the poor reception
in that part of Galveston—but because I wanted to look at the photo-
graph of the list of names I'd found in Gaynor Allitt's house.

David Durham's was one of the names on the list, underneath that
of Sara Espinosa.

⠿

At Quantico they teach you that people who are irritating are not necessarily wrong, but it's just common sense to bear in mind that they
might be.

Sometimes you have to hear your own arguments in someone else's
mouth to know how crazy you sound.

I began to consider the possibility that mine had been nothing
more than a contrarian's argument—an obsessive's wish to prove that
he was right and everyone else was wrong. I wondered if perhaps the
detective had caught the same skeptical bug I had; that perhaps he, too,
had lost his religious faith and had taken his newfound skepticism to
excess. Or if having cut God out of his life, he had found this left a
God-shaped hole at the center of his life that he needed to fill with
something he could believe in: himself, perhaps.

The circumstances of David Durham's death were unfortunate, even bizarre, but it wasn't unlikely that a man suffering from heart cancer was disturbed at a physiological level that manifested itself in all kinds of eccentric behavior such as shitting on your motel room floor. People do all sorts of weird things when they're ill and even when they're not ill. And if not physiologically disturbed, you could argue that Durham was already psychologically disturbed even before he wrote his last book. What kind of evangelist wrote a book arguing that the power of all religions derived from their "rigorous denial of common sense"? That sounded fucked up, by anyone's standard.

Of course, Durham's name was on Gaynor Allitt's list. Yes, there was that. But for the first time it came into my mind that other groups of religious neo-cons and friends of Fox News might well have compiled similar lists of their ideological enemies and that very likely many of these lists would have overlapped. Hadn't David Horowitz done something similar in writing his William Buckley–style book.

People die, of course, and the minute you compile a list of people, it stands to reason that some of them will die sooner than others. I suspected that the odds against five people on Gaynor Allitt's list being dead within twelve months of one another were lower than might have been supposed. The Portland police file had a list—photocopied from the book—of the one hundred and one professors that Horowitz had described as academics who were poisoning the minds of today's college students; and when I glanced down at this impressive list of names, I was hardly surprised to discover that almost a dozen of the names on Gaynor Allitt's list were also featured in Horowitz's book: namely Noam Chomsky, Eric Foner, Ward Churchill, Peter McLaren, Gayle Rubin, Caroline Higgins, David Barash, Angela Davis, Alison Jaggar, José Ángel Guttiérrez, and Joseph Massad. All of which prompted me to think that maybe it was time I got my act together and, in compliance with Gisela's wishes, put myself in the hands of the Head Fed, Dr. Sussman.

After that, I would report to her office and tell her humbly that she was right and I was wrong and that I wanted to drop the investigation of everything that was connected to Philip Osborne's death—or, to be more accurate, not connected with his death at all.

So I shaved, took a shower, hunted down a clean shirt, pressed my suit, polished my shoes—I even did some tidying up around the house—and went out onto the veranda and paused at the top of the steps. Even by the preternaturally inert standards of Galveston, it was a day of extraordinary stillness, without a breath of wind. It was not, however, a pleasant stillness with birds singing or the sea crashing onto the not so very far away beach. The air was a great hushed emptiness of noise. I went down the steps and opened the door of my dust-covered car. The midday sun hung in the blue sky like a burning clock face and it had turned the plastic interior of my car into an inferno; so I started the engine, turned the air-conditioning up to high, and then went back up the stairs and took shelter from the sun under the wooden roof of the porch while I waited. The interruption of that dead silence with the muffled roaring of my car's air-conditioning seemed to galvanize the whole street like a kind of generator summoning first an emaciated black cat to see what all the fuss was about, then a small lizard at my feet, and finally the sight of my only neighbor—the old man—walking barefoot down the sidewalk toward me. I could hardly believe my eyes, for he was the first person I had seen in the street since moving into the diocesan house.

"Good morning," I said.

"Not in Galveston."

"I'm sorry?"

"I must say, you don't look like a retired clergyman," he said, his eyes flashing about restlessly.

"I'm not," I said. "I'm just staying here temporarily until I can find somewhere more permanent."

"Permanent?" He sighed. "You won't find anything permanent around here," he said. "Not anymore. Not since Ike. This whole damned area feels like it's about to be condemned to destruction. And probably should be, too. The real shame is that Ike didn't finish the job. Some of these old houses aren't safe at all. Still, yours looks not half bad. I suppose the Catholic Church paid for everything? The way it always does. That's what comes of wearing liturgical vestments: they have very deep pockets."

His baritone voice sounded like he was from somewhere other than Texas; there was more than a touch of New York in it—the state, anyway—and something patrician, too, as if he'd been to one of those top universities where they learn how to rule not just themselves but other people, too.

"You live farther up the street, don't you Mr. . . . ?"

"I don't know that you could call it living exactly," said the old man. "It's more of a day-to-day existence. Subsistence, you might say. In fact, I have kind of got used to the idea that this whole street was my own private hell. Like that dreadful play by Jean-Paul Sartre."

"I don't go to the theater very much."

"Quite right. Neither do I. Always hated the theater. My ex-wife used to say, 'Charles Hindemith, you don't have the patience for the theater, they should ban you from everything except Shakespeare and Stephen Sondheim.' These days I don't enjoy any entertainment you can't stop with a button on a remote control. Everything else thinks it's fucking art and there's nothing entertaining about art. Art is something you have to endure. Like piles."

He was handsomer than I had expected—distinguished even—and not nearly as old as I had supposed; his silver hair shone in the sun like a newly minted coin but he hardly seemed to notice the searing heat. His navy blue cotton shirt was unstained by any sweat. He didn't even wince under the sun's malevolent yellow eye, as was my own habit.

"Are you actually living here on your own?" he asked, with something close to incredulity.

"Yes. I am."

"Then you must be mad. Young fellow like you stuck out here in this godforsaken ghost town. I'm old. Abandoned in this purgatorial place. It's expected that I should be here on my own. For all I know, I'm damned. But you're a handsome young man, with your whole life ahead of you. And living here is like being sent to Alcatraz Island. *Are* you mad?"

"My name's Martins," I said, ignoring the question. "Gil Martins."

"That isn't what I asked," he muttered.

I came down the steps of the house and held out my hand for him to shake, but he looked at it indifferently and only shook his head.

"Now really, what's the point of that?" he said. "There's no point. I mean, there's no point if, as you say, you're just staying here temporarily."

"Suit yourself."

"Well, no, not anymore," he said sadly. "Anyway, it's not you I came to see."

"Father Dyer is in an old people's home now," I said helpfully, although I could more cheerfully have told the old man to go fuck himself; he had that kind of manner. "In Texas City."

"After Galveston, that sounds like it could be an improvement."

"I'm afraid I don't know the address. But I could easily find out where it is if you wanted to visit him."

"No. That wouldn't be a good idea at all. I might actually like the place and want to move in there, too. Look, I didn't mean to disturb you. You're obviously about to go somewhere. I was just strolling by and I heard the car start. There's not much that starts around these parts. Plenty that finishes, of course, but not very much that starts. Suffice to say that it's plain you're not nearly ready for me. Not by a long way."

"I'm sorry, I don't follow you."

"No," he said pompously. "But you will. Give it time. You will."

And with a twinkle in his eye, he walked off.

"What happened to your shoes?" I called after him.

"Who needs shoes in Galveston?" Without turning his head, he waved back at me.

"Asshole," I muttered, and went down the steps and climbed into the car.

🙰

I drove north across the Galveston Causeway. This and the toll bridge over San Luis Pass to the southwest were the only two ways off the island. The toll bridge was nothing more than an improbable two-lane highway across the bay that connected one spit of shifting sand with another. In winter, when bad weather blew in off the Atlantic—which was often—it was altogether less reliable than the wider, higher, north-leading causeway.

As before, the minute I drove onto the mainland my cell phone rang. It was Ken Paris from the computer forensics lab.

"Ken," I said brightly. "Gee, it's good to talk to someone human again. Galveston is like solitary confinement in a desert island penitentiary. They've got me on forced leave so I can see the house shrink. I guess it was that or the bughouse."

"Yeah, Helen told me. How's that working out?"

"Matter of fact, I'm on my way in to see Dr. Seuss now."

"On a Sunday?"

"It's a fucking Sunday. I had no idea."

"I knew Galveston was cut off from the real world, but I assumed they still had television and newspapers."

"I wouldn't think it was safe to assume even that much. So if it is

Sunday—then what the fuck do you want, Ken? Don't you know better than to ring a guy when it's Sunday?"

"I don't tell everyone, but I like to work on a Sunday. The telephone doesn't ring. Nobody sends me any e-mails. And I don't get jerks coming in here with a plea for help because junior lost his homework on the fucking laptop."

"So I guess I should be honored that you called me."

"Not especially. But it being a Sunday and you being on forced leave 'n' all, I just figured no one else in the Bureau would give a shit if we met up for a while. It's about that laptop you dumped here last Sunday afternoon. Gaynor Allitt's laptop? The lady who did the Dutch on the Hyatt Regency blacktop?"

"Jesus, I'd forgotten all about that."

"Doesn't sound like the thing anyone forgets in a hurry."

"I mean the laptop. I'm not likely to forget her brains on the sidewalk if that's what you mean."

"Anyway, forced leave or not, Martins, I figured you were going to want to have this shit as soon as possible."

"Yeah?"

"Meet me at the Red Onion Café at twelve-thirty and I'll explain everything."

"What is it, Ken? What have you found?"

"She kept a kind of video diary, Martins. And get ready to be surprised."

❇

The Red Onion Café was halfway between the RCFL and the FBI field office, on the eastern edge of the Northwest Freeway. A pueblo-style, red concrete redoubt of a restaurant that looked a bit like the Alamo, it was a popular place with agents from the Bureau, except at

Sunday brunch, when the clientele was mostly overweight Texas families with a taste for Mexican food.

The waitress escorted me to a table in the back next to a window that looked out onto a parking lot filled with dozens of yellow trucks. Ken Paris was reading the *Houston Chronicle*. There was already a Corona beer and a plate of tortilla chips on the table and next to it an iPad with a pair of headphones plugged into the side that was obviously set up for me to look at Gaynor Allitt's video diary. As usual, Ken was wearing a loose, short-sleeve shirt that made him look as if he were going bowling. He chuckled as I sat down in front of him. I ordered a Dos Equis for myself and loosened my tie.

"Hey," he said, "you really did think it was a workday, didn't you, Agent Martins?"

"At Federal Plaza they used to say that terrorists always work on Sundays and that nothing says holidays like a pipe bomb in Times Square."

"They do like their fortune-cookie wisdom at Federal Plaza."

I clasped my hands tightly and pressed them down on the table, thinking it might help to stop me from rearranging the cutlery and condiments, or even reaching for Ken's iPad. Someone watching me might almost have thought I was praying.

"The diary? Is it on that tablet?"

"I was going to bring you crayons, but then I changed my mind."

"When I got your call this morning, I was in the process of changing my own mind," I told him. "I mean about this whole damn case. I've been seriously thinking of dropping it on account of how people have been giving me strange looks in the corridors at Justice Park Drive."

"They've been doing that for a while, Gil, before the case, only you didn't notice."

"You mean the OCD thing?"

"How's that going anyway?"

"I'm trying to keep a check on it. Of course, now that I do, it seems a lot worse than I thought it was." I paused a moment. "Feels really weird, actually."

"Good." Ken nodded. "I mean that you're trying to put a choke on that shit. It'll be a change to sit and have lunch with you and not watch the sugar packets get fixed into a neat little pile." He grinned. "The number of times I've wanted to reach across and mess it all up for you. Still, you might feel a little differently about the case when you've seen the video diary. About chucking it in, I mean."

"Let's take a look-see at what we've got."

"Let's get the important things done here first, okay? I'm starving." He waved the waitress back and we ordered our food.

"I did you a transcript to save you the trouble of making notes. And I've made a video copy for you on a flash drive. By the way, I might have called you before with this, but Gaynor Allitt wasn't using a plain-text password, but one with a hash value. That's when you apply a one-way algorithm to a password. Her password had eight characters and, with the hash, that gives you about eight billion combinations. It took our rainbow table software a while to crack. But more significantly, it would have taken someone who didn't work for the FBI or the NSA forever and maybe even longer than that."

"So, what does all that stuff mean?"

"The hash? It means she was very well informed about computer security and probably very nervous about someone stealing or breaking into her laptop, which is why she took such an unusually rigorous precaution."

"She was certainly scared about something," I said.

"Just who or what that is will probably become a little clearer when you watch the diary."

"Any evidence of sending self-destructing e-mails?" I asked.

"None at all. According to what's on the cache memory, I doubt she's even been on an SDE service site using that computer." He waited a beat. "As well as shooting the video diary, she liked filming herself naked and masturbating." He glanced around the restaurant. "But I figured they're not ready for that movie here in the Red Onion Café."

"You're kidding."

"Nope. You can look at that particular film on the flash drive if you're inclined. She might also have been using her video camera for Skype. As a matter of fact, she used Skype a lot, but her list of Skype contacts was kind of short. In fact, it had only one name on it, and that's a Skype name, so it doesn't mean much in a phone book. You could always try contacting this person by Skype to explain the problem, but that's got to be your call. Strikes me if she was Skyping while she was jerking off, then that person might be a little slow to reply."

"See the video diary first," I said. "Then decide about the Skype contact later. Did she send any of these diary entries as an attachment to an e-mail?"

"Nope. Not that I can see." He swiped the sliding arrow to unlock the iPad and pressed the video app icon to reveal a still image of Gaynor Allitt sitting in her chair facing the camera; the film was cued up and ready to view. I put the little rubber buds in my ears. Ken picked up his paper again and started to read.

Most of the front page was devoted to how the mayor had asked Houston's law enforcement agencies for a progress report on the serial killer. In spite of the very best efforts of Harlan Caulfield, the reporters had started calling the perp Saint Peter after all. Harlan was not going to be happy about that. For a moment, I pictured him angrily smoking one of his ridiculous e-cigarettes and then pressed the little arrow on Ken's iPad. But I wouldn't have minded one of those e-cigarettes myself.

あち

There were several entries over a number of days—all of the entries were conveniently dated on screen—but her appearance always stayed the same, more or less, which convinced me that the look was deliberate and calculated to create a certain impression in whoever it was Gaynor Allitt had intended the video diary for, and if that wasn't me, then it was almost certainly someone like me.

She wore a red flower behind her ear. It might have been a result of the almost indelible memory I had of her mangled body at the foot of the Hyatt, but the flower looked like a wound, as if she had been shot in the side of the head and the resulting eruption of blood had congealed in a whorl of red stamens and petals. No doubt it had been chosen to match the red nail polish, the red lipstick, and the red dress she was wearing. I wondered if perhaps the red had been symbolic— if she meant to imitate the Scarlet Woman. In the disapproving eyes of the Izrael Church of Good Men and Good Women, what Gaynor Allitt had to say would have guaranteed her the soubriquet even if the way she was dressed did not. It was just possible that she'd dressed like this when she went to church. I had my doubts, but I thought she looked good.

She sat in her study with a small clip-on microphone attached to her bosom. In her hand was a remote control on a cable. Speaking directly into the lens, she seemed nervous at first but quickly gained in confidence, with the occasional hint in her voice of Brooklyn, which was where she had come from before moving to Texas. But it was what she said that was important; and it contrasted sharply with what I'd heard her say at HPD headquarters on Travis Street.

If you're watching this video, then it means I'm dead, and either you're a member of the Izrael Church of Good Men and Good Women who has stolen my laptop or you're someone from Houston law enforcement, pos-sibly wondering what happened to me.

If you're the first, then fuck you; and please pass on my hate and de-testation to that arch practitioner of evil, Nelson Van Der Velden. In my opinion, he and the rest of you represent everything that's wrong with America and its perverted obsession with apocalyptic religion.

If you're someone from law enforcement, then welcome to my world and you have my thanks for taking the trouble to find out what happened to me. Hopefully this short film will help to answer questions you might have about my death. Please try to keep an open mind while you watch my video. I am not crazy; and I ask only for your patience while I explain myself. At the very least, make an effort to read the unpublished manu-script of a book written by me that you will also find on this laptop. The manuscript is entitled Prayer *and you shouldn't make the mistake of thinking this is some kind of religious tract and dismissing it as irrelevant to your inquiry—assuming that there is an inquiry; and if not, why not, and where the hell have you been? Didn't any of you notice that people— the enemies of the religious literalists and Christian theocrats—were dying?*

I am not a religious nut case. I'm not even religious. What you will have seen in my house is a show of religious conformity in case anyone from the Izrael Church showed up on my doorstep. Nelson Van Der Velden likes to keep tabs on all his followers and employs a thought police called the Shomrin to check up on the members of his church, to make sure that they are paying their tithes and generally living a life of which he approves. Believe me, the consequences of any nonconformity can be drastic, even lethal.

Which prompts me to counsel you to exercise caution in how you deal with these people. They're armed and dangerous, although not in any way I think you will have encountered before—but I'll get to that. I am not, however, an atheist. I want to stress that for reasons that will become clear. Yes, I do believe in God, but not for any of the usual mundane reasons.

By the way, at the end of the manuscript you'll also find a PDF file containing signed release forms that were witnessed in front of an attorney giving you formal permission to use my work as evidence in your investigation.

My name is not Gaynor Allitt, it's Esther Begleiter and I'm from Brooklyn, New York, where I was brought up as a Jew in a Satmar Hasidic Jewish family. I already knew a great deal about religious fanaticism when I came to live in Texas. I'm no longer in touch with this family so I don't suppose my death will come as the source of great regret to the parents who long ago gave up hope of my being a credit to them.

As a child, I attended Abraham Joshua Heschel High School in New York, and it had been assumed I would also attend Yeshiva University. But I had other plans, which included escaping an arranged Hasidic marriage with my second cousin because I had realized that I was a lesbian. Lesbians and Satmar Hasidism don't mix. The Torah views all homosexual behavior as an abomination. I remember trying to discuss this with my mother, who assured me that plenty of Jewish lesbians had put aside their personal feelings in the interests of becoming good wives and mothers. But I wasn't convinced, so, instead of going to Yeshiva, I broke with my family altogether and managed to get a scholarship to study psychology at Georgetown University.

After graduating, I stayed on to do research. It might have been my background but I had become particularly interested in the placebo effect of religion, which is another way of saying that I regarded all religion as an inert, medically ineffective pill intended to deceive the recipient. Being a psychologist, I was particularly interested in how prayer actually seems to change four distinct areas of the human brain: the frontal lobe, the anterior cingulum, the parietal lobe, and the limbic system. I was also intrigued to investigate claims that a specific amount of prayer each day could prevent memory loss, mental decline, and even dementia or Alzheimer's disease. It should be added, however, that none of this was prompted by a wish to prove to myself that God really existed. In fact, I was by then more or less convinced he didn't.

After handing in my research thesis, I decided to write a book about the Christian nationalist movement in America; to this end, I thought it might be a good idea to go undercover and, if I could, join a fundamentalist Christian nationalist church. Texas seemed to be the logical place to do that. During the course of my research on the neurological effects of prayer, I'd heard of a secretive Texas sect based near Houston that believed in a complete Christian theocracy and in turning the Book of Leviticus into law, and that was in favor of the execution of gay people, adulterers, abortionists, and atheists, and that not only believed in these things but actively prayed to bring them about. As it happened, the Izrael Church of Good Men and Good Women is rather more than a sect, with almost ten thousand members; and the prayers they give voice to go radically beyond what most people understand by the idea of prayer.

So a couple of years ago I left my home in Washington, changed my name, got a job in Houston as a court reporter—I figured that if I worked in psychology I might meet someone I knew and my new identity would be blown—and set about trying to become a member of the Izrael Church. Only it took a while for me to be accepted as an ordinary member of the church—which is what you are if you attend only the Sunday services— and then to become a member of a secretive prayer group called the Kavanot that has something in common with the Kabbalah and that ascribes a higher meaning to the purpose of prayer that is nothing less than an attempt to affect the very fabric of reality itself. Admission to the Kavanot requires first that you have been an ordinary member of the church for a year; second, that you pass an IQ test with a score of 132 or more—which supposedly denotes superior intelligence and makes you a *prayer power*—and third, that you are interviewed by Nelson Van Der Velden himself. He decides on whether you are suitably equipped—intellectually, spiritually, and morally—to join the Kavanot.

Having passed all three conditions, I joined the Kavanot about eighteen months ago.

Currently, there are approximately five hundred men and women in the Kavanot and Van Der Velden's aims are to make it larger and therefore more powerful. And here I'm afraid things start to become more fantastic. I could hardly believe it myself when I discovered the true character of the prayers that were being offered up to God in the Kavanot. But please try to remember, I'm not making any of this up. Just keep asking yourself if this amounts to my last will and testament, why the fuck would I lie about this?

But first let me tell you a bit about Nelson Van Der Velden.

First of all, he's the son of Robert Van Der Velden, who used to run the Prayer Pyramid of Power in Dallas. Originally, Nelson was Robert's anointed successor at the PPP, only there seems to have been a falling-out, the reasons behind which are now shrouded in secrecy. Some I know have speculated that Nelson wanted to turn the Prayer Pyramid of Power into something more than just a brand name, that he wanted to make it a spiritual reality; and it's certainly the case that the PPP was the inspiration behind the Kavanot. But others I know have suggested that it was all about money and that Nelson refused to advance his father the cash that would have staved off his creditors. Because, make no mistake about it, Nelson is a wealthy man. Each of his followers—me included—is obliged to donate a tenth of their annual income to the Izrael Church. And with a membership of ten thousand people, that quickly mounts up. I once calculated his yearly income as being between twenty and thirty million dollars. Why do his followers tithe so generously? Because Nelson prays for them. If that sounds like a poor deal, believe me, it isn't.

Nelson Van Der Velden is a very formidable intellect. As a boy, he went to Milton Academy in Massachusetts and then to Harvard Divinity School, after which he earned a doctorate in theology at Berkeley, which took him to study in Israel for a year. There he met and studied with several leading rabbis, including Rabbi Yitzhak Kaduri and the more reclusive mystic, Rabbi Shimon Dayan, who teaches his followers a means of directing the intent behind a prayer—to specify the path along which a prayer ascends in a dialogue with God in order to increase its chances of being answered favorably. In this way, every word of every prayer—indeed, every letter of every word contained in a prayer—has a precise meaning and measurable effect.

I am not sure how it was that Nelson was able to ingratiate himself so effectively with these two influential rabbis, and there is certainly some detective work to be done on this in Israel; but it may have something to do with the fact that Nelson's command and understanding of the Torah is close to perfect. He speaks and reads Hebrew fluently. Consequently, the story goes that he was able to impress these two rabbis in a way that no Jewish scholar had ever done. Now, I don't know very much about the Torah, but it seems that there are certain hidden, mystical aspects called Sitrei Torah and Razei Torah. And I believe there's another term that covers Jewish esoteric knowledge, which is called Chochmah Nistara. But the Hebrew names aren't important. What is important is that Talmudic doctrine forbids the public teaching of this esoteric knowledge; in the Mishnah—or Oral Torah, as it's sometimes known—rabbis were warned to teach the mystical creation doctrines to only one student who was found worthy. The gossip around the Izrael Church is that Nelson Van Der Velden was that student.

To be honest, I'm not sure what these secrets are that were supposedly revealed to Nelson Van Der Velden, but the quiet consensus among those within the Kavanot who are prepared to talk about these things is that these were nothing less than the secrets that God revealed to Adam. According to a rabbinic midrash—which is a homiletic teaching—God *created the universe through ten* sephirot *or* attributes. *This is also common to the Kabbalah.*

I hit the pause button on Ken's iPad and snatched out the earphones as the waitress arrived with my beer and our lunch. Ken put down his newspaper and glanced across at the screen to read the number under the progress bar. I forked some food into my mouth, replaced the earphones, and hit the play arrow again.

The secrets that were supposedly revealed to Nelson include the true nature of Adam and Eve and stuff about the Garden of Eden and the Tree of Life. I was going to have to get used to the idea that Gaynor Allitt's real name was Esther Begleiter.

But the really important revelation from Nelson's point of view was the seventy-two-letter name of God that was entrusted to him by Rabbi Dayan. This word was the same word that Moses used to speak to command the angels, to turn rivers into blood, to part the waters of the Red Sea and destroy the Egyptian army, to kill all the cattle in Egypt, and to kill all firstborn Egyptians. Jewish mystics used this word for meditation purposes. But, of course, no such constraints applied to Nelson Van Der Velden, and as soon as he had returned from the Holy Land to the United States, Nelson decided to use the name of God in prayer to suit his own ends. Having said all that, he keeps the name a secret known only to him. I myself have never heard him utter the name because he does so in a special little booth that stands in the center of the Kavanot, a little like the prayer closet I have here in my house. I'll say something about that, as well, in a minute.

Anyway, this kind of esoteric Hebraic prayer, or empowered prayer— that's what Nelson calls this—it didn't work at all; and it had to be pointed out to Nelson—perhaps by his father—that he wasn't Moses. It took further study of the Kabbalah to convince Nelson that what he needed was his own Prayer Pyramid of Power to add psychic energy—his words, not mine—to his own prayers. Thus, the establishment of the Izrael Church and the Kavanot.

When I joined the group, it was mostly devoted to its own profit and welfare. Van Der Velden would lead us all in empowered prayer to increase the wealth or health of the group. None of it made any sense to me, and I was Jewish. I mean, I'd heard of Kabbalah and the sephirot but never anything about the seventy-two-letter name of God and the Mosaic power of prayer. Of course, that might have been because I was a woman and that kind of knowledge would never ever be entrusted to a Jewish woman. But that's another story.

At first I was entirely skeptical. Frankly, I thought they were all mad. But then something weird happened that freaked me out. Actually, there were several weird things that happened, but the first was that one of the Kavanot members who was suffering from inoperable cancer got better after we all prayed for him. Then someone else won the Texas state lottery after we'd all prayed for his business to turn around. Of course, I was already disposed to think of this in the scientific terms I was used to as a psychologist, to dismiss all of this as a prayer placebo. Except for one thing that sounds ridiculous, I know, but it could hardly be denied that you could really feel a sense of a power moving among us when we took our prayers to God as part of the Kavanot. It was really quite uncanny. And quite inexplicable. After a while, it seemed that there were lots of good things happening to people who belonged to the Kavanot. Even to me.

The fact is I fell in love with someone; this was a woman, of course, so we had to be really careful as, like most Christian theocrats, Nelson strongly disapproves of homosexuality. The woman's name was Agnes. She had been a member of the Kavanot for longer than I had and she's what changed my mind about a lot of things. Mostly it was she who convinced me that I had been wrong about the Izrael Church because I'd never been in love with a woman who had been in love with me. So I put *aside my ideas of writing a book about Christian nationalism and threw myself into my love for Agnes and, by extension—for had he not brought us together?—God and the Izrael Church. I became like all the rest of them.*

But then Nelson began to grow more ambitious in the things he told us we had to pray for and in the way we prayed. First of all, we were taught to pray in shifts around the clock at the church and at home. Some of us were told to acquire a closet to pray in so we could pray undisturbed. Sometimes we prayed alone for hours on end, but sometimes we were allowed to have a prayer partner with us; naturally, I chose Agnes and there were times when we sat in my prayer closet, or hers, and our prayers ended with us in each other's arms. Those were happy times for Agnes and me. We felt that God could hardly disapprove of the great love we felt for each other.

But we were much less comfortable with what we had to pray for now. It had come to Nelson in a vision, he said, that we should start to bring about God's kingdom on this earth—his Great Reckoning, the Bible calls it—that we should begin the destruction of the unrighteous in order to prepare the way for the coming of the Lord. In retrospect, it seems to me that this idea of using prayer as a lethal weapon was always one of Nelson's aims. You see, the name of the church hasn't anything to do with the state or the children of Israel as might easily be supposed. Nothing like it. Izrael or Azrael—the name means He Who Helps God—is also the name of the archangel of death, not just in biblical tradition but also in Islamic theology and Sikhism. According to Nelson, Izrael is none other than a fallen angel who, in spite of being a demon—that's the nature of a fallen angel—is reverent of and subordinate to the will of God and has always done God's dirty work—from killing Egypt's firstborn, or annihilating those children who were foolish enough to laugh at the prophet Elisha for having a bald head, to killing those people who were unlucky enough to have caught a glimpse of the Ark of the Covenant.

This sounds crazy, I know, and I hardly took any of this seriously until the first prayer victim—that's what Nelson calls them—until Dr. Clifford Richardson died suddenly. He was one of the country's leading obstetricians and ran a private abortion clinic called the Silphium Clinic in Washington, D.C. That might just have been a coincidence, but when our next prayer victim, Peter Ekman, also died suddenly at his home in New York, I know that Agnes and I began to feel afraid. Not just of Nelson Van Der Velden, but of God himself. For it seemed that we had unlocked a dreadful power that had nothing at all to do with the Christianity we—or, to be more accurate, that Agnes—had embraced. This same fear and what we had read in Leviticus left Agnes convinced that we had been deluded in our notion that God might approve of our love. The more we studied the scriptures, the clearer became her impression that our love was damned. Agnes herself became very depressed about this, and with the death of a third victim, Professor Willard Davidoff, following our prayers for his destruction, she became suicidal.

You might ask why we simply didn't leave the church and move away. Well, two people did: Norris Clark and Brent Pitino, both of whom met untimely and horrible deaths that Nelson took great delight in announcing before a meeting of the Kavanot. Clark was found dead on a railway line after wandering in front of an express train, while Pitino was killed after falling off a motorboat and being chewed up by the screws. At least those are the official explanations of what happened. If you're still there, Mr. Lawman, then you might like to check out those two deaths for yourself. By all accounts, there wasn't much left for anyone to put in a casket. Which certainly fits with what Nelson has told us about Azrael. If he doesn't scare you to death, he tears you to pieces, just like those kids in the Book of Kings.

There had been no prayers in the Kavanot for their deaths; Nelson is too shrewd for that; but lately he has been able to identify those members who have the greatest capacity for powerful prayer and it is generally held

that Nelson has established an ultrasecret prayer group within the Kava-
not to carry out his express bidding in these matters. To punish those who
disobey him or try to leave the church.

After that, fear gripped us all. And three weeks ago, unable to live
with the guilt of what she thought we were doing or the terror of what
might happen to her if she left the church, Agnes took her own life. She
opened her veins in the bath.

Esther Begleiter swallowed stiffly and then stopped the recording
although, according to the progress bar, there were several more minutes to come, and I took the opportunity to pause the recording for a
moment and devote my attention to the food.

"You done?" inquired Ken.

"I got some minutes left here. We can talk in a minute."

I hit the play arrow again; the picture shifted with a cut that hardly
looked professional; and when Esther came back, the time ID in the
corner of the picture showed a whole day had passed.

Sorry about that, she said—it was almost as if she had been talking
directly to me and I wouldn't have been all that surprised if she had
addressed me by my name. *But it was the death of my friend and lover,*
Agnes Reilly, that prompted me to begin my book, Prayer, *again and to*
make this video. If you want to check my story, please do. You'll find
nearly everything I've said can be verified. That might even include this,
our latest prayer victim. Currently the Kavanot is praying for the death of
Philip Osborne. Check the time and date signature on this recording,
and by the time this is viewed, he, too, will perhaps be dead. But I guess
these things can be faked, can't they? So, to offer some more proof in this
regard.

Esther held up a copy of the *Houston Chronicle*.

To help verify today's date, here is a copy of this morning's newspa-
per and—"

Next she produced a small transistor radio and turned it on.

And this is KPRC AM 950 on the radio. She paused. *But there's a news bulletin coming up, so you can check that out, too. Remember what's being said here; I'm telling you that Philip Osborne, who's still alive, might well be dead by the time you view this recording.*

She paused as the news bulletin on the radio gave the date and time of day.

But I could have faked this, too, right? Yes, I'm sure it could be done. So maybe I need something else to prove what I'm saying is true. Okay. I think I have it. The answer is just a few blocks away, I think, and given that this is a Monday . . .

This time the cut looked more professional, to an exterior shot pulling back from a giant announcement board. Esther Begleiter was at Minute Maid Park, at a ball game between the Houston Astros and the Cincinnati Reds; and after focusing on the time and the score, she turned the little camera on herself. The game was sparsely attended; but that was hardly unusual for the Astros. She appeared to be seated in the club box area, right behind the diamond.

There, she said. *That should be easy enough for you to check. Maybe now you'll believe what I'm saying. Look, I hope I'm wrong. I sincerely hope it doesn't happen. But right now, July 25, I'm telling you that the Izrael Church of Good Men and Good Women is praying for the death of Philip Osborne. So if the poor bastard does die, then you'll have to believe me, right?*

The film cut back to Esther's study at her house on Gregg Street.

Look, I know this all sounds totally nuts. Nobody is more aware of that than I am. I'm a scientist after all. In spite of that, you probably think I belong in the bughouse and I can't say I blame you. But if you are a cop, then let me lay this out for you in a way that even a cop can understand.

You've got item number one: Three enemies of the Christian right— Dr. Clifford Richardson, Peter Ekman, and Professor Willard Davidoff— have died suddenly. Perhaps you've already written those three deaths off as nothing more than an unfortunate coincidence. But I'm telling you that Nelson Van Der Velden and members of the Izrael Church, including me, prayed for those deaths to happen.

You've got item number two: Two members of the Izrael Church—Norris Clark and Brent Pitino—have died violent accidental deaths.

You've got item number three: A third member of the Izrael Church, Agnes Reilly, committed suicide because she felt guilty about what had happened, guilty and terribly afraid that something similar might happen to her.

You've got item number four: Members of the Izrael Church are currently praying for the death of Philip Osborne.

You've got item number five: The manuscript of my unpublished book. Please read it; the book contains a lot more details about what I've described in this film.

And last of all you've got item number six: That's me. As I explained at the beginning of this film, if you're watching, then it means I must be dead. And if I'm dead, then you can bet it wasn't natural causes. You see, I've made this film because I'm frightened that something will happen to me the way it happened to Clark and Pitino. The thought police at the Izrael Church know that Agnes and I were close. They've already questioned me about her death as if they suspect I think the same way about things as she did and that I also feel terribly guilty, which I do. I can't tell you how bad I feel about everything. And, of course, I miss Agnes desperately. So much so that I'm not sure I can go on without her. I don't believe I'm a prayer victim myself. Not yet, anyway. I would have felt that, I'm certain of it. But it's what I fear the most. From what Agnes told me, I only know a little of what happens when you become a prayer victim. And she was genuinely terrified of that happening to her. She told me that Almighty God's tame demon Azrael doesn't strike immediately. At Nelson's instruction, he takes his time and prefers to strike the fear of the Lord into the soul of the nominated victim. Sometimes Nelson takes a

hand in this process himself and through some complicated offshore In-
ternet service provider—I think it's in China—he sends his prayer victims
an e-mail informing them that the Angel of the Lord has marked them
out for death. After that, it's just a matter of time but never more than
thirty days. I'm not sure why that should be so, but it is. Richardson,
Ekman, and Davidoff were all dead within a month of their nomination.
Oh, yes, I didn't explain that, did I? You are nominated for death by the
Kavanot and then a vote is taken. I've made a list of everyone that has
been nominated so far, which I wasn't supposed to do; the whole business
of prayer victims is treated as a matter of great secrecy with the Izrael
Church and there are even people who worship there every week who
don't know about this activity. Anyway, you'll find the list in my Bible
inside my prayer closet. It's in no particular order, although the first four
names on the list are all prayer victims. After Osborne, it's anyone's guess
who'll come next.

Please. Stop them if you can. For me? But be careful, too. You have
no idea of what you're dealing with.

As Esther Begleiter's short film ended, I uttered a long bewildered
sigh and leaned back on my armchair. The Nelson Van Der Velden
described by her sounded as if he were a million miles away from the
guy pictured on the front of the *Chronicle* giving a million dollars to a
children's hospital. I sensed I was back where I was when I'd gone on a
month's enforced leave. There was no real evidence in what Esther
Begleiter had said. Not a word of it could have been substantiated to the
satisfaction of the assistant district attorney, let alone a grand jury. Even
the time ID prediction that Philip Osborne was going to die looked like
David Blaine street magic. There's a trick to foretelling the future like
that; and more often than not, when Penn & Teller have explained how
it's done, it always looks Homer Simpson simple. Surely no one in Justice Park Drive would ever believe I was on the way back to mental
fitness if I turned up at the office suggesting that we take her claim

seriously. I could hear Gisela Delillo now. *Go home, Martins. You are sick. See the Head Fed. Forget this stupid obsession of yours. The woman sounds as mad as you are.* The Chief Division Counsel would laugh me out of his office. Doug Corbin would tell Gisela I told you so, Gary Greene would mutter some crap about my not being a team player, and Chuck Worrall would write a damning comment in my personnel file that would effectively end my career.

I tugged out the earphones, tossed them on top of the iPad.

"What's your opinion, Ken?"

"She's crazy, of course. Has to be. Prayer isn't about getting six numbers in the lottery. The last time I prayed and expected a result was 1978, when my old man was ill in the hospital. I prayed real hard for him to get better. He didn't." He shrugged. "I never won the lottery, either."

I emptied the bowl of sugar packets into my hand and started to play solitaire with them.

"You won't find the answer there," said Ken.

"I'm looking to establish an order to how things are," I said. "And I'm beginning to see that this habit of mine is just a metaphor for what any detective does. So, what the fuck? Maybe when I've figured out what's happening here, I'll stop doing it. For a while, anyway."

"Whatever."

I scratched my head as if hoping that might provoke my brain to arrive at some sort of strategy on how to proceed. It didn't.

But it occurred to me that I might just provoke Nelson Van Der Velden. After all, it was a Sunday.

TWENTY

After lunch, I went to a movie at the Cinemark in Webster, just off the Gulf Freeway only a couple of miles west of the Izrael Church of Good Men and Good Women. It was somewhere dark to sit for a while and think, which in Houston is always difficult. There was a McAlister's deli next door to the theater, and after the movie had drawn to its interminable conclusion, I went in there and had a coffee and a pastry for supper. I read the first chapter of *Prayer*, which was on the flash drive that Ken had given me, but it was kind of dry and certainly not as interesting as her tape; then again, it was only the first chapter and it certainly didn't deter me from my intended course of action. While I'd been watching the movie, a number I didn't recognize had called my cell several times, but I hadn't heard the phone ring in my pocket. Whoever it was, I didn't bother to call them back. I had other things on my mind, like what I was planning to do when I went back to the Izrael Church. Almost certainly this was going to get me into trouble, one way or the other. I was full of doubt, of course, but only the stupid are always cocksure and certain of what the fuck they're doing. That's what I told myself as I drove into the church parking lot, which was full of cars and more or less empty of people because, according to my watch, the service was already well under way. For once it seemed as if I'd timed things perfectly.

"It's not that you're any better than a lot of other bastards in the Bureau, Martins," I said aloud, as I got out of the car and opened the trunk. "It just takes a while longer for you to give up on something. Dumb when it doesn't work out for you and smart when it does. Maybe that's what it takes to be good at this fucking job. I don't know. Hell, I haven't thought any of this all out clearly. I can't. I don't know enough. Not yet anyway. But this'll stir the pot, right enough. I'll be damned if it doesn't."

I took off my shirt and felt the sun like a laser on my bare skin before I slipped on a blue T-shirt with the letters FBI in clear yellow on the back and a Bureau roundel on the front. I clipped my gold badge to the front of my belt, put on my aviator sunglasses, checked the Glock on my hip, tucked Ken's flash drive into the pocket of my trousers, and walked calmly toward the front door. This time I wasn't looking to go unnoticed. I felt like a fox that was about to enter a hen house. I glanced up at the angel Azrael on the bas-relief above the front door. He looked rather less benign and even more muscular than before. This was an angel who did a bit more than just sing the glory of God and bring good tidings of peace and joy to all mankind at Christmastime; this was an angel with a fucking attitude. And if the expression on his face wasn't enough to make you wary of him, there was something about the broken manacle on his ankle that put me in mind of an escaped felon, like Charlton Heston in *Ben-Hur*.

One of the stewards near the entrance walked toward me with his hand held up in the style of a traffic cop. He was wearing sunglasses like mine and I could see the whole parking lot—myself included—reflected in each lens as clearly as if someone had drawn it on using Photoshop.

"I'm sorry, sir," he said, "the service has already started."

I opened my special agent's wallet and held it up in front of his face the way we'd been taught to do at the Academy. Show it like it means something, was what they told you, like it's a presidential fucking order.

"You can't go in," said the steward.

"This says differently," I said, and then put the heel of my hand on my holster for added emphasis.

But the greeter was already backing off; and now all I saw reflected in his sunglasses were the letters FBI so I knew he could see I meant business.

I pushed the heavy glass door open and walked inside. My footsteps echoed on the floor like the sound of a longcase clock and cool air brushed against my face as if the angel outside had just flapped his wings. Beyond a set of double doors I could hear that Nelson Van Der Velden had already started his sermon; in his smooth and folksy voice he was talking about the *Titanic* and how if they'd only heeded the warnings about all the icebergs then the fifteen hundred people who lost their lives might have been saved and how it was time that people started listening to God's warnings if similar disasters were to be averted. It was good advice and I might have done well to have listened to it.

I put an arm of my glasses into the neck of my T-shirt and stepped into the auditorium. At the sight of the several thousand people who were present, I paused and glanced around for a seat as near to the front as possible and, seeing one, walked down the aisle. It suited me just fine that my arrival did not go unnoticed; that was part of my so-called strategy. A lot of people did a double take as they saw me and I hoped that Ruth would be one of them who was wondering what the hell was going to happen when I reached the front. I was kind of interested in finding that out myself.

Nelson Van Der Velden saw me—by the time I neared the front, he could hardly have avoided seeing me—but to give him credit, he hardly

paused at all and, for a moment, carried on with his sermon as if nothing had happened.

I walked to the end of the row where I had identified a spare seat
and, as politely as I could, I pushed my way along to it. I sat down and
tried to make myself as comfortable as you can be when you're wearing
a Glock on your hip and everyone is looking at you, not all of them in
a kindly and Christian way. If there was one thing I'd learned from
Ruth, it was that the only guns that Texans really minded were the ones
worn openly in church.

"Don't make a big deal of your problems," Van Der Velden told his
congregation. "Make a big deal of praising God. That's what we're all
here for. Isn't that right? All of us come into God's presence with praise
because you've got to give him something to work with. If he's going to
help you, you've got to magnify his glory. You've heard what David says
in the Psalms. He says, 'The Lord is my very present help in times of
trouble.' That's right, he's always there to help us, but only because we
come here to give him what's rightly his: our worship and our praise. It's
true of most of us, although I'm none too sure about that gentleman
who just sat down in the third row." Van Der Velden chuckled. "The
guy from the FBI? Did you see him? You know, when I was a kid, there
used to be a TV series called *Dragnet*. So I've heard of Sergeant Friday;
but it could be that we've got ourselves a Sergeant Sunday. Let's
hope so."

Everyone, Van Der Velden included, thought that was very funny;
even I managed a smile.

"I guess that Sergeant Sunday knows more about times of trouble
than most. You might say trouble is his business. And it might just be
that he's in more trouble than any of us can imagine. And that he just
felt the need to come here and be with us all. So, you're very welcome,
Sergeant Sunday. Hey, mister, stand up and say hello. Come on, don't

be shy. Nobody gets to be shy in the presence of the Lord. Stand up and take a bow."

I fixed a rictus on my face and stood up, turned around, and bowed stiffly at the congregation before sitting down again. But Van Der Velden was hardly finished with me.

"You know, after Waco, the FBI is hardly the most popular institution of Big Government in Texas. You might say its agents are about as popular as the tax gatherers were in Jesus's time. Not that *they're* exactly popular now, either. Collecting people's taxes has never been the most respected career choice a guy could make. You'll remember what the Pharisees said to Jesus about them in Luke, when a tax gatherer called Levi decided to give a great feast in the Lord's honor. The Pharisees said, 'Hey, Jesus, why do you hang out with the tax gatherers and the sinners?' And Jesus said unto them, 'They that are whole have no need of the physician, but they that are sick. I came not to call the righteous but sinners to repentance.' So, I say again to our friend Sergeant Sunday from the FBI, 'Sir, you're very welcome here, to worship God with us this evening.' And I hope that everyone in this church will go out of their way after this service to tell him just that."

All of the people seated around me smiled or nodded in agreement; one of them shook my hand; and I felt real welcome—almost.

"Praise the Lord," said Van Der Velden. "One of the things I like most about the gospels is God's sense of humor. The way he turns stuff around on the people who are trying their hardest to trip him up. Me, I always imagine there's a twinkle in his eye when he outsmarts them. And it's one of the things that makes the Bible such a great book to read, isn't it?

"Yes, sir, I love my Bible. I read a lot of other stuff, too. Sports, of course. But I also read a lot about science: *Popular Science, Scientific American*. Richard Dawkins. Stephen Hawking. No, really. You might say that I like to keep a close eye on what the opposition is up to." He chuckled again; and so did the congregation. "One of the things that amuses me about scientists is the way they'll twist themselves into knots to look for a scientific explanation for something that is staring them in the face. You've heard of the expression 'nature abhors a vacuum.' Well, so does science, which has spent almost three thousand years trying explain the idea of empty space in the universe. Aristotle said the universe was filled with an invisible medium he called the ether. So did Sir Isaac Newton. If you'll permit me another joke, it was Newton who first made something out of nothing, with his laws of motion in space.

"Today, you've got quantum physicists trying to get us to take them seriously when they come up with what are some pretty nonsensical conclusions about that same space, which they now want us to call dark energy. They tell us now that a quantum vacuum is a vacuum that isn't really a vacuum on account of the fact that it contains an infinite amount of this same dark energy. Dark energy is what you'd have left after you take out all of the galaxies of stars and planets that—some of these scientists will tell you—amount to about 70 percent of the mass of the universe. And of course, some think that and some think this and about all they can agree on is that they don't agree about anything very much. More than a few of these scientists even want us to accept the idea that they may actually need to come up with a whole new physics just to reconcile all of the contradictions that exist in the physics we already have. And let's not mention all of the money they want to spend. They've already blown millions of dollars inventing something called the Large Hadron Collider to find out about, you guessed it— *nothing*. It's a mystery, they say, this nothing. Because while nature seems to abhor a vacuum, it doesn't seem to mind a quantum vacuum. So that's all right, then."

Van Der Velden chuckled again.

"Can you imagine the howls there would be if Christians did that?

If we came up with a whole new Bible to explain some of the things they say we can't explain? We'd never hear the end of it, would we? Now, if all of this seems like much ado about nothing, then you'd probably be right. Because I think you'll agree with me that Christians already know what to call this invisible energy in the universe. We already have an explanation for how to make something out of nothing. And we sure don't need a new physics to do it. There's nothing mysterious about the identity of this invisible force, is there? We sure don't call it dark energy, or a quantum vacuum, or the uncertainty principle, or the Higgs particle. Maybe one of those scientists was beginning to get the idea when he called it the God particle. But then we knew about that all along, didn't we? We've already got the best explanation in the world for how to explain what can't be explained. We're talking about God. If those scientists are happy with a big fat nothing in their lives, then so be it, but me, I prefer something better. If you want a reason for why everything happens in the universe, you sure can't beat Almighty God. They've all been looking in the wrong place. Because all of the answers to the universe and everything are right under our noses. They're in the Holy Bible. This Bible."

Van Der Velden grinned and held up his Bible, which seemed to be the cue for everyone in the congregation to stand and do the same, and to repeat a mantra that sounded as if he and they had said it many times before. I stood up and considered holding my FBI ID wallet in the air—in its black leather cover it was almost as big as a small Testament—and then rejected the idea as perhaps a provocative step too far; so I folded my arms and waited.

"Because I believe that this Bible contains the revealed and incorruptible word of God," they all said. "I believe what the Bible tells me—"

"That the Father Almighty created heaven and earth," said Van Der Velden.

"I believe what the Bible tells me," said everyone.

"That by him all things are made through Christ our Lord, who was crucified for our sins, that all prayers are answered," said Van Der Velden.

"I believe what the Bible tells me," said everyone.

"That Christ rose from the dead and ascended into heaven."

"I believe what the Bible tells me."

"That he shall come to judge the quick and the dead."

"I believe what the Bible tells me."

"About the resurrection of the body and life everlasting. Amen. Let me hear it: Did you receive the message today?"

"Yes," they clamored.

"Let me hear it: Did you receive it today?"

"Yes!"

"Amen and praise the Lord. Thanks for coming. Thanks for listening. Bless you all."

The organ struck up with something loud and grand, the choir joined in as if the Messiah had phoned in to say he was on his way, and the service was over. People started to shake my hand and to clap me on the shoulder as if I were the prodigal son.

"I guess you must have come straight from work," said one.

"You on duty after this?" said another.

"Something like that," I answered politely, and made my way toward the figure of Frank Fitzgerald, Nelson Van Der Velden's gatekeeper.

Fitzgerald was standing by an elevator at the back of the church auditorium that led up to the pastor's Bond-movie suite of offices. He was stockier than I remembered and, what with the black suit and the broken nose and the earpiece and the way his hands were clasped in front of him, he looked less like a church elder and more like a security guard in a nightclub. He regarded me with distaste and, given the way I was dressed, I couldn't exactly blame him.

"Kind of discourteous, don't you think—you dressed like that to come in here?" He turned and operated the elevator with a key. The doors opened immediately. "This is a church, mister, not a crack den." He inserted the same key, and when the doors closed, he pressed the only button.

"Haven't you heard, Frank? Religion is the opium of the people. Good for keeping people quiet."

"So is television. You might just as well ask people to stop being human as hope they'll ever give up the things that make them feel happy."

"Religion sure didn't make me happy."

"And so now you're what? An atheist?"

I nodded.

Fitzgerald snorted his contempt. "How's that working out for you?"

"Just fine," I lied.

Fitzgerald said something, but the sound of the doors opening again meant I didn't hear it; either that or I wasn't meant to hear it.

"You'll have to leave the hog's leg with me," he said. "If you want to see the pastor."

He ushered me to go ahead of him into Van Der Velden's office.

"No can do," I said. "This stays on my hip even when I'm in the shower. That's just Bureau regulations."

"The pastor's got his own regulations, too," said Fitzgerald. "This is where I come in."

I might have ignored him except that there was a SIG Sauer automatic in his hand. It had a little American flag engraved on the side and it was pointed at me.

"Guns make him nervous," he added.

"Maybe we have something in common after all," I said. "Guns make me nervous, too. So why don't you put that one down before you get yourself into trouble?"

"No, it's you who's in trouble, my friend. Mr. Brick Agent operating on his own. You're not supposed to do that, are you? Just in case someone gets the drop on you like this?" He winced. "I know. You see, when I'm not here looking after the pastor, I work for the Department of Homeland Security. Coast Guard."

"So you're kind of like a bodyguard."

"No, I am a bodyguard. About the only place I don't watch out for him is when he's preaching and when he's playing tennis at the Houstonian Club."

So that was where I'd seen Van Der Velden, at the Houstonian Club; and the reason I hadn't recognized him before was that he'd been dressed in tennis whites.

"I'd do as he says if I were you," said a voice.

I glanced around and saw Nelson Van Der Velden come into the enormous room.

"Mr. Fitzgerald can be a hard man to contradict. Especially with a weapon in his hand."

"That's not a very Christian outlook he's got there," I observed.

"On the contrary," said Van Der Velden. "In the Book of Nehemiah it says of the Jews who were building the walls of Jerusalem, 'Those which were building the wall, and those that did bear burdens, with those that loaded, every one with one of his hands wrought in the work, and with the other hand held a weapon.'"

"Well, gee, I guess that's all right, then," I said. "You know, if he takes his orders from you, then it could be said you're going to be in the same shit he is."

"Here," he said, coming over to my back and calmly taking the Glock from my holster. "Let me help you with that."

I might have stopped him but for the SIG that was still leveled at my head; and I didn't doubt that Van Der Velden was right about Fitzgerald; he had the air of a man who knew how to use a firearm.

Van Der Velden lifted the automatic, dropped the nineteen-shot magazine into his hand, and began to shuck the shells into his desk drawer. Clearly, he knew what he was doing, too, but then, in Texas even babies can handle a firearm and sometimes do. When the magazine was empty, he slotted it back into the Glock and returned the gun to me.

"You know, I can't remember if the Reverend Billy Graham employed a bodyguard, but I'm betting not," I said.

"I've had death threats."

"I'm beginning to understand why."

"I really don't think understanding is your strong suit, Agent Martins," observed Van Der Velden. "Otherwise you'd hardly have turned up in my church looking like that. What's the big idea? Were you trying to be offensive?"

"Maybe," I said.

"Are you wearing a wire, perhaps?" asked Van Der Velden. "Frank?"

I shook my head, but Fitzgerald went ahead and searched me for one all the same.

"He's clean."

Fitzgerald holstered his gun and, with much less grace, so did I.

Van Der Velden glanced at his bodyguard. "It's all right, Frank. You can go. I don't think Sergeant Sunday is going to try to arrest me now."

He shrugged at me.

"That's what it looks as though you were planning to do. Wouldn't you agree?"

"If it is, then you're resisting arrest, and you're in a lot of trouble, Pastor. Wouldn't *you* agree?"

"That's the second time you've suggested that," said Van Der Velden. "And it doesn't sound any more plausible the second time."

Fitzgerald nodded at his boss and left the room.

"You see, Agent Martins," added the pastor, "right now, it's your

word against a man of God's. A man of God who has some social standing in this state." He smiled and sat down behind the desk. "Somehow
I don't think that your superiors are going to take kindly to your being
here, dressed like gangbusters. After all, I've got about eight thousand
witnesses to your insensitivity. That's not the FBI way, is it? Not since
Waco. And aren't there some operational guidelines on how you people handle an investigation when a church is involved? I believe you're
obliged to seek the approval of your own legal counsel."

"You're very well informed, Pastor."

"After our last meeting, I had my lawyer check up on exactly what
you're allowed to do."

"I'll bet you did. But since you bring them up, I'd only be in breach
of those operational guidelines if I was investigating you undercover;
and I'm hardly that, am I?"

"No, I agree. You could never be described as acting undercover."
He nodded. "Yes. Now I begin to understand your thinking, perhaps."

"There's that," I said. "And the fact that maybe I wanted to get a
reaction out of you, Van Der Velden."

"Which begs the question, why? The last time you were here, I
think I answered all of your questions about the unfortunate Miss Allitt
very politely, did I not?"

"You were very polite," I said. "Just not very truthful."

"I don't doubt that you have a good reason for saying that, Agent
Martins."

I tossed him the thumb drive on which Ken Paris had made a digital copy of Esther Begleiter's recording.

"This is my good reason. A little home movie Gaynor Allitt made
before she killed herself. I made you a copy of your very own."

"I assume this movie has something to do with me," said Van Der
Velden.

I nodded.

"I also assume that you mean me to watch it now, is that right?"

"That's right, Pastor."

"And I will gladly do so, if only to humor you, sir; after that, I will even answer any tiresome questions you may have regarding this unfortunate woman and put your mind at rest regarding my relationship with her, following which we can perhaps both get back to our respective lives as quickly as possible. Is that satisfactory to you?"

"Entirely. You express it very clearly, Pastor."

"That is my calling, Agent Martins. Just as it is yours to be a royal pain in the ass." He held up the thumb drive. "I can just plug it in, right?"

"That's right."

"Computers are not my strong suit."

Van Der Velden flicked the cordless mouse on his enormous desk and awakened the screen of his computer; then he leaned below the desktop to fit the thumb drive into a USB port.

"I'd have thought it would take some expertise to be able to send one of your prayer victims an anonymous self-destructing e-mail," I said.

Van Der Velden ignored me for a moment. He moved the mouse on a mat that said TAKE IT TO THE LORD IN PRAYER: BUT DON'T GET UPSET IF HE DOESN'T SAY YES, clicked on the file containing Esther Begleiter's video, placed a pair of gold-rimmed glasses on his face, and leaned back in his expensive office chair.

"Is that what she alleges? Miss Allitt?"

I had to hand it to him. He looked as cool as if I had just accused him of arguing that the Earth is round.

"Watch the video."

As the film began and Van Der Velden heard Esther describe him as an "arch practitioner of evil," the pastor shot me a reproachful look that was about as fake as his alleged visions of the Messiah.

"I don't mind listening to some criticism of myself and this church—we live in a democracy, after all—but I really don't see why I should be abused while I'm doing so."

"Just watch the video," I said patiently.

Van Der Velden made a holy-looking steeple out of his fingers and tapped them together thoughtfully. Most of the time he paid the film close attention and, once, he even wrote something down. It was probably a note for his lawyer when he contacted the Bureau to complain about me, to tell Chuck that I was a disgrace to the Bureau and sacrilegious, too—that I deserved to be suspended or investigated myself. I was ready for that. I figured that my so-called mental condition—occasioned by too much overwork leading to the successful arrest of the HIDDEN group and the prevention of a terrorist atrocity on the streets of Houston—would probably be enough to get me off the hook with maybe not much more than a severe reprimand. Maybe.

What I wasn't ready for was what happened next.

Please, said Esther Begleiter, in her last words to camera, *stop them if you can. For me? But be careful, too. You have no idea of what you're dealing with.*

Van Der Velden nodded as if in appreciation of what he had just sat through and then switched off his Windows Media Player. He was smiling a strange sort of smile.

"That's for sure," he said.

"I'm sorry?"

"You undoubtedly will be, Agent Martins, before this week is out."

I grinned. "This is the bit where you tell me that you're going to report me to my superiors. Go right ahead, Van Der Velden. I'll take my chances."

Van Der Velden laughed. "I'm not talking about any earthly superior, Agent Martins. After watching Miss Allitt's home movie, surely you must realize that."

"Oh?" I smiled.

"I thought you believed in God."

"Whatever gave you that idea?"

"You did. The last time we talked you said you worshipped over at Lakewood Church."

"No, I said I went there. But I stopped worshipping there a long time ago."

"Why? Because you ceased to believe in God?"

"Do you?"

"Do I believe in God? Hmm. What kind of God? The God of Jesus? Some bearded, grandfatherly figure who holds the whole world in the palm of his big hand like some heavenly Santa Claus? Slow to anger, abounding in love and compassion?" Van Der Velden smiled a wry sort of smile as if that image amused him and took off his glasses. "Or the God of Moses? I assume you must have read enough of the Old Testament to know what that particular God is like, Agent Martins. He's a very different proposition. What does Deuteronomy say? For the Lord thy God is a consuming fire, even a jealous God. The kind of muscular God who hardens the pharaoh's heart against allowing the Israelites to leave Egypt just so that he can destroy the whole Egyptian army—'that the Egyptians may know that I am the Lord.'"

"I take it that's the kind of God you believe in."

"Oh, yes. And obviously so did Miss Allitt. Or Miss Begleiter, as I suppose I should now call her. She believed. She believed very much. She was certain that what we're doing here is real. Or did you really think that there was some more scientific explanation for what happened to Mr. Osborne and those other godless men?"

"Isn't there?"

"If there was, then surely the FBI would have found it. Instead, you're here, sniffing around like a baffled dog without the slightest clue about what you're up against. By the way, if I were you, I really wouldn't go around saying he doesn't exist. God doesn't like that. It might be better for you if you stopped saying such misguided things."

"Take my advice, Van Der Velden, and stick to Sunday sermons. The people you preach to are more gullible than I am."

"You think I'm just another cracker-barrel evangelist, like your own pastor at Lakewood, Mr. Osteen. But you won't think that when the angel of death comes for your soul tomorrow evening." He bowed his head for a moment, pinched the bridge of his nose, and closed his eyes. Then he said, "Amen." After a deep exhalation, he opened his eyes again and nodded.

"Threatening a federal officer with death is a serious crime." I smiled.

"Oh, it's no threat. You will die as I said you will die. Tomorrow evening at midnight. If you've made any plans for Tuesday, I would change them now if I were you."

"You're serious, aren't you?"

"Normally, I allow the enemies of the Lord longer than twenty-four hours to get used to the idea. It amuses me to think of them trying to be rational in the face of something as extraordinary as God's avenging angel. But I've decided to make an exception in your case. Whatever trouble you can stir up will be forgotten by your colleagues when your body is found. It goes without saying that I'll have an unbeatable alibi. I'll be leading a prayer meeting tomorrow evening in front of five hundred people. As a matter of fact, we'll be praying about you." He paused. "But I certainly wouldn't take any comfort from that."

"I'm to be killed by the Lord's winnowing fork, is that it? That's one exhibit I'd like to see in a court of law."

Van Der Velden became less playful all of a sudden, tired of my incessant mockery; the perfect smile disappeared and his eyes narrowed malevolently.

"I'm sorry you remain so skeptical, Agent Martins," he said. "But as the hours elapse between now and midnight tomorrow, I think you'll find you will start to feel a lot less sanguine about any of this. In the beginning—which is any time from now on—you'll experience psychological breakdown; your mind will be beset with doubt and uncertainty about the things lurking in the shadows that formerly you took for granted were not there; then you will feel horror as irrational fear grips your soul. Fear of the dark, a reluctance to switch out the light before you sleep. Whatever happened to common sense? Are you alone as you thought you were? What was that noise you heard? Why did that curtain move? Is there someone there? Could someone be downstairs?"

"Someone or something?"

Van Der Velden laughed. "You say a lot more than you know. At least more than you know right now. Because the psychological breakdown that awaits is nothing like the real ordeal before you. The physical one. To be killed by a demon from hell is no easy thing. Perhaps it's the worst thing there is."

"I thought you said it was God who was going to kill me."

"Oh, but he is. God is going to kill you through the medium of his own archangel of death, Azrael. Azrael is a fallen angel. A demon over which God has power like everything else. You know, for an FBI Special Agent, you seem oddly ill informed about all this. Or weren't you paying attention to Miss Begleiter? How did she put it? God uses such beings as Azrael to carry out his dirty work?"

"You're crazy."

"Do you think so? Or are you just saying that because you would prefer to believe I'm crazy, because that makes it a lot easier to dismiss what I'm telling you? Come now, Agent Martins. We both know I'm as sane as you are. Although perhaps that's not saying very much. Because I have the distinct impression that this investigation of yours might already have hit the buffers and caused you some difficulties at work. Perhaps you've already been accused of being a little crazy yourself. Well, who could blame your colleagues for being even more skeptical than you about these things? Yes, that would explain a great deal. Such as why you're out on a limb and working on your own. And why you're no longer living at home. I telephoned the people at Lakewood and gave them some story about how you'd turned up here asking to join our membership. They told me about you and your wife."

I was on the edge of mentioning that I'd seen Ruth in his church the previous Sunday, but I hardly wanted to get her into trouble; I had no reason to do her a favor. But then she was more susceptible to the pastor's kind of suggestion than I was, and she was also the mother of my son.

"You know," he said, "you should thank me. No, really, you should. Not many people are given the fantastic opportunity I'm about to give you, my poor deluded friend. I'm going to restore your faith in the existence of God. Overnight. Because he's there, Agent Martins, he's there. He's always been there, but you were just too frigging dumb to realize it."

"That's very generous of you, Pastor."

"You're being sarcastic, of course. But I don't do any of this for myself, you know. Really, I don't. Everything I do I do out of fear of God. Real fear. It's the one thing that people never understand about God. That he's capable of some really terrible things. Not that it should be a great mystery. It's all in the Bible. Perhaps, at the end—your end—you will understand that, too."

"You actually believe this bullshit, don't you?"

"Already the Lord's angel of death is leaving hell to come for you. That is what I believe. That is what you will believe. And you will die before tomorrow night at twelve as sure as we're standing here talking right now."

I'm not exactly sure how Van Der Velden managed it. Perhaps there was an odorless narcotic gas that I inhaled in the elevator. Or maybe there was some electronic means of bringing about the same result—a hologram or a projection—I don't know. But there had to be a simple and straightforward explanation for what happened as I retraced my echoing steps through that empty modern church, although, to be honest, there were none that left me feeling even half convinced.

Walking toward the huge main door, I was absolutely certain that none of the flip-down seats on either side of the gently sloping gangway ahead of me was occupied; then, almost in the blink of an eye, it seemed that one seat was filled after all. My own double take at this discovery was enough to stop me in my tracks as momentarily I was almost convinced that my mind was playing tricks on me and, for several seconds, I just stood there dumbly, looking straight at the only vaguely defined figure now occupying a seat immediately by the exit.

Just as peculiar as the suddenness of the strange figure's appearance was the odd way he or she—it was hard to be sure either way—seemed to shimmer like a heat mirage. We're used to these in Texas. Sometimes the air above the blacktop shifts like a belly dancer. Inside an air-conditioned church, however, this must have had another explanation: I was suffering from heat stroke and dehydration, perhaps. That's easy when the summer days are over a hundred degrees.

For a moment, I rubbed my eyes, the way you do when you think you're seeing things that aren't there. The next second I heard my own name whispered behind me, close up to my ear. Turning quickly, I expected to see someone standing behind me; but finding no one there, I decided I must have imagined it—and when I turned back to look for the person in the seat beside the exit and found him no longer there, I had to consider the possibility that I had only imagined that, too.

The strangest sensation now overtook me as I suddenly wanted to get out of Van Der Velden's church as quickly as possible and into the bright light and hot certainty of the baking Texas sun. I hurried toward the door, increasingly anxious to be outside. But I paused beside the chair that I was almost certain had for just a second been occupied by some ill-defined figure and found my left hand reaching to flip the seat down as if some trace of the mysterious occupant might remain.

Almost immediately I snatched my hand away, for the seat was hot—as hot as a saucepan on a stove—and if I'd ever doubted this, there was the evidence of the continuing pain in my fingertips, which for a long time afterward remained as red as if I had actually burned them on a hot iron. This was, of course, impossible because the seat—made of wood and wool and the presumably flammable stuffing that made it comfortable to sit on—could only have been as hot as it felt to the touch if it had been on fire. The seat must have been impregnated with some kind of acid that burned skin and flesh without corroding the upholstery.

Holding my hand, I glanced around angrily.

"That's a good trick, Van Der Velden," I said aloud, assuming that the pastor was watching and listening via some secret camera high up in the roof, and presumably also enjoying my obvious alarm and discomfort. "But it's still a trick and it doesn't convince me you're anything but a cut-rate Elmer Gantry. D'you hear? I'm not buying the idea that your little bit of David Blaine street magic might be the real thing."

I waited for some response, but none came.

"Fucking asshole," I said, pushing open the big church door.

These were brave words. Because I could hardly deny the pain I was feeling in my own hand or the persistence of the memory of my own name being whispered by someone who wasn't there and, if I'm honest, I can hardly deny that I was very relieved that the door to the church was not locked.

TWENTY-ONE

I n the parking lot, under the big blue sky, I breathed a little more easily. The heat on my face seemed reassuringly normal, but only just. There were times when the heat of Texas felt like hell and the grass broke up when you walked upon it and the air was filled with the humid breath of a million different souls and human will was shut down to nothing much more than an animal's impulse to find the mercy of some shade. Perhaps in this place of all places, where only a few miles away men with slide rules and ancient computers had sent other men to the moon, the heat was meant to bow the heads of men and keep them humble. But I stared right back up at the angel over the door of the church, full of loathing; and if I could have reached it, I would have spat in his eye.

I walked quickly to my car—the last one left on the lot—keen to be away from the Izrael Church. It would have been obvious to Van Der Velden and his followers that this was my car. For one thing, it wasn't a very nice car, and a cursory inspection would have revealed the pass on the windshield that allowed me entry to a space underneath the Bureau on Justice Park Drive. So, before I drove away, I checked my car for a bomb—the way we'd been trained to do at the Academy—before putting it in gear and driving, slowly, away. It seemed unlikely that Van

Der Velden would try to kill me so close to his church, but you never can tell; better safe than sorry.

In any other circumstances I might have wanted to check my car for tracking devices, too, although that would have meant driving all the way back to the office in Houston and leaving the car in the FBI garage with the resident electronics technician. But this was a very different situation; I wanted Van Der Velden's people to know where I was so that they might make an attempt to kill me at home in Galveston. Because now I was intent on being ready to receive visitors. After what Van Der Velden had said, surely he had to try to kill me. The only question that remained was exactly how he was going to do it. If all of this sounds commendably hard-headed and practical, it was. In spite of everything I'd been led to believe, I had to think there was a perfectly logical explanation for everything that had occurred and was yet to occur. To that extent, I was still behaving like the brick agent I was trained to be.

That was what I thought; and yet I felt something different. It was like I was on a seesaw of rational thoughts and irrational ones, although, in truth, there were only a few of these that were probably nothing other than a normal reaction to being threatened. I have to admit that there was also a very small, superstitious part of me that was half inclined to believe there really was an angel of death or a demon called Azrael, and that because of the pastor's silent prayer, this supernatural being would kill me before midnight the following night. Yes, the time limit I had been given made me feel odd, too. The best way to describe all of this is to say that I have an imagination like anyone else.

In this preoccupied state of mind I drove back onto the Gulf Freeway.

But worse was to come.

As I throttled back to seventy miles per hour, it seemed that in my rearview mirror I could see something red begin to appear in the sky behind me. At first I thought I was looking at a series of distant airborne objects—balloons, or even something more sophisticated; after all, the Johnson Space Center was just a few miles to the east, and while almost all NASA flights had taken place in Florida at Cape Canaveral, you always had the impression when you were anywhere near the JSC that you might see something unusual in the sky.

It was another minute before I realized that what I was actually looking at were the red letters of a message and that far from being written on the sky they were actually taking shape on my rear window. It was several more seconds before the words fully materialized on the glass and I was able to read them.

YOU WILL DIE BEFORE MIDNIGHT TOMORROW.

The next moment I was loudly summoned from my contemplation of the message as a truck horn blasted me back to full concentration. I had drifted badly out of my lane. I swerved quickly—too quickly—and narrowly missed a collision with another truck on the passenger's side. Several tire-squealing, heart-stopping seconds passed before I had the car fully under control again.

When I'd stopped swearing at the massive rear wheels of the truck and calmed down a bit, my anger gave way to a cold sweat of fear at this near disaster. I quickly turned off at the next exit, by which time the message had disappeared as mysteriously as it had appeared; I pulled up on the side of the road, and leaped out of the car and tried to make out any trace of the letters on my window. But there was none, not so much as a smear; and in the hope that I might send them for some forensic tests to determine the chemical Fitzgerald must have used—he could easily have applied the message to my rear window while I was

talking to Nelson Van Der Velden—I spent the next few minutes rubbing sheets of paper and pieces of tissue on the glass—inside and outside. I even rubbed some tissues on the rearview mirror in case
Fitzgerald had somehow tampered with this.

Yet somewhere inside my brain I knew all this activity was probably
futile; I knew a little about this kind of thing from my time at Quantico—
enough to know there wasn't any kind of chemical writing that could
appear on glass and then vanish without a trace.

A little reluctantly—what other surprises lay ahead for me on the
drive back to Galveston?—I got back into the car and drove on. A few
miles on, I stopped at a gas station where I bought some cigarettes and
groceries. While the clerk added up my bill, I went into the men's room
and tried to pull myself together.

Inside the cubicle I suddenly knew I was not alone in the wash-
room. It wasn't that I heard the door open or heard someone moving
around. I felt it, as if someone had opened a large refrigerator, alarming
and subtle at the same time; and so immediate was the effect in my
blood that it almost felt as if I'd been strapped onto a crucifix-shaped
gurney and injected with sodium thiopental in the execution chamber
at Huntsville. Still sitting on the john, I leaned forward, hardly breathing at all, like I was some junkie shooting up into my own thigh mus-
cle, powerless to resist the presence from doing exactly what it would.

I am here, the presence seemed to say, *I am coming for you, as it was
of old, and you can do nothing to stop me. I am here to do his work. As it
was of old, in the beginning and in the Bible.*

It was several minutes before the cold departed and I dared to
breathe again.

"Get a grip," I told myself. I flushed the toilet and came out of the
cubicle, glancing one way and then the other. "He's messing with your
head. You're imagining this. D'you hear? It's all in your head."

I washed my hands, splashed some water on my face, and went back to the checkout, where the clerk gave me a look. He was a skinny kid with a gloomy expression, as if he might have been planning to hang himself with one of the drive belts that were dangling like so many nooses on the wall behind his head.

I handed over a twenty. He opened the cash register, took out my change, and laid it on a little ashtray that was the shape of Texas and decorated with the state's six national flags. I collected my change, turned to walk out, and then turned back.

"Wait," I said. "When I was in your men's room, did you see anyone go in there behind me?"

"Mister," said the clerk, "you're the only customer who's been in this gas station for the last two hours. There are quiet Sundays and there are Sundays that make you think God's trying to tell you something. You know what I mean?"

I wished he might have expressed himself some other way. "You're sure about that? That no one else went in there?"

The clerk nodded at the CCTV monitor. "Take a look," he said, pointing at a clear view of the men's-room door. "Sure I'm sure. I always watch fellows who go in there in case they're up to something."

I went outside and put the groceries in the trunk of my car. I looked up at the sky and met the full power of the sun on my face. The sky held no clouds, not a breath of wind nor the promise of any rain, just more unrelenting heat. Two or three hundred feet up, a large buzzard wheeled around immediately over my head as if it knew something about what had gone down in the men's room.

I am here to do his work. As it was of old, in the beginning and in the Bible.

That voice again. But was it inside my own head or somewhere else? I surveyed the parking lot and the gas station and the other buildings that were grouped next to it: a photocopy shop and a CVS pharmacy. The buzzard was still there above my head. Shielding my eyes against the sun, I watched it as it circled slowly in the cloudless sky, and I decided it looked less like a bird and more like something else. The wings seemed not to move at all.

"What is that?" I muttered. "Couldn't be another Switchblade, could it?"

But when the wings seemed to move, I decided it was a buzzard after all, or perhaps an eagle. I don't know why exactly, but the sight of that bird made me feel anxious. It reminded me that I was probably dehydrated so I went into the CVS to buy some cold vitaminwater. Inside the drugstore's cool interior, I paused for a moment as I waited for the ghost image of the Texas sun to clear from my retinas.

Except that it didn't. Instead, the afterimage began to slowly grow in size. I closed my eyes and shook my head, but the ghost image continued to expand and unfold like a rolling green cloud. I hadn't encountered this kind of visual disturbance as something that ever lasted for longer than a few seconds, and I reminded myself that this was only a well-understood optical illusion caused by the cone cells in the eyes as they tried to adapt from overstimulation to light. I must have been staring at the sun for longer than I had supposed. But when the ghost image not only continued to grow in size but took on a real shape, I began to grow more alarmed. I felt my breathing grow faster and a cold sweat start on my skin.

Instinctively, I backed away, only it's hard to back away from something that's inside your own eyes and head. I rubbed my eyes furiously and blinked several times, but the illusion continued to become larger and more strongly defined; then I closed my eyes again, but to no avail.

The green image seemed to be taking on a very definite oval shape.

"Holy fuck," I heard myself say out loud.

My next curse sounded more like a cry of fear. I backed into a display of shampoo bottles, knocked it over, and then fell onto the hard floor. Still lying on the floor, I tried to crawl away backward as if my life depended on it.

The shape became a man's face, only this was not the kind of bullshit satanic face some people claim they saw in the smoke from the World Trade Center, this was something else, only I had little time to describe its features as the face quickly closed in on mine until all I could see was a huge eye hovering over me. The eye was the color of the night, with an iris that seemed to be made of a dark sky filled with thousands of stars, and the dilated pupil at its center was a great black hole that was the size of a planet that seemed to look right into the very innermost part of me.

And then I was inside that pupil and looking into the depths of something infinite that filled me with horror. Darkness enveloped me as if a hood had been thrown over my head. At the same time I felt clammy hands pick me up and strap me down; the next second I felt the prick of something sharp in my flesh and then my veins filled with fire. My body let out a shriek and writhed like a snake, but the straps held me firm and in my bones I knew that only prayer could help me now.

As it was of old, in the beginning and in the Bible.

"Are you all right?"

I blinked and opened my eyes. The terrifying afterimage was gone. I sat up on the floor and looked at a young black woman wearing a lab coat. She was regarding me with understandable anxiety.

"I think I must have fainted."

She nodded. "It's a hundred and five out there," she replied, as if that was all the explanation that was needed. "You should drink some water."

I stood up, took a deep breath, and nodded. "I'm all right." I took a step. "Actually, I think I just had a panic attack."

"Have you had them before?"

"Yes," I lied.

"You should go to a hospital. There's one up the road from here in Webster."

"Thanks, but I think I'll be okay. Although maybe you could recommend something for anxiety that I can buy over the counter? Like Xanax. But not, if you know what I mean."

"Have you been prescribed Xanax before?"

"No, but I know plenty of people who have and I know how it works. I just need to calm my nerves, that's all."

She shrugged. "You could try kava," she said. "It's an herbal sedative. I've heard that some people find it quite effective." Pointing over my shoulder, she added, "You'll find some in our vitamin and supplements aisle."

I bought a packet of two hundred pills and a cold drink to help me swallow a handful.

"If I were you, I'd still go see a doctor."

"You're probably right."

I went back to my car and tried to gather myself. Instinctively, I felt I needed to speak to someone—someone who knew me—and with my mind still on what had happened in the drugstore, the men's room at the gas station, and back at the church, I completely forgot my previous stricture about not contacting Bishop Coogan because of the tap that DCS Net was running on his telephone and called him on my cell.

He wasn't there, but by the time I had remembered the impropriety of my speaking to him at all while an FBI investigation was ongoing, I had left a long and garbled message on his answering service, apologizing for not having contacted him to thank him for the use of the diocesan house and explaining that I was on forced leave. A minute or two after hanging up, I saw my mistake.

"Damn it all," I said, angry with myself for having let the cat out of

the bag regarding the house. Now I really would have to look for somewhere else to live.

About the only good thing I could see ahead as I neared the end of
the freeway was some thick gray cloud blowing in off the ocean, which
meant that we were in for some cooler weather and possibly even some
very welcome rain. There had been none for almost four months now.
The sudden appearance of the cloud ought to have surprised me, but I
was still too much on edge to find it unusual. I had to make an effort to
calm myself or I was certain to have another car accident. I started
breathing deeply through my nose until I felt the closeness in my chest
start to clear.

About a mile short of the Galveston bridge, the cell rang. Thinking
it was Bishop Coogan, I didn't answer it right away. Then I glanced
down at the caller ID and saw that it wasn't him but the mystery person
who tried calling me earlier. I slowed the car a little and answered it.

"This is Sara Espinosa."

"Hi there, Doctor. How are you doing?" My voice concealed all of
the jangled nerves I was feeling; that was a courtesy to her; you called
the FBI to get reassurance, not a dose of someone else's paranoia and
angst.

"I've been trying to call you all day. You're a hard man to get."

"I've been driving all over the place today."

"Working Sunday, huh?"

"Yes, but it's not normally like this." That certainly felt like the un-
derstatement of my week. "Sundays usually last about a month for me.
Sometimes I think God made Houston to encourage people to go to
church."

"Then he probably made Galveston to encourage people to go to
Houston. I've never seen a city look this deserted."

"You're in Galveston?"

"I called you earlier on to say I was going to be down here. And now here I am. This place—it's like being in a disaster movie."

"Is everything all right?"

"I was down here to see an old friend so I thought I'd look you up, that's all."

I slowed the car again as I neared the bridge. It felt good talking to her. The prospect of seeing her felt even better. Being with an attractive woman might be a better treatment for my own anxiety than what the doctor in Webster would have ordered.

"Listen, Sara, I'm about to lose the signal on my cell. So come to an address I'll give you. It's where I'm living right now. Come over and we can have some coffee."

"Thanks. But I'm there already. Your colleague, Helen Monaco, gave me your address. Her cell phone number was on the back of your card." She paused. "I'm afraid I lied to her. I hope you don't mind, but I told her you'd asked me down there to see you but that I'd lost your address and you weren't answering your cell phone."

"I'll be there in about ten minutes."

As I put my foot down, I glanced at the clock on the dashboard. It was nine-fifteen p.m.—kind of late for anyone to be making a social call in Galveston, especially when they lived in Austin; Austin was a four-hour, two-hundred-mile drive. Even if Sara Espinosa stayed for an hour, she wouldn't be home before at least two a.m. It seemed curious. Then again, by the standard of everything else I'd experienced in the last couple of hours, it hardly seemed curious at all.

As I neared my own front door, I saw a beautiful sky-blue Bentley Continental Supersports convertible that was parked out front, with Sara Espinosa in the driver's seat, and I reflected that maybe she just liked driving. If I owned a car like that, a four-hour drive at night might seem like a pleasure.

I pulled up onto the short driveway. Sara got out and walked toward me, looking shapelier than I remembered. She was wearing a white trouser suit and matching sneakers with little gold stripes, not to mention several gold bangles and a gold watch. She looked like one of those Kremlin churches with the rounded gold and white towers—something involving worship anyway.

"Nice car," I said. "I guess there's a lot more to human biology than I thought there was."

"Oh, that," she said, turning to look at the car as if "that" were a pet cat or a birthmark and not a $300,000 car. "Yes, biology's been good to me."

"I didn't need to see the car to know that," I said.

She blushed a little, which surprised me, because even as I'd said it, I thought it was probably the kind of sexist remark that a woman like her would find disagreeable. Which told me something in itself; she was a little less combative than the first time we had met, a little less self-assured.

I took my eyes off her and then the car, and fixed them on the horizon for a moment. As well as some significant-looking clouds, the wind was getting up, too; it stirred her blond hair as if she were still driving her car with the top down. Had there been a weather report I'd missed? Maybe that was the problem. Somehow a TV weather report was always more a description of what had happened instead of what was going to happen. But then, as a famous physicist once remarked, prediction is always difficult, especially when it's about the future, although clearly Nelson Van Der Velden had no such qualms.

"Could be a storm coming in," I said.

"Oh," she said, turning to follow my eye line. "Yes, you could be right."

I yawned. The kava seemed to be working now.

"You're tired," she said. "You've had a busy day, I can tell. I should really go."

"No," I said. "No. Come in. I insist. Before the neighbors start to talk."

She followed me up the steps to the front door.

"Are they terribly nosy?"

"That was a joke," I said, ushering her into the hallway. "There aren't any neighbors. Not really. Most people in this neighborhood upped and left a while ago. Or died for all I know. There's just me and the grumpy old man up the street. You're the first visitor I've had since I moved into this dump."

I frowned because it seemed to me that the musty smell that had always filled the diocesan house had been joined by something else. I'd come across a smell like that once before, at Driscoll Street, when we'd come back from vacation to find that the house had suffered a power outage and all the meat in the freezer had spoiled.

"What's that smell?" I said.

"I can't smell anything."

"You can't?"

"No." She stepped into the sitting room and looked around politely. "It's not a dump at all," she said.

"If I'd known I was going to have a visitor, I'd have cleaned up a bit before I left this morning."

"No, really, it's nice. Comfortable. And very masculine. I even like the picture."

I shrugged. "The guy who lived here before me was a priest, so it's his taste, not mine."

"It's by Stanley Spencer, isn't it?"

"That's what it says on the back of the frame."

"He married a lesbian who refused to consummate the marriage."

"It can happen to anyone," I said.

"How does an FBI agent come to be living in a priest's house, anyway?"

"It's a long story," I said. "Have a seat. I'll make some coffee."

"I'd prefer a drink. White wine if you have any."

"There's plenty of wine. Good wine. The priest was a bit of a connoisseur. There's a small wine cellar and a special chiller cabinet with what looks like some quality stuff that I haven't dared touch. A bottle always seems a bit too much when it's just for one."

That was a lie, of course; when you're drinking on your own, wine just seems to take longer than scotch to work its anesthetizing effect.

Still sniffing the unpleasant air, I threw open some windows and went into the kitchen, checked the garbage disposal and the trash. But finding nothing that seemed to explain the smell, I went downstairs to fetch the wine. I was half inclined to lecture Sara about drunk driving but that seemed less than honest, given the empty bottles of liquor in the trunk of my own car; besides, I hardly thought one glass of white wine was going to do her any harm, even at the wheel of a Bentley.

I carried the bottle upstairs, opened it, and poured us each a large glass, burying my nose in the floral bouquet of the golden wine. I wondered how it would mix with kava, but mostly I didn't care. I downed a glass and poured myself another. It wasn't every day an attractive woman turned up on my doorstep. Especially in Galveston.

She sipped the wine. "Delicious. White burgundy is my favorite. And this is the perfect temperature, too. Most people in Texas serve white wine much too cold. And too young. 1995. Well, that's perfect."

"You know cars, you know art, and you know wine," I said. "About the only thing you don't seem to know is interior decoration. This place is a dump and you know it."

She took another look around the room and sighed. "Perhaps it's a little monastic," she observed. "But that's what you'd expect with a priest. Even one who enjoys Puligny-Montrachet."

She swallowed some more of the wine. It did taste good; and I had to admit the wine looked like the Holy Grail, it was so golden in the glass.

"That's much better," she said. "Gosh, I needed that more than I thought I did."

"Me, too." The wine was mixing well with the kava. I felt good. Better than I'd felt in several hours.

For a moment, neither of us said anything. I glanced awkwardly around the room, wondering what she really thought of the place and, by extension, me.

"Would you like something to eat, perhaps?" I asked.

"With this?" she asked, meaning the wine. "Oh, no. There's nothing I could possibly eat with wine as good as this. But don't let me stop you, Agent Martins."

"No," I said. "I had lunch. And please, call me Gil."

"All right. I will. Your accent, I've been meaning to ask."

"I lived in Scotland until I was fourteen."

"Wow. What was that like?"

"It always feels like a previous personality I left behind."

"And you like Galveston better?"

I grinned. "No. But I liked Boston. That's where my family went after Scotland. I'm thinking of moving back there. To Boston. Not to Scotland."

This was possibly the first moment when I realized that I was considering it. Surely Houston was finished for me. Ruth and Danny were no longer in my life; and probably I'd have to leave the office when Chuck found out that I'd called a suspect who was under surveillance. With any luck, I might persuade the Boston field office to take me on. Or perhaps the Massachusetts State Police.

"I think I was happiest when I was living in Connecticut."

"Meaning you're not happy now?"

"Meaning it was where I grew up. I think the place where you grow up always has an extra importance in your life. Don't you?"

"I never really thought about it," I lied.

She shivered.

"Are you cold?" I asked.

"A little," she admitted. "Aren't you?"

"Maybe the weather is changing," I said, glancing out the window. To me it still felt really humid, but I wasn't about to argue with her. "Here, let me fetch you a blanket or something."

When I returned from the bedroom with a blanket, I found her staring anxiously out of the window.

"The car's all right there," I said. "I can guarantee it. The one advantage of living in a ghost town is that there's no crime. You could leave a thousand bucks on your hand-stitched leather seat and it'd still be there in the morning."

I wondered if all that was about to change; if someone from the Izrael Church was planning to turn up the next day and murder me in some anonymous way.

"Oh," she said. "It wasn't that at all."

"No?"

She shook her head and smiled a sad little smile as I hung the blanket on her shoulders. We sat down on the sofa. She swallowed some more of the wine.

"God, this is good wine," she said.

"Isn't it?" I lifted the holster off my belt and laid it on the table.

She looked up at the ceiling as if my small talk was becoming just too minute to bear; or maybe she just couldn't bear to look at the gun. I picked it up and moved it onto the floor beside my foot.

"Don't you find it lonely, living here?" she asked. "I mean, it's so very quiet. I've been sitting outside for a while and saw no one."

I nodded. "Yes, it is quiet," I said. "Very. But right now I don't have much choice about where I live. My wife is divorcing me and I'm going to need all my money for a good lawyer. Or, for that matter, a bad one. This house comes rent-free. I have a friend who's a bishop. He lent me this house while I'm looking around for something else."

"Sounds like a good friend to have."

I smiled thinly. I hardly wanted to open up that one for discussion, either.

"You're very brave, I think," she said, "living here among all this—this disappointment and ruin. I couldn't do it. I think I would probably be afraid of all kinds of things."

"I have a gun," I said. "All kinds of things can usually be shot."

"Yes. There is that, I suppose. You don't have to hide it, you know. I don't mind the sight of it at all. The gun, I mean. It makes me feel secure." She smiled. "And so do you."

"I'm very glad to hear it." I placed the holstered Glock on the coffee table in front of us, which strangely seemed to bring her comfort. "There. How's that?"

"It's getting dark." She got up again and went to the window and looked one way and then the other as if she expected to see someone she knew.

"You've come a long way for a shooting lesson," I joked. "If that's why you're here. And I really do think Mr. Hindemith might complain if we start shooting in the backyard."

"Did you say Hindemith? Like the composer?"

"Hindemith. Yes, that's what I said. Although I didn't know about the composer. He's the old man who lives up the street."

She lifted her eyebrows and shook her head.

"What about him, anyway?" I asked.

"It's odd, but my first husband's name was Hindemith. Charles Hindemith."

"Oh, yes. I forgot about all your husbands. Do you have one living in Galveston?"

"No. It's just that it's hardly a common name."

"If you say so."

"But then Charles was hardly a common man. Which is why I married him. He was a professor of English literature, at Yale."

"I'm guessing he was older than you."

"Oh, yes. Much. I was twenty-one, he was sixty-five. Charles was very stimulating to be with. He had a brilliant mind."

Carefully, I asked her what had happened to him—carefully because I had the very strong recollection that the Mr. Hindemith up the street had said that *his* name was Charles, and I hardly wanted her to think that her first husband was living less than a hundred yards away—especially as Sara seemed so very obviously nervous about something else.

"He died. He had a heart attack not long after I married him."

I felt a small sense of relief, which was enough for me to give way to the crude thought in my head.

"It figures," I said. "Hey, I'm sorry. That wasn't necessary."

"No, that's all right, Gil." She smiled a wry sort of smile. "It is actually accurate. He fucked himself to death. And not always with me. I wasn't the only student he messed with."

"My own wife kind of ran out of interest in that side of things. At least with me."

"No, that's all right," she said firmly. "There's no need to creep around this, Gil. You want me. That's natural. Almost as natural as the way I want you to do it."

I felt my jaw slacken a little at that. The woman was almost as fast as her car, and much more beautiful.

She came back to the sofa and sat beside me again, only closer this time. "As a matter of fact, that's why I'm here. The last time we met there was something between us and—well, you must have felt it, too, right?"

I nodded dumbly. I was out of practice with this kind of thing. The last time I'd contemplated a relationship with a woman she'd told me that she was a lesbian.

Sara took my hand and pressed her face into its palm before kissing the heel of my thumb.

"So why don't you kiss me," she said, "and then we can both relax?"

I still felt a long way from relaxed, but I kissed her for a very long time, and when I stopped, I could feel that she didn't want me to stop; in fact, from the way she held on to me I formed the strong impression that she didn't want to let me go at all.

"The last time we met I also felt that I managed to blow it," I said. "I scared you."

"Yes, you did rather," she said.

"What changed your mind?"

"Oh, the usual stuff. Biology. You shouldn't ever underestimate the power of biology."

"I try not to. Lately, however, I've been underestimating the power of all kinds of things."

"Such as?"

"It's another way of saying that things haven't been going all that well for me these last few months."

"Your wife."

"Among other things, yes."

"She must be crazy. You're really a very attractive man, you know? And very kind. As soon as you'd left my office, I regretted making you go. You were only trying to look after me. I can see that now. I sat there for a long time wanting to call your number right away. And every night since then."

I kissed her again, but this time I did it with my own skepticism ringing in my ears. I hadn't forgotten the strong and obvious discomfort I'd seen in Sara in her office at UT when I'd told her about Esther Begleiter's prayer list; only now she seemed to be trying to play that down. There was something odd about her being with me in Galveston, about her whole demeanor, not to mention her sudden desire to sleep with me, but I couldn't help myself. I wanted her desperately—it was ages since I'd made love. Besides, I'd already blown it with her once and wasn't about to blow it again.

"You seem a little tense, Gil," she said.

"It's been that kind of a day." I shook my head. "But I'm feeling better already." I tried to kiss her again but found her sliding out of my embrace and down between my legs.

"You're only saying that," she said, coolly unzipping her trousers and then mine, "because I haven't done this yet."

In other circumstances I might have stopped her. For one thing, I was too exhausted to resist and for another, I hardly thought I was taking advantage of her; she knew exactly what she was doing. Besides, what she was doing hadn't been done in a long time and I felt absurdly grateful for it; as if, like some Good Samaritan, she had found me injured by the side of the road to Jericho and was now nursing me back to health. So I just lay back and tried to give myself up to it and put all of my being into my prick, which, all things being equal, wouldn't normally have been very difficult; but it took a while for me to relax. Indeed, she had to pause for a moment and fix me with her beautiful eyes and tell me to lie back and let her take complete charge of my pleasure.

"No," I said. "Not this way. Not the first time."

That was my cue to pull Sara onto my suddenly inspired lap, and my strength must have taken her by surprise because she gasped, and then gasped again as my hand pushed between her thighs until it met the soft silk and lace of her panties and half pulled and half tore them down her long tanned legs. Untangling her bare feet from these delicate shackles, I pried her thighs apart and pushed my face deep into the very essence of her. All I wanted was to smother myself with the most intimate flesh of this beautiful, beautifully clever woman whose attraction for me seemed as unlikely as it was welcome. I pushed the lips of her apart until my nose and tongue were fucking her and my face was soaked with her delicious wetness. A shrink might have suggested I was trying to hide myself inside her in some Oedipal way; all I knew was that this was a true act of worship. I hardly cared about my obsession with cleanliness, either—not anymore. I had found a cure for that; my growing fear and the desperate need for the holy sanctuary that was close contact with another human being now conquered all. If I could have swallowed a living part of her, like the Eucharist, I would have done so.

Sara uttered a sigh that was also a deep, almost tectonic shudder, as if she, too, was suffering from shock; and that was my second cue. I was quickly between her legs, molding them around my waist and steering myself into the center of her body with the urgency of one who has almost forgotten what it was like to cleave unto a woman—as the Bible describes it rather wonderfully—and be one flesh with her; until, at the moment when I felt my hardened prick nudging right up against the neck of her womb, I let go of everything inside me—not just semen, but all sense of who and what I was—and, I think, she did, too.

For a long time after, we lay intertwined like the roots of a prehistoric tree of knowledge that had existed long before us and would continue long after we were both gone. Then I felt myself gradually shrink inside and then out of her, which was the moment for imperfection and reality to return. We talked for a while about nothing in particular before I returned to what was bothering me.

"Sara," I said carefully. "Has something happened to you since we met in your office?"

A smile twitched faintly on her mouth as if it were hooked on the end of a very fine length of fishing line.

"No. Nothing at all." She paused. "Well, yes. Perhaps."

"Why don't you tell me about it? The reason why you're here. The real reason, not the role you've been playing since you walked through the door."

Sara frowned. "Why can't you do your thinking with your dick like any other man?"

"Because normally the FBI Academy at Quantico teaches us to keep it holstered until the moment when we really need to use it." I waited for a moment. "There is no old friend here in Galveston. Am I right?"

"No," she said quietly. "I drove down here this morning. I've been hanging around outside your house for most of the day."

"Why?"

"To see you, of course. Why the fuck would I come to Galveston for any other reason? I just can't be at home right now. I can't be alone, either. I'm scared, Gil."

I bit my lip. I was still feeling a little scared myself, but I wasn't about to tell her that.

"You're going to think I'm crazy."

"What could be crazier than spending three hours in the car to get to Galveston?"

Sara let out a long unsteady breath.

"This isn't like me," she said. "I'm a scientist, for Pete's sake."

"That might make you immune to human feelings, but it doesn't make you immune to human failings."

"Listen to you, Michel Foucault."

"Just tell me the rest of your story."

"You're just like my first husband. He never had the patience to hear anyone out. He was always jumping to the end of someone's story. And films and plays. He could always predict the end of every movie I ever saw. And taking Charles to the theater was a nightmare. He couldn't abide the stage. I don't think I ever saw a second act of anything for as long as I was married to him."

I felt something like a frown on my face, and although the light in the room was now almost gone, she must have seen something in my eyes.

"What?"

I switched on a lamp, telling myself that she wasn't the crazy one, I was; it was either that or the uncomfortable possibility that my own senses and memory had become very unreliable.

"Nothing. Please go on."

"The day after you came to my office at UT, I decided to check on my ChoiceMail program. Much to my surprise, I discovered some rather curious threatening e-mails. They were the usual crap about how God was going to kill me because I was an ungodly bitch. What made them curious was the way they disappeared almost as soon as I had read them. Like someone had programmed them that way. Computers aren't my field. I don't install the latest Windows version without help. But even I know that's unusual. I asked a colleague about it and—"

"I know about this stuff," I said. "So you can skip the e-mail for dummies explanation. Get to the meat."

She looked at me with some disappointment at my being so short with her, which prompted a muttered apology on my part; this was, of course, a lot easier than giving her an explanation for the disturbed feeling I had from the recollection of what the old man who lived up the street had told me that same morning. Surely there was no way he could have known Sara Espinosa.

"All right," she said. "Well, then some strange things started to happen. I mean outside cyberspace. I had the idea I was being followed.

Footsteps in the underground parking lot at UT and my apartment building, that kind of thing. Footsteps that stopped when I stopped and started when I started walking again. And a very strong sensation that someone was standing behind me, when no one was. I asked Smith Protective Services to keep a closer eye on my apartment, which they did; and so imagine my surprise and alarm when one night I thought I heard something in the hallway outside my apartment door. I checked the picture on the entry phone and then the peephole and there appeared to be someone standing there in the shadows. No, that's not entirely accurate. I couldn't make the figure out in detail, but it wasn't standing so much as squatting. Also the person—I can't say for sure that it was a man—had bare feet."

"Bare feet?"

"Yes. Bare feet. And bare legs. I called the people at Smith and they checked the entry-phone CCTV for the hallway and told me that there was nothing on the camera. And certainly not a man with bare feet. But they sent a security guard anyway to check it out and he came up to the ninth floor where I live and found nothing. The guard rang my doorbell, and while he was there, I checked the hall for myself."

"That does sound weird."

She shrugged. "That happened on three consecutive nights, so now they think I'm crazy. If I called them again, they'd probably tell me to take a sleeping pill. Or ask me what the fuck I was smoking."

"Did you call the police?"

"No. I mean, how could I? What would I have said? I'm seeing things in my hallway that a private security company has already checked out and told me aren't there? Bad enough to have the people at Smith thinking I'm nuts without the police thinking that as well."

"So why didn't you call me?"

"That's a good question." She sighed. "And I'm a little ashamed to answer it. I suppose, if I'm honest, in a strange way I thought maybe it might have something to do with you. After all, these things happened only after you'd come to see me."

"So what changed your mind?"

"I'm coming to that. On the third night I saw the figure in the hallway, I realized I would have opened the door and challenged the guy myself except that I was so terrified. Maybe if I'd had a gun, I might have. Which is why I bought one. It's in my bag now. Anyway, on the day I bought one, he'd gone. The guy in the hallway. Thus far, he hasn't reappeared ."

"So that's all right."

She gave me a sarcastic smile. "Well, at least you didn't tell me I imagined it."

"No." How could I have told her that?

"Thank you."

"Describe your apartment building, please."

"There are ten floors. Each floor is one whole apartment. Mine is on the ninth floor. The hallway I'm describing is in front of the elevator. There's a doorman downstairs who's there until midnight and then from six a.m. Security is tight as a drum. Each floor is accessed by a key in the elevator car, which means the elevator won't stop unless you have the key. There's a fire escape, but you need the same key to access that."

"Any balcony? A terrace?"

"No."

"So what happened then?" I asked. "What happened next that was enough to persuade you to drive two hundred miles to be with me? And please don't say it was my kind brown eyes or I'll know you must have also imagined the man with the bare feet outside your apartment door."

"But your eyes are kind," she insisted. "And I know very well they're not brown, they're blue." She stood up. "Oh, this was a stupid idea.

Coming here. I don't know what came over me. Really, I don't. I should go. I'm well aware of what I must sound like: a woman living on her own, frightened of her own shadow. Except that I never have been before."

I reached out, took her hand, kissed the wrist, and pulled her back onto the sofa beside me. "So you didn't imagine it. I believe you. Go on. Let's hear the rest of it."

"Last night I was in bed and something woke me. I had the strong sensation that someone was in the apartment. There was a very strong smell of something rather horrible. I mean really foul. As if a large animal had died and gone bad in there."

Sara shook her head. What color she had was slowly draining from her face as she replaced it with the dreadful memory of what had happened.

"I don't know how long I lay there, but finally I couldn't stand it any longer. So I took the gun out of the bedside drawer and got up. I went from room to room with the gun in my hand, turning on every light. I would have opened some windows except I was too scared to go near them. Anyway, it didn't matter as the foul smell disappeared just as suddenly as it had arrived. Thinking I must have imagined it, I fetched myself a glass of water and then had a pee. I switched the lights out and went back to bed. I read for a little and then turned out the light. Almost as soon as I did, I heard a series of very loud and deliberate knocks on the window beside my pillow. Which really freaked me out. Like I said, I'm on the ninth floor. I mean there's no one who could have been out there tapping like that."

"Describe the knocks you heard."

She leaned forward and demonstrated on the coffee table. "One, two, three," she said. "Just like that. At regular intervals. It happened maybe six or seven times." She shivered again and then leaned back into the fold of my arm. "I think I screamed the first time. Then I was angry. I pulled back the curtains, although I don't know what I expected to see." She shrugged. "Peter Quint? I don't know. But there was nothing. All I could see were the lights of the city." She paused. "I'm sorry. Peter Quint is a character in a novella by Henry James called *The Turn of the Screw.* It's the story of a young governess who goes to look after two children at a remote English country house and becomes convinced that she can see the ghost of her predecessor and her employer's dead valet: Peter Quint. He has a very nasty habit of peering in at the window."

"I've read it."

"You have?" She sounded surprised.

"Peter Ekman mentioned it in his diary. So I thought it might provide me with an insight." I shrugged. "But it didn't. At least not until now."

"Anyone peering in my window would have to have been holding on to a rope."

"Maybe they were. Is there a window cleaner's platform?"

"Yes, but I'd certainly have seen it; or perhaps I'd have seen the cables that support the platform. It wasn't that dark." She shook her head firmly. "No, someone was trying to frighten me and I know that because—I heard someone laughing."

"Where? Outside the window? Inside the apartment?"

"Outside the window."

"I see. This happened when?"

"Friday night."

"What happened yesterday?"

"Yesterday I went to see a friend who's a shrink. She heard me out and then wrote me a prescription for sleeping pills and tranquilizers."

"Which you didn't take?"

"Is it that obvious? No."

I drank some more of the white wine. Oddly, it tasted even more delicious now than before and, in the lamplight, it was hard to imagine how something that looked so beautiful could contain a substance as hazardous and intoxicating as alcohol. Sometimes it's a little hard to see the danger in ordinary things. Similarly, it was difficult to decide what to do about Sara. Sending her home seemed out of the question. For one thing, she'd drunk too much wine to be safely driving a two-hundred-mile-an-hour car and, for another, she'd probably have become hysterical at the idea of being on her own. But given the threats made to my life by Nelson Van Der Velden and what had happened to me since then, was it wise to let her stay with me? Again I wondered how much to tell Sara about that, and once again I decided that it was probably best to avoid the subject altogether.

Of course, I was also troubled by what she had told me because of the way it seemed to defy any logical explanation. And not just what she had told me; if the Charles Hindemith I had met in the street outside my own front door was indeed her first husband, who was dead, then it wasn't just Sara who needed urgently to see a psychiatrist, it was me, too. But how was I to find out more about him without alarming her further?

If all of that wasn't enough, what was now nagging at my mind once again was the uncomfortable thought that the only rational explanation for what had happened to Sara Espinosa—and by extension to Osborne, Richardson, Ekman, Davidoff, Esther Begleiter, David Durham, and even, perhaps, me—was something irrational; that the impossible had suddenly become possible after all.

"Look, you're very welcome to stay here with me," I said. "But if you don't mind, I'll change the sheets. It's been a while since I made up the bed."

She started to protest. "Do you want me to sleep with you?" she asked. "Just say if you don't."

"Of course. I wouldn't have it any other way. Not now. Why? Don't you?"

"It's just that some men prefer to sleep alone," she explained. "Luis, my third husband, couldn't bear to sleep with me after we'd had sex. I think I disgusted him."

"Nothing about you disgusts me," I told her. "I reserve that privilege for myself."

"But Giles—do you mind if I call you Giles? I don't care for 'Gil' very much . . ."

"Not at all. It's my name."

"Why do you feel like that?"

"I'm a bit OCD," I explained. "I know it doesn't look like it now, but sometimes I get a bit freaked out by germs and by the need to impose order on the world." I shrugged. "I probably need to see a shrink. That's what my boss thinks."

"A God complex," she said. "That's just a normal part of the human condition. You have germs to worry about. God had Lucifer."

"You make it sound reassuringly normal."

"It is. There's nothing really wrong with you, Giles. Nothing that a good woman can't fix."

"Are you volunteering for the job?"

She paused as if she really was considering that possibility.

"It wasn't really a sensible question," I said.

"Oh, but it is, my darling man. It's an excellent question. I don't know why, but I feel very safe with you, Giles."

"It's the badge and the gun. Makes me look like Gary Cooper." I grinned. "Do not forsake me, oh my darling. Here, I'll show you up to the room."

I led the way up the creaking stairs and opened a linen cupboard in the corner. On each shelf was a set of beautifully ironed sheets from when Father Dyer had employed a housekeeper, and on top of each set of sheets were a small bar of scented soap and a label indicating the particular bed they fitted. I picked out a set and she helped me to make up the bed in my room.

"What was he like? Your first husband?"

"Charles? Very handsome in a mature sort of way. His hair was like platinum. I used to love running my hands through it. He was witty, arrogant, opinionated, and, on occasion, the most infuriating man I ever met. A typical upper-crust New Yorker. Like Gore Vidal with a bad smell under his nose."

It was also an excellent description of the man I had met in the street.

"There's a bathroom next door," I said, handing her a clean towel and trying to contain my growing sense of disquiet. "And you'll find a new toothbrush in the cabinet."

"For a man who hasn't had any guests since he moved in, you seem very well set up for visitors."

"Not me," I said. "Father Dyer. And you're quite safe here. If you hear any tapping on the window, it will only be branches of the tree in the wind." I certainly hoped that was true. "Can't seem to find any tree surgeons here in Galveston. Like everyone else, they all seem to have moved out."

She looked only partly reassured by this information.

I held out my hand. "Give me your car keys and I'll put the top up on your Bentley."

She glanced out of the window—the last light was gone and even the moon was covered with clouds—and then blankly at me.

"In case it rains," I added. "Unless you'd prefer to do it yourself."

She shook her head silently. She didn't need to say so, but I could tell that she was obviously afraid of the dark.

It was a good thing I wasn't.

"I might be outside for a while," I lied. "I have to check my own car."

It sounded plausible enough, I thought.

"All right," she said. "But don't be too long."

"It's okay," I said. "Really. Nothing's going to happen to you here. Why don't you take a bath? There's plenty of water. We've got lots of water in Galveston."

TWENTY-TWO

It was absurd, of course, and I was beginning to suspect that I might be as mad as my poor uncle Bill. They do say that madness runs in families and I was now facing up to the possibility that in mine it was sprinting toward total insanity.

I was walking up a deserted Galveston street to visit the eccentric Mr. Hindemith; I wanted to satisfy myself that when I'd met him the previous day I hadn't been talking with the dead man who was Sara Espinosa's first husband. Could anything have been more ridiculous than that? No. But I knew that I faced a sleepless night unless I was able to prove to myself what the remaining rational part of my mind told me was obvious: that there are no such things as ghosts and very probably I would find some ordinary and sensible explanation for all that was crowding into my unruly mind.

Everything in the moonlight looked black-and-white, like an old movie, and I half expected to see a desperate-looking Jimmy Stewart rush out of a house that a well-meaning angel had conveniently arranged to empty of all traces of his ever having lived there. I felt a little like George Bailey myself, wide-eyed, a little scared, not sure of anything, hardly knowing what to believe in and what to doubt, a fish out of water.

It was true, the coincidences seemed uncomfortable, to say the least: the name of Charles Hindemith; the description Sara had given of the man and his tastes; the bare feet of both Mr. Hindemith and the figure Sara imagined she had seen outside her apartment door; the way the man had refused to shake hands with me as if—well, as if such a simple action as that might not have been physically possible. And yet the coincidences also seemed unreasonable: the barefoot Mr. Hindemith I had met would hardly have haunted the apartment of his former wife in Austin while also haunting a house close to me, two hundred miles away in Galveston. And why come and introduce himself? Most of this made even less sense than my late-night visit to the man's house.

"You really are a crazy fucking bastard, Gil Martins," I muttered out loud. "Gisela got that right. You should have seen the Head Fed when you had the chance."

Besides, it was no longer the ideal night to do anything except stay at home. The dry breeze that had stirred Sara's hair outside the diocesan house had turned into a mild gale. It whistled along the desolate street, banging the gates and doors and broken shutters of the dilapidated empty houses and shifting the tall weeds in their small front gardens. At times the wind lifted in pitch so that it sounded like something that had once been human but was not human anymore. Even a deaf man would have been happier without that wind. It seemed to hurry me along as if it were anxious that I should I find out the truth, especially if that truth turned out to be an uncomfortable one. Curiously, there were a couple of moments when the pressure of the wind was so strong it felt almost as if someone had pushed me and I actually turned, half expecting to see the person who had stumbled into me, or even Hindemith himself.

The shadow of something large passed low overhead. It was probably a pelican, a spoonbill, or even an ibis: Galveston's birds were about the only living things to have profited from the exodus of humanity from the city. I actually felt the air from the bird's wings flapping up and down.

As I neared the large and rambling wooden house's exterior, I now rehearsed—so that I might not seem as peculiar as Hindemith himself— an explanation for why I was calling on him at such a late hour.

"I had the sudden idea that you were not well, Mr. Hindemith," I muttered out loud, which is another sign that you're losing it, of course. "Perhaps it's just the sudden change in the weather. But I thought it was only neighborly to come and see that you were all right. Especially as neighbors are in short supply around here."

It sounded lame, but it didn't sound as bad as "I just came around to check out that you're not a fucking ghost."

I'd brought my Glock, which I'd reloaded; I'd also clipped a little tactical flashlight on the muzzle, because all of the houses were dark and there were no streetlights. When the clouds made a black fist around the moon, it was hard to see very much at all. But as I neared Hindemith's front door, I saw there was a very faint light in a turret room on the third floor, as if a single candle had been burning there instead of an electric light. That wouldn't have surprised me. If anyone looked like the kind of person to light a room with a candle, it was Mr. Hindemith.

I walked up the steps onto the porch where a wheel-back rocking chair stood moving gently in the wind; whenever I had driven past the house, this was where I had usually seen Hindemith, and it was tempting to imagine that only a few seconds before he had stood up and gone inside the house. A set of Corinthian bells and chimes hung like a miniature church organ from the porch ceiling immediately above the chair as if designed to catch the dreams of the chair's occupant, and they seemed to resonate continuously, adding a surreal, angelic touch to the night. I searched for a doorbell and, not finding one, moved a screen so that I could knock on the door. It was wide open, so I shouted into the hallway several times and then stepped inside onto a bare wooden floor that creaked like an old galleon.

Right away I encountered a feeling of strong foreboding. I took out the gun and switched on the flashlight. Then I looked around for the electric light, but like many of the houses in that part of Galveston, the electricity wasn't working; probably it hadn't worked in that house since the hurricane, thus the candle I thought I'd seen upstairs.

My footsteps seemed to arouse something on the garbage-strewn floor that scurried off into the darkness. An enormous leaning tower of pizza boxes stood in one corner of the room as if someone had eaten a pizza next to it every day for five years. The place smelled like an open grave.

"I should have brought a fucking Domino's," I said.

In spite of that, it was hard to imagine anyone living in such a curious place. Everything else was under dust sheets except for a cobweb-strewn glass-bowl light that hung over my head, which seemed to be full of dead insects. There was a long dirty mark along the wall that showed the high point of the floodwater and reminded me of just how devastating Ike had been in Galveston. A large but empty fireplace occupied the center of the wall with enough white marble in it to have kept Michelangelo supplied for a lifetime. Below the floodwater line, the marble was as green as if it were covered with seaweed.

"Hello," I called. "Mr. Hindemith? It's Gil Martins from down the street. I saw the door was open and I stopped by to check you were okay, sir."

I walked toward the stairs and mounted the first steps, which were wider than the rest and led up to a short mezzanine floor that gave onto a large and dirty window; on the dusty glass someone had very skillfully drawn an ascending, ethereal staircase that reminded me of the biblical story of Jacob, although, as things turned out, there were not nearly enough of them to have been useful.

As I approached the center of the mezzanine, the clouds cleared from the moon to light up the dust drawing on the window and I felt my heart stop for a moment as I saw a human figure—a naked man who appeared to be standing on the stairs of this almost heavenly ladder; and it was another second before I realized that the naked man was actually standing outside in the backyard, although it was more like a small park; the next moment the man glanced my way and moved quickly in the opposite direction.

"Mr. Hindemith," I exclaimed, although I wasn't exactly sure it was him. The figure had silver hair like Hindemith's but was, I thought, more muscular than the man I had met; then again, that man had been wearing clothes. "Wait a minute, please. I need to talk to you, sir."

Thinking I must have scared him out of his bed and out of the big house—it was hardly the kind of place that anyone visited, least of all late at night—I realized I'd have done better to have waited until the morning. Now all I could think of was the need to apologize to the old man for having disturbed his sleep and perhaps tell him that I would fetch him safely back to his bed before he injured himself.

I saw a dilapidated set of French windows and went through them into the back garden, immediately regretting it. I found my face covered in a large cobweb that made me think no one had been through there in a long time and that there must have been some other way out I hadn't seen. Something crawled on the back of my neck and I clutched at it several times before I was able to cure myself of the sensation that I had a large spider underneath my shirt collar. At the same time I caught a glimpse of the same naked white figure running down to the bottom of an unkempt lawn before it disappeared into a thick grove of trees.

"Hey, Mr. Hindemith," I shouted. "Don't be afraid. It's me. Gil Martins. Come back, sir."

I ran after him across the overgrown lawn and was swiftly among the trees; I could still hear him running ahead of me and it surprised me that the old man should be so quick on his toes and that his bare skin should be so apparently careless of the branches and bushes that pulled and tugged at my clothes. His footsteps were hardly light; the noise of his naked feet on the ground was like the sound of galloping hooves, which was enough to convince me not only that the old man was made of solid flesh and blood but that he was younger and more vigorous than I'd thought. This fact alone left me feeling a little reassured that the man I was pursuing was real and could therefore have nothing to do with Sara's ex-husband. Clearly I was on a wild-goose chase after all.

"Fuck this," I said.

Perhaps it was this fact that slowed me down; or perhaps it was just that I've pursued enough fugitives to know that it's easy for someone to injure themselves when they're being chased; there was that, of course, and the strong possibility that I would have injured myself; either way I stopped running.

"You're going to break your leg or take your eye out running in the dark like this, Martins." I laughed out loud as if the sound of my own amusement might make what I was doing seem more normal. "This was a stupid idea. The guy's probably nuts anyway. Almost as nuts as you are. Anyone who can eat that amount of fucking pizza belongs in the bughouse."

I looked around, trying to make out which way I had come. A grackle shrieked in the darkness, which did little for my nerves and seemed to set off some laughing gulls. Like the wind, wild birds at night have a capacity to make even unimaginative people such as I am feel very uncomfortable. The battery in my tactical flashlight was dying already; it had been months since I'd bothered replacing it. In the shifting darkness of that small and overgrown forest there was no sign of the near-derelict house. I wasn't exactly lost, but I had no idea which direction would lead me back to the house and the street. I holstered the gun and looked hopefully at the sky in the hope of seeing the curtain of cloud part to reveal the way back.

Hope did not last long because a second or two later the wind dropped suddenly, the birds stopped their noise, and I heard a heavy, inhuman panting sound in the surrounding bushes that chilled my blood. It was slow and steady and—there can be no other word for that sound—frightening. The panting sound turned into a thick, salivating swallow that gradually became a low growl.

"Mr. Hindemith, is that you, sir?" I paused. "If that's you fucking around with me, I should warn you I'm armed and nervous and that's not a good combination."

Even as I spoke, I was sure it wasn't a man. No man ever sounded like that. I might have said it was a dog except that it was too large; and I might have said it was a big cat—perhaps a mountain lion—except that even the biggest cats know how to move through undergrowth with great stealth. I struck a match and held it over my head in the hope of seeing some sign of a trail I'd made that might afford me a way of escape.

What I saw in the flickering light drew such a horrified cry of disgust from my own lungs that I dropped the match and, stepping instinctively backward, I tripped over a thick bush and fell heavily onto the ground. I might have found another match and lit it but for the strong desire never again to see what I had seen a moment or two before. This was the supine naked figure of a large and powerful man; only it had not been Charles Hindemith I saw but someone else, the malevolence of whose horrible but intensely bright face and penetratingly awful gaze was now vividly attached to the back of my retinas. It

was an extraordinary moment, for it was as if I had glanced into the
dead silence of another unnatural world and seen something hideous
that was human and yet was like no human I had ever seen. I can't express it any better than to say that I instinctively knew I had come face-
to-face with something unspeakably evil that seemed to regard me
as—for want of a better word—*prey*.

"Who are you?" I heard myself bark.

I reached for my gun and found to my horror that it had slipped out
of its holster. I twisted around and, ignoring a branch that scratched my
face, patted the ground around me in a desperate and ultimately futile
search for the Glock. If I had found it, I would without hesitation have
started shooting, so great was my fear and horror. But not finding it in
the dark, I had little choice but to address the thing again.

"Who are you?" I repeated dumbly because, in the core of my being, I found I was suddenly aware of an answer to this question that si-
multaneously flashed the answers to several other questions, too, an
awful insight that even then, perhaps, served to restore my faith in the
Church of Rome. Had something like this happened to Philip Osborne
and those others? Was this the reason that Willard Davidoff had tried
to climb a forty-foot tree in Olmsted Park?

The wind dropped again. In the darkness the growling sound persisted for a moment and then stopped completely; and the darkness and
the palpable silence that followed became the real source of my terror.
To be alone with something as horrible as that in the dark was like all
my childhood nightmares made living, loathsome flesh.

And the smell—the smell was of something long decayed from the
bottom of a deep well or unfathomable pit. It was the same smell that I
had encountered in the diocesan house down the street.

As it was of old, in the beginning and in the Bible.

The next second I picked myself up and ran. I didn't know where, I
just knew I had to get away from that terrible spot.

And now I had the certain knowledge that whatever I had seen was running after me. The chaser had become the chased. I ran as if the shadows themselves were in pursuit of me; and perhaps they were. Panic took hold of my whole self as I crashed into a tree before going around it and running on. Once again I tripped and sprawled on the ground and, glancing around, heard something following close behind me. I picked myself up and this time I was more fortunate because the clouds parted and the moon appeared again, illuminating my position and the direction I needed to go. I sprinted toward the back of the house and, reaching it, went through the French windows and slammed them shut behind me.

For a moment, I stood there with my foot jammed against the bottom of the frame, panting loudly and shaking with terror and staring through the dusty windowpanes at the moonlit garden where something in human shape hovered on the edge of the tree line. My heart felt as if it were going to leap out of my chest and take off on its own. Never had I felt fear like this, not once since joining the FBI had I felt myself actually physically sick with dread. It was as though my whole personality had changed from man to boy. My heart was such an afflicted thing and my breathing so labored that at any moment I thought the very life would flee from my terrified body.

"Jesus Christ, what the fuck was that?" I muttered. "What the fuck was that? What the fuck was that?"

I stayed there, staring out of the window for several minutes before the movement in the trees ceased altogether and my heartbeat and breathing returned to something like normal.

"Get a grip," I whispered, almost angry with myself for being so afraid of something I couldn't explain. "And that's all it is. Just something you can't explain. For all you know, that could have been someone in trouble, lying on the ground. Maybe it was Mr. Hindemith. Maybe he also fell and hurt himself. Perhaps he's still lying there, hurt, waiting for you to come and help him. Perhaps he's in need of an ambulance. Instead, you're cowering in here like a fucking pussy. So much for all your FBI training. Jesus, you're such a fucking pussy."

I started to laugh.

"You're such a fucking pussy, Gil Martins."

I paused, still running in my head the film my brain had shot in the split second when I'd lit the match and seen the weird-looking man lying on the ground. Was it really a man I'd seen? There was no getting away from the fact that something about that man I'd seen was not right. Yes, the expression on the man's face had been extraordinarily hostile. And there was also the way the thing had groped at my feet. But it wasn't so much that as the fact that the long, bony fingers had been more like claws.

"So, he needs a fucking manicure," I said. "Come on, Martins, anyone looks like shit when they're hurt. If he looked pissed off, it was because you chased him through his own back garden, you dumb asshole. And I bet you'd look pretty damned evil if someone came wandering into your house in the dark."

I swallowed hard and finally caught all of my breath.

"Just don't go believing that shit Nelson Van Der Velden told you. This has got nothing to do with that. You hear? Come on, man. Let's see what you're made of. Get back out there and do your fucking job, okay? You're an FBI agent, not a lingerie designer."

I opened the French windows once more and stepped out onto the overgrown lawn. The wind dropped again and the night seemed to hold its breath as if keen to see the outcome of this act of lunacy on my part.

This time I walked slowly down the lawn.

At the bottom of the lawn I turned and looked back at the house, just to get my bearings and then, with my heart in my mouth, I stepped cautiously into the woods and struck several matches, one after the other, but I didn't see anything.

I stood still for a moment and listened carefully. "Mr. Hindemith? Or whoever you are, please identify yourself. I'm an FBI agent and I'm armed." That part was a lie, of course; my gun was still lying on the ground somewhere in the garden.

But I heard nothing by way of a reply. Just the wind in the trees. And an owl hooting somewhere in the darkness.

A minute passed and then another until I figured I was wasting my time and moved again, only this time I disturbed something else that was lying on the ground—probably the ibis or the spoonbill I thought I'd seen earlier; it flew up into the air with a great beating of wings and then was gone, leaving me with a stupid grin on my face and the beginnings of a terminal cardiac condition.

I walked back to the house and out the front door, and jogged my way back down the street—all the time looking around to see if I was being followed by something—toward the lights of the diocesan house and home.

The wind had picked up again and this time there was some rain in the air; it cooled my face and dampened my shirt and felt good against the skin on my forehead as if the water had been taken straight from the font. But my hand on the doorknob of the diocesan house was such a trembling thing that it looked as if I had Parkinson's disease, and I wondered if it would ever be still again. Inside the house I tried to close the door quietly, but at the last second the wind seemed to catch it and the door banged shut with a loud and reverberating noise.

I let out a breath and then fetched myself a drink from the cabinet, downing it quickly.

"That's better."

The scotch collected what human spirit I had left, fortified me a little so that I was able to resist the true implications of what I had experienced for just a while longer. Surely I had mistaken what I had seen.

"Of course you did. You imagined it."

Yes. My own imagination had carried me away for a moment. Nothing could have been what I had thought. Such things were impossible. For me, especially. I had made a choice, after all. And I should stick with that choice. There was no self-respect to be had in abandoning that earlier, rational decision, especially on such flimsy evidence. Fuck that. If I changed my mind now, it would just be from fear, and all that would be left would be that same fear and self-loathing. Nobody could live like that, could they?

"Jesus Christ," said a woman's voice.

I spun around to see Sara in the doorway. She was wearing a T-shirt and not much else other than a severe look of alarm. The look on her face was all due to me.

"What the hell happened?"

I shook my head. "Nothing much," I said, fixing a sort of smile onto my face. "The wind is picking up. I think there's a storm coming. It caught me by surprise. I went into the backyard to close the gate and it blew back into me and knocked me flat on my back, that's all. Stunned me for a moment." I touched my face and found some blood on my fingers. "Shit. Must have cut myself, too."

She swallowed noticeably. "That's not what it looks like."

"Really, I'm fine," I said.

"Come here." Sara took me by the hand and led me back into the hall, then placed me in front of a full-length mirror that hung on a wall, and switched on the overhead light.

She didn't accuse me of lying, not right away; she didn't have to; all she did was let my appearance speak for itself.

I was quite a sight. My hair was standing on end as if I'd been electrocuted; the irises in my staring eyes were so dilated I looked as if I'd been taking drugs; and my face and chest were covered in blood. There were five parallel scratches on my face and my chest—deep enough to have torn through my shirt—as if a large and fierce animal had lashed out at me with razor-sharp claws. I looked as if I had been mauled.

"Holy Christ," I whispered.

"You'd better let me put something on those claw marks," she said quietly.

"They're not claw marks," I insisted. "Where do you get an idea like that? The gate left me stunned, that's all. In the dark I walked into a tree and scratched myself on the branch. Let's not get carried away here, Sara."

"They look much more like claw marks than anything a tree might have done."

I shrugged. "What, you think there's a mountain lion out there? This is East Texas, not Arizona, Sara. It was a tree. I walked into a fucking tree. It was my own stupid fault."

She pointed at my holster.

"Your gun is gone."

"It must have fallen out when I fell over. No harm done, I'll find it in the morning."

"Which begs the question why you took it in the first place."

"Oh, I see. There's a flashlight on the muzzle."

"Do you have any iodine?" she asked. "Or antiseptic?"

"Under the kitchen sink, I think."

I fetched myself another drink and knocked it back quickly. Glancing down at my chest, I tried to recall the moment I had received the lacerations; surely it had just been the branch of a tree, after all—a branch with five smaller branches that only resembled the fingers and claws of an outstretched hand. That's all it could have been. In my panic to be away from that man lying on the ground I had simply run into the clawlike branch of a tree. And yet, somewhere inside my soul—for I think such things do exist—I knew differently. After all, how could I account for that man lying on the ground?

"Yes, a tree," I said. "That's all. I'm not really injured, you know. I think it looks worse than it is."

I could see that Sara didn't believe me. She didn't say so. Perhaps she, too, knew but didn't want to know. I understood what that felt like.

"After I brushed my teeth," she said from the kitchen, "I went outside to ask you something and you weren't there."

"Like I said, there's a storm coming. That's why I probably didn't hear you."

She came back into the room with a bowl and a roll of paper towels.

"I appreciate that you're trying not to scare me," she said. "Really, I do. But from now on, I think it's best if you don't lie to me. Even for the best of reasons."

"All right," I said.

"You'd better take that shirt off so I can dress those wounds. And then you can tell me what really happened."

I took off my shirt; then I sat beside her on the sofa and let her wipe the wounds with antiseptic-soaked paper towels. For some reason, I started to tremble.

"I think you're suffering from shock," she said.

For a moment, I almost laughed. *Shock*, I wanted to say, *that's not shock, lady, that's fucking terror.* But I restrained myself just in time. I could see no point in adding to Sara's considerable store of terror with a large spoonful of my own.

"I don't suppose this will help very much," she said, and then she kissed one of my scratches. "In fact," she added, "there's probably"—she kissed another—"a very good chance"—and another—"that what I'm doing now could even infect them, the average human mouth being as dirty as it is."

I took hold of her dimpled chin, looked at her generous lips, and then kissed them with lingering appreciation.

"There's nothing dirty about your mouth," I said, licking her sharp little teeth and under her upper lip. "In fact, it's just about the nicest mouth I've ever seen."

Rain pattered against the window as if reminding us that there was still a real world outside.

"I should go put the top up on your car like I meant to do earlier. Be a crime for the rugs in that thing to get wet." I kissed her some more. "Did you have your bath like I told you?"

"Not yet."

I nodded at the ceiling. "You go up and have one, and I'll be along in a moment."

"All right," she said, but she insisted I kiss her before letting me go.

I went outside. I still had the Bentley's key in my pocket, and it was only a matter of a few seconds to operate the top. I had just turned back to the house when I heard Sara scream.

My chest immediately tightened again and I ran with limbs made clumsy by fear, and then I fell, half crawled, and then scrambled up the steps into the house.

TWENTY-THREE

She was huddled up into a ball in a corner of the bathroom, hugging her knees to her chest, with her eyes closed and her beautiful face pressed against the wall. I knelt down and, for a moment, I looked closely at Sara's head and body for some injury or sign of what had scared her, but found nothing that gave a clue as to what had happened. The bathroom looked the same except that the bath was running. I turned the tap off and came back to her side.

"Hey, there," I said gently. "Take it easy. What happened? What's the matter?"

Sara didn't answer, but as soon as I put my hand on her head, she threw her arms around me like a little child and held me tight and started to cry. I let her hold me like this for several minutes before she became calm enough to tell me what had frightened her.

"You said we're alone here," she said. "Didn't you?"

"That's right. We are alone. I promise. It's just the two of us."

"Yes, I saw you make up the bed," she said haltingly. "I saw you. I helped you. We did that, didn't we?"

"Yes," I said. "We did. Now, take it easy."

She nodded and wiped her face with a towel I gave her.

"Yes," she sniffed. "When you went out the first time to put the top up on my car, I came in here, to the bathroom, to brush my teeth and stuff. But I didn't go to bed. Just now I came in here again to run a bath. But before I did, I glanced in the bedroom. Which is when I saw the bed."

She was calm now, but her face was a sickly color of gray.

I nodded and then stood up and put my head around the bedroom door. Her pants, jacket, and shoes lay on the floor by the bed where she had dropped them and a big Hermès handbag was open beside her watch and jewelry on the dressing table. The TV was on, but the volume was turned down and the remote control lay on the floor next to her shoes. The blind was drawn, and even though the rain sounded heavy against the window, everything looked normal to me.

"What about it?" I asked.

I came back into the bathroom and knelt down at her side.

She shook her head. "Tell me that this is not some kind of sick joke," she said.

"I don't understand," I said. "There's no joke. I'm not in the mood for jokes, nor are you, I think. But forgive me, I really don't see what the problem is here, Sara."

She swallowed a brick and then let out a big, teary sigh. "The problem is, my darling man, that the bed has been slept in, but I didn't sleep in it."

"What?"

"Yes. Which means, if you didn't sleep in it and I didn't sleep in it, then who did?"

I got up and put my head around the door of the bedroom again. There was no doubt about it: the sheets and quilt that I had carefully arranged on the bed were now disordered as if someone had slept there for a good eight hours, which made no sense at all.

I was thoroughly disturbed by what she was suggesting. On top of everything I'd just been through in Mr. Hindemith's back garden, this was a lot more than I had bargained for. Was she part of some mad conspiracy to fuck with my head? And if so, why? And why her? Someone with her background could never have been one of Nelson Van Der Velden's followers; and besides, if she was to be believed, someone had been doing a very good job of fucking with her head, too.

I went back into the bathroom and sat on the toilet.

"Tell me everything that happened after I left the house the first time," I said patiently.

She nodded and, resting her head against the wall, stared up at the ceiling light. "The first time you went out I was in the bedroom about to get undressed. I wanted to ask if you had a hair dryer so I could wash my hair so I went downstairs again and opened the front door to ask you about that, only you weren't there. Which scared me. It's very quiet around here. So I came back upstairs and sat around for a moment or two wondering what to do and if I might have made a mistake coming here. After a while, I got undressed, like you see. I took off my clothes and my shoes and socks, and came in here, and then when I heard you return, I went downstairs again. And you looked like you'd been attacked by a wild animal and were hitting the whiskey bottle."

"Yes, I remember."

"So, when I went downstairs, the bed—the one we'd made up—it hadn't been slept in, and now it has." She shrugged. "It's as simple as that."

I nodded.

"You don't think that you could have sat on the bed and sort of messed it up while you were waiting for me to come back in earlier?" I suggested. "Sort of absently? The way you do when you're preoccupied with something?"

"No," she said. "I remember. I sat on the chair in front of the bed-room TV. I watched it for about fifteen minutes. Not once did I sit on the bed."

I went back into the bedroom and pressed my hand onto the bottom sheet of the bed; it wasn't warm but a chill passed over me all the same. The bed was damp to the touch, as if someone had jumped out of the bath and got straight into the bed.

"You'll be relieved to know it doesn't actually feel like it's been slept in," I said as coolly as I was able.

"I don't know if that helps or not," she said.

Instinctively, I glanced at the window, which was shut, and then I looked up at the ceiling to check for a leak; I even stood on the bed and pressed my hand against the plaster, but it was dry.

"That is, I mean, the bed's not warm. All the same, I think I'll change it again. To make you feel more comfortable."

When I was through, I came back into the bathroom. "It's okay now. I've made it up again."

"You think I'm crazy, don't you?" she said.

"No, not at all, Sara."

"In view of what's happened these past few days, it's a wonder I'm not; but if someone is trying to drive me out of my mind, then I'm not going to let them, do you hear? I've got a first-class mind and nothing and no one is going to be allowed to fuck with that."

Some of that sounded as if it was directed my way, so once again I knelt down beside her and took her hand. "Sara, please believe me," I said. "I had absolutely nothing to do with this."

"I do believe you," she said. "Actually, that's half the problem."

"What do you mean?"

"After I came downstairs, you were never out of my sight. I really don't see how you could have come up here without my noticing it. Either there's someone else in this house or—I can't think of any other explanation; at least there's not one I want to think of." She swallowed uncomfortably. "As a matter of fact, I think I'm going to be sick."

She crawled over to the toilet, lifted the lid, and then retched into the bowl. If she was acting, then she was worth a Golden Globe.

When she'd finished, she flushed the toilet and I helped her to wash her face and drink some water.

"Feel better?"

"A little."

I led her into my bedroom and tried to make her comfortable under the sheet. Next I switched on all the lamps to eliminate any shadows. It was just a pity I couldn't do anything about the overgrown tree outside my window that was tapping at the pane more insistently than usual because of the wind.

"I've never slept in a cop's bed before," she said. "Or, for that matter, a priest's." She smiled a thin halfhearted smile as if she was trying to recover her sense of humor.

"With three husbands, you surprise me," I said, rising to the challenge.

"Not that I think I am going to sleep," she admitted. "I'm very tired, but I'm not at all sure yet that I'm going to stay here."

"No? It's hardly a night to go anywhere on your own."

"I was thinking you could come with me," she said.

"Yes, but where? A hotel?"

"Maybe."

"In Galveston?" I made a face.

"Good point. Well, maybe we could drive to Houston. Or find a motel on the way."

"All right. If you want. I'll drive you wherever you want to go. Houston. Austin. You name it. Just say when and where. Your car or mine. Although your car does look a lot nicer."

She shook her head. "No, that's all right. Let's stay here for now. I just wanted to hear you say it. I guess if you were planning to murder me here you wouldn't do that."

"Until you called me this evening, I thought I wouldn't ever see you again," I admitted. "So I don't know how I could have been planning anything that involved you."

"Really?"

"What I mean to say is, you called me, remember?"

"Yes." She smiled again. This time it looked more convincing than before. "And I'm very glad I did. You're very sweet. Where the hell were you all day, anyway?"

"I had lunch with a guy from our computer forensics lab," I said. "And then I went to see a movie at the Cinemark in Webster just off the Gulf Freeway."

She nodded.

"Look," I said. "I need to fetch another gun from the car. Just in case. And to lock up around here."

"I'd rather you didn't leave me alone."

"I'll be no more than a minute."

"There's a gun in my purse," she said. "You can borrow that if you like."

"All right." I handed the bag to her and watched as she brought out a little Walther P22 compact pistol from its capacious interior.

"Here," she said.

"Nice little gun," I said.

"You can only say something like that in Texas."

"Yes, I suppose so. But it feels good in your hand."

"Ditto."

I checked the magazine. Then I tucked the gun into the waistband of my trousers. I might have let her keep it if I hadn't been worried she was scared enough to shoot me by accident.

"Are you expecting trouble?" she asked.

"I don't know," I said. "I mean, there's what happened with the bed to consider, isn't there?"

"I'd rather not, if you don't mind. But I'm not sure how you're going to shoot someone that neither of us can see."

"Fair point." I smiled, but only to conceal the fact that suddenly I was convinced she really did believe that someone other than us had been occupying my bed; and it made the hairs on the back of my neck stand up.

"On the other hand, I still don't really know what happened to you earlier." She nodded at the scratches on my torso. "I mean, those don't look like they were done by anything invisible."

"I already told you about that. It was the branch of a tree that did this."

"If you say so. But look." She held up her hand.

"What am I looking at?"

"My nails."

"They're very nice."

"I got them done today in Galveston. While I was waiting for you to come back."

"For Galveston that counts as the return of civilization. I'm impressed. "

"Yes, they do look nice. But they're also sharp. I've scratched enough men in my time—in anger or while having sex—to know what the effect of a human scratch looks like."

"I can count myself lucky, I guess."

I turned the volume up on the TV so that she'd have company while I was out of the room, and then walked to the door. Leno was still on.

"Where are you going now?"

"To lock the front door. Like I said."

"You won't be long, will you?"

"I'll be just a minute."

"And you won't be going outside or anything?"

I shook my head. "I'm coming straight back up to make love to you again."

TWENTY-FOUR

As I went downstairs, I had the strongest sensation of there being something unwelcome in the house and immediately noted a trail of very wet footprints that led in from the front door along the parquet floor. Were they mine? I might have said they were except for two things. The footprints led into the sitting room whereas I was quite certain that on entering the house in response to Sara's scream I had run straight upstairs. The other thing was much more disturbing—these were large, barefoot, Man Friday–style prints and I was wearing shoes.

For a moment, I just stared at them as if doubting the existence of the shoes that were still on my feet, but the very instant that it registered that these could hardly be my own footprints, I drew Sara's gun from the waistband of my trousers and quietly worked the slide. Was this the man I had chased in Mr. Hindemith's garden—perhaps Mr. Hindemith himself? The man who had scared the living crap out of me? If it was, I owed him a hard slap in the mouth with the Walther. But suppose the intruder was armed? Suppose he had found the Glock I'd dropped in the garden? Suppose I ended up getting shot with my own gun?

Then three things happened—they were practically simultaneous, but they seemed to occur in slow succession, as if time had decelerated to allow me longer to feel more afraid than I was already—these were accompanied by several missed heartbeats, a prickling on my skin, and a sort of vacuum around my head and shoulders that seemed to suck the sound right out of my ears.

First of all, the power went out, plunging the entire house into darkness; the next instant I knew without any doubt that there was a figure standing by the window in the sitting room; and the third was that Sara screamed again. This time I could guess the reason for her fright, and stiffening myself, I took a step back onto the stair and called up to her.

"Sara? Listen to me. It's just a power outage caused by the storm. I'll fix everything just as soon as I find another flashlight and the fuse box. So take it easy, honey, and close your eyes and everything will be cool. I promise."

I wish that could have been true; but I knew this was now highly unlikely. The air was still as a stagnant pond, and much as I tried, I could hear no clue for the sight that was awaiting me now in the sitting room; at the same time I knew I had to confront whatever it was just to prove to myself that I was still in the real world where a mad evangelical pastor's prayers did not come true.

As it happened, there was no other flashlight at hand; but being a priest, Father Dyer had left several beeswax candles about the place, and I quickly lit two with the matches in my pocket and very cautiously carried one into the sitting room, where I noiselessly closed the door behind me with my elbow so as not to alarm Sara any further. I hardly wanted her to come down the stairs and find me facing a barefoot intruder. I was a little less concerned about the figure still standing in the darkness and I'd have happily shot whoever or whatever it was just out of sheer annoyance.

"Who's there?" I snarled. "Speak up, you bastard."

The candle made little impression on the shadows, and the silent figure remained just a silhouette beside the window, his head jerking one way and then the other for no apparent reason. But this was accompanied by an odd sound that seemed to be coming from the figure itself: it was as if I were listening to someone—a man, perhaps—violently exerting himself to be free from some sort of bond or restraint.

"I've got a gun," I said quietly. "And I won't hesitate to use it. Now, slowly step into the light so I can see you."

That might have worked on a real person, but after everything else that had occurred, I already had the impression that this was something different, for wouldn't a real person have said something by now? And done what they were told? After all, the gun in my hand was clearly visible to whoever was in the shadows.

"I'm losing patience with you. Now who the fuck are you?"

I stepped forward and felt my own jaw drop at least an inch as the yellow light from the candle lit up the intruder's twisted face. And seeing him, I felt as if some unseen hand had picked me up like an hourglass and turned me upside down, with all the sand inside me now reversing. Everything I had believed—which is to say, everything I had come to believe about belief—was wrong. I was beginning to see that now. You might say that it was the moment when my life changed forever. And the impact of this dreadful knowledge quite literally disarmed me because I put the gun down on the mantelpiece and then covered my mouth, possibly to stop myself from crying out or even puking with terror.

"Holy shit," I breathed through my fingers. "Holy fucking shit. I don't believe it. What the hell are you doing here?"

I had not seen the weird little man standing in front of me for years and yet I recognized him instantly. He twitched uncontrollably for several seconds, snarled a silent remark at some unseen devil, and then appeared to calm a little.

It was my mad uncle Bill, hardly changed from when I'd last seen him almost thirty years ago, wearing a pink nylon shirt, loose gray trousers, and thick, ill-fitting glasses that so badly needed cleaning they were almost opaque. He was thin, too, as undernourished looking as he'd always been, eaten up with raw, nervous energy and bughouse madness.

"Hello, Gil," he said, in a strong Glasgow accent. "How are ye, son?"

"Bill." I shook my head. "Jesus, it can't be you. You're five thousand miles away. You're in Scotland."

"Not anymore, son," said Bill. "As a matter of fact, I'm dead. Just a few minutes ago, as it happens."

"I'm sorry," I said, as if I were in a dream.

"No, no. Don't be sorry, son. Wis nae your fault. I've had more enough of the fucking Dykebar Hospital. Had enough of myself, too, if ye ken what I mean. There's so much of that shite you can stand; fucking psychiatrists and other mental cases who're in the bin with you." He started to twitch again for a moment and then addressed the invisible figure near him, just like always. "Stop it. Let me fuckin' tell him my own way."

"Bill," I said. "I just wish there was something we could have done. I wanted to visit you. Really I did, but—" I sighed. "This can't be happening."

"No problem, boy. Really. I was never one tae hold a grudge. I wasn't what you'd call a people person, know what I mean? Your father tried his best, but he could nae cope and so he did what he thought was best. Which was put me in the hospital. To be fair to him, he did try to get me out of there again, but it was no good; by that time I was what they call institutionalized. And that was me fucked, right enough. I don't suppose anyone thought I'd last this fucking long. Least of all me. Matter of fact, that's why I offed myself with some pills. I'd been saving them up for a while so that I could do it properly." He shrugged. "That and a large injection of methadone, just to make sure. Can't beat it, son."

"Bill," I said, closing my eyes. "This isn't real. You can't be in Texas. I hear what you say and some of that makes perfect sense but you can't be in this house. Not now. I must be imagining all of this. Yes, that's it. Something must have happened to me."

I closed my eyes and opened them again, but Bill remained in front of me, as clear as the picture of the angels on the wall.

"Oh, I'm here all right. Wherever the fuck here is. That I don't know and don't ask me to explain it. Awright, fair enough, I'm not real in the way you or that nice wee lassie upstairs would understand, son. No, you could nae say I was real like she is. By the way, son, that's a nice bit of cunt you've got there. Nice one. Wouldn't mind stuffing that bird myself."

I looked away. "No, no, no. This isn't happening. It can't be."

"You've said that already. Repeating yourself is the first sign of madness. Take it from one who knows. You know what I am. And why I'm fucking here, son. It's no good listening to your head with this one, Gil. That isn't going to help. You have to listen with your heart. That wee still voice that we all have inside our heads. The one that gets drowned out by the all the shite that we learn in life about what's real and what isn't. You know what I'm talking about. You've heard that fucking voice yourself, Gil. You just stopped listening tae it for a while, that's all."

"This isn't real."

"Aye, it's difficult. I'll admit that. But think of it like this, if you will. I've returned to this world from the depths, not exactly alive but next best thing, to say just this: that what you hear is true, Gil. And you can speak and believe it all without being shamed, forever and ever, amen."

"Speak and believe in what?" I demanded. "I don't understand."

Bill grew angry for a moment and, lifting his fist, he seemed to beat the air for several seconds before he could speak again.

"In God, Gil," he said. "What else would I be here to talk about? Almighty fucking God. But there's not much time. For either of us. And I just slipped away to give you this warning, see? That you're fucking dead unless you can get yourself back in with him. His angel of death has got you marked out, Gil, and believe me you do not want that bastard to come and get you. You've met him already, I think, so you must know what I'm talking about. He's more demon than angel if you know what I mean. Look, son, it's just best you do as I say. Make your peace with the big man. Everyone gets a second fucking chance. But not everyone is wise enough to take it. Those other poor bastards who died—the ones who got you started down this road—they didn't have a way of seeing the truth that was right in front of their noses. But you do. You've got me. Frankly, I think a lot depends on the messenger. On who gets the fucking job to come back and say hello. Despite all that happened, you and I were once close. That could be it. Aye, that's right. I was always fond of you, Gil boy."

Bill shook his head, which seemed to produce another fit of twitching and silent shouting before he added calmly: "Or, I don't know, maybe it's just that it takes a fucking loony to make any of this sound sensible. Know what I mean? Aye. Maybe that's it, son. That it takes a fucking loony to make almighty God's message sound sensible." He nodded. "Aye, looking back on it—the whole religious thing—I think it probably always did. When you consider it objectively, all of the great religious leaders have been crazies like me, son."

"This is crazy," I said. "That's true at least."

"One last piece of advice, son. Don't think about this too long. There are three stages in your re-integration into God's plan for mankind, Gil. There is learning, there is understanding, and there is acceptance. You're still at the second stage. But there's less time than you think to get to the third stage. By my reckoning, you've got rather less than twenty-four hours. And it might get very rough before it gets better. God's a vindictive bastard, Gil. That's one important truth I've learned already."

"You're not my uncle Bill. I must be mad."

"Look, I'll spell it out for you and then that's me done and away from here. You'll be on your own after that. God doesn't want to destroy you, but he will if he has to." Bill snapped his fingers; it sounded like a thick twig breaking. "Just like that. Only it won't be as quick as that. It'll be something horrible. The way God likes these things done. See, he wants your compliance, your obedience, Gil. He wants you back on his side, genuinely, heart and soul, but especially your soul. He wants you back in the fold like he did the lost sheep or the prodigal son. Because it is intolerable to God that unbelief should exist anywhere, but especially in one who has believed, like you. The seed that fell on the stony ground, so to speak. You have to take it to the Lord in *prayer*, as soon as possible, Gil. *Prayer*. Read that daft woman's fucking book, if you doubt me. Esther Begleiter. She'll tell you the same thing as I am. *Prayer*. That's your only possible recourse. Sorry to sound all fucking preachy, son, but that's how it's got to be. No deviation is permitted. Not anymore. Not now that Pastor Van Der Velden has called this shit down on your head. God is not reasonable, Gil. God is God. He's terrible, just like it says in the bloody Bible."

Bill glanced out of the window. I closed my eyes and let out a long sigh.

"My time with you is almost up," whispered Bill. "If you don't do it out of obedience, Gil, then do it out of fear. And I mean fear because that's how it will be. I would nae be in your shoes, son. Not when that fucking angel starts to plague you. Gil, you've no idea what Azrael is capable of, the terror he can inflict. He's a demon, Gil. A real fucking demon. Shit, I've always known that. When people thought I was a loony, that's what was disturbing me. God and all that comes with him."

Bill still looked like a lunatic, but the earlier ferocity of his words had gone and his voice had grown almost dreamy. That might just as easily have been me, however. And when I opened my eyes again, he had disappeared and I stood there facing a great emptiness as if there were some sort of space behind the air in front of the window where he had been standing. I reached out and put my hand into the dead silence in front of me as if to make sure that he was no longer there.

"Holy shit," I breathed. "What's happening to me?" I felt such a rush of goose bumps across my whole body that I had to grab the blanket Sara had dropped onto the floor when I had first made love to her and wrap it around my shoulders to stop me from shivering. Was it the kava that made my heart feel enlarged? Or my breath so short?

"Holy shit."

I don't know how long I stood there. After what I'd seen—or what I thought I'd seen—I wasn't sure that time had any real meaning, but when I glanced at my wristwatch, I saw that I couldn't have been there longer than a minute or two. I was still holding the candle in my hand as if it were a heretic's taper. Sara's gun was on the mantelpiece where I had placed it. Everything except my loudly beating heart was now quiet. It was the quiet that made everything now seem more horrific to me. Even the rain had stopped.

Surely I had imagined it all. Like Bill, I had become the victim of my own crazed mind. Wasn't the clue to that the very fact that I was on leave to see the FBI psychiatrist? I was nuts. This was beyond OCD and playing solitaire with sugar packets. This made me almost certifiable, within the meaning of the law. I was the one—not Gaynor Allitt— who needed to obtain a magistrate's order for emergency mental health protection; for all I knew, it wasn't just me who was at risk of harming

myself in some indefinable way, it was the poor beautiful woman upstairs. Assuming Sara really was upstairs and was not, like Bill, a fig-
ment of my own imagination. Yes. Hadn't there been a certain wish
fulfillment about the way she had arrived and jumped into bed with
me? And a dreamlike quality about the perfection of our lovemaking?

I sniffed my fingers, which to my relief still smelled of her. I could
hardly imagine that, could I? Sara had to be real. Surely she was still
waiting upstairs in my bedroom and all I had to do was fix the fuse and
go back to bed with her.

As I turned to go and look for the fuse box, the lights came back on.
I looked around the room and found there was very little that was as
different as perhaps it ought to have been. I blew out the candle, picked
up the gun, tucked it back under the waistband of my trousers, and
trudged back upstairs, not really knowing what I expected to find there.

But Sara was exactly where I had left her, still sitting up in bed, her
head resting in her forearms. She looked up as I came in the room and
bit her lip, and I saw that her exquisite face was pale and full of
concern.

"You fixed it then?"

"The fuse?" I said innocently. Surely she would leave if I told her
the truth. Anyone sensible would. "Yes. I fixed it."

She nodded. "You were a long time doing it."

I shrugged. "I'm not an electrician."

"I thought I heard you talking to someone."

I took off my trousers and my shorts, and climbed into bed beside
her, smiling as if nothing were wrong and my heart did not feel as if it
were about to appear on the roof of my mouth.

"Myself. I always talk to myself when I'm trying to fix something.
Mostly it's just swearing on account of the fact that I don't really know
what the fuck I'm doing."

"Kevin was the same. My second husband. He couldn't change a lightbulb without swearing like a trooper. I think he took the failure of all household appliances personally. As if they'd insulted him."

"I can understand that. We can leave the light on if you like."

"Yes, please," she said, throwing back the covers to reveal her nakedness. "Yes, I think you should see it all."

TWENTY-FIVE

Making love to her took my mind off a lot of other things, the way it does—for both of us, I shouldn't wonder. It was a way of forgetting and I badly needed to forget almost everything that had happened to me. From the noise Sara made while my impudent tongue played around with her, I don't suppose she was thinking very much about what had persuaded her to drive all the way down to Galveston. In fact, I don't think she was thinking about very much at all. She just lay there on the bed in front of me, her back arched like a longbow, trembling with helpless abandon as if possessed by some insistent, gentle spirit or like a beautifully undulating landscape that was being affected by some long, slow earth tremor. When I was satisfied that she was satisfied, I climbed back up between her cool creamy thighs and, with her kisses smothering my intimately perfumed face, I took care of my own pleasure.

When I'd finished, I yawned loudly.

She kissed me fondly on the head and then added, "You may put the light out now, if you want."

"Are you sure?" I wasn't sure about this myself. I feared the darkness as if I were a small child.

"I'm here with you. What can happen?"

She was right. What indeed? What could possibly happen that had not already happened? And if anything else did happen, then at least we would try to meet it together. At least that was my thought, although I was trying very hard not to think of anything much other than Sara and when I was going to fuck her again.

I leaned across the bed and switched out the bedside light. I thought of the diocesan house and how long it had stood on that street and how it had withstood the battering of Hurricane Ike and the biblical flood that had followed. Could I withstand as much? It was beginning to seem unlikely. Nelson Van Der Velden's calmly uttered threat that I would be dead before twenty-four hours had elapsed was beginning to seem quite possible—my heart already felt like someone had used a defibrillator on me while the blood in my veins must have been pure adrenaline. I thought of Philip Osborne and Peter Ekman and what had happened to them, but somehow I gradually fell into a restless, troubled sleep that was full of shadows and dread and foreboding, not to mention Uncle Bill and the loathsome creature I had wrestled with in Mr. Hindemith's overgrown garden.

※

My heart had stopped beating altogether. I was quite certain of that. I had no breath, nor the possibility of breathing. I tried to cry out for help, but not the least sound came from my mouth. There was just a silent, cold, all-enveloping blackness that threatened to stifle me as though I were at the bottom of a very deep well, with something pulling me down into thick and slimy silt. I tried to push myself up and found myself sinking deeper, with strong, sharp hands pulling at my feet and then my legs. I kicked hard and tried to swim my way back to the surface that I instinctively knew was life, for I had the strong sensation that if I did not quickly escape the place I was in, I would certainly die. I sank and kicked again. And this time I felt a strong jolt and, taking a deep loud breath that could have been heard out at sea, I knew I was suddenly alive and awake.

Seconds passed and I just lay there panting loudly like a dog and enjoying the feel of air in my chest, which was lathered with sweat. A ringing in my ears gave way to what was happening in the room.

Sara had got up and was washing herself in the bathroom. But I knew I was wrong about that because I turned over and, finding some strands of her long hair on my pillow, stretched out my hand and patted her small skull. In the very same moment that I put my hand there, I thought her head seemed a little colder than I was expecting so that I half wondered if a window was open; then I heard someone moving again in the bathroom—a toilet flushed and then a tap was running—and, leaning across her inert, sleeping body, I fumbled in the darkness for the Walther I had left on the bedside table.

"Who's there?" I asked.

Sara stirred underneath my body and then seemed to shrink against my side. She moaned a little, too, as if she was already crying with fear.

"Ssssh," I whispered close to what felt like her ear. "There's someone in the bathroom."

Her tall, muscular body hardened noticeably as if it was now prepared for flight.

"Who's there?" I asked again, louder now because I had the gun in my hand.

"I didn't mean to wake you, Giles," said a quiet but cheery voice from in the bathroom—it was Sara's voice. "It's just me. You were having a nightmare, I think. Your legs were moving like you were a dog in a race. Hey, I'll be there in a minute. I'm afraid I couldn't find the light." She hesitated. "Wait a minute. I think this must be it."

As it was of old, in the beginning and in the Bible.

"No," I cried. "Don't."

Even as she spoke, I felt with absolute, revolting certainty the awful knowledge of a different human figure next to me—not hers—and then a cold, clammy mouth descended onto my hip. I leaped from the bed as if it contained a rattlesnake; hearing a loud cry of horror that turned out to be my own, I flew to the bathroom as Sara switched on the light. Turning back to face the bed, I fired three shots at the space I had just vacated.

"Holy shit," she yelled, cowering on the floor and covering her ears with her hands.

I stood there staring at the bed that the bathroom light now revealed to be empty, unless you count the three bullets that must have been lodged somewhere in the mattress. Gunsmoke and some feathers from an exploded pillow hung in the pungent air, which seemed to be mixed with something earthy and old. The smell reminded me of an exhumed grave I'd once witnessed.

"What the hell?" screamed Sara. "Have you gone fucking crazy?"

"I don't know," I replied, trembling with fear. "I don't know."

"Well, that's honest, I suppose. Jesus Christ. You might have fucking killed me. And with my own gun."

I frowned. "What do you mean, killed you? You were in here. I was aiming at whatever the fuck was in the bed."

She paused, becoming less irate now as she realized that I had an automatic weapon in my hand that was cocked and ready to fire. "Please, Giles. Please put down the gun. It's making me very nervous."

"Believe me, you can't be nearly as nervous as I am."

"Put it down and tell me what happened."

After a very long moment, I eased the hammer down to make the gun safe, flicked on one of the Walther's two safeties, and placed the gun back onto the bedside table. Then, as best as I was able—I was still shaking with fear—I told Sara what had happened.

"You must have dreamed it," she said.

"Oh yeah? In the same way you dreamed that someone had slept in our bed?"

"You'd been asleep. So perhaps you were still confused. Suppose that it had been me in the bed."

"Sorry, but I'm still trying to deal with the idea that if it wasn't you then what the fuck was it? Jesus. What the fuck was that?" I wiped my arms with my hands—I could still feel the touch of the thing on me.

"What do you think it was?" she asked calmly.

"I don't know, but I am certain of this: it was something—repulsive. I had my fucking arms around it thinking it was you for about ten seconds. And I felt something bite my ass as I got out of bed."

"Here, let me see."

I twisted around to look at my bare ass. There was a large human-size bite on my hip. The sight was enough to make my hair stand on end. My heart did a pretty good job of trying to stand on end, too.

"Christ," said Sara, shaking her head. "That couldn't have been me."

"I didn't say it was you, did I?"

Horrified, I staggered weakly into the bathroom and put my head under the cold tap for a long moment. The cold water seemed to slow my feverish brain. While I kept my head under the water, I felt Sara's hand on the bite mark.

Sara turned away from looking at my ass to examine the catch on the bathroom door.

"You don't think you could have done it on this?" she asked. "When you came barging in here?"

"It's a bite, not a scratch."

"Sure about that?" She shrugged. "Could be a bruise. Perhaps you banged yourself on the door?"

"Does that look like a bruise to you?"

She touched my behind with her finger. "No, not really."

"Listen, sweetheart, it's my ass and I can still feel whatever it

was—its goddamn clammy mouth on me. I just shot the fucking mattress on account of that feeling. What happened to me just now—it was
like being in bed with a corpse."

"And you thought that could be me?" She shrugged. "That is a
natural mistake for anyone to make, I suppose." She folded her arms
and looked thoughtful for a moment. "How much do you know about
this house anyway?"

"What's to know? Look, I thought you were a scientist. Surely you
don't believe in all that *Amityville Horror* shit."

"I don't. I just wanted to hear you say you didn't believe it."

"I don't know what I fucking believe."

"But there is something you're not telling me."

There was, of course. But trying to figure out where to begin convinced me that it was probably a lot better not to begin at all.

"No," I said. "I think I told you everything when I was in your office
at UT. And you didn't believe it then. About the only thing that's happened since is that I've been to the church. The one I told you about,
where they pray for the destruction of God's enemies. And now they're
praying for me." I shrugged. "As a matter of fact, I was there earlier this
evening and the pastor—Nelson Van Der Velden—he told me that I had
twenty-four hours before the Lord's angel of death came for my soul."

"And you believe *that*?"

"Like I said, I don't know what to believe. But things have happened tonight that I can't explain."

"Such as?"

"Just—things I can't explain."

"Not yet, you can't. But just because we can't see a rational explanation doesn't mean there isn't one."

I sighed. "Sara, I work for the FBI. Before that, I trained as a lawyer,
okay? I was weaned on admissible evidence. So you don't have to give
me the skeptic's notes on this. I've got a pretty hard head of my own."

Sara seemed to think better of making her next remark; instead, she said, "It won't help to argue about this."

I nodded. "You're right. But please try to remember how you felt when you saw the bed, Sara." I pressed both hands on my chest as if trying to calm my heart. It didn't work. "That's how I'm feeling to the power of ten right now."

"Meaning what? That I was making something out of nothing?"

"I didn't say that. Listen, I think we've each had a severe fright. My nerves are in shreds."

"Well, mine aren't much better," she said. "This past week has been a fucking nightmare."

"There's no monopoly on nightmares," I said. "Not here." I took her hand. "What I mean is that there's no point in taking this out on each other. We need to keep calm so we can figure out what to do."

We were both of us naked and Sara went into the bedroom to fetch her T-shirt and put it on.

"Well, I think I know what to do," she said, glancing around the floor.

"You do?"

"Can you remember where my panties are?"

"They're downstairs. I took them off when we were on the sofa." I frowned. "You're getting dressed? Why?"

"Yes," she said. "I'm getting dressed because I'm leaving. I can't stay in this crazy house tonight. Not anymore. Not after all that's happened."

"You say 'crazy house' in a way that makes me believe you think it's me who's crazy, not the house," I said.

"No, I don't think that at all," she said. "But I probably will think you're crazy if you don't leave with me." She shook her head. "You can't stay here."

"You think it's any better out there?" I pointed at the window. "Outside? Anywhere else?"

She frowned. "But there is something you're not sharing with me, isn't there? It might just be that you don't want to scare me any more than I'm scared already, but we both know that you didn't get those scratches on a fucking tree."

"If I tell you everything, I don't want you going into a tailspin," I said.

"Oh, God," she said, looking sick. "I was just bluffing in the hope there isn't any more to know. But there is more, isn't there?"

I nodded. "Yes, I'm afraid there is. But mostly I'm just afraid."

TWENTY-SIX

We went downstairs to find her underwear. I started to tell her about the events of the day, but I hadn't gone very far with my halting, sheepish explanation when she shook her head and, for a brief moment, covered my mouth with her hand.

"No. I don't want to know. I just said I did, but really I don't, Giles. I'm scared enough as it is."

"You're right," I said. "It won't help."

"Look, all I want to do is get the fuck out of here. Will you come with me?"

"Sure, but where are we going to go, Sara?" I glanced at my wrist-watch. "It's two a.m."

"Anywhere there are people," she said. "We'll just get in the Bentley and drive north across the state line. Washington, D.C. Yes, that's it. We'll go to Washington."

"Washington? It's twelve hundred miles to Washington," I said. "What the fuck . . . ?"

"So? We can be there in a day. Look, Martins, shit like this doesn't happen in Washington. People are normal in Washington." She held up her panties and then proceeded to put them on.

"Why do you think that?"

"I don't know. All those fucking lawyers probably. They're all of them godless skeptics like you and I are. I kind of think that if you're surrounded by people who believe in a lot of fucking nonsense like ghosts and gods and Christ knows what then it's easier to believe in those things yourself. That's why we've got to get the hell out of Texas."

"You could have a point," I said, although I was hardly convinced. I was doing my best to humor her; she was close to breaking down altogether and I figured that the best thing to do was just play along with her for now. Maybe a few miles down the road with the top down and some fresh air would help to bring her to her senses. There was a decent-looking motel just off the Gulf Freeway near Texas City where I figured we could probably stay. I'd been planning to stay there myself when I moved out of the diocesan house.

"Sure, I have a point." She sighed loudly. "Now I have to go back to the bedroom to fetch the rest of my clothes. Will you come with me?"

We went back upstairs where I found some clean clothes and she put on the ones she'd been wearing. I also took her gun, my FBI ID and badge, a couple of bottles of water, and my keys. While Sara finished dressing, I rolled up the blind and stared out of the window at the street, which seemed to unnerve her.

"You're looking out there like you expect to see something," she said.

"It's what I'm not expecting to see that I'm worried about."

"That's a comforting thought. Could we not do that kind of thing?"

"I can't help it, Sara. I can still feel that thing in my arms." I shivered and rubbed my scalp furiously. "Makes my hair stand on end just thinking about it."

"All the more reason for us not to delay," she said.

I do his will. As it was of old, in the beginning and in the Bible.

"Switch off the light," I told her.

She switched off the light. "What is it?" she asked nervously.

"There's someone out there," I said.

"What?" She came over to the window and looked outside. "Where?"

"He's standing in the driveway of the blue house on the opposite side of the road. Just by the mailbox."

"I can't see."

"Maybe that's because you're not wearing your glasses. You're a little nearsighted, aren't you?"

"How did you know I wear glasses?"

"They're on the dashboard of the Bentley," I murmured. "I figure you only wear them for driving."

"That's right. I do." Sara screwed her eyes up tight and made an almost painful-looking effort to see what I could see, but without success.

"Take my word for it, he's there."

"Well, what's he doing?"

I wasn't exactly sure. There was someone there all right, but with the amount of rainwater on the windowpane, it was hard to determine if the figure was naked like the man I'd met in the back garden of Mr. Hindemith's house.

"At the moment, he's doing very little but standing where he is, looking across the street at this house."

Sara shook her head. "Well, this is a free country, isn't it? People can do what they like, surely?"

"It's not exactly a night for stargazing, Sara," I said, as a brief squall of rain hit the glass in front of my nose like a handful of gravel and reminded me of Nelson Van Der Velden's stupid poem about prayer. But I didn't want to think about him.

"No, perhaps not," she said. "So, what are we going to do?"

"You're still determined to leave?"

"God, yes. I don't want to stay a minute longer in this house than I have to."

"It'll be dawn soon. We could go then if you like. Maybe the weather will have cleared up. And I'll be able to see clearly across the street."

"No, Giles, please, let's go now."

"Then perhaps I'd better go out there first."

"Suppose something happens to you?"

"I've got your gun." I shrugged. "And when I've opened the trunk of my car, I'll have another gun. Two more, actually."

I turned and, folding her in my arms, kissed her freshly perfumed forehead fondly. "It's all right," I told her. "You won't have to stay up here. You can wait inside the front door. Or on the porch if you prefer. When I judge things are safe, I'll open the car door and you can run straight into the driver's seat."

"That's on the other side of the car," she observed. "On his side." She shook her head. "Perhaps you should drive, Giles."

I shrugged. "All right. If you're sure. But if that was my car, I wouldn't let anyone drive it but me."

"Right now, all I care about is getting out of here as soon as possible."

We went downstairs.

"Here," I said, handing her the Walther. "You hang on to this."

"What happens if you need it?"

"I told you. I've got another one in the trunk of my own car. It'll take me just a second to fetch it. Just leave the front door ajar, and when I'm ready for you, I'll call you."

She nodded.

I opened the door, stepped out onto the wooden porch, and went down the steps. Warmish rain showered my face, stinging the scratches a little and soaking my clean shirt. As I walked to the rear of my car, I glanced across the road at the house opposite. The man was still there, not moving, almost as if he were a statue. And this time I was quite sure it was the same figure I'd seen in Mr. Hindemith's garden: the man was muscular and quite naked.

I do his will. As it was of old, in the beginning and in the Bible.

For a second, I remembered the terrible face I had seen in the light of the match I'd struck. And the dreadful, malevolent expression on that face. I wasn't ever likely to forget it. Not ever. I've met some real psychopaths in my time with the FBI, but his was the most awe-inspiring face I'd ever seen.

I quickly opened the trunk. With the courtesy light on, I swiftly surveyed the array of weapons and protective clothing I kept there. I didn't think I'd need the vest, but I took my other Glock and the FN self-loading shotgun that was part of an agent's arsenal. I put the Glock into my empty hip holster and laid the shotgun on the ground before locking up the trunk. Then I picked up the shotgun, racked one up from the six-shot magazine, and turned to face the house opposite.

For a moment, I just stood there, dumbly rooted to the spot, glancing one way and then the other and feeling a little foolish with the shotgun in my hands. The man was gone.

"Is he still there?" called Sara.

She was standing on the porch with the Walther in her hand. Cursing myself for not springing the live round from the automatic's muzzle before returning the weapon to her, I realized that all that was going to prevent me from getting myself accidentally shot by her was the Walther's ambidextrous safety catch.

Toting the shotgun, I walked across the street.

The blue house was derelict; and I could see no sign of anyone having been there for a long while. Not even a set of footprints I could follow into the backyard. There was only a tremendous sense of loss and time passing—a sensation that was not uncommonly felt almost anywhere in Galveston. But perhaps I also felt a sense of mortality and human insignificance—most likely my own.

I came back to the Bentley, opened the passenger door, and waved Sara down the steps.

"He seems to have gone," I said. For some reason I found myself reluctant to use the word "disappeared," although that was certainly what it felt like.

She ran to the car even though it seemed to have stopped raining.

When Sara was safely in the passenger seat, I went quickly back up the steps, closed and locked the front door of the house, and then returned to the blue Bentley.

"Where did he go?" she asked.

"I have no idea," I said. "But it really doesn't matter now. We are out of here. Shit, why didn't I think of this before? All these weeks I've been staying in this hellhole of a town by myself, it's a wonder I've not gone fucking crazy."

"Who says you're not?"

"It's crossed my mind more than once in the last twenty-four hours."

I put the shotgun safely in the backseat, shifted my Glock onto the floor of the car, and hit the ignition button that started the big six-liter engine.

The seat belt warning alarm began to toll like a church bell, only it seemed to be prompting me not to buckle on the belt but to address the loaded Walther that was still clutched in her hand about ten inches from my neck.

"Here," I said, taking the gun gently from her. "Just in case you don't like my driving."

I took the Walther and looked around the car's sumptuous leather interior. I put the gun in the glove compartment.

"There," I said. "That's better."

I shifted the seat a little with an electric button and then reached to adjust the movie theater–size rearview mirror, which was when I found a length of silver chain and a medal hanging from it like a cabdriver's lucky charm.

"What's this?" I said.

"I don't know," she said.

"This is your car," I said, unthreading the chain. "You must know."

"It wasn't there when I arrived here earlier."

I switched on the courtesy light and turned the medal in my fingers, confirming what I already strongly suspected. The Scottish design was unmistakable; the head of St. Christopher quite distinct; if anything, it seemed more sharply defined than I remembered, as was the inscription on the back. Only it couldn't have been that medal. Not in this world. I felt the faraway faint flash of another life in another time that someone very like me had lived in a parallel universe. My chest tightened and a cold sweat appeared on the back of my neck and my hands.

"It must have been there," I whispered. "You must have . . . surely . . . It doesn't make sense . . ."

But even as I spoke, I knew she really didn't know anything about the medal; she couldn't have. The medal wasn't hers. It never had been. It wasn't anything to do with her. I was quite certain she'd never even seen it until she'd got into the car alongside me.

The medal was mine.

"Oh, God," I heard myself mutter, and I sank weakly back against the leather seat as if my whole spine had simply disappeared from my torso. The medal couldn't have weighed more than a few grams, but it seemed as if it weighed a ton in my hand.

She took the medal from me and examined it more closely on the palm of her hand. "It's a St. Christopher's medal," she said.

"At least I'm not imagining that, I suppose."

"What the fuck do you mean?"

I shrugged, but it must have been clear that I didn't dare answer her for fear of sounding like a lunatic.

"Wait a minute," she said. "G. Martins. April 5, 1988." She frowned. "This is your St. Christopher medal."

"Yes." My voice was full of dread. "It is."

She handed the medal back. I looked at it sadly, remembering the events of that distant day in Glasgow. I saw my mother's face so full of pride; I felt the cold in my thin white cotton shirt; I could even taste the host on the roof of my mouth. I remembered peeling it off my palate and then spitting the thing into the center of my handkerchief as if it had been a piece of spent chewing gum. I remembered the sickening sense of loss when I returned home after the confirmation and found my medal was gone and the frantic and ultimately hopeless search to find it again. I remembered it all as if it had been yesterday.

"Well then, why ask me about it, Giles? I don't understand."

I sighed. "I don't understand, either," I said. "This is my medal all right. I got it on the day I was confirmed. Which was also the day I lost it. In Scotland, when I was just a kid. I haven't seen it since, Sara."

"Giles? What the fuck are you talking about?"

I groaned. "I don't know," I said, and switched off the engine. The silence between us was as thick as a fog. And I knew we were already drifting apart again, like two lost ships.

"*You* don't know. Well, that makes two of us."

"Sara, I'm absolutely certain that this medal wasn't hanging on the mirror when I came outside to put the top up."

She glanced across at the blue house. "The man who was over there—the one you claim was there." She shrugged. "Perhaps he put it there. Well, why not? I suppose it's just about possible. He could have got into the car somehow, although I really don't see how. He must have had something to do with it."

"Look, I know this sounds crazy, Sara, but until just now, I swear to you, I hadn't seen this medal for, what is it?" I sighed. "More than twenty-five years." I closed my eyes. "I honestly thought it was lost forever. And now here it is again, five thousand miles from the place where I lost it, looking as clean and untarnished as the day it was minted." I shook my head and wiped a tear from my eye. "It's as if someone is trying to tell me something."

"Tell you what?"

"Something pretty terrible, I guess." My breath was unsteady now, almost as if I'd suffered a bereavement. "Something that's as awful as anything anyone was ever told."

Sara looked pained and suddenly very small in the seat beside me. "I really don't know why you're telling me this, but . . . you're scaring the shit out of me."

"I don't mean to, Sara, really I don't, but if you didn't put the medal there, then—"

"Giles, just think about it," she said calmly. "You must have put it in here yourself when you were looking at my driving glasses and deciding if I was farsighted or nearsighted. Any other explanation doesn't make sense. You came out here to put the top up. Remember? That's when you must have left the medal here." She smiled, like she was trying to humor a madman. "Perhaps you wanted to keep me safe when I was driving. St. Christopher is the patron saint of travelers, right? Yes, that's it. If you did, that's nice. Thanks. I appreciate the thought. No, really I do."

The way she outlined this very reasonable explanation it sounded like one with which she'd have been well satisfied; and why not? All I had to do was nod it through and we'd have been fine; we might still have salvaged something of our relationship; but that was not meant to be.

"Honestly? I believe you're telling me the truth, Sara. I don't see how you could have put my medal there since I was last in this car.

Unless you sneaked out while I was asleep. But of course, that just begs the question of how you came to have it in your possession in the first place. You simply couldn't have had it. Not after so long. And from so very far away. It really was lost forever. Like me, perhaps." I shrugged hopelessly. "And now it isn't lost at all. That leaves only one explanation, which, however crazy it sounds, is the only explanation that works."

"And what's that?"

"Someone else put it there. Not you. Not me. And not some passing stranger."

And then I spoiled everything, as if I had rubbed a half grapefruit in her face.

"I think God might just have put it there," I said.

Her nose wrinkled with horror. "God? What the hell are you talking about?"

"God. Or perhaps God's angel."

Sara uttered a deep sigh and then laid her forehead on the dashboard as if we had just escaped a serious collision or, perhaps, as if we had just suffered one.

"Sara, please. Just for one minute put aside all your scientific beliefs and your understandable need for empirical evidence and consider the many strange things that have happened to you: the man who you claim was outside your apartment door and outside your ninth-floor apartment window; the feeling of dread you said you had; the bed in my room that had been slept in by someone who wasn't there. And that ghost you mentioned? *The Turn of the Screw*? Yes, you know what I'm talking about. None of this makes any sense unless we admit that there are no explanations for any of this. At least not the kind of explanations that work in a laboratory and rely on hard evidence."

"Those are the only explanations that make sense, Giles. Everything else is just bullshit. I thought you knew that, too. I thought that was our point of real understanding, you and I. That both of us were fellow skeptics."

"Please, Sara. Try to remember that all of these things have happened since that lunatic Nelson Van Der Velden started praying for your death and mine. Except that he's not a lunatic at all, of course. Christ, I'm beginning to realize that. Because I can't help but believe in God now. I believe he's not a God of love at all, but a terrible God of anger and vengeance. I believe that in a few hours' time God's angel of death is going to come for me. In fact, I believe I've already met him earlier this evening. He left these scratches on my face and chest. He bit me. You've seen the bite on my ass. It was God's angel of death who was standing across the road when we came out of the house. And it was God's angel of death who was standing outside your apartment door."

"Stop it, Giles, please. I find all of this laughable. And really quite offensive."

"But there's a way out of this, Sara," I said. "For both of us. Earlier on this evening, my uncle Bill visited the house. You might say that it was a kind of vision."

Sara laughed. "At least it wasn't Hamlet's father. At least you're not trying to tell me that."

"Bill told me he was dead, but that he'd come to give me a warning. That's who you heard me speaking to, Sara. It was my uncle Bill. I don't know how, but it was him all right."

"This is insanity." She hugged her hands between her knees and then hooked her fingers onto the glove compartment. "Only it's not just you who's insane, it's me, too."

"It was my uncle Bill who told me that there's a way out of all this. That all we have to do is pray to him, Sara. That's right."

"I'm insane for getting involved with a maniac like you. I had an idea you were crazy when you came to my office at UT. That you were looking for your own way back to God, and it looks like that first instinct was right."

"Our only possible way out of all this is through prayer. So, please, come back into the house with me and we'll take it to the Lord in prayer. We'll ask his forgiveness for not believing in him. Really, I think it might be as simple as that."

She quickly opened the glove compartment and then the Walther was in her hand. It was pointed at me.

"Get out of the car," she said firmly.

"Sara, please," I said. "I really mean you no harm."

"Get out of my fucking car, asshole."

"But your only chance now is prayer."

I saw her thumb move on the safety.

"Don't make me shoot you, Martins," she said. "But if that's what it takes to get you out of this fucking car, I will."

The last part of her sentence came out in a loud and violent scream that was also quite eloquent and more than enough to persuade me to do what I was told. I elbowed open the Bentley's heavy door and stepped quickly out.

"Now back away from the door," she said. And pressing a button, she lowered the top, which made it easier for her to climb across the central console into the driver's seat. Then with the gun still pointed my way, she reached over and pulled the door toward her. "Stay back or I swear I'll shoot."

"Don't leave, Sara," I said, backing up toward the porch of the house. "You're in danger. I think you know that, too. I realize it sounds crazy—I was every bit as skeptical about all this as you—but prayer is our only chance."

"You bet it sounds crazy, you loony fuck! To think I actually went to bed with a creep like you. Jesus Christ, it makes my skin itch all over just to think about it. You know something? I hope that angel does fucking kill you, you creep. I hope he tears you to fucking pieces."

She started the engine and her curses were lost in the sound of the Bentley's powerful engine for a moment.

"You know what I think? I think it was you all along. Who creeped me out. Who put these stupid fucking ideas in my head. I think you're some kind of fucking stalker, Martins. And as soon as I get back to Austin, I'm going to report you to your superiors."

"Please, don't go like this. I can help."

"I'll leave your fucking guns up the street. I suggest you use one of them on yourself and save me the cost of the phone call."

But she was crying as she drove away in a loud squeal of tires. And I wondered if I would ever see her again.

TWENTY-SEVEN

D awn crept up onto the edge of the horizon like a thin trail of blood seeping slowly through a dull gray blanket.

It had stopped raining. but my shirt was still wet and I was acutely aware of my own mortal coldness and the sense that I might never again be warm. If Nelson Van Der Velden was right, this was to be my last day on God's earth. That was beginning to seem like a good thing because my own company had become a burden to me. For a moment, I actually contemplated fetching the guns Sara had thrown out of the Bentley up the street and using one of them on myself as she had suggested.

I'm not sure what stopped me; perhaps it was the St. Christopher's medal I still held in my hand; or perhaps it was the birds in the overgrown trees above my head. It certainly wasn't any sense that suicide was wrong. More likely what stopped me was that I was hardly in a hurry to meet a God who now filled me with such dread.

I hung the medal around my neck, recovered the abandoned weapons, including her little Walther P22, and went back to the house; I moved quickly because thoughts of suicide were soon replaced with the idea that I might pursue Sara in my own car; however, I couldn't see how doing that wouldn't end badly. She was scared enough without my driving after her. A car chase along the Gulf Freeway could only have resulted in an accident. Besides, I hardly thought that my own car was up to catching a speeding Bentley. The best I could hope for was that when she had calmed down a bit I might speak to her on the telephone. Assuming I was still alive, that is. There was the small matter of almighty God's angel of death to consider first. Because he was there. I knew that now, as certainly as I felt the skin on the palms of my own hand or the inside of my mouth. He was outside somewhere, and he was waiting for me.

I shivered, but it wasn't just from feeling cold. Being restored to my former belief in God was like finding that an infection I thought I'd thrown off and to which I thought I'd developed immunity was still there. But what I mainly felt was fear. It was the wrath of God I believed in, not his peace and understanding.

I do his will. As it was of old, in the beginning and in the Bible.

As soon as I was inside the house, I switched on the lights and went through what remained of Father Dyer's priestly possessions. If I was going to pray again, I was going to need some of the props that went with it. There was a drawer in a rolltop desk that contained a Bible, a rosary, a few candles, some vestments, and a vial that looked like holy water, which was what you might have expected in a priest's desk drawer. I took the Bible and the rosary, and knelt down on the floor of the sitting room and bowed my head to pray. Or at least I tried to pray. My head was still brimful of Sara Espinosa.

"Lord . . ." I muttered. "Lord, hear my prayer."

It still wasn't the Lord I was thinking of, however. Not by a long shot. I shook my head and tried to rid my mind of these insistently erotic thoughts, and yet I hardly wanted to give up the taste and smell of Sara so soon. Not now that she had gone, possibly forever. How could I close my mind to the thought of her naked, pliant body when the chances were I wouldn't ever see her again? I closed my eyes tight and knocked on my own skull with a hard knuckle.

"Come on, Martins," I said. "You have to concentrate on putting your mind right with God." I paused and then began. "Heavenly Father . . ."

But still none of my thoughts were at all conducive to coming before him. It was as if I had almost forgotten how to pray. Or as if something insistently human was preventing me from doing so. Perhaps that's what Paul meant in the Acts of the Apostles when he says, "And why now do you wait? Rise and be baptized and wash away your sins, calling on his name," or in Galatians when he says, "Now the works of the flesh are evident: sexual immorality, impurity, sensuality."

If Ruth could only have seen me, her triumph would have been complete. Why hadn't I listened to her? Why had I ever doubted in his existence? She was right about that, of course, although not without some qualification. He was hardly the God of love she thought she knew so well; he wasn't the heavenly father most people imagined him to be. Yes, I could see that there had to be a God because there was so much misery in the world; a God who was indifferent to all human suffering—it couldn't have worked any other way. He was a God who demanded total obedience; a God who punished unbelief as cruelly as the cruelest tyrant ever did.

I stood up and poured myself a stiff drink and tried to think of how I had prayed as a boy, before I came to America and discovered the childlike evangelical faith in the benign, paternal God of Lakewood Church. That was no good. It was no use praying to him like he was someone who loved me. He didn't. That much was obvious. He was going to kill me before the day was ended. His angel was going to come for me and tear me to pieces unless I managed to persuade God to relax the hand of his angel, as it says in Samuel II 24:15–16.

If I doubted that, I only had to look out of the window.

I do his will. As it was of old, in the beginning and in the Bible.

"Jesus Christ."

The man I'd seen across the street was back; he was certainly the naked man I'd seen in the garden of Mr. Hindemith except that now, in the early-morning light, I could see he was a little less of a man and a bit more of a beast. Certainly there was some animal-like power in his musculature, but it was his face that seemed particularly bestial and that reminded me of a hungry-looking wolf. And when he moved, *he moved on all fours.* It was hard to imagine this creature relaxing his hand for anything. Instinctively, I knew he wasn't going away and that each time I looked he would be a little closer than he was before, as if he was biding his time before he killed me; and I understood the real stomach-churning fear that had possessed those others before me— Richardson, Davidoff, Ekman, Osborne, Durham.

"No wonder Davidoff tried to climb that tree," I murmured. "Or that Ekman locked himself in his panic room."

I turned away and made two strong fists and pumped the air in front of me as if I'd been holding the reins of a chariot.

"I have to pray. I have to fucking pray."

But how? Perhaps, after all, it was better to pray in the old Catholic way.

"I need help. The help of Mary the Mother of God, perhaps. Surely she will help me."

I lit the candle and, with the rosary wrapped tight around my fist, I knelt again.

"Hail Mary, full of grace, the Lord is with thee. Blessed art thou amongst women and blessed is the fruit of thy womb, Jesus. Holy Mary, Mother of God, pray for us sinners, now and at the hour of our death. Amen."

Uttering a quiet sigh of satisfaction that I'd managed one prayer at last, I brought the rosary to my lips and kissed it and then snatched my hands away as the smell of something foul stayed in my nostrils.

"What the hell?"

I sniffed my hands again and recoiled once more as the strong smell of shit filled my head. Sara's smell had disappeared completely and, worse, had been replaced with such an awful fecal stink that I was obliged to go immediately to the bathroom to wash my hands. I had to do this several times, and it was only when I had virtually scrubbed off the skin with soap and a nailbrush that the smell of shit finally disappeared.

God was hardly satisfied with that, however. When I tried to picture Sara in my mind's eye, her naked flesh seemed vile and degraded, like that of a leper; her beautiful body was covered in warts and boils and hairs; it was as if suddenly he had made all memory of her disgusting.

"No," I shouted at the ceiling. "Please don't take her away from me so soon."

But it was too late. All human traces of my former pleasure in her body were gone.

Exhausted, I sat down on the floor and allowed myself the respite of a brief moment's recollection of happier times with Ruth and Danny. It seemed so long since I had seen my son and I wondered if he was missing me. What had Ruth told him about me? That I was a godless sonofabitch? I would have given anything to see his sweet face again and hear him call me Daddy.

I frowned and shook my head.

"No," I said. "This isn't fair at all."

A terrible series of images now afflicted me with even greater suffering. I saw myself twisting my son's hair in my hand and slapping him hard on the cheek so that he cried with pain; kicking him down a whole flight of stairs; burning his eyeball with a hot cigarette; stamping on his face; punching him on the side of his head; and knocking out his teeth with my fist.

I knew these images were false, and yet I could not get them out of my mind. I knew where they came from, too, and as I tore my shirt, I heard myself say, "Naked I came out of my mother's womb and naked shall I return: the Lord has given and the Lord has taken away; blessed be the name of the Lord."

I knew he would hardly be satisfied with that, so I smashed a cheap-looking vase on the mantelpiece next to the still burning candle and rolled up my shirtsleeves and, using a piece of broken pottery, began to scrape the skin of my arms until the blood was running down my hands onto the floor, just like Job's had.

"You want to fill my mind with your hate. You want me to curse the day I was born, don't you? Well, I do curse it. You want to rob me of everything that makes me a man."

I glanced up from this position of abject self-pity as I saw something appear on the sidewalk right in front of my house. I stood up and saw his demon waiting there, closer now, closer than before; and in a horrible way it was as if I had always known this creature from a time before I'd even existed; he stared back into my face through the window and then bared his sharp yellow teeth in what might have been a smile but was more likely a snarl.

"What am I to do?"

And once again I knelt down and closed my eyes and bowed my head in prayer.

"Our Father, which art in heaven, hallowed be thy name, thy kingdom come, thy will be done, on earth as it is in heaven. Give us this day our daily bread and forgive us our trespasses as we forgive those who trespass against us, and lead us not into temptation but deliver us from evil, for thine is the kingdom, the power, and the glory, forever and ever, Amen."

What else could I do? That was all I could do now. Just recite Our Fathers, by rote, like a parrot, as if I'd been back in Scotland doing penance after the confession of my imaginary sins.

"Our Father, which art in heaven, hallowed be thy name, thy kingdom come, thy will be done, on earth as it is in heaven. Give us this day our daily bread and forgive us our trespasses as we forgive those who trespass against us, and lead us not into temptation but deliver us from evil, for thine is the kingdom, the power, and the glory, forever and ever, Amen."

Would this be enough to spare me from the horrible fate that surely awaited me when God's fallen angel came for me, just as he had come for the others before me? Probably not. When is a prayer not a prayer? When the prayer is recited as a penance. I scraped some more skin off my arms with the piece of broken pottery. I could see why unbelievers like me were required to suffer. But why do the righteous have to suffer, too?

I recited the Lord's Prayer a third time.

The absolute freedom of God to inflict suffering was his, all right. No question about it. And he was proving that to me now. God wasn't required to give justice. Or understanding. Or any of the other theological nonsense. He did not need the approval or love of his creation. All that was required was that we believed in him.

I do his will. As it was of old, in the beginning and in the Bible.

But it still came as something of a shock when I heard a terrible banging on the front door. You could feel it through the walls and the floor, and it was almost as if the whole house had become an enormous drum.

"You're earlier than expected," I shouted, "but that's okay. That's okay. I'd rather get this over with."

More loud banging, which I seemed to feel inside my own head, and I realized to my shame that I'd wet myself, probably out of fear.

I stood up and, gathering what remained of my courage and dignity, I went to open the door, to admit the Lord's demon into the house.

TWENTY-EIGHT

In the gloomy hallway I paused for a moment as the knocking became louder and more insistent. It seemed to match the noise my own racing heart was making. Then I took a deep breath and, resigned to my fate, opened the front door with a shaking hand.

To my surprise and considerable relief it was not God's angel of death standing on the porch in front of me, it was Bishop Eamon Coogan. But if I thought that opening the door would put an end to the banging, I was wrong. The banging seemed to be continuing ominously upstairs, as if some builders were working there oblivious to the effect that their effort was producing.

"Eamon," I said. My relief was almost palpable.

"What the hell happened to you? Jesus. You're covered in blood."

Instinctively, I pulled down my shirtsleeves in an effort to cover the scratches on my arms.

"It's a long story." I glanced over his shoulder, but for the moment, the angel of death was gone from the street out front; I assumed that he was probably responsible for the muffled jackhammer sound that filled the house. "You'd better come in. If you can bear it."

I showed Coogan into the sitting room, and he winced a little as more pounding from upstairs jolted the ceiling. Some dust fell from the plaster molding, tinkled against the light fixture, and then fell into the dust that already covered the wooden floor; dust to dust, just like it says in the prayer.

"What's with all the noise?" he asked.

I saw little point in enlightening any normal person—even one such as the bishop who probably believed in such things as demons and angels of death—as to the real reason for the noise. Sara's reaction proved that any normal person would have assumed I was mad. It was bad enough that I almost believed this myself without alienating someone who was possibly my last friend in the world—not to mention the one friend I had who might conceivably be able to help me.

"Plumbers," I said glibly. "Toilet is blocked. They're trying to fix it."

Coogan nodded warily. "Plumbers, is it?" He didn't look convinced. "Did you argue about the bill, perhaps?"

"I had an accident, that's all. Nothing serious. I fell down the stairs. I slipped on a wrench that someone left on the floor."

Coogan looked even more disbelieving.

"I've seen emergency rooms that looked better than you."

"Leave it, will you, for fuck's sake? I'm fine. I'll find a Band-Aid in a minute, okay?"

"Sure, Gil. Whatever you say."

I swallowed my fear—or as much of it as I could manage in one gulp—and smiled patiently. "What are you doing here, Eamon?"

"You telephoned me last night," he explained. "Remember? I tried calling back on your cell and on the house phone, but with no result."

"Yes, I think some of the lines are down because of the storm," I said. "And there's no cell reception here to speak of. At least not on my network." I smiled. "But it's a long drive from Houston just to find out why the phone isn't working."

"The message you left sounded rather peculiar," said Coogan. "So I decided to come down here first thing this morning and see that

everything is all right." He glanced up at the ceiling as the steady banging seemed to grow even louder, shifting a small shower of dust onto his
large head. He brushed it off irritably. "And now that I'm here, I'm not
sure it is."

"Everything is just fine." I poured myself a drink. "Want one?"

"It's a little early, but you know, I think I will, with all the terrible
things that have been happening to me." He shook his head.

"Oh, yes. How's that thing going for you?"

"What thing?"

"The grand jury indictment."

"Oh, I see. I wasn't referring to that, Gil. Although, now you come
to mention it, it seems they—they being the FBI—are now bringing
charges against the diocese instead of me personally. I suppose that's
why you've been avoiding me."

"Yes, it is."

"I understand. It was a difficult situation. But it's a tremendous relief to me that at least I won't be going to prison."

"Well, I guess that all worked out for you."

"I swear I thought we were doing the right thing, Gil. For the sake
of the Church, that is."

It struck me as funny—almost—that my last friend in the world
should be someone who had helped a pedophile escape justice.

"So what were you referring to?" I said, quickly changing the subject. "What you said just now, about all the terrible things that have
been happening to you?"

"Well, perhaps it was just one terrible thing."

I handed him the drink. He drank some scotch, lit a cigarette, and
looked around. The guns caught his eye, but he didn't mention them.
He glanced up at the ceiling again as the light fixture began to sway.

"There was a terrible accident on the Galveston Causeway that
slowed me down coming here. That's all."

I frowned, already thinking the worse. "On the bridge?"

He nodded. "A young woman drove a sports car right over the edge of the northbound road into the bay just short of Virginia Point."

I felt my blood slow down as if someone had locked me overnight in a meat freezer.

"Uh-huh."

"I stopped at the scene to ask the Galveston police if there was anything I could do, but they said they thought the poor woman had already drowned."

"Did they happen to say what kind of car it was?"

"A blue foreign convertible. Apparently a witness saw her traveling at almost a hundred miles an hour. She braked to avoid something in the outside lane, hit the central concrete barrier, and then lost control. The cops were still looking for the body when I left." He toasted the air. "Well, here's to her, whoever she was, poor lass. God rest her soul." He crossed himself with the hand that was holding the cigarette, which seemed to add an almost infernal touch to his Catholicism.

"Yeah, here's to her."

With my eyes and throat filling up with tears and emotion, I sighed and sat down heavily on the arm of the sofa where less than ten hours before I had been sitting beside Sara. Her lipstick was still on a half-finished glass of Puligny-Montrachet. If I picked it up and put it to my lips, I could surely taste her again; so that's exactly what I did, mingling the thick pink fingerprint of her mouth with the warm golden wine and for a second it really did feel as if I had kissed her again.

None of this mixed easily with the whiskey in my hand and, to Coogan, it must have looked like I was a hopeless alcoholic, but I hardly cared.

So, that was that. There's nothing like the death of someone you love to make your own continuing existence a matter of small consequence. I expected nothing from the world now. Not from this world, nor from the one to come. And I understood the point of the pounding; it was the sound of doom.

"Did you know her, Gil?"

"She sounds very like a friend of mine who stayed here last night."

"Merciful God," he said.

I smiled at that one.

"We argued and then she lost her temper and drove off. I tried to stop her, but she pulled a gun on me and I had to let her go. It was let her go or get fucking shot, I think. At the time, it seemed like the right choice—to let her go, I mean. But now I'm not so sure." I smiled bitterly. "I kind of wish it had been me and not her. She was so very clever and I think the world will miss her."

I wiped my face with my forearm.

"That's awful, Gil. Really awful. I'm sorry." He shook his head sadly. "But if you don't mind my asking, why did she threaten to shoot you?"

"Because she thought I was fucking crazy."

"All this banging would make anyone crazy." Coogan glanced angrily at the ceiling. "But why did she think that about you?"

"Simple. Because I told her I believed in God."

"That's no reason to shoot someone. Especially in Texas. But forgive me for asking, Gil, but I was under the impression that you'd become an atheist."

"So was I. But I changed my mind. Or rather someone changed it for me."

"For this thy brother was dead, and is alive again; and was lost, and is found. I'm very glad to hear it, Gil." He toasted me and swallowed some scotch.

"I wish I could agree with you, Eamon. But I'm afraid I can't. Well, I'm afraid, anyway. That much is certainly true. Either way, I'm almost certain I'm as lost as you can get with a head still on your shoulders."

"I don't understand."

"No. Well, let's just leave it there for now, shall we?"

"All right, Gil. If that's what you want. I can see you've had a shock, right enough. But you should really get some of those cuts and scratches seen to." He glanced up at the ceiling as the banging seemed to become more persistent. "Look, do you think you could tell your plumbers to stop for a while. Just while I'm here. This is important, Gil. I can't hear myself think."

"Actually, that's the point of it, I believe. To stop you from thinking. Or me."

"If we're talking about your soul, I'd rather not have this bloody racket to contend with."

"Oh, me, too. But I'm afraid there's not much I can do to prevent that, okay?"

"All right, all right. Take it easy."

"There's a lot of things I wish I could do. Like go back to my previous state of ignorance. These people who believe in God. Jesus, I wonder what they'd think if they found out what he's really like. If God or one of his angels turned up at Lakewood or the cathedral one Sunday. If the Second Coming really did happen. Man, I'd love to see the look on their fucking faces. You take all kinds of things for granted when you're in church: that God is your heavenly father and that he has the whole world in his hands and shit like that. All things bright and beautiful. Jesus loves you. Only it isn't like that at all. Let me tell you it's a lot easier to worship that God than the God who really exists. It takes more than fucking prayers to make things right with him."

"Gil, Gil, what on earth are you talking about, man? You're making no sense."

"Oh, I'm making sense, you just don't realize it. Actually, it's good you're here, Eamon. I'm glad you came. Even if you are kind of a dirty priest, you know? I mean, tipping off a jacko that he was about to get busted. That was just wrong, Eamon."

"Hey. I told you. I thought we were—"

"Doing the right thing, right. Well, that's what I'd like to do now. I'm sorry I brought that other thing up. I apologize." I grinned at him. "Look, I really do need your fucking help here, Eamon. Some urgent spiritual advice?"

"Well then, just tell me what the problem is."

"Eamon. How would I go about being received back in the Roman Catholic Church?"

"You never left, Gil. Once you're baptized into the Roman Catholic Church, you remain a Catholic forever. The only thing that can stop you from being a Catholic is if you are excommunicated. And I hardly think you've done anything bad enough for that. No, as far as the Catholic Church is concerned, once a Catholic always a Catholic. That's one of the great things about being a Catholic. The Church can forgive all sorts of iniquity."

"So it would seem," I said pointedly.

"Just because you might have called yourself an evangelical Christian, or even an atheist, for a while, it really makes no real difference to the Catholic Church."

"Then how do I make my peace with God?"

"The same way as always. The sacrament of penance. Scripture tells us that three things are required of the penitent. Contrition, confession, and an act of penance and the making of amends for your sins. It's as simple as that, Gil. This sacrament—which is also called the sacrament of reconciliation—is the outward sign of an inward grace and reconciles the penitent to Almighty God." He nodded firmly. "Yes, it wouldn't be a bad idea at all for you to take that sacrament. You must receive the Holy Spirit, as it says in the Gospel according to St. John."

"Would you hear my confession, Eamon?"

"Of course."

"I should like to be reconciled to God. If it's possible. I'm not sure it is. But I should like to try."

I do his will. As it was of old, in the beginning and in the Bible.

More muffled banging from upstairs. Coogan paled a little. "Is that what this is about? Oh, Jesus, Gil. What the—? It's not the devil you've raised up there, is it?"

In all other circumstances I might have laughed, but now his question seemed to serve my purpose. In Coogan's world it was only the devil and not God who was capable of creating terrible suffering in this world. Telling him that God's angel was going to destroy me would surely have encouraged some ridiculous theological argument; but telling him that the devil was planning to do it was just what was required. And ultimately, what's the fucking difference?

"Yes," I said quietly. "It is, I'm afraid."

Coogan crossed himself hurriedly and finished his drink.

"Look, I'm sorry, Eamon, but a great evil has descended upon me and this house."

"Holy Mother of God," he said. "What's been going on here?"

"I can't explain. It would take too long. A lot of it you would hardly believe anyway. But that's why my friend with the sports car took off in such a hurry. Because she was terrified of a demon, Eamon. The demon in this house."

"I'm not sure I even know how to do an exorcism," said Coogan.

"No, an exorcism is not required." I took hold of Coogan's enormous shoulders and shook him. "I need to find that state of inward grace you were talking about, Eamon. I need you to hear my confession. And quickly. All right? Could you do that, please?"

He lit a nervous cigarette and glanced anxiously at the ceiling as the banging persisted.

"Is that him? The devil?"

"No, not the devil but certainly one of his demons. Azrael, I think."

Coogan crossed himself again. I grabbed the big man by the lapels of his black jacket and hauled him roughly toward me.

"Will you please stop crossing yourself and listen to me, you stupid Boston Irish fuck? I need you to confess me." I shouted into his face. "Will you confess me?"

"Yes," he said. "Yes. Yes, I will."

"But not here, I think," I said. "Somewhere else."

"No problem," said Coogan. "I have the keys to the old cathedral. We can go there right now if you like. In fact, I insist upon it."

TWENTY-NINE

oogan was even more scared than I was. His big brown hands were shaking as he searched his crowded key ring for a Yale that fit the lock of the cathedral door, and much of his usual color had disappeared from his now pasty-looking face. He was breathing noticeably, too, which is always a bad sign in a big man, as if at any moment he might keel over clutching his chest. By this time, I was a little surprised I had not suffered a heart attack myself. I felt like my chest was beneath a concrete block and my head was tight with pain.

Fumbling the key into the lock, he said, "What the hell were you thinking about, Gil, messing around with that kind of thing?"

"I wasn't thinking," I said absently. "Okay? It just happened."

In truth, I was hardly listening to this admonishment and it wasn't just because it was inaccurate. Most of my attention was reserved for the empty window of a derelict building on the other side of the road where my naked tormentor was watching us. Although he was at least thirty or forty feet away, I had the clearest view of him yet—if it really was a he, because there was something unpleasantly asexual about the creature who was observing my desperate and possibly futile attempts to escape destruction at his knotty, taloned hands.

I do his will. As it was of old, in the beginning and in the Bible.

He was on all fours, like a kind of great ape, with the upper half of his hairless body disproportionately large and muscled. The skin that covered it had a strange incandescent aspect as if it glowed with some internal fire, and here and there on the surface were strange patches of what looked to be ash, like eczema, as if the heat from its body had actually burned through into the air. His feet and hands were outsize but human enough, although he seemed to be without sexual organs. Before, I had thought his face to be like a wolf's, but this was not the case as the sun, shifting from behind one of the cathedral's twin white towers to illuminate his features, now clearly revealed: it was a primordial face, like some species of ancient man, from a prelapsarian time when man had probably eaten raw what he killed with his own bare hands. The prognathous jaw was filled with large teeth and the slavering tongue seemed too big for its gaping mouth. A demon he truly seemed to be; however, it was an impression that was strongly confirmed in me not just by the creature's loathsome and restless and protean features but also by some primordial sense of intuition.

The door to the cathedral was now open and Coogan was patiently awaiting my entry. But then he caught the look on my face and where the trail of my eyes led; he was just in time to see something, but exactly what he could not say, which was just as well.

"What was that?" he asked. "I swear I saw something up at that window, but now it's not there."

"Never mind." I walked into the cathedral and Coogan banged the door shut behind us, locking and bolting it as if that might save us both from what was outside. "You don't need to know."

For a moment, I wondered if Sara's car accident really had been a car accident; if her losing control of the Bentley had been caused by something other than speed and poor control; if perhaps the demon outside had chosen that particular moment to appear in the seat beside her, which would have made anyone crash. It was a horrible thought and I tried to put it out of my mind in the interests of self-preservation; I make no apology for that. Earlier thoughts of not wanting to live were gone, at least for now; there is nothing quite like sunshine and another new day to make a person want to cling to life—even in Galveston. Perhaps, if I made confession, I might achieve a state of inward grace and be reconciled with my creator; for hadn't my mad uncle Bill promised as much? Would a confession give me the second chance he had mentioned? There seemed to be no other way ahead for me now.

It seemed only fitting that my confession should be heard in Galveston's crappy old ruined cathedral. Ever since sustaining significant water damage during Hurricane Ike, the St. Mary Cathedral Basilica had been closed for repairs, and certainly it seemed likely to stay that way. Inside the basilica all was chaos and decay, and to that extent the building provided a suitable picture of the state of my own abandoned religious faith. The original wooden floors were gone, many of the pews had been removed, the sacristy was ruined, the stained glass heavily mottled with mold, and most of the statuary, including a fine pietà, badly water-damaged. It was more like entering the mausoleum of some long forgotten Gothic king than a church that as recently as 2008 had been the distinguished center of a thriving Catholic community. We stepped through the door and immediately felt like trespassers, our footsteps echoing through the wooden rafters as if we were a couple of ghost hunters. Perhaps that wasn't so very far from the truth. Something paranormal was abroad in the street outside. Only it was hunting me. Of the original confessionals, only one was in a fit state to be occupied, although the threadbare green satin curtains were draped like beach towels rather than hung on proper rails. Coogan pointed at the confessional and we went inside, each to a different side. I sat down on a dusty shelf and crossed myself several times very deliberately; it was the first time I'd done this in a very long time. I hesitated, trying to remember the proper form of words that was used here.

"Bless me, Father, for I have sinned. My last confession was . . . at least ten years ago."

Coogan was straight down to business; he read a passage from the Bible.

And again he entered Capernaum after some days, and it was heard that he was in the house. Immediately many gathered together, so that there was no longer room to receive them, not even near the door. And he preached the word to them. Then they came to him, bringing a paralytic who was carried by four men. And when they could not come near him because of the crowd, they uncovered the roof where he was. So when they had broken through, they let down the bed on which the paralytic was lying. When Jesus saw their faith, he said to the paralytic, "Son, your sins are forgiven you." And some of the scribes were sitting there and reasoning in their hearts, "Why does this man speak blasphemies like this? Who can forgive sins but God alone?" But immediately, when Jesus perceived in his spirit that they reasoned thus within themselves, he said to them, "Why do you reason about these things in your hearts? Which is easier, to say to the paralytic, 'Your sins are forgiven you,' or to say, 'Arise, take up your bed and walk'? But that you may know that the Son of Man has power on earth to forgive sins"—He said to the paralytic, "I say to you, arise, take up your bed, and go to your house." Immediately he arose, took up the bed, and went out in the presence of them all, so that all were amazed and glorified God, saying, "We never saw anything like this!"

I sat still for a moment, trying to think of all my sins; after ten years, there were a lot of them to consider; and, in no particular order, I opened the case for the prosecution.

"Father," I said, "I accuse myself of the following sins. I have denied my faith. I have placed my trust in substitutes for God. I have despaired of God's mercy. I have taken the Lord's name in vain. I have used profanity. I have broken my promise to be a good Catholic. I have failed to honor Sundays and to celebrate Mass. I have neglected prayer. I have abused alcohol. I have supported the idea of abortion and suicide. I have been impatient, angry, envious, revengeful, and lazy. I have not forgiven others. I have not been chaste in word and thought. I have had sex outside marriage. I have looked at impure images. I have spoken ill of people. I haven't always told the truth. I have not been faithful to sacramental living. I have not contributed to the support of the Holy Mother Church. I have not done penance by abstaining and fasting on obligatory days. I have resisted God's will for me." I paused for a moment and then added, "Father, I am sorry for these and all the sins of my past life."

"I want you to say three Our Fathers," said Coogan, assigning me my penance. "And three Hail Marys. And while you're doing it, I want you to consider the profound gravity of your sins and the mercy of God."

"O my God," I said, "I am heartily sorry for having offended thee and I detest all my sins because of thy just punishments, but most of all because they offend thee, my God, who art all good and deserving of all my love. I firmly resolve, with the help of thy grace, to sin no more and avoid the near occasions of sin. Amen."

Then Coogan spoke the words of absolution: "God, the Father of mercies, through the death and resurrection of his Son has reconciled the world to himself and sent the Holy Spirit among us for the forgiveness of sins; through the ministry of the Church may God give you pardon and peace, and I absolve you from your sins in the name of the Father, and of the Son, and of the Holy Spirit. Amen."

"Amen."

"Give thanks to the Lord for he is good," said Coogan.

"For his mercy endures forever," I replied.

I stepped out of the confessional and found my legs were trembling.

Feeling a little faint, I sat down on one of the remaining wooden pews to begin my prayer penance.

Coogan left me alone for that; I heard him as he went for a walk around the cathedral. Perhaps he prayed, too. Perhaps he prayed for me. But more than likely, from the smell, he was smoking a cigarette.

Prayer. I hoped it would work for me and, remembering how months before I'd gone to the Cathedral of the Scared Heart in Houston to pray for God's help that I might believe in him, I reflected that perhaps it always had done. Hadn't that prayer I had made been answered? Because didn't I now believe in God as never before? *Truly, when God wants you to suffer, he answers your prayers.*

After I was through with my Our Fathers and my Hail Marys, I went to look for Coogan. He was sitting in the ruined sacristy among the warped and broken drawers of the beautiful wooden cabinets that once had held stoles, altar clothes, and altar furnishings. In that cold derelict room it was hard to imagine that God's church had any kind of future.

"Okay?" he said, quietly stubbing out his cigarette on the bare wooden floor.

I nodded. "Yes," I said. "I think so." I glanced at my watch. "Time will tell."

But when we went outside again, the demon was gone.

THIRTY

The Magnolia Tree Café on San Jacinto Street was almost empty, which suited me very well. It was cool and almost dark in there, too, which suited me even better. It was three o'clock in the afternoon. A saccharine-flavored woman's voice echoed out of the wide-screen television.

I was sitting at my usual corner table, staring into my coffee. Now and again I glanced up at a big smiling face that was eyeing me in high definition from the wall next to the washrooms. The face belonged to a woman who was blond and beautiful; she was wearing a floral-print dress and holding a leather Bible as big as a telephone book. GOD IS WATCHING YOU, the caption said at the bottom of the screen. A fat waitress wearing a paper magnolia behind her ear came and filled up my cup with scalding hot coffee. It tasted like burned cork and smelled even worse, which was how the people who went to the Magnolia Tree Café seemed to prefer it.

I was listening to the TV but not really watching. It was *Pastor Penny Black's Messiah Matinee* and she seemed to be speaking directly to me; and, naturally, the news she had to tell was really wonderful. God in his infinite mercy and graciousness had chosen me to be there to watch her show; and even though I'd acted like the prodigal son, I'd been marked by God; I'd been chosen by God and forgiven by him; he'd ordered my footsteps; he'd given me an opportunity and the spirit of God was now drawing me to him; all I had to do was say "in the name of Jesus" and I'd have free access to God. This was good. Free access to God sounded just fine. Kind of like free Wi-Fi.

Of course, I ought to have felt a warm glow of satisfaction flare up in me at this thought. But I didn't. Not in the least. Pastor Penny made God sound like he was the nicest guy in the world. A nice, eccentric old man with a bushy beard and a generosity of spirit that was almost unknown among humankind. Only I knew different.

Seeing me turn my nose up at Pastor Penny's message, the waitress might have assumed from my sneer that I didn't believe in God. But I did believe in God—absolutely—only my belief in God was no longer a matter of blind faith like Pastor Penny's, but a matter of revelation and knowledge; it was based not on God's grace but on fear. I was afraid of him as I would have been afraid of a man with a loaded gun, a dangerous dog, a rampaging grizzly bear, or a sepulchral voice emanating dramatically from inside a picturesque burning bush. Fear was the key to my whole belief system. Put your trust in the Lord is what someone like Pastor Penny would tell you; but I say it's a lot better to put your trust in your fear of the Lord; you can't go wrong with that. If you doubt what I'm saying, then take another, closer look at the Old Testament sometime; Noah, Abraham, and Moses do what they're told to do—no matter how unreasonable—not because they want to do it but because they're terrified. Abraham goes through with the whole charade because he's afraid of the consequences if he doesn't. Knowing God the way he did, he had to figure that there were many worse fates than having your throat cut. Simple as that. It's the same with me. If you will forgive the comparison, I'm like Abraham; I do what I do out of fear and nothing else. Fear of the Lord is the only reason I'm still alive.

As always, the thought of God and his capricious, tyrannical power made me feel a little weak inside and my stomach turned over. I sipped some hot coffee, which was as bitter as wormwood, but at least it helped dispel all thoughts of love and forgiveness. It tasted like shit. My whole life tasted like shit. And now that I was reconciled with my creator, possibly it always would. God just wanted it that way. And out of fear I went along with this. Fear of the Lord was what was going to guide me now for the rest of my life. But that was okay. You know where you are with fear.

I got up and fetched a copy of the *Houston Chronicle* from the rack by the coffee counter. That was part of my afternoon ritual. I would have several cups of coffee, read the paper, and then head to the Cathedral of the Sacred Heart a couple of blocks away. Mostly I just read the sports and TV section. On this particular occasion, however, the headline on the front page really caught my eye. To be honest, it did more than just catch my eye; it made my heart skip a beat, as if the angel of death were parked outside my front door again.

It wasn't the kind of bullshit good news that Pastor Penny retailed; it was actually a story I was keen to read.

"Houston Serial Killer Slays Clear Lake Pastor," read the headline.

There was a large color shot of Van Der Velden—such a handsome, photogenic man; he was holding a Bible and wearing a smart suit. Harlan Caulfield appeared in a smaller monochrome picture at the bottom of the page, smoking one of his stupid e-cigarettes. I started to read, although I'd already seen the report on the previous night's TV news.

The Texas evangelist Dr. Nelson Van Der Velden has been shot dead on the grounds of the exclusive Houstonian Club.

The incident happened yesterday shortly before 8:00 a.m. as the 37-year-old preacher was preparing to play his daily game of tennis with a member of his controversial Izrael Church of

Good Men and Good Women, located in Clear Lake, near Galveston.

Witnesses described how Nancy Myerson, 25, ran screaming into the Houstonian Club reception area and told shocked staff that Dr. Van Der Velden had been shot. Bill Leggero, 41, the senior club tennis professional, said that when he went to investigate Miss Myerson's report he found Dr. Van Der Velden's body slumped in a chair on an outside court and covered in blood. It appeared that Dr. Van Der Velden had been shot three times in the back of the head, although no one at the club reported hearing gunfire. Dr. Van Der Velden was pronounced dead at the scene.

A .22-caliber Walther automatic pistol was found by police in a discarded towel bin in the men's changing room.

Hundreds of people gathered outside Van Der Velden's Art Deco–style church in Clear Lake to grieve the pastor's death, and also at his $10 million home in River Oaks. Van Der Velden's estranged father, Dr. Robert Van Der Velden, who until recently ran the Prayer Pyramid of Power church in Dallas, paid tribute to his son.

"My beloved son has been gathered to the Lord," he said. "We didn't always see eye to eye but truly this man was a man of God. Right now, I know he's in heaven with Jesus."

The Prayer Pyramid of Power closed last year and filed for bankruptcy with debts of more than $20 million.

Meanwhile, police have sealed off the blood-stained tennis court and the men's changing room at the Houstonian Club, where membership costs $10,000 a year, while they search for further evidence.

Tributes are pouring in from many leading members of the community, among them the governor of Texas, who described

Nelson Van Der Velden as a leading citizen and great humanitarian. "It's a tragedy," said the governor, "that such a decent, moral man and pillar of the Houston community should have been taken from us so cruelly." The mayor of Houston, John Ortiz, praised Dr. Van Der Velden's ministry and philanthropy.

It has been only four weeks since Van Der Velden donated the sum of one million dollars to the Texas Children's Hospital in Houston. Doctors at the Fannin Street hospital spoke warmly of the late pastor, among them a professor of pediatrics, Dr. Gerry Soule, who said that the religious figure was "a great Christian who practiced what he preached."

Speculation mounted last night that Dr. Van Der Velden was the latest victim of a serial killer who has murdered six people in the Houston-Galveston area in less than a year. The victims of the multiple killer, nicknamed Saint Peter, had in common their great work for charity and devotion to the welfare of others and also the manner of their deaths: all of them were shot at close range with a .22-caliber pistol.

Ballistics experts at the FBI are conducting tests on the gun found at the Houstonian Club to determine whether the weapon used to slay Dr. Van Der Velden was also used to kill any of the other victims. Harlan Caulfield, the FBI's Assistant Special Agent in Charge of the task force investigating the killings, expressed the Bureau's sorrow at Dr. Van Der Velden's death; he also told the *Chronicle*'s reporter that Houstonians had nothing to fear from Saint Peter because he was very confident that the Bureau would soon apprehend the killer.

However, others remain critical of the Houston FBI's failure to apprehend the killer, most notably the writer and broadcaster Gene Haugen Olsen, who has called on Senator Bryant Hinman to meet with the Department of Justice and see what can be done to facilitate a new investigation. To date, there are no new leads, no suspects have been interviewed, and in an editorial today the *Houston Chronicle* lends its support to Mr. Olsen's calls for a new initiative in an investigation that appears to this newspaper to be going nowhere.

In truth, I never thought much about the FBI. Not since I'd quit the Bureau. And to be honest, I didn't miss the work. Not as much as they missed my doing it. Several times Gisela asked me to reconsider my resignation; and several times I told her no; the Houston FBI SAC, Chuck Worrall, also asked me to reconsider; I told him to go fuck himself. He said he wanted to know who was going to protect the people of Houston from domestic terrorism; I replied that it wasn't my problem and again told him to go fuck himself; headquarters in Washington, D.C., also called to offer me a training post at Quantico; I told them to go fuck themselves, too. Something had died in me when Gisela had sent me on leave. I'd lost the sense that the Bureau was as loyal to me as I'd always been to it.

You might even say I lost my faith in the FBI the way I'd once lost my faith in God.

I might not have missed the Bureau, but I did miss the guys who worked there. I especially missed Helen Monaco. I missed carrying the badge—for a few days I felt naked without that gold shield and the gun that went with it. I missed the money, of course. Not that there was ever much of that. Since leaving the Bureau, I'd managed to get the OCD under control. I no longer started to play solitaire with sugar packets whenever I was in a restaurant or a coffee shop. All of that stopped when I stopped thinking about animal-rights activists and Christianists and Islamists and far-right militias and what they might do to the city of Houston and, by extension, my family; these days, all of my thoughts are about me, and God, of course. Let's not ever forget him. And believe me, I won't. Not ever again.

A couple of times Helen came down to the Magnolia to have a coffee with me; and we talked.

"Why this place?" she asked. "It's a dump."

"It's convenient to the cathedral," I said.

"Do you spend a lot of time there?"

"Quite a lot. I feel at peace in the cathedral."

"I like it there, too. Especially after a day in the office. I get pissed off sometimes with the other guys. The dyke jokes. I have a wife now. Did you know that?"

"Congratulations. I'm really pleased for you. What's her name?"

"Toni. We got married in Los Angeles. Texas doesn't yet recognize same-sex marriage."

"Nor does the Catholic Church, but I wouldn't let that stop you."

"Don't you miss it? The Bureau? The work?"

I shrugged. "I used to think we were doing good work. Now I don't think it matters very much one way or the other if we catch this killer or that terrorist. It certainly doesn't matter to God if we catch the bad guys or not. There's always another one to take his place."

"You don't really believe that, do you?"

"A hundred years ago people were worried about anarchist bombs. Now we worry about bombs from al-Qaeda. Jack the Ripper murdered five prostitutes in London's East End. Now we have Saint Peter murdering people here in Houston. Nothing changes very much."

"That's not very encouraging. Priests are supposed to be encouraging."

"Whatever gave you that idea?"

"Tell me, Gil. Do you really believe in what you're doing, or is going to church again just your way of trying to get Ruth and Danny back?"

"It's a little too late for reconciliation, I think. No, Ruth and I, we're through. I know that."

I'd seen Ruth and Danny by then—at our old house on Driscoll Street. It was actually quite amicable. I'd spent a whole evening with them after taking Danny to a ball game; while I was there, Ruth apologized for having treated me so badly, which kind of took me by surprise. I wasn't expecting that. But I had a few surprises of my own for her and among these was my new calling.

"I didn't behave like a good Christian," she declared.

"I know I certainly didn't."

"You had an excuse, Gil. You weren't actually a Christian at the time. You were an atheist."

"It must have been very difficult for you, living with me and my very ungodly questions. Faith is kind of hard to sustain even at the best of times. I used to think it was easier to believe in God than not to believe in him. But now that I'm certain he exists, I find I don't believe in him at all. At least not the way most people believe in him."

"I don't understand. You say you know he exists but—"

"What I mean is—" I paused. "Forget about it. Just take my word for it, Ruth. For me, it's no longer a matter of faith. I know God exists, all right? That's all you need to hear from me on the subject."

"Really? Are you joking about this?"

"No joke. I'm perfectly serious."

"I do believe you are," she said. "Well, what do you know? Jesus, I certainly didn't see that coming." Ruth smiled thinly. "And where does this new certainty come from?"

"Let's just say that something happened to me that convinced me I'd been completely wrong. Like Saul in the Acts of the Apostles. It was my road to Damascus moment, Ruth. Except that I wasn't struck blind. Quite the reverse, as a matter of fact."

"I wish I had your confidence, Gil."

I frowned. "You're not having doubts?" I said. "Surely not? Not you, of all people?"

"Sometimes I think that the real reason I left you was because you were only saying what I was afraid to say myself. As a matter of fact, I've stopped going to church while I try to figure out what I really do believe."

"Which one? Lakewood or the Izrael Church of Good Men and Good Women?"

"Both." She shrugged. "Nelson Van Der Velden was charismatic, of course. When he died, I guess I began to change my opinion of the church in general." She smiled. "I've been thinking. About us. Maybe you and I could see some more of each other again."

"Oh? What about Hogan?"

Ruth shook her head impatiently. "He was nothing to me. Just a friend, that's all. Forget Hogan, okay?"

"Okay."

"Perhaps I was too hasty about you, Gil. You know something? I think I was clinically depressed. That's what my doctor says. I'm on Xanax now and I feel much better about a lot of things." She sighed. "I guess what I'm trying to say is that I'd like us to give our marriage another shot. For Danny's sake, if nothing else."

I smiled and laid my hand fondly on her cheek. "I'm afraid it's a little too late for that," I said.

"Are you seeing someone else?"

"No. There's no one, Ruth."

This was not quite true, but I hardly wanted to mention his name in this context. His name should rarely be mentioned, ever—certainly not without a great deal of precaution. I have Nelson Van Der Velden to thank for that.

"It's not that I don't love you or Danny."

"What then?"

There was no way of making it sound any less peculiar to Ruth than it would sound—although I don't think it's any less peculiar than turning down a well-paid job with a top firm of New York attorneys to join the FBI because of what happened back in 2001. What happened to me in Galveston had been as traumatic and affecting as 9/11. Maybe more so.

"It's just that I've decided to become a Catholic priest, Ruth. I've joined St. Mary's Catholic Seminary."

"But why, Gil? Why?"

"At the time I didn't have anywhere else other than the seminary to go to, Ruth. Physically and spiritually. I'd come to the end of myself, if that doesn't sound like too much of a cliché. But now that I've thought more about it, I've made the decision to enter the priesthood just as soon as I can. I think it's the right decision for me. In fact, I'm sure of it."

"Gil Martins, what possible use is there in your becoming a priest?"

"Oh, I don't know." I grinned. "Time will tell. But I think Bishop Coogan is relieved to have at least one priest who isn't a pedophile or gay."

"My God, I certainly didn't see this one coming."

"No, neither did I, although I think maybe God did." I patted her on the arm. "I had hoped you would be happy for me, Ruth. But I can see you're a little upset by the idea. Well, if you can, pray for me."

"I don't think I will." She shook her head. "Oh, I don't mean that I don't wish you well, Gil. It's just that I'm not sure that prayer is all that effective."

"Oh, it is," I said glibly. "Take it from one who knows."

"I prayed for you before," she said. "I prayed that you would believe in God again."

"Well, I guess your prayers were answered then."

"We get what we pray for and then find out that we didn't want it after all."

"Isn't that so right?"

"Now that you do believe in God, I find that I don't believe in him so much anymore. Weird, isn't it?"

"There's no sense in trying to understand God," I said. "'Touching the Almighty, we cannot find him out; he is excellent in power, and in judgment, and in plenty of justice; he will not afflict. Men do therefore fear him; he respecteth not any that are wise of heart.' That just means God doesn't like a smart-ass. Job 37:23–24."

"Is this what our conversations are going to be like from now on, do you think?"

"Ruth. It's what our conversations were always like. The only difference is that now it's me who's quoting scripture, not you."

When I left, she tried to kiss me on the mouth, but at the last moment I turned my face so that her lips just brushed my cheek. It wasn't deliberate on my part, more instinct, really—the way you duck something that might injure you, like a hornet. But it hurt her, for sure, although that wasn't my intention. As I walked away from my old house and got into my car, there were tears in her eyes. I wondered if the tears came from the fact that she still loved me or if they were because she regretted what she'd put me through. Then again, maybe her tears were for our son and the fact that I wouldn't see him grow up the way most other fathers do. But I didn't care. I'd lied when I told her I still loved her; that was just to make her feel better. Me, I didn't feel the same about anything anymore. Not about her, not even about Danny, and certainly not about myself. Myself least of all.

In the Magnolia Tree Café, an unexpected peal of laughter trickled out of the television for a moment. I looked up from doing the crossword in the *Chronicle* to see what was happening up on the screen.

Pastor Penny had cracked a joke; and just to make sure we all got it, she cracked it again.

"Forget Pilates, forget the gym, forget yoga, and forget working out. The best exercise you can get is to walk with God," she trilled.

Encouraged by the congregation's reaction to her little joke, Pastor Penny decided to try another.

"You know, the other evening I was stopped by a traffic policeman who informed me that I'd broken the speed limit. He informed me that I'd driven at thirty-five miles per hour in a thirty-mile-an-hour zone. I apologized for my thoughtlessness several times—I'm not used to being stopped by the cops—and I guess he wasn't used to this, either. I suppose most people in these circumstances get more annoyed than I was. Anyway, he asked me if I was under the influence of alcohol. And do you know, I was so surprised I said no, I'm under the influence of God."

More laughter. Did anyone of them, I wondered, ever have any idea about the real nature of God? Probably not. And that was probably just as well.

"And you know why I'm under the influence of God?" she yelled—Pastor Penny was kind of in your face with her preaching. "I'm under his influence because God is love."

Absently I wrote "God is love" on the edge of my newspaper.

But when Pastor Penny's TV audience laughed, it seemed like they were laughing at me, so after a moment or two of consideration, I crossed out the word LOVE and replaced it with FEAR. Now, that was a lot more like the truth. I looked at the slogan and nodded to myself. There could be no love where first there was fear. Not ever. And still nodding, I said out loud, "Behold, the fear of the Lord, that is wisdom."

Hearing me speak, the waitress smiled and said, "Amen," and then, as a reward, she brought me some more of the terribly bitter coffee that tasted like wormwood.

"I'm glad you like Pastor Penny's TV show," said the waitress. "I like to watch it, but sometimes the customers object and I have to change the channel."

"There are no other customers," I said. "So that's all right then."

"Bless you," said the waitress. "God loves you, brother."

I restrained my first impulse, which was to laugh out loud in her face, and just politely nodded my thanks.

❀

A couple of days after Van Der Velden's murder, Harlan Caulfield came to see me at the seminary. We talked in my room, with me sitting on my single bed and Harlan seated in the only armchair.

Harlan's face looked even more lived-in than usual: the furrows on his forehead now looked so deep that his cranium seemed about to detach from the rest of his head. The space between his always quizzical eyebrows, above the bridge of his nose, was a Gordian knot of anxious skin and sinew. He looked like a human question mark. I didn't offer him anything. I had nothing to offer except some Salem cigarettes, which would hardly have been fair given his attempt to give them up. I offered him one anyway and then lit one myself when he declined with a curt shake of his head.

"You started smoking again?"

"Why not? Considering everything else that you have to give up, I figure I've got to have some pleasures in life."

Harlan nodded sadly. "Might be worth it at that," he said. "Just to have a smoke again. My life has no real pleasures. Not anymore."

"I'm sorry to hear that. So what can I do for you, Harlan?"

"You know why I'm here."

"It isn't to beg me to come back to the Bureau," I said.

"You're right. Somehow I think we'll manage to get along without you."

"Then I suppose it's about Saint Peter," I said.

"I wish people wouldn't use that name," he said, looking away. "Given your new priestly calling, I'm kind of surprised you do."

I shrugged. "But you do think it was the same sub who killed Van Der Velden?"

He shrugged. "Could be. Bears all the hallmarks of."

"A million dollars buys you a nice shiny halo in this town."

"But you don't think he deserved it."

"That depends, Harlan."

"On what?"

"On what you're fishing for."

"All right. Fair enough. Where were you on Tuesday morning at about eight o'clock?" he asked.

"You mean on the morning of Van Der Velden's murder? I was here. In bed. Just me and my newfound celibacy."

"I thought priests were supposed to get up with the larks."

"That's monks you're thinking of, Harlan. Besides, I'm not yet a priest."

"Can you prove you were here?"

"No. I guess someone might have seen me at breakfast. But I don't remember talking to anyone in particular. One morning is kind of like another in this place. But it'd be kind of weird if I could actually prove it, don't you think?"

"You can see why I'm asking though, can't you, Martins?"

"Of course. I knew your killer's modus operandi. I'm still a member of the Houstonian Club. And I knew Nelson Van Der Velden. Frankly, I didn't much like him, either. On top of all that, before his death I suffered a nervous breakdown. In your eyes that makes me borderline mentally unstable. I'm surprised you didn't come to see me yesterday, Harlan."

He nodded. "Did you kill him?"

"Thanks for asking, Harlan, I'm a lot better now."

Harlan stared at his hands and then knotted his fingers as if he was about to pray.

I laughed.

"Did I say something funny?" he asked.

"I guess the *Chronicle* was right," I said. "You really don't have any new leads, do you?"

"The way I see it, you might have had a motive to kill him; and you could easily have facilitated the opportunity."

"And the other killings? You want me to provide an alibi for those murders, too?"

"Right now, I'm only talking about one murder."

"Well, thanks, buddy."

He looked momentarily sheepish. "I don't say you did do it, Martins. Merely that you could have done it."

"Fair enough. But where do you want to go with this?"

Harlan shook his head. "I could bring you in for questioning."

"You could at that. And just so as you know, I'm waiving my rights. As a favor to an old colleague. I can't afford a lawyer anyway."

"Gil, you look good for this murder."

"That's going to play well with the media. When all else fails, accuse one of your own."

"You walked into Van Der Velden's church wearing a gun."

"Didn't you ever take your gun to Lakewood?"

"Maybe."

"I know I did. My wife used to tick me off for it. Besides, I wasn't the only one at Clear Lake wearing a hog's leg. Dr. Van Der Velden had a bodyguard. Although not so as you would have noticed. Not on

Tuesday anyway. Guy named Frank Fitzgerald. You might like to run a few checks on him. Claims he's Homeland Security when he's not moonlighting as the pastor's tough guy."

"Frank Fitzgerald, huh? I didn't even know Van Der Velden *had* a bodyguard."

"I would imagine he's lying low right now. Out of professional embarrassment. Or maybe he's just worried about getting thrown out of the U.S. Coast Guard."

"Uh-huh. HPD found the probable weapon. Twenty-two-caliber Walther. Same as all the others. It was in a laundry basket at the club alongside a pair of evidence gloves."

"I saw. It was in the paper."

"They traced the weapon back to Dr. Sara Espinosa. That biologist you knew from the University of Texas in Austin?"

I nodded coolly.

"Dr. Espinosa is missing," said Harlan, "presumed drowned following an auto accident last month in which she appears to have driven her $300,000 Bentley convertible off the Galveston Causeway into the bay near Virginia Point. That's not far from where you were living before this place."

"I know."

"You don't happen to know what she was doing in Galveston, do you?"

This was a trick question; I knew he knew the answer. Helen would have told him she'd gone there looking for me.

"On the morning she died? Sure. She turned up at my house claiming she had a stalker at her apartment in Austin. This was about three or four in the morning. She'd been drinking. We talked for a while and I'm afraid I told her I couldn't help. That it was a police matter. Then she drove away. I didn't hear about the accident until a while later."

"Hardly very gallant of you. To let her drive off like that."

"It was the middle of the night. I wasn't feeling very gallant, Harlan. Or maybe I should just have called the Galveston PD and let them handle her."

"Austin PD is investigating the possibility that Dr. Espinosa's gun may have been stolen by an intruder in her home in Austin. In the days leading up to her death, Dr. Espinosa had become fearful of her own safety and had recently contacted a private security firm monitoring her safety with concerns about a possible stalker."

"That's what she told me when I went to see her in Austin. And again when she turned up in Galveston. She seemed very disturbed."

"Did she mention she had bought a gun? The Walther P22?"

"No. But then buying yourself a gun is hardly news in Texas."

"No, I guess not."

For good luck, I fingered the St. Christopher's medal I wore around my neck while I waited for Harlan to say something.

I could tell he didn't believe me; he was a much better detective than the newspapers gave him credit for; but we both knew there was no evidence to contradict my story—certainly not from the daily records at the Houstonian Club. Avoiding the entrance and exit used by everyone else meant that I was almost never on the club's computer. Slipping into the club without being seen at seven in the morning and waiting in some thick bushes near the tennis courts was a relatively simple matter. It's not just the detection of crime they train you for at Quantico; it's how to carry one out, too.

If killing Nelson Van Der Velden could ever be called a crime.

Harlan glanced around my room. "So this is where you've ended up," he remarked. "Wouldn't ever have figured it. Your becoming a priest 'n' all." He frowned. "I'm curious. What changed your mind? About God, I mean?"

"Why do you ask?"

"Why? Isn't it obvious?" He shrugged sheepishly. "I want to believe in him myself, Martins. If I can. Life is so much easier if you believe in something other than yourself." He paused for a moment. "I figure if a sonofabitch like you can believe in God then there's hope for me yet. So, what was it?"

"Sometimes it seems I had very little to do with it," I admitted.

"Honestly?"

"Honestly. You could say I had a vision. And that wouldn't be so far from the truth. So, maybe there's hope for you yet."

"That's what I keep telling myself."

He nodded and stood up, and then he left without another word.

⊞

I was in the Cathedral of the Sacred Heart.

I'd been wrong to think of it as looking like a maximum-security prison. It looks more like a modern theater where they put on the kind of big show that's designed to persuade you of the same thing—that God is love. It wouldn't do to let too many people know the awful truth about God, which is that he is despicably cruel and capricious and indifferent to good and evil, that he is a God who keeps all of us in a state of drunken distraction and malevolent intoxication. It would have done no good to have told people like the fat waitress in the Magnolia Tree Café the truth that I knew. The truth would have frightened them away as if they were rabbits.

Inside the cathedral I knelt in the nave and waited my turn in the confessional, and while I knelt there patiently, I listened as the church organist played an uplifting piece of music that was quite at odds with what God is really like.

Muffled footsteps echoed underneath the enormous ceiling of the cathedral as if we were already in some celestial place awaiting an appointment with a saint or an angel about a position in the hereafter—if such a thing could possibly exist; about that I don't know, but I wouldn't put it past God to have conceived of the whole idea of heaven as a really sick cosmic joke.

I looked up at the stained-glass window of a rather muscular, bare-chested Christ depicted as the light of the world and reflected that this was only half the story; because the true face of God—the God of darkness—was not shown here. He would have frightened people—scared the living shit out of them; that was the God I knew. Then again, I doubt that there's a stained-glass window designer in America who's equal to the task of depicting the gnostic, Manichean God whom I now worship, albeit in secret. If Michelangelo had painted the real face of God on the ceiling of the Sistine Chapel, they'd probably have hung and burned him at the stake, like Savonarola.

A Hispanic-looking woman holding a rosary came out of the confessional and sat down, muttering the string of prayers that were her simple penance and that seemed to afford her some comfort. Well, of course, she didn't know the difference between the true God and the one that people pray to. Otherwise, I daresay she couldn't have managed it. How do you pray to a God who keeps the light trapped inside the dark, whose kingdom is one of fear?

It's all a matter of knowing to whom and to what you're speaking. Once you realize this, then prayer is easy. That's what Nelson Van Der Velden understood. He worked out whom he was praying to, that's all. He learned that real prayer, effective prayer, is about direction. The true God has nothing to do with the material world or the cosmos and so praying to the benign avuncular God of the Church is useless; it gets you nothing—as if you couldn't have worked that out for yourself. Wars continue to be fought. Murderers—murderers like me and Saint Peter—remain unpunished. That's how it's always been and how it always will be. People go hungry. Diseases run amok. Natural disasters such as floods kill thousands. So what?

My own crime seems so insignificant it's hardly worth mentioning. So you'll excuse me if I don't try to justify it now.

I thought back to the time when I had come into the cathedral to look for spiritual guidance—like a hungry cartoon mouse—and before that, to the time when I had been confirmed, and I laughed at my old innocent self. It had taken me all these years to figure the cruel misunderstanding that had been forced on humankind.

The God delusion, Richard Dawkins called it. Well, it is a delusion, of course it is; only it's not quite the delusion anyone imagines.

AUTHOR'S NOTE

If there is a God, I rather agree with Randolph Churchill, who, having been persuaded by Evelyn Waugh to read the Bible, exclaimed, with no small incredulity: "Isn't God a shit?" To which, in support of that same proposition, I would only add the following:

"Think not that I am come to send peace on earth: I came not to send peace, but a sword. For I am come to set a man at variance against his father, and the daughter against her mother, and the daughter-in-law against her mother-in-law. And a man's foes shall be they of his own household."

MATTHEW 10:34–36

"I form the light, and create darkness: I make peace, and create evil: I the Lord do all these things."

ISAIAH 45:7

"The Lord is a man of war: the Lord is his name."

EXODUS 15:3

"But those mine enemies, which would not that I should reign over them, bring hither, and slay them before me."

LUKE 19:27

"If a man also lie with mankind, as he lieth with a woman, both of them have committed an abomination: they shall surely be put to death; their blood shall be upon them."

LEVITICUS 20:13

"Backbiters, haters of God, despiteful, proud, boasters, inventors of evil things, disobedient to parents. Without understanding, covenant-breakers, without natural affection, implacable, unmerciful: Who knowing the judgment of God, that they which commit such things are worthy of death."

ROMANS 1:30–32

"The wicked, through the pride of his countenace, will not seek after God: God is not in all his thoughts."

PSALMS 10:4

"The wind of the Lord shall come up from the wilderness, and his spring shall become dry, and his fountain shall be dried up: he shall spoil the treasure of all pleasant vessels. Samaria shall become desolate; for she hath rebelled against her God: they shall fall by the sword: their infants shall be dashed in pieces, and their women with child shall be ripped up."

HOSEA 13:15–16

"Remember, O Lord, the children of Edom in the day of Jerusalem; who said, Rase it, rase it, even to the foundation thereof. O daughter of Babylon, who art to be destroyed; happy shall he be, that rewardeth thee as thou hast served us. Happy shall he be, that taketh and dasheth thy little ones against the stones."

PSALMS 137:7–9

"Behold, I will cast her into a bed, and them that commit adultery with her into great tribulation, except they repent of their deeds. And I will kill her children with death; and all the churches shall know that I am he which searcheth the reins and hearts: and I will give unto every one of you according to your works."

REVELATION 2:22–23

"And it shall come to pass, that as the Lord rejoiced over you to do you good, and to multiply you; so the Lord will rejoice over you to destroy you, and to bring you to nought; and ye shall be plucked from off the land whither thou goest to possess it."

DEUTERONOMY 28:63

"Then the earth shook and trembled; the foundations also of the hills were moved and were shaken, because he was wroth. There went up a smoke out of his nostrils, and fire out of his mouth devoured: coals were kindled by it. He bowed the heavens also, and came down: and darkness was under his feet. And he rode upon a cherub and did fly: yea, he did fly upon the wings of the wind. He made darkness his secret place; his pavilion round about him were dark waters and thick clouds of the skies."

PSALMS 18:7–11

"I will meet them as bear that is bereaved of her whelps and will rend the caul of their heart, and there will I devour them like a lion: the wild beast shall tear them."

HOSEA 13:8

"It is a fearful thing to fall into the hands of the living God."

HEBREWS 10:31

"Shall a trumpet be blown in the city, and the people not be afraid? Shall there be evil in a city, and the Lord hath not done it?"

AMOS 3:6

"Though they bring up their children, yet will I bereave them, that there shall not be a man left: yea, woe also to them when I depart from them!"

HOSEA 9:12

ACKNOWLEDGMENTS

I am very grateful to the men and women in the Houston office of the FBI for their help in the research of this book. They were unfailingly courteous and accommodating, and they will probably thank me if I don't mention them by name. Any mistakes that remain in the novel about the operations of this dedicated organization are mine. I am equally grateful to the people at the Lakewood Church in Houston, who made me feel very welcome at their services, and to the people of Texas. I should also like to thank Dr. Nick Scott for sharing with me memories of our respective religious upbringings in Edinburgh. Thanks are also due to Jane Wood and Steve Cox in London and to Christine Pepe in New York for reading the text so closely. As always, a writer needs a good editor. I should also like to thank my wife, the author Jane Thynne, for braving a Texas heat wave and accompanying me to many of the locations in this book—most notably Galveston. I also want to thank Caradoc King, who always believed in this book when others, like the apostle Thomas, had their doubts. Thanks also to Ivan Held, Marian Wood, Mark Smith, Katie Gordon, Lucy Ramsey, Nicci Praça, Michael Wolff, and Robert Bookman. While in Houston, I stayed at both the Hotel ZaZa and the Houstonian Hotel and can unreservedly recommend both.

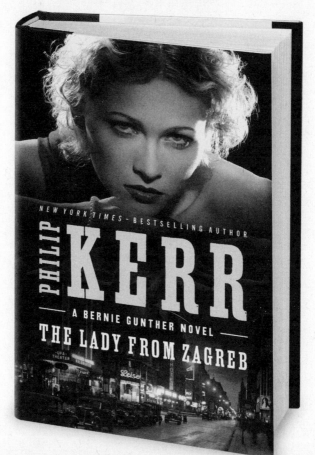

AVAILABLE FROM PENGUIN

IN THE BERNIE GUNTHER SERIES

A Man Without Breath

Prague Fatale

Field Gray

If the Dead Rise Not

A Quiet Flame

One from the Other

German Requiem

The Pale Criminal

March Violets

Berlin Noir

ALSO BY PHILIP KERR:

A Philosophical Investigation

Hitler's Peace

**PENGUIN
BOOKS**